MORGAN COUNTY PUBLIC LIBRARY
110 SOUTH JEFFERSON ST
MARTINSVILLE, IN 46151

P9-DDD-292

WITHDRAWN

FIC
MCM

McMillan, Terry.

I almost forgot about
you.

# I Almost Forgot
# About You

# I Almost Forgot About You

## A Novel

## Terry McMillan

CROWN

NEW YORK

This is a work of fiction. Names, characters, places, and incidents either are the product of the author's imagination or are used fictitiously. Any resemblance to actual persons, living or dead, events, or locales is entirely coincidental.

Copyright © 2016 by Terry McMillan

All rights reserved.
Published in the United States by Crown, an imprint of the Crown Publishing Group, a division of Penguin Random House LLC, New York.
crownpublishing.com

CROWN and the Crown colophon are registered trademarks of Penguin Random House LLC.

Grateful acknowledgment is made to the Charlotte Sheedy Literary Agency, Inc., for permission to reprint "The Uses of Sorrow" from *Thirst* by Mary Oliver, published by Beacon Press, Boston. Copyright © 2004 by Mary Oliver. All rights reserved. Reprinted by permission of the Charlotte Sheedy Literary Agency, Inc.

Library of Congress Cataloging-in-Publication Data is available upon request.

ISBN 978-1-101-90257-8
Ebook ISBN 978-1-101-90258-5

Printed in the United States of America

*Book design by Lauren Dong*
*Jacket design by Elena Giavaldi*

10 9 8 7 6 5 4 3 2 1

First Edition

*For my son, Solomon*

*We dream of times that are not and blindly flee the only one that is. The fact is that the present usually hurts.*

—BLAISE PASCAL, *Pensées* (47)

THE USES OF SORROW
*(In my sleep I dreamed this poem)*

Someone I loved once gave me
a box full of darkness.

It took me years to understand
that this, too, was a gift.

—MARY OLIVER

# Contents

# Running Out of Time?

IT'S ANOTHER EXCITING FRIDAY NIGHT, AND I'M CURLED UP in bed—alone, of course—propped up by a sea of pillows, still in my lab coat, the sash so taut it's suffocating the purple silk dress beneath it, but I don't care. After a grueling day of back-to-back patients, I'm a few minutes away from being comatose, but I'm also hungry, which is why I'm channel-surfing and waiting for my pizza to get here. I stop when I come to my favorite standby: *Law & Order: Criminal Intent,* even though I've seen almost all of them—including the reruns. These days I usually just watch the first five or ten minutes, long enough to see Detective Goren stride onto the crime scene in his long trench coat, tilt his head to the side while he puts on those rubber gloves, rub the new growth on that beautiful square chin, and bend down to study the victim. It's at this moment, before he utters a word, when I usually pucker up, blow him a kiss, and then change the channel. I've lusted over Detective Goren and yearned to be held against shoulders like his long before my second marriage bottomed out.

Truth be told, over the years I've fallen in love every Wednesday with Gary Dourdan's lips as CSI Warrick Brown, and even though I was no Trekkie, Avery Brooks's deep baritone and sneaky smile made me say "Yes" aloud to the TV. I also let myself be seduced for hours in dark theaters, hypnotized by Benicio del Toro's dreamy eyes, even though he was a criminal. By Denzel's swagger when he was a slick gangster. Brad Pitt as a sexy young thief. Ken Watanabe as the most sensual samurai I wanted to ride on a horse with, and I wanted to be a black geisha and torture him until I finally let him have all of me.

I hate to admit it, but if I had the energy, I'd kill to have sex with the first one who walked into my bedroom tonight. I'd let him do anything he wanted to do to me. It's been centuries since I've had sex with a real man, and I'm not even sure I'd remember what to do first should I ever get so lucky again. In fact, I think I'd be too uncomfortable, not to mention scared of getting all touchy-feely, and don't even get me started on him seeing me naked. Hell, this is why I sleep with the remote.

When I hear the doorbell, I glance over at the broken blue clouds inside the clock on the night table. I've been waiting forty minutes for this pizza, which means they're going to owe me a free one! I roll off the bed on my side, even though the other side has been empty for years. I walk over to the door and yell, "Be right there!" Then I grab my wallet out of my purse and beeline it to the front door, because I'm starving. That is so not true. I'm just a little hungry. I'm trying to stop lying to myself about little things. I'm still working on the big ones.

I open the door, and standing there sweating is a young black kid who can't be more than eighteen. His head looks like a small globe of shiny black twists that I know are baby dreadlocks. His cheeks are full of brand-new zits. His name tag says FREE.

"I'm so sorry for the delay, ma'am. There was a accident at the bottom of the hill, and I couldn't get up here, so this one's on the house."

He looks so sad, and I'm wondering if the price of this pizza is going to be deducted from his little paycheck, but I dare not ask.

"I don't mind paying for it," I say. "It wasn't your fault there was an accident." I take the pizza from him and set it on the metal stairwell.

"That's real thoughtful of you, but I'm just glad this is my last delivery for the night," he says, leaning to one side as if he's pretending not to look behind me, but of course he is. "This a real nice crib you got here. I ain't never seen no yellow floors before. It's downright wicked."

"Thanks," I say, and hand him a twenty.

He looks as if he's in shock. "Like I said, ma'am, this pizza is on the house, and I also got some drink coupons you can have, too," he says, pulling them out of the pocket of his red shirt.

"It's a tip," I say. "Is your real name Free?"

"Yes, ma'am."

"How do you feel about it?"

"I dig it. I get asked all the time about it."

"So how old are you, Free?"

"I'm eighteen." He's still staring at the twenty but then quickly shoves it inside the back pocket of his jeans in case I come to my senses and change my mind.

"Are you in college?" I'm hoping he says yes and that he's taking English so one day soon he'll stop saying *ain't*.

"Almost. That's why I'm working. You really giving me this whole twenty?"

I nod. "Do you know what you want to major in?"

"Mechanical engineering," he says with certainty.

"That's great."

"Your husband rich?"

"What makes you think I'd have to have a husband to be rich?"

"Everybody that live up in these hills is. Even them two dykes that live next door. And they married."

"Those *dykes* aren't just my neighbors, they're also my friends, and they're *lesbians*."

"A'right. My bad," he says, flinging his arms up like *Don't shoot*. "I didn't mean no harm."

"I know. Anyway, I'm divorced. And I'm not rich. But I also don't struggle."

"You cleaned him out, then, huh?"

"No."

Then he gives me the once-over. "You some kind of doctor?"

I look down at my lab coat. "Yes. I'm an optometrist."

"Which one is that?"

"I help people see clearly," I say, so as not to complicate it.

"Who helps you?" he asks with a smile, which throws me off completely. What a loaded question to ask a woman old enough to be his grandmother. "Just fooling with you, Dr. Young. No disrespect intended."

"None taken, Free."

Who helps me see? See what?

"Cool. Well, look, I gotta dash and get this car back to my cousin, but major thanks for the mega-tip, and I have to say it's nice somebody black gave it to me. Most of the white folks up here ain't big on tipping, except for them lesbians."

What he just said was a little on the racist and sexist side, but I know he meant well. He runs down the sidewalk and jumps into that raggedy car of his, removes the pizza sign displayed on top, and disappears down the hill. I lean against the doorframe watching him go. I really should've praised him for working to pay for college, and if he hadn't been in such a hurry, I would have loved to tell him that he might find his calling in college and he might not. But I'd also tell him to search until he did. Otherwise he could end up doing something he just happened to be good at, something respectable that might guarantee him a nice income, but one day, when he's older, like, say, fifty-three soon to be fifty-four, when his kids have grown up and he's twice divorced and bored with his profession and his life and the thought of trying to change it all—or even where he lives—scares the hell out of him because it feels like it's too late, I'd tell him to please figure out a way to do it anyway, since I'm an excellent example of what can happen when you don't.

I turn off the porch light, close the door, and I can't believe all of this is flooding in. I walk across these cool yellow concrete floors and sit on these cool metal stairs and look out at the light jutting up through those soft navy blue waves in the cool black-bottomed pool, and I look up a flight where both of my daughters used to sleep, and I look down to where the library and the guest room are, and I sit here and eat this entire cheese-and-tomato pizza.

I am full of regret.


MONDAY MORNINGS are the worst, which is why I left a little early. The freeway is still slow going. But I'm used to it. I crack my window, although it can't be more than fifty degrees. The dampness coming from the bay can't eclipse the clarity of this morning as thousands of us slowly descend around a curve, and there waiting for us like a giant postcard is the Bay Bridge and right behind it the San Francisco skyline. This is a beautiful place to live.

But then, as typically happens at least once a week, the traffic suddenly comes to a screeching halt. I can see the reason up ahead. A four-car pile-up is blocking two of the five lanes, and everyone is trying to move over to make room for the fire trucks and ambulances I now hear. I just pray no one is hurt. I roll my window all the way down and put the car in park. Some have already turned off their engines. I leave mine running and call my office.

When my cell phone rings, I know who it is before I even glance at the screen. "Hello, Miss Early," I say to my mother, for obvious reasons but also because her name is Earlene.

"Hello back to you, Miss Georgia."

Of course I was never any Miss Georgia, because I was born in Bakersfield, where she still lives, and I was named after my late father, whose name was George. There's hardly a day that goes by when someone doesn't ask me if I'm from Georgia. In college I just started lying and said yes: Macon. But then they wanted to know why I didn't have a drawl.

"What can I do you for, ma'am? Are you feeling okay?"

"I'm probably healthier than you. Anyway, I'm calling for two reasons. I'm going on a cruise for seniors with my church."

"That's nice," I say, trying not to laugh, because I'm thinking this is going to be one wild and scandalous cruise.

"That's all you have to say?"

"I'm thrilled for you, Ma. I know you go to one of those megachurches, but are there enough seniors in the congregation to fill a whole cruise ship?"

"Of course not. There are ten churches, and we're not going to be the only older people on it."

She's eighty-one. Soon to be eighty-two.

"When and where are you going?"

"We leave two weeks and one day from today. For ten whole days! We're going to four or five islands in the Caribbean that I can't remember right now. One of them is the Grand Cayman."

"That's a whole lot of numbers, Ma, but it sounds like so much fun. It'll be good for you."

"I know. I still miss your brother and your dad, and I get lonely in this condo, and I'll just go on and admit that I get tired of going to church just so I can have a social life and I don't have to get dressed up to worship at home. Anyway, I'll be doing a lot of praying standing in front of those slots." She laughs.

"Okay, Ma, what's the other thing? Because I'm stuck in traffic, and it looks like it's about to start moving."

"Well, you know it's almost time for my annual eye exam, and my cruise conflicts with the date I have on my calendar."

"Ma, it's not set in stone."

"I know. So I'm hoping to get a rain check to see if we can make it after the holidays, unless you think I need to have it sooner."

"Ma, you don't have to have the test on the same day every year, but around the same time is just smart to do at your age."

"I'm not senile yet, Georgia."

"I'm not even going to respond to that. And who is *we*? Please don't say Dolly."

"Well, it's not safe for me to drive that far alone anymore, so Dolly is willing to do the driving."

Why me, Lord? Dolly is my older second cousin, whom I love but don't like that much, because she's got a nasty attitude and never has anything nice to say about anybody, especially me. I know this to be true, because gossip travels faster within families. She has convinced herself that I think I'm hot shit because I went to college and live in a nice house with a pool. Some relatives I can live without, and Dolly's on the top of that list.

"The boys want to come, too. They haven't seen you in years, and they've been having a hard time finding work."

The boys are over thirty. And haven't worked in years either. Last time they were here, they smoked marijuana in the bathroom and tried to drink up half the liquor in the bar.

"I'm about to start remodeling, so there'll be no place for them to sleep," I lie.

"Well, it's about time. And I hope you tone it down some. I feel like I'm walking into a rainbow every time I come through your front door."

"Gotta go. Love you." I usually give her smooches, but she just hurt my feelings, so I don't much feel like it.

I RUSH PAST the tall wall of windows, and Marina, our six-foot Japanese receptionist, waves at me. She's on the phone, sitting behind the long maple counter. In the four years she's worked here, she's worn black every single day—including on her fingernails. From here you can see only her shoulders. She waves, then gives me a slow thumbs-up that all is fine. I wasn't really worried, but I don't like to inconvenience patients, even though the situation is more often the reverse.

Unlike home, the office is serene. The walls are a pale gray, a warm yellow, and one is white. My mother approves. Nine chairs are white, except for one that's yellow. Four oblong purple tables are scattered around the area meant for fitting eyewear. Almost every inch of wall space is filled with frames and sunglasses to suit almost every taste and price.

One of my most annoying but favorite patients, Mona Kwon, rushes to open the door for me. "Thank you, Mona!" I say, and head on over to Marina. Mona sits in *her* chair; the one next to the door if it's empty, or else she'll stand. She'll be seventy-five soon. She only needs strong readers but claims she can't see the tips of her fingernails when she holds them out in front of her. She comes in to have her glasses adjusted at least twice a month. She has forty pair and counting. The techs think she's probably suffering from dementia. I think she's just lonely. She also doesn't like the techs to warm her frames; she insists I do it. After lifting them out of the hot sand and slipping them behind her ears, I watch her stare into the mirror a few minutes too long, as if, or until, she's satisfied she looks like whoever she wants to be.

"Although it'll soon be afternoon, good morning," I say to Marina as well as to three other patients I know are waiting for Lily, my partner, who doesn't come in until eleven. She parties a little too hard, and even though she dresses like a hooker under her lab coat and wouldn't be caught dead in heels less than four inches, she's a damn good optometrist.

"So," I say to Marina, "what's the verdict?"

"You've only missed one appointment, and I rescheduled."

"Thank you much. Is someone in my chair?" I ask without looking over the schedule.

"A newbie. And not to sound corny, but she really is black and beautiful. First name Cleo. Last name is Strawberry. How cool is that? We must thank our lovely florist for the referral. Cleo just wants new contacts, and Ms. Kwon has made it very clear she'll wait. You need a tall Peet's?"

"It won't help. But thanks, Marina."

She hands me my appointment list and the patient's folder. Strawberry? I head to my office, grab a clean lab coat from the closet, slip it over my boring blue dress, then sanitize my hands. I read over her chart quickly and head two doors down. I tap lightly on the door. When I hear an energetic voice say, "All is clear!" I feel better already. Marina was right. She looks like a black princess. Probably in her mid-twenties. She closes the *Dwell* magazine in her lap like a child who's been caught reading something illicit. She reaches over to set it on the instrument table but knows that's wrong, so I hold my hand out along with a smile and take it. She looks up at me and smiles back.

"Good morning, Ms. Strawberry. I'm Dr. Young, and I'm so sorry I'm late."

"Good morning to you as well. I was probably right in front of you, because I just got here about fifteen minutes ago. So no need to apologize, Dr. Young. I just pray no one was seriously injured."

"I hope not, too. Apparently we're going to have to thank Noelle for the referral. Her floral arrangements are like sculpture. We never know what to expect from one week to the next. So. Your last name is Strawberry. That's not a very common name."

"No it isn't. That's why I like it!"

"Eons ago, when I was an undergrad, I had a good friend with that same last name."

"What college?"

"UCSF."

"My dad went to UCSF for undergrad, too!"

"I graduated in '76."

"He was the class of '75! His first name is Raymond."

I can't believe what she's just said. Ray Strawberry and I always thought of each other as Best Friends with Benefits, because his girlfriend was at Harvard and he was madly in love with her. I wasn't really attracted to him at first. Ray and I were both studying our butts off and lonely and needed some relief, so we made a pact that we would call each other up for sex with no strings attached, which at first we did once a week, but then it got up to twice weekly and then whenever we could steal a half hour. All was going well until his girlfriend came for spring break and I realized I was jealous, because unbeknownst to me I had accidentally fallen in love with him.

"I can't believe you're his daughter! We kind of lost touch after he went off to Yale. Ray was serious about becoming a surgeon. So did he? And is he practicing in the Bay Area? How is he? I'd love to say hello. Wow. What a small world this is."

"Well, he's passed on."

I gently put the ophthalmoscope back on the instrument tray. It doesn't matter that I haven't seen or thought much about Ray in all these years. I can't believe his daughter is sitting in this chair, in my office, and has just told me that the first man I fell in love with is dead.

"It's been five years now," she says as she brushes her fingers through those thick black tendrils. "A six-car pile-up. A deer."

Shit.

"I am so sorry to hear this. So very sorry."

Shit.

I grab a Kleenex for myself and then hand her one. I give her the exam, measure her vision, and dilate her pupils in total silence. She starts to tell me her father's history but suddenly stops. She knows. When we're finished, I write her a prescription for new contacts, tell her how nice it was to meet her, that her vision will probably be blurred for the next few hours, and to avoid direct sunlight. On her way out, she hugs me like it's good-bye, and I know she won't be coming back.

I'M MELANCHOLY for the rest of the day. I don't feel like driving in rush-hour traffic and don't feel like going home. I walk six blocks toward Fisherman's Wharf. Even though it's only six o'clock, it's almost dark, and the breeze coming from the bay bites. No matter how warm it is in San Francisco during the day, the temperature is guaranteed to drop as much as twenty degrees by evening, which is why I have on my lined trench coat with a wool scarf wrapped around my neck four or five times. My hands are in my pockets. I turn left on the Embarcadero and almost bump into a homeless woman blocking the sidewalk. She's wrapped in a grimy green blanket. Her hair is colorless, and her face is dirty. I can't tell how old she is, but what I do know is right now this sidewalk is her home. I open my purse and pull out a bill that happens to be a twenty. I put it in her can and keep walking. I do not feel generous.

I have no destination in mind. I'm just trying to register the fact that someone I was once very close to, and loved, is dead. It doesn't seem to matter that it's been over thirty years since I saw him. It doesn't seem to matter that I can't remember the last time he even entered my mind. What's making me so sad is he never even knew that I loved him.

I cross the street and go into a restaurant that's holding happy hour. A handsome host asks if I'll be having dinner, and I tell him I'm not sure. He asks where I'd like to sit, and I point to outside. I follow him and luckily am seated right under a giant heater. Almost all the tables are full of professionals who work nearby. The water in the bay looks black, and the waves are high and heavy. Ferries to Sausalito, Tiburon, and Larkspur are crossing paths out there. They pass right by Alcatraz. The Oakland and Berkeley hills twinkle on the other side of the bay, and to the left, through light fog, the Golden Gate Bridge still looks red even at night. I take off my coat. Instead of white wine, I order a cappuccino.

I should've told Ray I loved him before he graduated. I should've taken the risk of finding out he didn't love me. And what if he did? When my coffee arrives, I sip the foam and then wipe the rim of the cup with my index finger. As I listen to the waves crashing against the dock below, I'm now wondering where the other men I once loved might be. Whatever happened to them? What are they doing? How did their lives turn out? And are they happy? And are they alive? I've done a pretty good job of airbrushing most of them out of my memory, but now I wonder if they've erased me, too.

I've been in love at least five or six or maybe even seven times. Two, I married. Three were full-throttle love, but then the transmission died, and the other two were over before we got started. This doesn't include the men I only had sex with. That number is much higher.

Over the years it became clear that sometimes you fall in love only to realize you don't even like the person. I liked Ray before I loved him. Respected him. And he certainly respected me. He had integrity. He was honest. We talked about anything and everything. He was also a good listener. I learned to be one, too. I didn't put on airs and didn't have to work to impress him. He liked me as is. Which is why we didn't play any silly games. In fact, he was probably the first guy I could say I was friends with. After Ray graduated, he went on to Yale and disappeared from my radar.

I became a better person because of the time I spent with him, knowing him. I never got a chance to tell him that. But I think I would like to let the other men know what I gained from loving them, maybe even hating them. Right now I don't exactly know, because I've never thought about it before. What I do know is that men have occupied almost thirty-five years of my entire adult life. That's a whole lot of time. It now seems obvious that the way we're raised has a major impact on what kind of person we turn out to be, but so does who we love.

I want to find them.

I want them to know they were once important to me.

I want to tell them what they gave me.

I want to find out what I gave them.

I want to remember why I loved them.

I want to find out why they loved me.

I want to understand why we stopped loving each other.

I want to find out why we stopped caring for each other.

I want to find out why we hurt each other.

I want to apologize.

I want to explain.

I want to forgive them.

I want to find out if they've forgiven me.

I want to figure out why it's so hard to forgive.

I want them to know I didn't forget about them and I just chose now to remember.

But more than anything, I really want to know if they're still alive and healthy and happy and thriving and if they've become the man—the person—they wanted to become. I hope so. And I thank Raymond Strawberry for helping me see this.


ON THE WAY HOME, there's no traffic. I feel different. Lighter. Clearer. As if I've just opened a lane for myself and I'm about to enter it. When we're young, we think we're always going to be young. We thought life was going to be one long party. One thrill after another. We knew we could get over heartache and disappointment and failure in a snap, because we were going to have hundreds if not thousands of opportunities and do-overs. We knew that success and happiness and love were in the cards. We didn't worry about the future. We were more worried about the next time we were going to get laid.

Now you fall across the bed when you're not sleepy but just tired of the way you live—or aren't living. From the outside you shouldn't be complaining, but success and a good credit score can't love you. Or give you an orgasm. You even empty the trash and wonder what you're really throwing away. You comb your hair and put on makeup and buy something pretty to wear and get your nails and toes painted hot pink even though you don't feel hot, and you wonder who will even notice. You shave your legs and under your arms and get your eyebrows waxed, and you wonder who will notice. And then one day, out of nowhere, you stop wondering and start worrying that the best part of your life is behind you. Is this how it's going to be forever? Is this all there is?

God, you hope not.

ON FRIDAY NIGHT I decide not to help Detective Goren solve any murders. Fuck him. In fact, I don't turn the television on at all. I take a bubble bath. I shave my legs and my underarms. I give myself a mud facial. I pluck my eyebrows. I put on a comfy pair of pink cotton pajamas that I folded quite nicely last week. They still smell clean. I fall asleep before ten.

On Saturday I decide not to go to Costco or Home Depot or Target or the grocery store for anything, because there is really nothing I need.

I go to the movies.

I buy a ticket to see *You Will Meet a Tall Dark Stranger* not realizing it's a Woody Allen movie, and as usual it's smart and entertaining but there's not a single person of color in it. I manage to laugh anyway.

Afterward I walk outside and into a nice restaurant and have lunch: butternut squash soup and a Caesar salad.

When I get home, I decide to reread *The Alchemist*.

Oh. What a night.

On Sunday morning at seven o'clock sharp, I text Wanda, *meet you at the reservoir. i'll be there at eight.*

She replies, *will meet you there! hooray!*

Wanda happens to be my cheerleader. She's worried that her best friend might die a lonely spinster, which is why she's the nostalgia queen and continues to remind me of when we were hot young things who used to make men take a number. Well, now my number is 175 pounds. She's been happily married to Nelson for thirty-two years. They chose not to have children and never apologized for it. "Three's a crowd," she told me right after they eloped in Maui. Wanda's been my best friend since college. And even though she's opinionated, often misses the mark as well as the point, it's also the reason I love her. She stands her ground, and I can count on her getting on my nerves at least once a week. She's the sister I never had. She pretends to golf for a living but has yet to earn a dime. Not that she needs it. Wanda's also the only black person I know who was born with a gold spoon in her mouth, which is probably why she's on so many benevolent boards. There isn't a week that goes by she's not at some dull dinner celebrating or honoring someone worthy, but Nelson just stopped coming up with excuses and just started saying, "I don't want to go." He's an accountant who spends most of his free time reading espionage novels and watching reruns of *Star Trek*. These banquets are also an excuse for Wanda to get dressed up. But for some pathological reason, she's cheap as hell, can't dress to save her life, and doesn't buy anything unless it's on sale. She spends most of her free time in outlets.

Wanda decided over pizza one night to major in psychology, which is probably one reason she was unemployable. But she's enjoyed not working and is addicted to a number of old-lady hobbies. Scrapbooking is one, and because they had zero children, her scrapbooks are full of pictures of all the dogs she and Nelson have rescued from the pound over the years that have since passed on. Creepy. Then there's needlepoint: ugly needlepoints are scattered all over their house, and three loud, shivering, newly purchased Chihuahuas sleep on the ones they can reach. I have never been able to sit there and watch her do it without needing a drink. I don't understand the purpose of needlepoint, because none of the pictures are ever interesting. In fact, I find most of them to be depressing and eerie. But because she's my best friend—or BFF, as my younger daughter, Frankie, has reminded me to call her and Violet—I've lied and said I loved them, since she gives me one every single Christmas regardless. But so as not to hurt her feelings, I put them in low-traffic areas.

They say you should never tell anyone what you're going to do until after you've done it. I disagree, because there's something to be said for intention. Plus, I've always had a hard time keeping my mouth shut when I'm itching to share what I'd like to think is good news.

I drive up the entrance road lined on both sides with giant oak and pine trees. It feels like an enchanted forest, and when I reach the top, where the parking lot is, a huge blue body of water is surrounded by hundreds of acres of green-and-gold hills. I spot Wanda stretching on a park bench and pull in to a parking space. To my dismay, Violet and Velvet pull up right next to me. Why didn't Wanda bother telling me that Violet was coming and bringing her daughter? I wave and smile and don't get out of the car. This spoils my plans. How can I have a personal, grown-up conversation with a hip-hopper right next to us?

Before I can figure out how to handle this, Velvet jumps out of Violet's white Range Rover, runs over, opens my door, and gives me a big hug. "Hi, Auntie! Thought I'd join you guys this morning."

"It's been too long," I say with as much enthusiasm as I can muster. She runs over and does the same thing to Wanda. Like mother, like daughter. She's in skintight orange leggings and an even tighter white tank top. She has about a thousand blond braids that hang down past her shoulders. She runs back to the SUV and hops back in.

Wanda turns and waves, hunches her shoulders, and I can tell she isn't thrilled to see Velvet either. Velvet not only runs her mouth nonstop like her mother, but she's loud.

Violet is my other college friend whom I love like a stepsister, but I'm not crazy about her standards. For being so smart, she's dumb as hell and gets on my nerves, but I just can't bring myself to divorce her. She won't let me. We've gone months without speaking, but eventually she always calls back. Or I break down and call her. She's the youngest of nine and apparently had a lot to prove, because she's competitive and hates to lose. Her brains and beauty merged quite well and she became a top sports attorney, but I still wonder how she managed to pass the bar. In her heyday Violet probably slept with half the NBA, MLB, and the NFL in her quest to represent players. She finally cooled her jets when word got around she was a legal slut and her client list started diminishing. This, however, hasn't stopped her from dressing like one. Even after three children and at fifty-four, she still has the body of a thirty-six-year-old.

Violet is married to Violet. She never believed in the institution, but she did believe in cohabiting. For the last five or six years, she's been what she calls a free agent, except that Wanda and I think Velvet has been cramping her style. At twenty-five, Velvet has yet to find a college she likes or a college that likes her, so she's been trying to figure out why, while living rent-free and asking, "Do you want fries with that?" Violet treats her daughter more like a girlfriend and is stupid enough to confer with her on things that Velvet knows nothing about. One son lives with his father in Toronto, and the other one plays basketball in Spain. Neither of them visits, and Wanda and I know why. Because Violet was not a great mother.

Of course she's on her cell and holds up her index finger to give her a minute. I text Wanda, *i'm going to call you in a sec. answer it, but don't look up or at me.*

I dial her number and pretend I'm getting an incoming call. I put a glad-to-hear-from-you look on my face. "On our walk this morning, I had planned on telling you that I'm seriously thinking about putting my house on the market and I'm considering selling my share of the practice and trying to change professions sometime in the near future and not necessarily in that order, and, Wanda, I just found out that Ray Strawberry died five years ago, which has really broken me up, and even though it might sound like a crazy thing to do, I've decided I'm going to look up all the men I've loved just to let them know I'm glad I had the opportunity to know and love them and just to see if they're alive and well. I know it may be a lot to take in, but now that Violet has brought Miss Thang, you know we can't talk about anything real, so I'm hanging up and we can talk about this another time." I end the call, get out of the car, and smile as if I've just received the best news.

Violet and I trot over toward Wanda, and I can't believe she's wearing loose brown sweats and a beige zip-up jacket. She must be depressed about something, but I can't tell because she's also wearing Ray-Bans. "Hi-di-ho, ladies. After we warm up, I'm going to jog on the upper trail for a half hour with Velvet, and then we'll meet you guys on the lower one for the last twenty. Okay?"

"Fabulous!" Wanda says, trying not to sound too relieved. She and I do not jog.

The three of us do a few stretches while Wanda leans against the railing. The reservoir is in the background, and people are already out in pedal boats, rowboats, and even a few kayaks. Some folks are fishing from the shoreline. It's a Kodak moment for sure. I'm a bit stunned when Wanda gives me a smile like I just performed in a school play and did a great job. She then claps her hands and puts on her white visor. Of course she's sporting one of the five identical last year's no-brand exercise outfits she bought at an outlet last month. This one is mint green. I like it.

Violet and Velvet give us a see-you-later wave and jog away toward the upper dirt trail, which is off to the side of the asphalt one we're about to walk on. They disappear within minutes, which is when Wanda walks over and gives me a hug. "I'm so on your team," she says.

"I know that, but let's get warm first."

"Whenever you're ready. I'm all ears."

We walk in silence for the first ten minutes. There are joggers, and quite a few elderly folks are being pushed in wheelchairs. We wave to them. Those who can, smile back. Lots of people with leashed dogs stop and go. Bicyclists whiz by us in their designated lane. Almost everyone we pass or who passes us says "Good morning" or "Hello, and how are you today?" or "Another perfect day" or "Stay fit." When we finally reach the boathouse on our left, it means we've made it to the top of the first steep incline. We walk slowly on the now-flat path a few minutes, long enough to catch our breath.

"So," I say.

"Wait, Georgia. I've got to ask you something first."

"Of course."

"What made you decide to do all this?"

"Sometimes you know in your heart it's time to make a change, but the longer you just think about it, the longer the change takes. If ever. I'm finally tired of just thinking about it. But let me ask you a question."

"Ask away."

"You're happy with your life, aren't you?"

She nods.

"Well, I'm not. I'm bored with mine. And since my life is the only thing I do have any control over, I want to start changing some of it."

"I'm listening."

"Don't you have any regrets?"

"We all have regrets, Georgia."

"Well, I feel like I have too many. I'm getting old, Wanda. We're all getting old. Not old-old, but older, and at some point we need to be honest with ourselves and do what excites us instead of what looks good on paper. I think that's how I ended up in optometry. I was good in science. And I wanted to impress my father by proving how smart I was, since he was a doctor. But I just kept on proving it only to learn later that he didn't care what I did as long as I loved it. So now here I am *not* loving it, and even though there're some things I *do* love to do, I'm not sure if it's too late to find out how good I might be at them. But so help me God, I'm going to find out."

"Well, finally! This is the Georgia I've missed."

"Hold on, now. This isn't *I Dream of Jeannie.* One step at a time. First you have to have the dream before you walk inside it. Let's keep walking."

Of course, if I had it to do over, I would have tried my hand at decorating or designing. I'm pretty sure my father would've hit the roof if I'd said, "I'm thinking about majoring in interior design, because one day I'd love to make homes uniquely beautiful." Ha. That's right up there with telling your parents you want to be a writer and you're going to get a degree in creative writing. Back in the day, I didn't know that *real* people designed furniture. I thought you had to have a gift or something. I can't draw, but I've always been full of ideas and had a knack for playing with color and textures.

I fell in love with paint in college. Learned how to make old things new. I bought a used wooden futon that came with a matching chair at a yard sale to fill up my tiny apartment. They were willing to throw in the cushions, which I passed on because they were filthy. I bought batting and some loud upholstery fabric and made my own. And then I forgot all about beauty.

After fifteen minutes Wanda finally says, "Let me say this. Hearing you say you're putting that house on the market is music to my ears."

"Why?"

"Because you don't need it. You've raised your kids. Fuck grass and flower beds. Fuck a two-car garage. Get a loft. With a whole new view. This way your relatives will have to stay in a hotel when they visit."

"I don't trust apartment living, Wanda. Anyway, I just need a new venue, but there won't be a For Sale sign in the front yard next week, that much I can tell you."

"I know, honey. But this is all just so fucking exciting! And as far as giving up your practice goes, I say right on. I always thought it was a pretty dull profession with no real payoff, not to mention a little creepy looking inside folks' eyes all day long. I never really thought it suited you."

"Well, why didn't you ever say so?"

"Because that's right up there with parents trying to tell their kids who not to marry. You have to find out for yourself that you erred. It just takes some of us longer than others to figure that out. You need to find something more creative to do. Make me some more of those god-damn pillows. They were gorgeous. I still get compliments on them all the time."

"Well, I'm not whipping out the old Singer anytime soon, but last week I found myself walking into an unfinished-furniture store like a shoplifter and came out carrying a tall wooden stool I intend to do something magical to. Just don't ask me what yet."

"And what are you going to do to it?"

I crack up. The only thing I know how to sew anymore is a square and a rectangle, and one Christmas we all agreed to make one another's Christmas gifts, and Violet gave me a dried-flower arrangement but forgot to take the price tag off the bottom, and of course Wanda made me a needlepoint. I whipped out my old sewing machine and made her and Violet silk pillows. Apparently I was on cruise control, because I went a little overboard and made them for everyone in the office and even some patients, and of course Mona Kwon wanted me to sell her four, which I refused to do and just gave them to her. Then my sewing machine broke down and no more Martha Stewart.

We walk around a curve in silence until it straightens out.

"So how'd you find out about Ray?"

I tell her. And all the reasons I've decided to look these men up.

"As long as you're not trying to be slick and rekindle an old flame that burned out a century ago."

"Please. You should know me better. I understand that you can't go back."

"I'm not sure if I could do it, but hey, this is why people go to shrinks! To get perspective. And that old cliché known as closure. Plus, what do you have to lose? Oh, hell, I see Velvet coming down the path. I would hold off telling all this to Violet, because she'll probably miss the point. So tell me real quick, who's up first?"

"I think I should start with Abraham."

"Well, I would hope so."

# From the Waist Down

NO MATTER HOW DRUNK YOU GET, DON'T COUNT THE guy you meet at the club and sleep with the very same night as a potential husband. It'll never happen." I'm trying to remember who said this, but I'm drawing a blank. Anyway, who was looking for a husband? We came to party. Which is why Wanda, Violet, and I, all underage and relying on fake IDs to get us into the club, were dressed in hot pink and orange and silver hot pants to make sure the fellas wouldn't miss our curvy behinds or our A- to D-cup cleavage in those thin, tight tank tops. Our white platform boots with fake goldfish in those acrylic heels also didn't hurt us any, which is why when we strolled toward the back of the long line, freezing our asses off, we pretended not to have any idea how good we looked and had the nerve to act surprised when the fellas started checking us out and "Hey, girl" and "Hey, baby" and wink-wink and "Please let me be yo' man." The big bouncer strolled down the line, reviewing all the girls like this was the Westminster Kennel Club Dog Show, and by the time he got to us, he said, "Y'all cover charge been covered." Some of the girls left outside looked at us like they wanted to kick our asses. We strutted right on past them. We never paid when we wore these getups. And I, the only one not drowning in department-store cologne samples, rubbed a dab or three of oils I bought, and occasionally stole, from the health-food store meant to lure and intoxicate a fella or at least make him curious enough to ask, "What's that you wearing? You sure smell good, girl."

I remember that as soon as I heard the first few chords of "Get Down Tonight," I jumped up from my chair and ice-skated out onto the dance floor and started boogying by myself, and before I could sit down, "Boogie On Reggae Woman" ran right into it, and then "The Hustle," and that's when this tall, black, handsome fella walked out and just started doing the Bump with me. "You sure smell good," he said, looking down at me, and I looked up, smiled as innocently as possible, and said, "Thank you." Violet was dancing with an android, and Wanda said she remembered this like it was yesterday, because no one had asked her to dance, and that's because she looked like she was mad about something. When "I Wanna Do Something Freaky to You" started in, the strobe lights were just spinning away, and I kept on dancing, and finally he said, "I'm Abraham, and who might you be?"

"Georgia," I said, and ordered my hips to give him one strong bump, then left him out there and strutted on back to my empty chair, where Wanda and Violet were sitting with their legs crossed, staring at him and then at me.

I should've known right then and there when Abraham didn't offer to buy me a drink that he was not meant to be on my Most Wanted List. But boy, oh, boy, how wrong I would be. He disappeared into the crowd, although I could see his blue or red or yellow Afro from time to time, and then he reappeared and asked me if I had come alone. When I pointed to my girlfriends, that's when he asked me if he could buy all three of us a drink, and Violet said, "Hell yeah," and I kicked her under the table, which meant to pretend like she had some class, and then he and I danced all night and drank all night, and I was so toasted that when he took me by the hand, I followed him into the men's room and inside a stall and fucked him.

Wanda and Violet dragged me out to the parking lot right before the club closed, and he followed, asking for my number, and I remember thinking his name sure was appropriate, because he looked like he had just stepped right out the Bible. I wrote my phone number on his long arm, but he was so dark and hairy he couldn't read it, so I wrote it on both palms.

He called the very next day and asked if he could come over. Back then we didn't really "date," because no one had any "date" money, and dinner was usually a hot dog and a drink at the movies, so the fact that

Abraham actually called made me feel special. Of course Wanda and Violet reminded me the following morning what I had done off the dance floor with a guy whose last name I still didn't know. But like a fool I gave him my address and then made something perfectly clear. "I am not an alcoholic, and I'm also no slut. I'm a college student." He said he didn't understand what would make me think he would think that about me. Please. Playing hard to get was a complete waste of time, and at nineteen I really just wanted to get laid in a horizontal position. This time not only did I want to remember it, but my fingers were crossed that Abraham would be able to make me feel and act like those women in the movies who're drowning in ecstasy. I was hoping he had the skills to make me slither, grit my teeth, dig my fingernails into his back, cause me to look like I was in agonizing pain when in fact it was just the opposite, and pretty much lose my mind. It would also be great if he told me he loved me, since no one ever had, and I wouldn't even care if he meant it.

When I opened the door, I almost couldn't breathe. All I remember thinking was, *Thank you, Jesus,* because my blackout was gone and I instantly remembered how unbelievably beautiful his lips were and how white and straight his teeth were and how long and hairy his arms were and how shiny and black his Afro and mustache and goatee were, and he even smelled heavenly. He handed me a purple hydrangea he'd stolen from someone's yard. We sat on my cheap tweed sofa, which was really a love seat. My studio was small. My bed folded up into the wall. I remember being nervous, and I figured we should talk about something light, something that would put us in the mood, which turned out to be the fog in San Francisco. He pretended to be interested in what I was majoring in, and I lied and told him architecture, because it wouldn't make him think I was too smart to handle, even though I knew it was going to be biology or physics or something in the physical sciences. I remember not caring what *his* major was, because tonight it was going to be me, Georgia Louise Young. We both knew why I let him come over, and I figured I'd find out his last name when I needed to know it.

I remembered you were always supposed to have a bottle of wine in the fridge in case you had unexpected guests, so with my fake ID I dashed to the corner and bought a bottle of cheap white wine that claimed to have real grapes in it.

This night would be a turning point in my life. After that first time with Darnell and then with Patrick and Jimmy, I just liked the fact that we were naked and trying to move in sync until we, or I should say "they"—in a matter of minutes—acted like they were being electrocuted and then suddenly collapsed on me. I never even broke a sweat and wondered when and if I was ever going to tremble like that.

After the wine Abraham took me straight to heaven. He seduced me just like in the movies. I will never forget the way those big hands gently slid my bra straps down my arms. That's when I stopped thinking. I remember not having time to turn off the lights. I remember being kissed like I was a baby and then a grown woman, and I remember him picking me up from my love seat and laying me down on the floor, on top of my thick shag carpet, and he kissed me slower than slow, and I started to move like I was in a race, because I was trying to prove to him that I was just as good a lay sober as I was drunk, but he whispered in my ear, "Slow down, baby," and I didn't know what speed that was, so I said, "Show me," and he put those hands on my hips and moved me like I was a slow roller coaster, and then the lights went off and I started losing control over my own body. At first I was embarrassed, and then when I started shaking and shivering and I yelled out, "Oh, God!" and Abraham said, "It's all right, baby," and then he got stronger and moved faster and collapsed on me, and started kissing me everywhere like I was something precious.

I had what felt like aftershocks, and Abraham held me and said, "It's all right, baby, I got you." Oh, yes, he did. And finally, finally, I understood what all the hoopla was about and knew without a doubt I wanted to feel like that as often as possible.

"Did you like that, baby?"

"Can you bottle it?"

He laughed like he was fully aware of his sexual power. All I knew was that I wanted to do it again just to see if I'd get the same results. And in the weeks and months that followed, I would discover I could have three and sometimes four of these magical moments back-to-back. It wasn't like I was trying. Abraham had become my real-life black Ken doll. And I wanted to keep him.

However. Despite my being smart enough to get a full scholarship, it had started to become increasingly clear that I was not that bright when it came to men. I thought they wanted a girl to be Wonder Woman. And me, like a damn fool, once Abraham started calling out my name during sex, I believed this to be a spiritual connection occurring between us and thus a sign of love. Abraham came over almost every day that first week, before or after his classes. Then one night we were lying on my Murphy bed and he was kissing my earlobe and said, "Look at all these goose bumps on my arm. I think I might be allergic to you, girl."

And I said, "That's impossible. I'm hypoallergenic."

"I like you," he said. "You're quick. Feisty."

"I've got better qualities, but I can't let you see them all at once."

"I'll wait," he said.

A week or so later, I finally asked him, "What's your major, Abraham?"

"Did I give you the impression I was in college?"

I just looked at him like he was joking. "I'm serious as a heart attack. What's your major?"

"It was horticulture."

"Was?"

I felt like I'd been conned. I sat up and moved away from him. All of a sudden, Abraham felt too big for this room. He was really too big for me, too, because I felt small in his arms. Not safe, just small. He didn't put his arms around me with tenderness; he pulled me into him like he was an octopus.

"I was going to San Francisco State, but then my moms got sick and I had to work, so I've been on leave for two semesters."

"What's wrong with your mom?"

"I'd rather not get into it," he said, as if she had some type of embarrassing illness, which made absolutely no sense. I would learn later that his sick mother was not only healthy but worked in the lingerie department at Macy's in Union Square, that and at twenty-five and not twenty-two like he told me he was, Abraham still lived at home, had three younger siblings, all of whom, as I would also learn, were in or had graduated from various universities in Northern and Southern California.

"Well, I hope she's going to be okay," I said.

"I pray every day," he said.

"Why do you hang out around a college campus if you're not enrolled?"

"I don't *hang* out around a college campus. These clubs are open to the public. Plus, I live very close to here."

"What do you do all day when you're not caring for your mother?"

"Are you interrogating me?"

"I want to know, Abraham."

"I work part-time for a nursery."

"Really? What do you do there?"

"I sell plants."

I wasn't trying to be difficult. I just wanted to know how he earned a living or if his sick mother was taking care of herself, since he'd been spending so much time with me. I was also hoping he wouldn't ask me to meet her, because my gut was already telling me we were probably not heading down any aisle except maybe at the grocery store.

He picked up the remote.

"I have to study for an exam," I said.

"Don't let me stop you," he said, and took off his shoes.

"I think you might not be able to spend the night, Abraham. I have to study, and I can't do it with the television on."

"Have you ever tried?"

"No, because it doesn't make much sense."

"Try it and see what happens."

"I need to be able to concentrate," I said, sitting at my scratched-up wooden desk in the ugly brown Naugahyde chair I'd bought at a garage sale.

The next thing I knew, he reached into his shirt pocket and

whipped out a joint and lit it. "A few hits of this and you won't have any problems concentrating, Miss G."

"I don't smoke marijuana, and I think you should've asked if I minded before you lit it."

"I'm sorry, baby. I respect you and your crib," he said, but not before taking two deep hits. "You should at least just take a puff or two. It's not like you're doing drugs. I promise you, if you don't like it, I'll never ask you again."

And he handed the joint to me. I also didn't like the way it smelled, and how anyone who didn't smoke real cigarettes could inhale smoke was beyond me. But I was about to find out. I didn't feel comfortable holding this thing and wasn't sure exactly how to inhale, and of course Abraham gave me yet another tutorial. I almost choked to death after the first attempt, because the smoke was hot and made the back of my throat feel like it was on fire. He encouraged me to take one more deep puff and hold it in, so I did, and the smoke traveled down on top of my esophagus and then did a U-turn up into where my brain was supposed to be. At first it felt like fireworks, and then I began to feel like I was floating down a stream. I liked it. And I took another puff and studied my ass off. The next morning, however, I would fail my very first Spanish exam, because I would not remember how to conjugate anything except Abraham.

"Can I move in?" Abraham asked one night. This. After not so much as having walked outside for three days. This was during spring break, if I remember correctly. I was now addicted to him, because I loved all the anytime-I-wanted-it sex. It was like having my very own action figure, and all I had to do was wind him up. Sex was my new major.

As much as I was in love with Abraham's body, I knew I wasn't in love with him. He only made me feel good from the waist down, but to be perfectly honest he had also started getting on my nerves. First of all, he wasn't the most stimulating conversationalist. When I would come in from a philosophy or a computer class and try to explain that some guys were developing new ways to use computers, he wasn't all that intrigued or even interested. He acted like he was afraid of books. He didn't seem very concerned about what was going on in the world, and he changed the channel when the news came on. I changed it back. I should've known he was missing a few links, the way he went into a trance watching anything that had to do with murder, combat, espionage, fire, floods, or horses.

This is precisely when I had to admit that Abraham was not that bright. In fact, he was boring as hell when fully dressed. I knew he was probably never going to appreciate the world that fascinated me and the role I might one day play in it, and there was no way in hell I was going to allow him to drag me down to his level, which was simply the mezzanine but had started to feel more and more like the basement.

"Did you hear me?"

"Yes, I heard you. And no, you cannot move in," I said firmly.

"Why not?"

"Because my apartment is too small." (He was six foot three—six-six if I included his Afro.)

"Then let's get a bigger one."

"But I don't want to move, Abe."

"Please don't call me Abe. I've asked you on quite a few occasions not to, because it makes me feel like Abe Lincoln."

"Abraham, I don't want to live with you."

"Why not?"

"Because my grades are dropping."

"And you're blaming that on me?"

"I'm blaming it on me, Georgia."

"I thought you said you loved me."

"I love a lot of things about you."

"What's the difference?"

"I don't know how to answer that."

I shouldn't have had to break this shit down to him. I had already begun to make the distinction between dynamite sex and love. One lasted a few minutes. The other was supposed to last years. My mama used to say, "A man can make you forget your last name." So far I was glad I still remembered mine. However, being with Abraham had started making me feel like I was shrinking and losing my focus. At that point in time, all I really wanted was what I could control and that was getting a bachelor's degree. My GPA had dropped, and I was not about to go into my junior year with anything lower than a 3.5. Period.

Which is precisely what I would end up missing for two months. My period. I was too afraid to tell Abraham.

On a night he wouldn't go home, I just sat there and looked at him while he watched *Sanford and Son*. He was so engaged he didn't even know I was studying him. He really wasn't all that handsome. In fact, he *was* starting to favor Abraham Lincoln. It was creepy. Every time he laughed, I started noticing that his teeth were getting beiger and that they'd only looked white because of his mustache and because he was also the color of a double espresso. Those lips, which had been so soft and warm and juicy and tender, now seemed to need more and more ChapStick. I had also started realizing he wasn't as concerned about personal hygiene as he should've been. The list of things about him that were getting on my nerves kept growing, but it's also very hard to tell someone you'd been having for dessert almost every single day and night that your taste buds were changing.

I DIDN'T WANT to have Abraham's baby. I didn't want to have anybody's baby while I was still in college. I was too scared to have a baby. It would change the entire course of my life, and it would also mean I'd always be connected to him. Wanda went with me. On the way to the clinic, she had to pull over three times, because I couldn't stop throwing up. What I was about to do terrified me. But I did it. And was grateful I wouldn't remember any of it right after I started counting backward. I pretended to be mad at Abraham for two whole weeks, even though he wouldn't stop bothering me. He apologized for whatever it was he'd done. Although he was an amazing joyride, I also knew he wasn't the only tall, handsome black man in the world with a penis worthy of a gold medal.

Instead of inviting him over to my apartment, I asked if he'd meet me at this amazing vegetarian restaurant that was the reason I was beginning to turn my back on hamburgers. When Abraham walked in, he was wearing an army green fatigue jacket. Everyone in the place seemed to notice him. He was one sexy militant, who looked like he lived by his own personal constitution. Like he stood for something important.

When he bent down to kiss me, I turned my head, and his lips brushed my left cheek. "So it's like that, then, huh?"

His voice didn't match the way he looked. It was too soft for a man his size. Something else I hadn't noticed before.

"Can I buy you lunch?" he asked.

"Sure," I said. "Everything here is meatless."

"Yes it is," he said. "Yes it is."

We didn't talk. We simply chewed. After he'd eaten every single piece of the thick wheat bread, he stood up, looked down at me, and let out a long sigh. "I think we just met at the wrong time."

I looked up into his black eyes. "I don't know if that's true or not, Abraham. But I have appreciated what we've shared."

He chuckled. "Can I at least give you a good-bye kiss?" he asked.

I nodded.

He bent down and kissed me softly on my forehead and then on my cheek, and then he pressed his lips against mine for two long seconds. "Good luck to you," he said, and took a few steps back. "You'll probably make some dude a great wife one day, Georgia. And I hope you keep his baby."

I went numb. I can still remember how ashamed I felt. I couldn't look at him, even though I felt his eyes on me. I stared down at the mishmash on my plate and closed my eyes until I heard him say, "Keep the change," and felt the cold air rush in after he walked out the door. I lifted my head, wiped my eyes with my napkin, and watched his thick, black Afro and those army green shoulders disappear as he got onto the cable car.

I'M NERVOUS JUST thinking about looking Abraham up as I sit in front of my cold computer. Maybe this wasn't such a good idea. In fact, maybe it's a stupid idea. I sit here for the longest time just staring out the window when I see Naomi and Macy, my next-door neighbors, sauntering up the sidewalk. I almost run to the front door.

They're both sexy blond lesbians who love white shirts and black pants and must have every color of slip-on Vans ever made. They got married on the steps of City Hall two years ago in San Francisco. I took them to brunch to celebrate. They're also crazy as hell, or I should just say wild and fun. Macy's a curator at the Museum of Modern Art in San Francisco, and Naomi manages a four-and-a-half-star hotel I've yet to stay at.

"What do you huzzies want? Hey, Rascal," I say, and rub her head the way she likes. She's a sweet pit bull.

"We were wondering if we could borrow twenty dollars?" Naomi says, and hands me a white box. I know there's something delicious inside, because there always is.

"No. And I'm on a diet. So whatever's in that box, I can't eat it."

"You've been on a diet since we met you, and what year was that, honey?"

"I believe that was 1886," Macy says.

"So you will eat this and enjoy it. It's my very own Key lime pie."

"And here," Macy says, handing me what I know will be another invitation to an opening I probably won't attend and do not know why. She must be six feet tall and could easily be a forty-something runway model if she just wanted to.

I open the envelope. I'm right.

"Thank you both. And I'll try. You want to come in?"

"No. Our goal was to disturb you. Did we succeed?"

"Yes, and I'm grateful. Now, beat it!"

And I slam the door. I can hear them laughing. This is our way. I'm lucky to have them as my neighbors, because the Russian family on the right has never uttered so much as a syllable when I say hello or good morning or good evening or happy holidays. They don't like to celebrate but are very good wavers.

I open the box and dig my finger into the mint green pie and scoop out a thick, smooth dollop. It's so good I do this three more times and then make a pot of coffee and push the rest of it into the garbage disposal for obvious reasons.

I take my coffee back to my office and find the password I keep hidden with all the other ones inside the big red Webster's dictionary and log in to Facebook. I've only been on this site twice in two years, because I have yet to see the point of it, but I understand you can find just about anybody on here, even though until today I haven't been looking for anyone.

I'm shocked when I see a photo of someone who looks like I did about ten years ago. I think Frankie put that picture of me on here when she signed me up. I forgot I had cheekbones. And only one chin. And a wig that wasn't synthetic; it was actually my hair. I looked happy, I looked good, and I can't remember why.

What will I say if I find him? "Remember me from the seventies? We spent some time together." That sounds lame, like I'm still stuck in the past. And what if all he says is yes? What if he has nothing else to say to me? What if he thinks I've only gotten in touch because I'm trying to hook back up after a thousand years? But then again, what if he's still in the Bay Area and happily married and would love to see me, maybe introduce me to his wife and kids (which I would love), or what if he wants to meet for a latte after thirty-four years? I forgot all about the possibility of seeing him in person. Shit. He would probably think I've let myself go. But I have.

According to Frankie, people put their whole lives on Facebook, so I should be able to see what he's done with his. I hope he finished college. But what will I tell him about me? That I've gone through two husbands? (I wouldn't admit to being traded in for a newer model or take any responsibility for being a bad judge of character.) That I'm a little on the fuller side and I also dye my hair intense auburn to avoid looking at the gray? That I'm an unhappy optometrist looking to make a career change when most people are thinking about retirement? And lie that I'm in a serious relationship but we're just taking it slow? And what if he asks what made me get in touch with him after all these years? What in the hell will I say that would make any sense?

I hit Escape.

Then Sleep.

Abraham's going to have to wait.


WANDA JUST HAD to open her big mouth and tell Violet what I'm planning to do, which is why Violet chose to leave me a long, sensitive voice-mail message: *"Have you lost your damn mind, Georgia? You must have. This is about the dumbest shit I've ever heard. What do you hope to gain from it? I say leave the bastards exactly where they belong: in the Relationship History Book. Of course I'm sorry to hear about Raymond, but if I were you, I'd think twice about selling my house in this fucked-up economy. But you have yet to take any good advice I've given you, and I don't expect you to start now, so forget everything I just said and do it your way. Bye."*

I'm forgetting it right now.

I go back on Facebook and type in Abraham's first and last names and push my chair away from my desk two or three feet and look down at the floor while my heart pounds like a jackhammer. When I glance up at the screen, I cover my mouth, because I only see one black face and he's a teenager.

I feel somewhat relieved.

But then, as if I'm on autopilot, I decide to Google his name, except this time I include his middle name, which I didn't even know I remembered. Well, I'm pretty sure Abraham wasn't a soldier in 1898, and he didn't drive a tractor-trailer in North Carolina, nor did he play the jazz trumpet with Jimmy Smith, and I'm hoping, for his sake, that the parking-summons warrant waiting for him in Alabama isn't his.


"MAYBE ABRAHAM is dead, too," Wanda says. We're getting off the Sausalito exit right past hundreds of houseboats, where Violet has lived for years. Black people don't live on boats. We live on land.

"Don't say that," I say.

Wanda's driving, which is a mistake, because she's not good at staying in her lane. "Everybody can be found somewhere on the Internet."

"Apparently that's not true."

"Did you ever meet any of his relatives?"

I shake my head.

"Not even his mama?"

I shake my head again.

"Then he's probably in prison."

"I don't want to think either one could be true."

"What would you have said to him anyway?"

"I don't exactly know."

"Yes you do," she says.

"I don't feel like telling you, Wanda, especially since it didn't happen."

"But you weren't even in love with Abraham, if I remember correctly."

"I didn't put that label on it back then, but I actually think I was. He scared me. And I scared myself. But so what? I'll be forever grateful to him for generating my first orgasm. You don't forget that."

"That's for sure. Not to skip the subject, but I'm skipping the subject for a minute. Have you done anything about the house yet, or are you already getting cold feet?"

"I can't lie. Ever since I decided to do this, I've been nervous as hell, but I've been telling myself it's normal to be scared when you're about to make a major change in your life. So, to answer your question, I've interviewed three Realtors and think I've settled on one."

"That's my girl!" she says, and gives me a high five right before she pulls into a parking space. Before us there are nothing but sexy white sailboats and fat yachts rocking in their berths. Behind us are steep green hills full of hip houses, some with giant windows jutting out and some on stilts that you couldn't pay me to live in, views or no views.

"Well, they all basically said what I already know. That because of the economy the real-estate market is taking a beating so it could be up to a year before the house sells. But I'm not in a rush. I've still got some other things to figure out."

"I think it's exciting. That you don't feel too old to do this. Seriously. I'm proud as hell of you, if you want to know the truth."

"Why, thank you, huzzy."

"Hurry up. Our reservation is in five minutes."

We finally jump out of the car and walk as fast as we can past shop after beautiful shop. I don't bother looking. Wanda doesn't either, because she wouldn't dream of buying anything over here, since the prices are way too high for her.

"So who do you want to look for next?" she asks.

"Listen, I'm not thinking about men right now. I'm thinking about lobster."

"What about Brad?"

"He doesn't count."

"Why not? You lived with him for three long months!"

I start laughing. "We were roommates."

"You slept in the same bedroom with that *roommate*."

"He stole money from me. Plus, I didn't love him."

"What?"

"I just never told you or Violet."

"You know we didn't like his ass anyway. He was below you, and he looked sneaky. With those little bird eyes. He was a waste of a perfectly good summer."

"It was forty-eight dollars."

"Delete him from your list."

"I don't have a list!"

"Well, why don't you make one?"

"First of all, Wanda, I'm only interested in finding the men I was in love with, not the ones I just slept with."

"I'll bet you a hundred dollars you can't count the ones you screwed."

"You are starting to piss me off."

"You can't even name them, can you? Because that list is probably too damn long. Ho."

"How many are on *your* list, huzzy?"

"Two. Because I found what I needed early. Anyway, I know who you loved, but I want to hear you say them just in case I missed some, since you were so sneaky."

"Oliver. David. Eric. Carter. And Lance."

"See what I mean? Who in the hell are Carter and Lance?"

"Well, like Ray, they didn't know I was in love with them."

"Why not?"

"Forget it, Wanda. Let me just say this, since you obviously don't get it. You can fall in love in a nanosecond, and there's really nothing you can do about it."

"Yeah, and how's that work?"

"I'm not even going to bother explaining it, but there's a reason so many of us act like we're possessed."

"Speak for yourself. Why aren't you including the ex-husbands? You did love them, if I remember correctly."

"Because I still hate Michael."

"You couldn't possibly after all these years, Georgia."

"He cheated on me."

"And he's the father of one of your children."

"He was a mistake. She wasn't."

"Where is he these days?"

"Last I heard, he moved to Chicago to work for some Big Eight firm. Estelle doesn't talk to me about him, because she knows it'll make me break out in hives."

Wanda shoves me through the door of the restaurant, which looks like the lower level of a giant old sailboat complete with portholes, thick wooden walls, long rubber sharks, and silver fish hanging on them. We can see straight out to the deck, which juts out over the water.

"And Niles?"

"Can you use social media when you're behind bars?"

"Shouldn't he be out by now? Anyway, I think you should start with the husbands and get them over with. Find out if Niles is a free man. But Michael should be next."

"Is this a directive, Lieutenant Jeffries?"

"Look, this whole mission was your bright idea, so if you're going to do it, do it in chronological order. That way you can see when and how and why you made such bad choices in men, which might help explain why you're still lost and confused."

"Go straight to hell, Wanda," I say, laughing.

"Been there once. Didn't like it."

"Look. In all honesty, I don't really care what Michael's doing or who he's doing it with. In fact, I think I'll skip him."

"You are such a hypocrite. I thought you said you wanted to get a new perspective, forgive them or yourself, and maybe tie up some loose ends."

"I did. But I think these would be called knots."

# Old Flames or Just Sparks

S O EVERYBODY'S NOT ON FACEBOOK. AND EVERYBODY can't even be Googled. Last night, before I went to bed, I took a peek at my home page, and apparently no one wants to be my friend. The only thing I see is a photograph of an old school and bold letters that say "40th Class Reunion!" Have I really been out of high school forty years? I'm almost ashamed to admit I've only been to one reunion, and that was the tenth, and I left early. By the twentieth I'd pretty much forgotten about high school, for the same reasons you don't reminisce about kindergarten when you're headed to middle school.

Nevertheless, I decide right here right now that I'm going to this one. Why, I don't know. I RSVP. Besides, it's a whole year away. I have no idea what to expect or if I even remember some of the nerds and sluts I graduated with. What I remember most about high school is heat, tumbleweed, and dust. I was popular but not well liked, because the word had gotten around that the reason I was in so many honors classes was that I skipped two grades in elementary school, putting me in the same grade as Roger, my older brother, who decided to skip college to join the army, which is how we lost him at twenty-two. There weren't very many black kids in my high school, and I often felt lonely. I'm so full of shit. I was just bored to death. By my senior year, I was tired of all the do-nothing clubs and couldn't wait to flip my tassel. I generated even more adversaries once the word got out that I wasn't going to Cal State Bakersfield but rather to the University of California in San Francisco. Bitch.

But that's all behind me. I now have a damn good incentive to lose twenty pounds by this time next year.

I log out.

Or off.

Whatever.


SO. SINCE WANDA opened her big mouth about the order I should consider looking up the five but probably seven men I loved, I'm also curious about how many I've had sex with. Since my social calendar isn't exactly backed up this evening, I've decided to dig out my old phone books to see how many of these guys I can resurrect.

Back in the day, I used to save every single phone book and bought a new one only when the pages started falling out or when so many folks had been crossed out because either they'd moved too many times or their number had changed so many times, which meant it had probably been disconnected for nonpayment—mine included— and sometimes I had to look in my own phone book to remember my new number. I always wrote the date the new book started and ended on the back cover with a Magic Marker, which is why I never bought a black book. I put my current address on the inside page so I'd be able to remember where I'd lived when I got old and nostalgic like I'm feeling now. Last but not least were the people I just wanted out of my fucking life for one reason or another, so I'd either draw lines through their names or a wide X or scribble so hard I'd sometimes rip right through the page and shred the person on the other side. This left many a phone book looking more like a scratch pad. Which is what forced me to buy a new one.

Times have sure changed.

As I grow older, I realize there's something to be said for nostalgia and not getting rid of stuff that holds memories, which is pretty much your personal anthropology and can document your evolution on so many levels. The same can also be said for all the photographs. I separated them by what I called my Wonder Years from all the branches and leaves that constituted my entire family. I have some cracked black-and-white photos of my grandparents' grandparents, who were slaves in Alabama and Mississippi. For stupid reasons I tossed my yearbooks a long time ago. I didn't want to remember those folks, and I also hated my pictures. I was not even close to cute when I was young. This was, of course, before I discovered makeup. And I don't want to question my hairstyles back then, because it'll just make me think about headbands.

I GO DOWNSTAIRS to the guest room and open the closet. And there's the cheap black trunk I took with me when I went away to college. Before I can slide it out, I have to move two big red boxes that hold all my special Christmas ornaments. I haven't had a tree in two years, since Frankie's been at NYU. I'm not feeling like a tree this year either. Santa doesn't stop at my house anymore. I still leave my porch light on at Halloween, because I don't ever want to think I've given away my last treats.

I figure I should probably get a little buzz to do this. And as much as I would love it if Wanda and Violet were here so we could stroll down memory lane together, I probably need to do this alone. Plus, they don't know everything I did or who I did it with. They only think they do. After I slide the trunk and a few boxes across this purple carpet, I run upstairs and pick out a decent enough bottle of chardonnay and grab a cheap wineglass and run back downstairs. I pour myself a glass and drink half of it standing up. I turn the intercom to Pandora, not really caring what genre it is, but as soon as I hear "Single Ladies" by Beyoncé, I do know I'm not in the mood for hip-hop, so I turn it to the channel that plays music that makes you feel like you're either floating in space or underwater. I kick off my Uggs and sit on the floor right in front of the closet door that now may never close until I move out of this house.

I reach over and lift the top of the trunk and look down inside and am shocked at how neat everything is. The first thing I grab is a big Ziploc that's full of cards and letters. Since my mother never wrote me any letters, I know these are either to or from some of *Them*. I toss this over near the blue bed. I have a feeling this is going to be fun.

My cell phone shivers on the carpet.

I pick it up. It's my oldest.

"Hi, Mom. What are you doing?"

I don't really know how to answer that, and I hate it when people ask me. What if you're not doing anything? Then you have to explain how you do nothing. But I also don't want to tell Estelle the truth. So I lie. "I'm reading."

"What are you reading?"

Shit.

Nosy Posy!

"*1,000 Places to See Before You Die,*" I say because it's on the table next to the bed. I want my guests to travel and then dream about it when they stay over.

She laughs. "And what page are you on?"

"It's *where*. I'm in Bora-Bora."

"That's in French Polynesia."

"See, it does pay to go to college. So what's up with you, honey-bunny?"

"Nothing. Just reaching out."

"You never just reach out, Estelle. What's going on?"

"Remember, you're my mother, and periodically it's normal for me to want to call and just say hi."

"Hi again. But we just talked a few days ago. Is there something going on?"

"No! Everything is copacetic. Have you heard from Frankie?"

"Not for a week. Why?"

"For some strange reason, she sent me a text and said she's madly in love. She never texts me."

"What's this one's name?"

"Hunter."

"Is he white?"

"The last two were, so why would she switch up now? You won't see me at her wedding. I don't care who she marries."

"Oh, stop it, would you, Estelle?"

"Frankie's the one who needs to stop. She didn't come to mine because she was supposedly studying film in Paris. She's also a dingbat and a spoiled brat with a host of undiagnosed issues."

I refuse to react to this. Estelle never has anything positive to say about her sister, and there's nothing wrong with Frankie other than being young and foolish. Estelle has been mad at Frankie since she was born and stole all Estelle's thunder—and attention—from Niles.

"So tell me, how are the twins and Justin?" I ask.

"Everybody's doing great. We might want to come visit you in the next couple of weeks, if that's okay."

"The whole clan?"

"No, just me and the girls."

Lord, help me. They're a handful, and they get on my nerves, but I probably shouldn't blame them for acting like kids when it's my patience level that seems to be diminishing right along with my hormone levels.

"That'll be fun," I say with as much enthusiasm as I can. "And you're sure everything is all right?"

"For the last time, everything's fine, Mom. I'd tell you if it wasn't."

"Okay, then. Let's talk again in a few days, and kiss the girls for me."

Estelle hardly ever calls just to chitchat, and her lighting into Frankie like this makes me think something else is going on. I just pray she's not having another baby, or she'll be stuck in that house forever.

Before I get a chance to take anything out of the trunk, the phone trembles again. This time I look to see who it is, and of course it's Wanda. "What do you want, huzzy?"

"I'm bored, and I need to get out of the house."

"Then go stand outside."

"Pour me a glass of whatever it is you're drinking. I'll see you in twenty minutes."

I finish pulling out all the scrapbooks and phone books and line them up to form what winds up being a very short history. I set aside the scrapbooks that have photos of my brother and the card he gave me when he left for the army. A few years ago, probably closer to five, Ma gave me four of these photo albums and said, "There's probably a million hours of my life and my parents' lives cracked and stuck to these pages," and I promised I'd have all the pictures and newspaper and magazine clippings scanned and digitized and some of them colorized. I'm ashamed I haven't done it, but I'm going to make good on that promise before it's too late.

I take a long, lazy sip of wine and decide I should just dive on into this trunk. I open it, and the first thing I pull out is a handwritten letter in what I can tell is my handwriting. "Oh, hell," I say to the empty room as I unfold it. I grab my glasses, which are parked between my breasts, and read:

> *Darnell: Do me a favor and do not call me ever again in life, since you seem to keep getting me confused with your other whores. I am not a cheap date. One day if you're lucky enough to grow up, maybe you'll learn what it means to respect the female species and not assume that just because you happen to be good in bed, it's enough, because it isn't. I've had better. You're one of the reasons the phrase "He's a dog" was invented. If there are ever any classes on self-respect and respect for women, I suggest you enroll in them both. Have a fucked-up life.*
> *Georgia.*

I tip over from laughing so hard. I should've made a greeting card out of this letter and used it for a whole bunch of these bastards. I set this declaration aside and continue my scavenger hunt. There are plenty of cards: Valentine and birthday cards from Michael's sorry ass, but these were when he was sweet and purportedly still loved me; then there's a separate, one-gallon freezer bag full of corny cards from Niles that I knew he put absolutely no thought into, because there were always white women with blond hair on the front of them.

When I hear the doorbell, I push myself to a standing position and head upstairs.

"Coming!" I yell while dancing to an unidentifiable beat that's obviously not coming out of the speakers. This is just one more reason I like wine.

I open the door, and Wanda walks past me in a blinding orange muumuu that must have once belonged to her mother. I close my eyes and put my hands on my hips. "Well, with that getup you've come to the right place, since I'm strolling down Nostalgia Lane. What has gotten into you, Ms. Thang?"

"I was sitting in my favorite chair just stitching away, and Nelson was snoring on the sofa, and the dogs were snoring at the other end, and some stupid football game was on, and I suddenly got this overwhelming feeling of boredom, so that's when I called you. Where's the wine, or did you drink it all?"

"Let's go see!" I say, and follow her to the bar.

As she stands on her toes to reach one of my fine wine goblets meant for real guests, I tell her what I'm doing and explain that I'm looking for the fish I had to throw back, and she just shakes her head and pops the cork on a good bottle. Then we head downstairs, the hem of that muumuu making her walk like she's in a beauty pageant or something.

"Throw that dress in the trash," I say. "Even my mother doesn't go this far, Wanda."

"You're right. I don't know what possessed me to buy it."

"Because you're possessed when you shop, that's why."

I warn her how the room looks, and when we walk in, she stands there with her hands on her orange hips and says, "So they're all in here somewhere, huh?"

I sit on the floor, and she sits in the white armchair.

"Why are you playing that funeral music?"

"It's called chill."

"Yeah, more like embalmed. We need some R&B music from the seventies and eighties, since that's where we're going."

I get up and change it to smooth jazz.

"Now we're going to need some reefer. Whatever. So who've you run across so far?"

"Nobody."

"I see you call yourself trying to hide that scrapbook I made for your and Michael's nuptials under the bed, and it's still beautiful if I do say so myself."

"It's falling apart. Those ruffles are crushed flat, and the plastic has cracked. And no, I do not want you to repair it!"

I hand her a scrapbook she didn't make, and after taking a sip she sets her glass on the little table and starts slowly flipping through the pages.

I do the same.

"What year is this?" she asks, turning it around. In the photo I have a giant Afro and a long denim skirt I made from old jeans and some kind of drapery fabric with giant flowers on it I sewed in the middle. Damn, was I skinny.

"The seventies. Don't you remember that skirt?"

"Where in the hell is your bra?"

I look a little closer. "You know that was when it was cool not to wear one. But I think you slept in your Playtex."

I fall over laughing and almost knock my wine over, but I catch it.

"Go straight to hell, Georgia. Wait a minute! Who is this headless guy?"

She holds up the book, and some tall guy in gray bell-bottoms and what looks like a Chubby Checker white shirt whose head I ripped off is standing with his arms around me. "That's Thomas. You never met him. He's from Bakersfield and took me to my senior prom and then left with another girl."

"You're lying, Georgia."

"If I'm lying, I'm flying. He was weird."

Her eyes ask, *What kind of weird?*

"Maybe I'll see him next year at the reunion! I can hardly wait. Keep turning the pages. You're bound to find another one." I pick up a phone book with a peacock on the front. The date on the upper right-hand corner is smudged. But I know that this was my first year in college, which meant it was also my very first phone book, because prior to leaving home I knew everybody's number by heart.

"You know what?" Wanda says, even though it's obviously not really a question. "This is boring as hell and feels like a complete waste of time."

"I was sitting here thinking the same thing. I mean, if I don't remember some of these guys, then they're not memorable."

"What do you have to eat around here? And please don't tell me chips and salsa. I can eat that at home."

"Well, you're in luck. I bought some smoked salmon and added watermelon radish and shallots and ginger vinaigrette and stuffed it inside two avocado halves. Take it or leave it."

"You have any crackers or anything to go with it?"

"Maybe. Check the pantry."

"When are you ever going to turn on your damn stove and invite somebody over for dinner?"

"It's no fun cooking for one."

"Then invite some-damn-body over! We all miss that weird shit you used to make. It was amazing. We want to be your guinea pigs again."

"Okay!" I say as she picks up her hem and starts heading upstairs. "By the time you get back, I'll have a list of the ones I had sex with, since I spotted quite a few of them in my phone books."

"Do you really care how many guys you've fucked?"

"Yes."

"Why?"

"Because I want to have a general idea how active I was back in the day."

"You were an *active* whore. End of story. Which is why this feels like a complete waste of time. Let's watch *King Kong*."

"I wish I could find a man like King Kong."

"Is that a no?"

"It's a no."

"I'm going to get a better bottle of wine while you come up with your long-ass list."

"You can't drive home with this much alcohol in your system, Wanda."

"Who said I was going home? I'm sleeping in Frankie's bed. I want Nelson to wonder if I've finally left him."

Yeah, right. Like that would ever happen. Their hearts are glued together. And off she goes.

I grab the yellow pad I brought down here and start writing as fast as possible. By the time Wanda gets back, I think I'm finished. She snatches the paper from me, starts counting softly with her index finger.

"You slut! There's like twenty fucking names here. My grocery list isn't this long!"

"I'll bet Violet's is twice this long."

Wanda goes down the list, shaking her head and laughing. "Tell you what. Let's play a new form of *Jeopardy!* There's only one category. We already know what it is, so I'll say his name and you try to describe him in one word—but no more than three or four—and just tell me why he struck out. Okay?"

"Nathan."

"Shouldn't have been the first."

"That's five words, Georgia."

I roll my eyes at her, stand up, and start walking in circles.

"Darnell."

"First one to break my heart."

"How old were you?"

"Don't ask me questions! You're ruining the flow."

"Okay! Dennis."

"Dumb as a post."

"David."

"No ambition."

"Wardell."

"Came in thirty seconds."

"James Number One."

"Ladies' man."

"James Number Two."

"Bisexual."

"Brad. We already know he was the thief."

"Mark."

"Mama's boy."

"Elijah."

"Pathological Liar."

"Thomas."

"Freak."

"Good freak or bad freak?"

I ignore her.

"Graham."

"Arrogant."

"Aaron."

"Boring."

"Abraham."

"Well."

"Phillip."

"Married."

"Frederick."

"Inconsiderate."

"Harold Number One."

"Another freak. And vain."

"Harold Number Two."

"Bad hygiene."

"Glen."

"Vulgar."

"Steve."

"Cowardly."

"Horace."

"No comment."

She tosses the list to the side. "Well, that was fun. These crackers are stale, and that avocado stuffing was cute but I'm still hungry. Who is Horace?"

"The only black man I've ever slept with who almost didn't have a penis at all."

She spits out my wine. "Shut up, Georgia."

"I couldn't even call it a pencil dick. It was a cocktail weenie. I felt sorry for the dude."

"What's Abraham doing on this list?"

"He probably shouldn't be. He was good at everything. Maybe because we didn't finish what we started."

"And that was a character defect? You're full of shit. I'm crossing him off," and she does. "What about that white guy you had a crush on in undergrad?"

"You mean Stanley?"

"Don't play dumb with me. Yeah. Stanley."

"I didn't have a *crush* on him. I had sex with him."

"Why isn't he on this list?"

"Because I didn't have a relationship with him. I told you back then how he wouldn't stop flirting with me, so I finally gave in, since he was fine and I wanted to see what it was like to have sex with a white guy."

"And you liked it, if I remember correctly."

"It was outstanding, and he was very nice, and I discovered the stereotype is just that, but it was a seventy-two-hour tryst I did under the condition that there'd be no strings attached. I tried to act like it never happened and did everything I could to avoid him, but it was hard, since he was in my Afro-American history class. That was one long-ass quarter."

"I forgot that's how you met. Back then a whole lot of white folks suffered from guilt."

"Okay, so now my secrets are out in the open. Time to put this list on Facebook?"

"You better not be serious, Georgia!"

"I'm just kidding, Wanda. Damn."

"Stanley should be on this list," she says, and hands it back to me.

I snatch it and scribble his name at the bottom but don't know what to put next to it except: "*White.*"

"So just for the record, would you ever consider dating a white guy now that we're in the twenty-first century?"

"I've never really thought about it. My daughter seems to prefer white boys, and I'm not mad at her, but you know I love me some black men and especially black skin."

"I do, too, but the only thing God made different about us is our skin color."

"Duh. You are too deep for me tonight, Wanda," I say as I toss the list into the trash can and step over the other stuff.

"All I'm saying is you'd certainly increase your odds if you thought outside that black box, Georgia. A man is a man. What kind of real food do you have around here? I'm starving."

"Frozen lasagna."

"As a guest do I have to microwave it myself?"

"Yes, and then go home."

"I'm spending the night, remember?"

I give her the finger.

She gives it right back to me.

# How to Stage

GREET AMEN, WHOM I REALLY LIKE, WITH GENUINE ENTHU-siasm, and Percy, whom I already don't like, with faux excitement. Amen is smart and knows the Oakland hills like the back of his hand. He lives higher up than I do. Where the fire was. He's also Greek. Tall. Good-looking. Happily married. Twenty years and counting. Two kids still in college, one on Wall Street. A winter home in Tahoe he's already offered to let me use this winter. For free! After the appraisal, which was lower than I'd expected, he made it clear that it's not just my home, it's all of them. Including his.

Percy, on the other hand, is irritating. I can tell he doesn't like me, and I wonder if it's because he's not used to dealing with people who have taste—and in my case a black person—or because I'm tall and he's short. Even with those loafers, he's about five-six. I'm five-eight. He should think stripes instead of plaid, and those Dockers could stand to be hemmed. His blond hair looks like it's so full of gel that a tornado wouldn't move a strand. His big Burberry notepad is pressed against his chest.

"So," he says after he walks in like a CSI tech, "are we ready to take a walk and let me share some of my ideas—which, I would like to make clear to you once again, Georgia, you can reject any of if you so choose?"

"Sure."

"Super. I'd like to start in the upstairs bedrooms and work my way down if you don't mind."

"I don't mind."

I follow the two of them up and down the three flights and get a kick watching Percy act as if he's on a game show. He likes to point.

"So I see your lovely ethnic pieces are still hanging, and I don't see any of the blue tape I left to indicate which ones you wouldn't mind storing. Of course, I know you're a busy person."

"It's on my list of things to do this weekend, Percy. But tell me, seriously, is this so a potential buyer won't think someone black lives here?"

"Absolutely not. We just want to think neutral and avoid themes with any cultural implications, because you want a potential buyer to fall in love with the home, not be impressed by your artwork or decorating skills."

"Really?"

I can tell that Amen isn't buying this bullshit, but he knows Percy's good at staging.

"As I said before, personally, I love your taste, but I'm not the one trying to buy your home, and although your decor is interesting and the kaleidoscope of colors is lovely, right now it feels more like a concert, and if you want it to sell quickly, we have to aim for a waltz."

Kaleidoscope?

"And just how do I waltz?"

"Well, chances are about three-quarters of the living-room furniture will most likely have to go."

"Go where?"

"Into storage."

"And replace it with what?"

"Rental furniture. We use reputable establishments that specialize in staging: everything from top-of-the-line bedding to sofas and lighting, plants, and even artwork."

I want to say, *No shit?* but instead I just say, "I understand, but can you at least give me more of a sense of what else you think I might need to do?"

And this is when Percy becomes almost orgasmic. "We'll need to dismantle all of the thematic rooms and make them more serene. We'll get rid of all clutter—especially the knickknacks, as I said before—and replace them with beautiful orchids wherever possible. The dining room needs a more traditional look, not artsy like what you now have. We'll group the rental furniture so that it's more musical. We'll shower the place with lighting—incandescent. I've noticed a few cracked windowpanes, broken doorknobs, and things of that nature. All of these items will need to be repaired. We'll probably have to hire painters and definitely change some of the bright carpeting. And the hardwood floors would do well to be refinished. I'm just giving you a general overview but I'm sure I've missed a few minor details, but not to worry. Wait! I forgot to mention plants! Giant areca palms and ficuses can do wonders for any room."

"What's wrong with the plants in here?"

"Some of them don't look as healthy as I'd like them to, and if you're having problems caring for them, I can also bring in artificial ones, which I don't recommend, or I'm sure the nursery we use would be happy to give you watering tips."

"About how much will all this cost me?"

"I haven't gotten to the outside yet. But suffice it to say that curb appeal is crucial, because it's the first thing a potential buyer sees. We'll probably need to hire a landscape architect to spruce up the flower gardens and around the entire pool area. That should about do it."

"So again, how much and how long will all this take?"

"Staging isn't cheap, Georgia, if done right, but think of it as an investment you'll recoup when you see how quickly your house sells and how close to the asking price you'll probably get. I'm estimating somewhere between ten to fifteen thousand."

"You're kidding."

He nods as if he's afraid of me now.

"And how long will it take?"

"Again, it all depends on how much you let us do."

"Everything you just mentioned."

"Anywhere from two or three weeks, providing there are no delays, which almost always happens."

"But how am I supposed to live in here when all this is going on, or is that a dumb question?"

"Well," Percy says, "do you have a vacation home?"

I would so like to slap him.

"No."

"Well, with a staging of this magnitude, most of my clients either rent a temporary apartment, check into a hotel suite, or take a vacation!"

Oh, fuck you, Percy!

"Are you thinking about where you'd like to live?" he asks. I'm beginning to wonder if Amen is even at this party.

"I'm not sure. Ideally, I'd love to live in New York, but it's far too expensive."

"Who needs winter?" Percy says.

"I'm tired of California," I say, just to piss him off.

"Everything a person could ever need is in California."

"That's so not true, Percy."

"Look, I'm going to have to bid you adieu, as I'm running late for my next appointment. I'll do my best to e-mail you the detailed breakdown by next week, as it takes time to figure all this out, and then you can let Amen know just how much you're up for. Fair enough?"

"Fair. Have a nice afternoon, and thank you, Percy."

Amen walks out behind him but stops on the top step. "And you're absolutely certain you want to sell, Georgia?"

"I'm positive, Amen. I told you, it's too much house for one person."

"But what if you remarry?"

I look at him like he's just asked a ridiculous question.

"Don't ever give up on love, Georgia. Keep the faith."

He sounds like a talk-show host, but I know he's being sincere, so I just say, "I have tons of faith."


"MOM! WE'RE HERE!"

Oh, hell.

I'm in my closet, sweating, naked, and frustrated from not having found anything I would want to be seen in at yet another cerebral party that Wanda has talked me into going to tonight, when I hear the sound of little hooves galloping into my bedroom. Before I have a chance to put my robe on, I feel four eyes on me, and there, staring the day away, are two brown midgets in shock.

"This is what you're both going to look like one day," I say while slithering into my terry-cloth robe and tying the sash tight. "But not if you exercise and use cocoa butter on your stretch marks."

Both of them start twirling their two thick braids.

"What are stretch marks?" the one in pink-and-white polka-dot leggings and pink T-shirt asks.

"They are marks that stretch, Scarlett!" Gabby says with authority. She's dressed to kill in orange leggings and an orange-and-white striped T-shirt. She looks quite pleased with herself and punctuates her pronouncement by putting her hands on her nonexistent hips. Scarlett looks as if she always believes her sister.

"Can Granny get a group hug?" I ask, and they run into me and pull on my robe and squeeze.

"Hi! We love you, Granny!" they say simultaneously.

"Hi there, girls! Granny loves you, too! Now let's go find your mom," I say, gently pushing them out of my closet, but when I try to take them by the hand, they shake loose and charge down the hallway. Little female puppies!

Estelle is standing there in one of two lululemon outfits I gave her for her birthday last year. This one happens to be lemon and black. She used to be a real yoga fanatic, but I don't think she goes much anymore. She's also as pretty as I always wanted to be. Looks more like Michael, the mistake I married right after grad school. I give her—or I should say *we* give her—another group hug. I kiss her on both cheeks and her forehead.

"You look good, Stelle," I say, lying through my teeth. She looks tired, thinner than I've seen her since college, stressed. She's one of these educated, New Age, stay-at-home supermoms who does everything, including working at home as a technical writer for Apple. She must do it in her sleep, because the girls are rarely out of her or Justin's sight line. They do all the things that television shows and books have told them to do to qualify as good parents. They didn't even trust day care. I'm surprised they trust me.

"Of course there was traffic, and I've only got fifteen minutes before my salt scrub. Thank you so much, Mom. How are you?"

"I'm fine, baby. Remember this house the way it looks now, because it's being staged, and in about a month or so it'll look like someone else lives here."

"So you're actually going to do it?"

"I am. How are you?"

"Excellent. Just thinking of going back to work, but I'll tell you more about that later. Girls, be nice to your granny and do what she tells you to. Do we have an agreement?"

They nod.

She hands me a bulging backpack. "Lunch, snacks, books, and DVDs. I should be back by six, if that's okay. And thank you so much for this!"

"Okay! Stop! Go! Relax! We go through this every single time! Now, beat it."

"Yes, Mom, just beat it!" Gabby in orange says as she chases after Scarlett in pink, both of whom are heading to my off-limits office. I tiptoe down and see them looking through my mother's scrapbook, and I lean against the door and just watch them.

"What's this?" Scarlett asks, trying to see through the yellowing plastic.

"It's a picture book," Gabby says before I do.

I believe I can now tell them apart. Gabby is the bossy one. Scarlett seems to rely on her for answers, and Lord, does she always have one.

"It's called a scrapbook," I say, and set it on my desk so they can see who's in it.

"Who are all these old people?" Scarlett asks.

"Relatives."

"Where are they?"

"Dead."

"All of them?"

"That's impossible," Gabby says.

"Most of them. Have you two ever heard of slavery?"

"I think we have," Gabby says.

"It's when black people had to work for white people and did not get a paycheck," Scarlett says.

"Which was silly, because you always need a paycheck," Gabby says. She once again puts her hands on her bony hips and then turns her palms up and says, "How were they supposed to pay their bills?" And hunches her shoulders.

"Especially their American Express," Scarlett says. "Daddy is always worried about that one."

"I'm just glad we don't have to be slaves and that Mom and Daddy and you aren't, Granny. Aren't you glad, Granny?" Gabby, of course.

"Yes."

"Why are all the pictures off the wall?" Miss Gabby asks, definitely living up to her nickname.

"Yeah. What happened to us?" Scarlett asks.

"Granny might be moving soon, so I had to put all the pictures in a safe place until I find a new home for them."

"Are you getting forked, too?" Scarlett asks.

"What do you mean 'forked'?"

"We have a sign in our front yard, and it says 'Forked' on it," she informs me.

"No it doesn't, Scarlett! It has an *s* and an *e,* but we don't know how to say it."

I cover my mouth.

"Where's your sign?" one of them asks, and I don't care right now which one it is.

"Granny doesn't have one yet, but my house isn't getting forked."

"Wanna know another secret?" Scarlett asks.

"We're moving, too!" Gabby yells.

"You are?"

"Yes indeed!" she says.

"We're moving into someplace cheap, because Daddy can't keep paying for the whole house—"

"Which we do not need anyways," says Gabby. "And Mom said when she finds a real job, we'll get to go to a real school."

"We want to go to a real school, don't we, Gabby?"

She nods.

"Can you keep a secret, Granny?" Scarlett asks.

"Absolutely," I say, thinking that apparently so can my daughter.

"Good, because we were not supposed to talk about this, and we don't want to get in trouble."

"I won't tell."

"Good. Now, what are we going to do for fun?" Gabby asks.

"Would you like to go for a walk?"

"Walk where?" Gabby asks.

"Up the hill," I say, pointing out the window.

"Not interested," Gabby says.

"How about down the hill?"

"Okay," Scarlett says.

So I change back into my sweats and sneakers, and we walk down the hill, but of course we have to walk back up, which almost kills me. Afterward we don't open that backpack Estelle sent. I let them eat forbidden snacks: unnatural cookies and potato chips, but when they see the Red Bull in the fridge, I draw the line. We watch two long cartoon DVDs, and they take turns reading me those silly but fun children's books I once loved, and of course I'm impressed with how well they can read and I applaud and applaud, and then I take them to In-N-Out Burger if they promise not to say they had that instead of the hummus and celery and the orange homemade soup that Estelle packed for them. Some people take all this healthy stuff entirely too far, and then one day you get cancer and die anyway.

We play hide-and-seek, but it's a bitch trying to find the two of them, and when it's finally four o'clock, I ask, "Do you guys ever take naps?"

They look at their little digital pink and orange watches.

"Is it Saturday?" Scarlett asks.

I nod.

"Not on Saturdays," Gabby says.

"But aren't you girls tired?"

What a stupid-ass question.

"Wait! I made a mistake! It's Friday!"

They run and sit back on the sofa, looking bored, waiting for the next activity. I turn on the television. "Have you two ever watched *Judge Judy*?"

They shake their heads no.

I turn to her show. "You'll like her. She's funny!"

They sit through two shows without moving an inch. They are mesmerized and probably too confused to ask me what a past-due notice is or a loan or a scam or why the people are fighting over a ten-week-old puppy.

"Judge Judy is mean," Scarlett says when it's over.

"What is a judge?" asks Gabby. "Is she like a preacher? And what is insurance, Granny?"

I tell them I don't know what insurance is but it's something I'm sure I should probably get. And on and on until I finally hear that door open and they jump up and run into their mother's arms like they haven't seen her in years, and I hug my daughter tight for trying to put on such a good front. I don't know what to say to her right now, and even though she looks refreshed and her brown cheeks are glowing, I can tell she's already thinking about tomorrow, next week, or next month. She uses rush hour as an excuse to head home, says thank you, and the girls give me a hug without being told, which means I may have finally scored some maybe-Granny-is-nice-after-all points. Estelle kisses me on the cheek and says she'll talk to me soon, and I hug her again, even harder this time, and say let's make it sooner.


WHEN I HEAR the phone ringing, I'm lying on the sofa in the family room, my mouth wet from drooling. It's dark outside, and the clock on the wall says it's a quarter past eight! Shit! It's Wanda. I spring up and start running toward my bedroom. "I'm getting dressed right now! Be there in an hour!"

"Are you all right, girl?"

"I'm fine. Those twins wore me out! After they left, I decided to close my eyes for a few minutes."

"Well, don't bother getting dressed. I'm on my way home. These folks must've all popped a Xanax or something. No one even laughed. It was boring. With one exception."

"What's that supposed to mean?"

"Well, they say you can talk a person up."

"You are not telling me Michael was there."

"I kid you not. He was with some cute Asian chick who looked like one of her parents must be black, but she was also young enough to be his daughter."

"He always liked them young and Asian, so what else is new? Wait a minute. Is this some kind of setup, Wanda?"

"Don't be ridiculous. He just moved back to the Bay Area."

"I'm thrilled. And?"

"And what?"

"So how'd he look?"

"Well, you know we've always had different taste in men."

"I mean did he look healthy?"

"Violet thought he looked old. She was talking his ear off when I left."

"Did he ask about me?"

"Of course he did."

"And what did you tell him?"

"That you're alive and thriving."

"Was he wearing a wedding ring?"

"No."

"Figures."

"He did give me his card and asked me for your number."

"You didn't give it to him, I hope?"

"Of course I did. And he's going to call you, and you're going to talk to him."

I slide down the wall to the floor. "I have nothing to say to Michael."

"Georgia, this was part of your plan. So look at this as divine intervention. And try not to be a bitch when he calls." She laughs.

I try to laugh, too, but I can't.

# Liar, Liar, Pants on Fire,
## You Son of a Bitch

T'S THE CRACK OF DAWN. I'M MAKING COFFEE WHEN I FEEL my cell phone vibrating in my bathrobe pocket. I know it can't be my mother, because she's not back from her cruise. It's probably Frankie, who only calls this early from New York when she needs me to help her with yet another unsolved mystery in the ongoing saga of why her checking-account balance is negative. Of course I'll send it. Then again, maybe Estelle wants to confide in me for a change. She should know she can trust me. Besides Justin, I'm her biggest ally. And I'll help any way I can.

But when I pull out the phone, I see MICHAEL MAYFIELD on the screen. You have got to be kidding me. It's one thing to call the day after, but 7:00 a.m. on a Saturday? I drop the phone in the sink like it's hot and watch it slide around the stainless basin until it stops.

I could kick Wanda's ass. He's still the same arrogant son of a bitch he always was. I haven't seen or spoken to him since 2002, but I was on my best behavior at Estelle's college graduation. I sat six chairs away from his not-as-pretty-as-I-thought-she'd-be wife at the luncheon, and I planted and replanted a faux smile on my face whenever I caught him looking at me. "I'm so proud of our daughter" were my last words to him before waving good-bye in slow motion. What could he possibly want to talk about? He must want something. And right this minute I don't want to know what it is, at least not before my frigging coffee.

I drink two cups. I water the plants Percy thinks I neglect. I empty the trash. I microwave a Hot Pocket and take my sweet time eating it. I chase it with a glass of orange juice. I put three towels in the washer and turn it on. I'm disappointed when there's nothing in the dryer that needs folding. I'm trying to remember if I have any pets I've forgotten I have that might need to be fed. When I finally pick the phone up out of the sink, it almost feels as if Michael can see me. I hop onto a barstool and listen to what he has to say: "Hey there, Georgia. It's me, Michael. I'm sure Wanda and Violet probably told you I moved back to the Bay Area, and I was wondering if you'd like to have dinner, just to catch up. They said you're doing great. Not that I'm surprised. It'd be nice to see for myself."

Dinner? He sounds more like an old friend than the ex-husband I still despise. I take a few minutes to figure out how in the world I would posture some oh-by-the-way-how've-you-been-doing-all-these-years? courage and some I've-been-good-no-not-married-but-in-a-blossoming-relationship courage.

I don't have any.

I walk into my room and fall across the bed and call my confidante.

"This is what you said you wanted to do, so cut the bullshit," Wanda says after I give her the lowdown. "Not including Michael makes you a hypocrite. So go catch up. It won't kill you. And let me know if you fuck him. Bye."

She loves to hang up after she makes her point, but she's right except for the sex part. I'd masturbate crossing the Bay Bridge before I'd even consider it. I sit up straight and dial.

"Well, hello there, Georgia. I didn't think you would call." He sounds the same as he did thirty years ago. His voice is heavy, raspy, still confident. Bastard.

"Why wouldn't I? How in the world are you, Michael?"

"I'm doing great. Just as I hear you're doing. But I wouldn't expect anything less."

"So what made you move back?"

"I was offered a partnership with my old firm, and I missed the Bay Area. As you may or may not know, Estelle refuses to give me any information about you except that you're alive, so I've stopped inquiring. But tell me what you're up to these days. I do know you remarried."

"I did."

"And are you happy?"

"I am. How about you?"

"Divorced."

"Me, too. Was it the same woman you left me for?"

"Oh, Georgia. Yes and no. Look, would it be possible to have dinner to see if we can call a truce? It would be nice to see you after all these years."

Without thinking about Wanda, I say, "Sure. Which side of the bay works for you?"

"Really?"

"What do we have to lose?"

"Should I wear my bulletproof vest?"

I burst out laughing at that.

"I can come over to the East Bay if it's easier," he says.

"No, I could use a drive."

"Does seven work for you?"

"That's fine. You want to choose?" I ask.

"No. You choose. Just text me and I'll be there."

"How will I recognize you, Michael?" I say with sarcasm.

"My hair and beard are salt-and-pepper. And you?"

"I look like Beyoncé's twin. See you at seven."

SO NOW I HAVE all day to kill. I go to the grocery store even though there's nothing I need. I get a mani-pedi even though I just had one last week. I choose hot pink for some reason. I get my eyebrows waxed. I have some individual lashes added. I go to Nordstrom and buy an uplifting black outfit that makes me look slimmer.

This kills most of the afternoon, which is why I need a nap. I lie down on the sofa in the family room and slide under a blue fleece blanket. I wiggle until my head rests on a pretty pillow I wish I'd made until I'm in a comfortable spot. I look around the room. It feels like I'm in a small museum. I stare at the furniture and wonder, if and when the house sells and I downsize, what I will keep and what I will let go. I watch the ceiling fan swirling slowly, and when I feel myself sinking, there is Michael. And me.

I MET HIM in the campus library. We were both studying for hours at a long wooden table. Me for optometry and him for finance. As I started gathering up my notes, he said, "So you're interested in how we see?"

That was a good one.

I tried not to blush, because I couldn't tell if this was a come-on or if he meant it. After all, I had, from the corner of my eye, been pretending not to notice he was almost handsome, the color of raw honey, his thick lips so perfect I would've been willing to pay for a kiss, and from what I could see through those thick lenses, his eyes were chestnut brown, and Lord, he smelled so clean, like he'd just showered in fig and mint leaves or something, but whatever it was, I couldn't stop inhaling him, and he'd been making it difficult for me to focus on anything ocular. I'd simply been turning pages without seeing what was on them.

"I am. And you're interested in money?"

His crooked smile emerged while he shook his head, and I believe it was at that very moment I crossed over.

"I'm interested in money management. And you."

We knew we were already possessed and stopped pretending we were studying and just packed up our books and highlighters and walked down Telegraph Avenue to a restaurant full of Boston ferns and spider plants and vanilla incense, and I said, "Wait a second. Before we walk into this house of ill repute, what's your name?"

That crooked smile again. "It's Michael. I don't have a last name. And what does one call you to get your attention?"

"Georgia."

"I'll bet you a burger you're not from there."

"I'll bet you some fries you're right."

We ate breakfast, lunch, and dinner in that restaurant and would probably still be there had they not been closing. In ten hours we discovered who we were. Where we came from. Why we were here. He looked into my eyes when he spoke, which made me uncomfortable at first until I began to soften. Then melt. He said please and thank you and "Would you mind if I . . . ?" and "Have you ever considered . . . ?" and "Did you know if . . . ?" and he rolled up his sleeves when we got to Malcolm X and Socrates and God and freedom and pain and love and beauty and honesty and why Berkeley and where on earth do we go from here?

He walked me to my dorm and kissed me on my cheek. Then he asked if I'd mind if he swore. And I said go ahead. And he said, "Damn."

And I said, "Damn is about right."

A year later I was honored to be his wife, and he said he felt lucky to be my husband.

> *This is what he gave me:*
> An open door to his heart.
> Peace of mind.
> A beautiful daughter.
> Joy.

> *This is what we did:*
> Traveled every chance we got.
> Went to church at least twice a month.
> Went to live concerts.
> Danced. Everywhere.
> Tried to read a book a week, but it ended up being every two
>     because parenting and work consumed us.
> Prayed.

> *This is what he taught me:*
> How to look beneath the surface, behind closed doors.
> How to ski downhill.

How to rub up against him in public without anyone
    noticing. We loved crowds. He'd put his hands on my ass
    and slowly slide them up and down like we had all day.
How to drive a five-speed and floor it and how to downshift.
How to appreciate foreign films. How to read the subtitles
    without moving my lips.
How to do nothing.

*This is how he loved me:*
In the morning, every morning, he kissed me on my cheek
    or my forehead or my lips or my shoulder or my eyelids or
    my nose and said, "Good morning, beautiful."
He kissed me good night every single night.
He held my hand everywhere we walked.
He always looked me in the eye when we talked, and he
    listened to whatever came out of my mouth.
He smiled at me, and sometimes I busted him smiling at me.
He read to me.
He let me fall asleep on top of him.
He took my braids out.
He spooned me almost every night.
He whispered in my ears. Kissed them.
He asked if he could take me out on a date.
He asked if I was married, and if so, he wanted to steal me
    from him.
He sucked my fingers.
He sucked my toes.
He squeezed my hand during romantic movies.
He wrapped his legs around mine.
He told me I never had to be afraid of anything.
He promised he would never hurt me.
He promised he would never cheat on me.
He promised he would never lie to me.
He promised me that divorce would never be an option
    for him.

For five years I didn't think it was possible to feel this good.
For five years I didn't think it was possible to be this happy.
But then he forgot all those promises he'd made. He forgot
    why he loved me. He simply stopped loving me.

*And this is how he did it:*
He stopped talking to me unless I spoke to him.
He stopped holding my hand.
He stopped kissing me good night.
He stopped kissing me good morning.
He stopped kissing me.
He stopped smiling at me.
He stopped laughing.
He stopped bathing and showering with me.
He stopped wanting me.
He started swearing at me.
He started lying to me.
He started cheating on me.
He hurt me.
And then he told me he was in love with another woman
    and wanted a divorce.
Oh, I forgot. He said he was sorry.

I wanted to blow his fucking brains out. But instead I just kicked him out and signed the papers in my pajamas when I got served. I became a ghost of myself. My mother helped with Estelle, because I couldn't get out of bed for almost two weeks except to go to the bathroom and bring in the paper. But I couldn't read it. I called the hospital where I worked at the time and told them I'd had an emergency and wasn't sure when I'd be in. I would end up using all my vacation time to recover from the hole that had been drilled into my heart. I didn't comb my hair. I didn't shower. I had no appetite and forced myself to eat yogurt. Saltines. Wanda almost broke the door down when I wouldn't answer the phone. She wanted to shoot Michael. Violet said this shit was like recovering from a C-section and that it could take up to a month before I'd be able to walk without wobbling and holding on to something.

I ran out of tears. And by the time I went back to work, I realized I wasn't angry. I was numb. I felt as if he had killed me and this is what it felt like to be dead.

But then as weeks and months passed, something funny started happening. I stopped missing him. I stopped mourning the loss of him, and in fact he was the one who became dead to me. I was relieved to have our condo to myself. I started feeling like I was on vacation in my own home. I did whatever I wanted to do without needing to clear it with him. I learned how to stop editing my every move. I stopped apologizing for being myself. Because I liked who I was. It took a year before I had the desire and the courage to even go on a date, and then the next two years were nothing but a series of false starts and fuck-fests, and then along came Eric, who was the balm I needed. But then he had to up and move to Paris to learn how to cook, and I couldn't go, which made my heart feel like a valley again. That's when I decided I needed to take a break from men, because their stock was too damn high and I was tired of not getting a return on my investment.

I CHANGE MY MIND about the new black getup and opt for the chocolate brown outfit I was going to wear to the party. I'm not trying to inspire Michael. I just want to look inspired. God, I hope he has a big fat gut and his teeth are rotting and he can't stand up straight because his penis has fallen off and he smells like mustard.

Not even close. He looks like a new and improved, older version of his younger self. He smells light blue, and before I know it, he puts his arms around me and hugs me as if he once loved me. "You look wonderful," he says, lying through those beautiful veneers.

"You look old," I say, and we both chuckle.

I chose a twenty-star Mediterranean restaurant in the Financial District with no view. I'm not the least bit hungry, which means I'm going to have to pretend.

"Would you care for a cocktail or wine?"

"I'm afraid to drink this evening, Michael, so I'll just have sparkling water."

"Afraid of what?"

"That it might make me say something I'll regret."

"It's the reason I called you. To let me finally have it."

"It's ancient history. But seriously, what *did* make you call me?"

"Honestly? I want to make amends. What made you come?"

"Honestly?"

He nods but looks a little nervous.

"Because this is the twenty-first century and we're old and I'm trying to be more civilized. To be very honest, I was thinking about looking you up on Facebook at some point just to see how you were doing and maybe to remind you I still hate you, but after thinking about what we once had, I was going to tell you I would be ever so grateful if you would clear up some things, because I'm still not sure what happened to us, but for starters I'd really like to know why you loved me and what made you stop. And I think I will have a manhattan."

I can't believe I just said this.

Michael leans back in his chair and crosses his arms. "Wow. You are serious, aren't you?"

"I am."

He uncrosses his arms and places his palms gently on the white tablecloth. "I loved you because you were beautiful inside and out. Because you were honest and patient and sensitive and smart and sexy and you had opinions about things and you liked helping people and you were good in bed."

"Is that all?"

"I loved the way you cooked. The way you made eye contact when we talked. You weren't afraid to try new things. I loved the way you laughed. That you were a good mother. How you used to hug me. For no reason."

"Okay, stop. Let's get to the ugly stuff."

"Can we order first?"

"Certainly, Michael."

"I still love the way you say my name."

I roll my eyes at him.

He orders my drink, and all I can handle is a salad, so he orders two Caesars.

"Well, this sure is a perky reunion," he says.

"It's better if we get the ugly stuff out of the way, don't you think?"

"I'm on your side."

"What if I told you I cheated on you?"

"You wouldn't have."

"You don't know that for sure, now, do you?"

"I'm pretty sure."

"Well, I did."

He looks at me like I've just castrated him. "You didn't. You couldn't have. Who was it? When was it?"

"Hold your little ponies, now, soldier. See how worked up you're getting? And we're talking about American history here."

"Did you?"

"I probably should have, but no. It takes a lot for a woman to cheat."

"Like what?"

"Misery. We do it to escape marriage hell, and when we do, most of us don't break up our families. In fact, sometimes that can invigorate things."

"Wow. You learn something new every day."

"But you guys cheat and expect to be forgiven. You can dish it out, but you can't take it. See how worked up you were getting at the mere thought?"

"I do."

"Have you learned not to make promises you can't keep?"

"I've gotten better."

"You promised me you would never cheat on me, that you'd love me forever and we would never get a divorce."

"I still love you, and I hate that I cheated on you, and I wish we'd never gotten divorced."

He sits there looking down at his glass, then twirls it around and looks directly into my eyes.

I believe him. And almost feel sorry for him. "Then what made you cheat, Michael?"

"Because I could."

"What kind of an answer is that?"

"It's the truth."

"You have to do better than that. I've waited a long time to hear this."

"Is it really that important? After all, we're sitting here thirty-five years later like old friends."

"But we're not old friends. You were my husband, who lied and cheated on me, and I want to know why."

"I just told you."

"Did you fall out of love with me?"

He nods his head, slowly up, then down.

"Why? How? When?"

"I don't really know why or how, and I don't even know when. You were the same wonderful woman I first met, but then after a few years there was a sameness to us, and I began to get bored with our life, and you seemed more interested in being a good mother, and you were so into your practice—"

"What?"

"Let me finish. I've never really thought about this until now, as ridiculous as that may sound, but I wasn't thinking about you when I first did what I did. I was only thinking about me."

"When you *first* did what you did? You mean it was with more than one woman?"

He nods.

"How long?"

He's quiet, and I feel myself getting worked up all over again.

"About the last year and a half of our marriage."

"Oh, really? You sneaky, lying son of a bitch!" I remember we're sitting in a restaurant, so I lower my voice and say, "You lying sneaky son of a bitch," again.

"I was conflicted."

"Con-*what*?"

"It's hard to justify it, Georgia. Almost impossible."

"Did you marry one of them?"

He nods.

"Did you have any children?"

"A daughter. I brought her to the party."

"Wait. Wanda said you were with a woman young enough to be your daughter."

"That was Ming. This happened when we were married, and I never had the heart to tell you."

I lean forward and ball up my fist like some young hoochie, then catch myself. "Let's stop right here, Michael. There's some things a person is better off not knowing, and I think this qualifies."

"I couldn't agree more."

"Other than our daughter, is there anything you got from me that you're thankful for?" he asks.

"Let me think."

He looks worried.

The waitress brings our salads and my drink, and I take a long, slow sip.

"I'm super grateful for how well you taught me how to manage money, how to invest it, and how to hoard it. Thanks to you, my credit score teeters around eight hundred."

"That's it?"

"Does Estelle know she has a sister?"

"Yes, she does."

"When was the last time you spoke to her?"

"Yesterday."

"Really?"

"We talk on a somewhat regular basis. I just don't think she wants you to know how much we're in communication, because I believe she senses you still despise me. Do you?"

"Abso-fucking-lutely," I say, laughing. "And I've enjoyed reminding myself of it whenever you cross my mind, which is hardly ever."

"I'm sorry to hear this."

"I'm overstating it, Michael. And I'm sorry for saying it. Did Estelle mention anything about her living situation?"

"As a matter of fact, she did. She said they're thinking of moving closer to your neck of the woods, maybe Walnut Creek."

"Really? And did she tell you when and why?"

"It sounds like you're not aware of this, Georgia."

"Of course I know about it, but I was just wondering why she told you."

"Because I'm her father."

I wish I could eat, but I can't. I wish I could tell him that those years he took up space in my life and my heart were magnificent. I wish I could tell him that I tried to give him everything I could, everything I had to give, everything I thought he wanted and needed, but mostly what I thought was good. I want to ask if he ever thinks about when we met in the library. How he held my hand walking down Telegraph Avenue? How tenderly he kissed me on my cheek? Did he forget how much joy and beauty and love we shared? I want to ask him when did we stop floating? When did we lose the fucking delight? Instead, this is what comes out of my mouth: "I'm glad I met you and glad I loved you, Michael."

He looks at me like he can't believe I just said this.

"I'm grateful for the years you made me happy. The years you made me feel safe. Cared for. The years you weren't the cause of my worries. The years you made me feel valuable. The years you put our daughter and me first." I sigh and lean back in my chair and take a sip of my water.

"Don't stop now!"

I toss my napkin at him. This is starting to feel like some sentimental made-for-TV movie, but I'm not going to change the channel.

"I can't believe you just said that. I needed to hear this, Georgia. Thank you so much for forgiving me."

"What makes you think I've forgiven you?"

"Haven't you?"

"I'm considering it."

He starts laughing, but I don't.

"To be honest with you, Michael, I had decided to hate you forever and hoped that somehow you'd feel it and suffer because of it. But you obviously weren't affected, and it took me a long time to realize I was poisoning myself with that anger. It made it impossible for another man to get anywhere near my heart."

"Well, I'm glad you did finally realize that."

"I was on the verge of conjuring some of it back up tonight, but then I just thought how pathetic it was."

"I do regret what I did to you, and although you may not believe me, I hated myself for how I did it and have prayed all these years that you'd forgive me."

"Pray a little harder," I say, and I feel a smirk emerge. "So tell me what you liked least about me."

"Wow. Seriously?" he asks.

I look at him like, *That's a yes.*

"You always had to be right. You always wanted things to be done your way, as if it were the best way. And—"

"Wait! That's enough! Okay. One more and that's it!"

"You were impatient."

"Who isn't, Michael?"

"Well, you'd get a little unhinged when things didn't go the way you thought they should go or the way you planned."

"Who doesn't?"

"And you had almost zero tolerance for people you didn't think were as intelligent as you."

"And these are character defects?" I start laughing. "Don't think I haven't figured some of this out—even though the things you mention are only minor imperfections."

"What about me?" he asks, looking a bit scared.

"They were minor things and not deal breakers. However, you were a little on the lazy side and had no household skills, but other than that I would have to put being dishonest and sneaky on the top of this small list."

"I've gotten much better at being honest. And learned it's not half as expensive as being dishonest."

"You know what I've figured out?"

"No."

"Men are stupid."

"Georgia," he says, nodding as if I'm right, which I am. "I'm sorry for hurting you, for disappointing you, and for breaking the promises I made to you," he says. When I see the whites of his eyes turn glassy pink, I feel mine stinging, too.

"I've waited a long time to hear you say that."

"I hope you haven't made other men pay for what I did."

"Believe me, you're not the only one on that bus, dude, but at least you seem to have finally gained a modicum of insight based on your fucked-up ways—or is this all staged?"

"I'm almost saintly," he says, trying to relax and head back to being serious. "I'm still hoping to meet someone like you, Georgia."

"You met me a long time ago, Michael."

"It's too bad we don't get do-overs."

"If that's a question, I think you're right. Don't you have someone in your life?"

"No," he says. "And you?"

I'm tempted to lie, but since this has become a damn honest party, I say, "No."

"Well, it's not over," he says.

"That's the word on the street," I say, and he stands up and just smiles, and I say, "It's nice to see you, Michael, and I'm glad we have more good memories than bad. So let's just cherish the goodness we shared and consider it an amazing chapter in our lives. Deal?"

"Deal," he says, and walks over to pull my chair out as I stand up. This time he wraps his arms around me and squeezes so hard I think he squeezes all that ancient anger right on out of me.

# Geography

YOU SOUND DIFFERENT," WANDA SAYS AS SHE DEVOURS the chips and salsa I just set out for her and Violet, who shocked me by apologizing after I didn't return her calls and said she still meant what she'd said, just maybe not the way she said it, and I just told her that it's my life to live it the way I want to and that I didn't need her approval to do anything, and then we hugged through the phone. This is nothing new.

"Hold on," Violet says. "Where'd you buy this salsa? It's delicious."

"I made it just for you two huzzies."

"Where'd you get the recipe?" Wanda asks. "You know Nelson loves salsa."

"I made it up. It's just heirloom tomatoes and lots of other stuff. I'll write it down."

They're helping me pack all the photographs in tissue paper and Bubble Wrap as well as making labels for some of the art leaning against walls all over the house.

"You do look a little composed," Violet says. "Did you make any sangria or what?"

"She saw Michael."

"What? Did you finally curse him out? Did you punch him in the nose like you've been wanting to do all these years?" Violet never tires of animal prints, and today she's in cheetah leggings and a tight black tank top. I'll be glad when she realizes that animals come in solid colors, too.

"And?" Wanda asks, staring me in the eye.

"I swallowed it."

"What'd you just say?" Violet yells from the kitchen, actually sticking her head around the corner. A giant areca palm standing in the corner makes her look like she really could be in a jungle. If only.

"You heard me," I say as I pick up a picture and continue wrapping.

"Did he put something in your drink?" she asks as she comes back and sets a tray on the table. "Don't tell me you slept with the son of a bitch, Georgia. But if you did, how was it?"

"Are you nuts?"

"So what if she did, Violet? It's her damn business, and we could say a whole lot about some of the aliens *you've* crawled under."

"So what'd you do with the anger?"

"I left it there."

"Left it where?" Violet asks.

"At the restaurant," Wanda says.

"You mean you had dinner with him?" Violet asks now that this story sounds like it's getting interesting.

"I did."

"I don't know how you do that, but you should market the shit," Violet says.

"I don't need any details," Wanda says, looking pleased.

"I'll just say this. I'm glad I loved him. Glad I married him. But also glad I divorced him."

"Where in the hell are you hiding the violins, Georgia?" Violet asks after downing what looks like a double shot.

"Why don't you shut up and wrap something," Wanda says, and hands her a black-and-white photograph of me at eight months old, which is what's written on the back. I was not a cute baby, and why they tinted my lips pink I'll never know.

"Did he happen to mention his young Asian girlfriend?"

"She's his daughter, Violet."

"Okay. Oh, she's the love child. I get it."

"Are we done with this conversation?" I look at them like I'm at a tennis match. I love them to death, but sometimes I don't want to hear the truth. Sometimes I want them to lie. Or just agree with me. Or be neutral, though that would be asking too much. But since we're BFFs, I suppose I'm stuck with them.

"Well, just because *you've* decided to let bygones be bygones, that doesn't mean *I* have to like his ass. The only reason I spoke to him at the party was I was trying to be civilized."

"People make mistakes," I say.

"Mistakes can be corrected. Most men know exactly what they're doing before they do it. And that's called intent."

"Okay, let's skip the subject for real," I say.

When we hear the beginning of a song I recognize as Lady Gaga, we know it's Velvet calling her mama. Violet yanks her phone out of her purse, frowns, and says to us, "Lord, what does this child want now?"

Wanda and I know Velvet *always* wants something.

"What can I do for you?" she asks, listening and nodding her head as she walks around the room in those stupid stilettos.

She so thinks she's still thirty. She presses Off and throws the phone back inside her purse.

"I don't even want to know," I say.

"Me either," Wanda says.

And out she goes. We are so used to this kind of drama that we aren't even moved.

"So," Wanda says, "this idea is turning out to be healthy. I'm glad. I always liked Michael."

She picks up two pieces of the packing paper and starts wrapping it around my mother and father celebrating their fiftieth wedding anniversary.

"And please don't ask me who's next, because I've got quite a few other things on my mind. I think my daughter and her husband are having major financial problems."

"A lot of people are, Georgia."

"True, but I think Estelle and Justin might be brand-new casualties on that foreclosure list, too."

"But Justin's a frigging designer at Hewlett-Packard! What kind of money problems could a Silicon Valley–employed Stanford grad be having?"

"Your guess is as good as mine."

"Who told you?"

"Scarlett and Gabby."

"Holy shit. They are smart. Why haven't you asked Estelle about this?"

"I don't want to embarrass her."

"Oh, so if they're about to be homeless, you'll discuss it then? Come on, Georgia. Sometimes you need to act like you came from Bakersfield."

"I'm thinking about how best to bring it up."

"Just tell her those big-mouthed twins spilled the beans, and then she can either enslave them or be glad you're able to help them."

We wrap and tape in silence for a few minutes.

"This may not be the best time to tell you this, Georgia, but Nelson and I are thinking of buying a condo in Palm Springs and possibly retiring there."

"What! Why?"

"Nelson's arthritis will be better in a dry climate."

"I never knew he had arthritis."

"I'm lying. We just like it there, and we're tired of this cold weather, and plus we both want to golf anytime we want to."

"You'll burn up down there."

"We're black. We can take the heat."

"Well, you two might be the only black faces you see for days at a time, because there's nothing but gay men and rich white people down there, and most of them are Republicans."

"Ask me if I care."

"Do you care?"

"No, I do not. I like gay men who don't hate women, and I don't mind being around rich white people, because there's plenty of them in the Bay Area, and I know how to ignore Republicans."

"Seems like everybody's moving, huh?"

"So what if your house sells really fast? Where in the world would you move?"

"I don't know."

"You have to have some idea."

"Costa Rica."

"Yeah, right."

"Dubai."

She cuts her eyes at me. "What about New York?"

"I just told Percy that's where I wanted to live to piss him off because I could tell he's a die-hard San Franciscan. But as much as I love New York, I feel too old to live there. And I'd only be able to afford a studio apartment, which would probably be more than my mortgage. I'll visit. Plus, I love sleeping in hotels."

"Miami?"

"Florida is boring. Too many accents, and half of them you can't understand or they can't understand you. I hate that humidity, and I've got beaches and sunshine right here, and let's not forget those hurricanes. No thank you."

"What about Arizona?"

"Do I look like I would want to live in a desert?"

"Denver?"

"Can't breathe there. That altitude kills me. And it's boring as hell unless you're into nature. Nature scares me. I don't understand the point of hiking, and I can't remember how to ski."

"Seattle is nice."

"I'd need to be on antidepressants. That rain is romantic and refreshing for a few days, but not nonstop week after week. Granted, it's full of smart, educated people, and they've got the best coffee, but so does the Bay Area."

"Would it occur to you to just stay right here?"

"Maybe. But to be honest, I don't think I want to be more than driving distance from my mother and my grandkids."

I look around at all the taped boxes. We've made a lot of progress.

"My work here is done," Wanda announces.

I thank her with hugs, but at the front door she does an about-face. "Wait!"

"What now?"

"Two things. You want to stay in the guesthouse or with us while this place is being staged?"

"No. But thanks for the offer, honey."

"I know you're not thinking of staying in a hotel for two or three weeks."

"I don't know what I'm going to do, but I do know I want to do something I haven't done before and maybe go somewhere I haven't been."

She looks at me like she's worried, and I push her out the door.

THE RAIN WAKES me up. And then people talking. It sounds like a conductor on a train. I must've fallen asleep on the remote's Pause button and now apparently rolled over on Play. I sit up. Julie Delpy and Ethan Hawke are sitting across the aisle from each other on a train. He's American. She's French. They're both young and smart. I saw this film when it came out in 1995, and decided to watch it last night for reasons I do not know. It's called *Before Sunrise*. I do know. I love implausible romantic movies that become plausible. This one felt more like a peek into the souls of two characters who got a once-in-a-lifetime opportunity to share their thoughts and opinions and they had nothing to lose and it was just a train ride but as they talked it started becoming clearer and clearer that both of them were discovering themselves at the same time they were discovering each other. It was not the typical boy-meets-girl-and-they-fall-in-love love story. It's a very talky movie, although I appreciated the things they talked about, but what fascinated me even more was the train ride itself. The whir of it speeding over those tracks. What they saw out the window. What they missed. The medley of colors. Those open fields. Horses. Cows. Sheep. And homes, farms, buildings. Even a city here and there.

I rewind the film to the point when Ethan tells Julie he's been riding this train for two weeks and doesn't exactly know where he's going. But at least he's moving. Right now I'm right there with him. I grab a handful of popcorn from the bowl sitting on the nightstand and then chase it down with a sip of lukewarm ginger ale, and I say aloud, "How frigging cool would that be?" A long train ride? Why not? I can afford to take the time off. I could ride up to Vancouver and maybe across Canada all the way over to Toronto and then down to New York and hang out with Frankie and fly back home. I could buy one of those passes that lets you get on and off in different cities. I could get one of those sleeper cars! I could read. I could wonder. I could relax. I could even think about my future on a blank screen until it comes into focus. I wouldn't be hoping to pick up an Ethan Hawke. That was a movie. I'd be starring in my own. I pull the duvet up under my chin, decide to get in touch with a good travel agent, press Off on the remote, and then close my eyes.

All aboard.

THE RAIN FINALLY STOPPED. But before I can brush my teeth, the phone rings. Without looking at the caller ID, I know who it is. "Good morning, First Lady of Bakersfield." This is often how I greet my mother.

"I *wish* I could be Michelle Obama for a few weeks!"

"Well, it's certainly one for the history books all right. So how was the cruise?"

"Duller than a cheap steak knife. I was so sick of being around old people I didn't know what to do. That was my last cruise. Traveling with folks who don't want to do anything but pray can drive you crazy. God can hear your prayers on land and at sea. Plus, they acted like if they touched a slot machine, they were going straight to hell. They should've stayed home if they didn't want to have any fun. Anyway, I was calling to tell you I don't feel like rushing up there anytime soon, and it doesn't feel like I'm about to go blind, and when will they be finished with the remodel?"

"The what?"

"Isn't the house being remodeled, or did you just make that up because you didn't want Dolly and Sons staying there?"

"Yes and no."

"We can wait until it's finished."

"But I don't know how long it might take."

"Do you have to move out of your house while they do it?"

"That's one way to look at it."

"So is anything exciting going on in your life?"

"Well, yes. You'll never guess what I'm thinking of doing."

"I'm too old to guess, Georgia, and it's too early to play guessing games."

"Taking a train ride."

"I like trains. Where to?"

"Anywhere."

"That's the same as nowhere. Be more specific, please."

"Vancouver," I blurt out, surprising myself.

"So is this like some kind of an adventure?"

"Yes. That's exactly how I'd describe it."

"Can I come with you? I could use an adventure."

"Not this time, Ma."

"Why not?"

"Because."

"Are you going with somebody?"

"No."

"You shouldn't travel on a train by yourself. People get killed on trains."

"Only in the movies, Ma."

"This is why you need a husband."

"As soon as I get off this phone, I'm going on Amazon and see if I can find one in the men's department."

"Ha, ha, ha. What made you decide to do this all of a sudden?"

"I'm selling my house."

"Well, why didn't you just say that instead of beating around the doggone bush? It took you long enough. I don't know how you've lived on three floors all by yourself since Frankie left for college, and you know once they leave, they don't come back. Get yourself a condo in San Francisco close to Fisherman's Wharf."

"Ma?"

"Did it sound like I hung up? I'm still here."

"I'm also planning to sell my share of the practice."

"Me and your dad never understood why you chose that field. Not exactly a thrill a minute, but it was respectable. And do what?"

"I don't know yet."

"Well, you're never too old for change. Did I tell you I'm going to be starting a cooking class?"

"No you didn't. What kind of food?"

"Who cares? It's free, and it's right here in my complex. You should go back to college and learn how to do something that's interesting. And this time make sure it's something fun. Love you, dear."

"I love you more."

"That's not true, or you'd invite me on your train ride."

"Bye, Ma."

Smooches this time.

# A Definite No, but Maybe

S THAT THE DOORBELL? I LOOK OVER AT THE CLOCK. IT'S almost midnight. I'm a little scared, because whoever it is, they're pressing that bell over and over like it's some kind of an emergency. I put on my robe, tiptoe across the room, and crack one of the shutters just enough to see a yellow cab in the driveway. All I know is that whoever it is chose me to rescue them, so I run out to the front door and pull on the handle hard enough that I almost lose my balance, and standing there like she's just been evicted is my daughter, Frankie, in tears.

"Frankie? Baby, what's wrong? Has something terrible happened? Are you okay?" I grasp her by the shoulders to make sure she's not hurt and then lift her chin up so I can see her face and what's in her eyes. I can't tell what, but something has happened, or she wouldn't have just shown up like this.

"Mom, moving to New York and going to NYU were the two biggest mistakes of my life, and it's taken two whole years for me to realize I don't care about the theory and history of cinema, and I'm confused about what the real purpose of my life is, and I also broke up with Hunter because he cheated on me and the girl is pregnant, so I just needed to get as far away from them and him as possible, so I decided to come home to get my head together. And I need a hug."

And then she collapses in my arms. I squeeze her hard and am relieved it's not a life-or-death situation even though it feels like one to her. She looks homeless in her fake brown velvet coat and scruffy

purple boots. But she's my daughter and a casualty of love and confusion because she's changed her mind about her future. Like mother,
like daughter.

"It's going to be okay, Frankie. I promise you."

"I hear that a lot on television. Which is why I don't believe it."

"Why's the taxi still sitting out there?"

Her tears suddenly evaporate. "Oh. Mom. Could you please let me
borrow a credit card to pay for it? I'm over my limit, but I promise I'll
pay you back as soon as I get a job."

Did she just say "as soon as I get a job"?

I then feel her rocking my left shoulder back and forth. "Mom!" I
look down and see one, two, three pink-and-black giraffe suitcases, a
navy blue duffel, and one, two, three, four boxes. So she really means it.
She has come back home without as much as a phone call.

She turns and holds up her index finger to the driver and shakes it
like she's got a nervous tic. I reach inside my purse and hand her the
American Express.

"Thanks," she says, and runs out to the taxi.

I start pulling the luggage inside as she dashes right back. "He
doesn't take American Express. Visa, MasterCard, or Discover." Her
big eyes are onyx, her hair a kinky black halo. Her lips are thick and
heart-shaped, and her teeth—thanks to braces, and she better be wearing that damn retainer at night—are bright, white, and straight. I hand
her the Visa. She forges my signature and seconds later darts back and
wipes the sweat beads from her brow. She then starts kicking the boxes
into the entry as I try and fail to pick up the duffel. When all her pos-
sessions are inside, I walk over to the stairwell, sit down, rest my elbow
on my knee, put my chin in my palm, and just look at her.

"You're not pregnant, are you, Frankie?"

"I wouldn't ever. Children are so overrated."

"So why didn't you call first to give me a heads-up that you were
coming?"

"Because I didn't want you to talk me out of it, Mom. You're such a
pragmatist."

"You don't know me as well as you think you do, sweetie. If you want to drop out of college, why would I try to stop you?"

"Do I detect sarcasm? Anyway, I dropped out of NYU, not college in general. I just have to figure some stuff out."

The house is dark. She doesn't bother turning on the lights but disappears into the kitchen and comes back with a Corona and proceeds to guzzle close to half the bottle.

"Mom, would you mind terribly if I just went up to my room and crashed? I'm wiped out. It's tomorrow for me. I'll bring all my stuff up in the morning if that's okay."

"It's fine," I say, and she walks over and hugs me and runs up the stairs. Moments later I hear the shower. She has not noticed anything out of the ordinary. And I'm glad, because it's tomorrow here, too.


IN THE MORNING I hear a tap-tap on my door.

"Whoever it is, come on in."

Frankie walks in wearing an NYU T-shirt and looking baffled. "Good morning, Mom," she says, then gives me a hug and collapses at the foot of my bed. "Are you painting?"

"Nope."

"Did I miss something?"

"You passed right by the sign, honey. It's under the evergreen."

"You mean you're selling our house?"

I nod.

"Why? And where are we going to move? And why didn't you tell me? What does Stelle think about this?"

"Hold your little ponies, daughter. I told you this summer I was thinking about putting the house on the market, and I did. It's too much space for one person."

"But *I'm* here now. That makes two. Please don't sell it, Mom. I grew up in this house."

"Look, Frankie. You just scared the hell out of me by coming home unannounced in the middle of the night, and I apologize if I'm not ready to start changing my plans because you're changing yours. And you're not the only one with memories. I'm just tired of living here. Alone."

"Wow, this is major."

"It is. So you're only going to be able to stay here for about two or three weeks, but I'll figure out where to put you up."

"Are you serious? You're kicking me to the curb? Wow. This is too deep for me."

"I'm leaving, too."

"What? Why? Did someone already buy it?"

"No. The house is being remodeled, or what's called 'staged,' and no one can be here while they're doing it. It could take up to three weeks, but even after they finish, the house has to look like a showroom at all times until it sells."

"You are serious, then, huh? And BTW, I've gotten much neater." She looks around like she remembers living here. "So where are you going?"

"On a train ride."

"What?"

"A train ride."

"For three whole weeks?"

"Probably not the entire time."

"Then I'll just go with you."

"No you won't."

"Why not?"

"Because I want to go alone, and besides, I've already made a reservation and I can't change it." I lie.

"You mean you want to sleep with strangers on a train or something? Come on, Mom. People get killed on trains. Haven't you read Agatha Christie? This sounds insane to me."

"I don't think I really need to explain any of this to you, Frankie."

"Well, that's true, but I'm your daughter, and I've come home lost and confused, distraught and brokenhearted, and all you can say is 'Hasta la vista'?"

"I'm not abandoning you, Frankie. I'll do whatever I can to help you figure some of this out."

"So where're you going on this train ride?"

"I'm not sure yet."

"Then how can you buy a ticket if you don't know where you're going?"

She is already getting on my nerves.

"I'm considering a few options. From here to Vancouver. Toronto. Montreal. Niagara Falls. I don't know yet. But to answer your question, it's called a rail pass. College students all over the world do this. I can stop in a city, stay in a hotel for a day or so, then get back on the train."

"Wow. This sounds so cool. Maybe I can change your mind, but if not, I can probably stay with Estelle and Justin. Help with those little munchkins."

"I don't think that's going to be doable either."

"Are they moving, too?"

"They're thinking of downsizing. Speaking of which, have you heard from your dad lately?"

"No. But I think he's mad at me. I haven't written him in a while."

"Would it kill you to drop him a line every now and then? He's still your dad, Frankie, and he was a good one. Just because he did something stupid, that doesn't mean you have to punish him when he's already paying for it."

She just looks at me as if all this is too much to handle and walks out, not closing the door behind her.

I hear her in the kitchen. Can smell coffee all the way down here. She's banging pots and pans to get my attention. I tiptoe across the hardwood floor into my bathroom and gently close the door. I turn the faucet on low so it doesn't make the small waterfall sound. I brush my teeth, leaning on the sink with my palms. What am I going to do about her? I can't just kick her to the curb, as she put it. I hear another tap-tap and: "Mom, I made a pot of strong coffee and soft-boiled eggs and toast if you're up to it."

My baby girl. She knows what I like.

I walk into the kitchen, and there's my chocolate daughter, her thick hair piled on top of her head into a ponytail that looks like black cauliflower. She's twirling around slowly on a stool at the island.

"Did you sleep okay?" I ask.

"As a matter of fact, I didn't, Mom. I think I may have made a mistake just dropping in on you this way. I forget that parents have lives, too, that don't necessarily include us. So. I'm sorry."

"You don't have to apologize for anything," I say as I pour myself a cup of coffee and pretend I don't see the cracks in the brown eggshells.

"What should I do?" she asks.

"I haven't had enough time to think about what you should do, Frankie. What do you *want* to do?"

She shakes her head from side to side. "I don't know. I don't know what I see in my future."

"Well, let me say this. I'll do whatever I can to help you find temporary housing until we both know for sure you're not going to run back to Hudson after I've put my name on a lease."

"It's Hunter. And I'm not running back to him or New York, and that's real. Thank you for offering to help. Again. I hope one day it's money well spent. And that you'll be proud of me."

"I'm already proud of you, Frankie, but I just can't fix every problem you come up against."

"I know. Let's go to Paris and get on the Eurostar and zigzag all over Europe and then come back to a new home!"

I just look at her. And then, "Are you not listening to me? And do I look like Wells Fargo?"

"You're just too frugal, Mom. At some point in your life, you should give yourself permission to splurge."

"What do you think I'm trying to do?"

"Speaking of splurging," she says, getting up and walking over to the door that leads to the garage and coming back with my still-unpainted stool. "What's this about, Mom? It certainly doesn't look like your taste, and it doesn't match anything."

"I'm going to paint it."

"Why?"

"Because I want to."

"But why?"

"Because I want to, and it's called fun, Frankie."

"Like the fun you had for about a month making all those pillows? Why'd you stop? Everybody loved them."

"We were talking about your lack of direction, not me trying to find one."

She looks at me as if I've said something wrong. "Last time I checked, you were like a legitimate and successful optometrist, Mom. Duh."

"Maybe not for much longer. And don't ask."

"OMG! I wouldn't dare. I'm already on information overload."


FRANKIE'S DOING LAPS when I get home. She's also naked. She glides through the dark water like a baby dolphin. I wish she could do enough butterflies and backstrokes to propel her pain and confusion out into the cold air. I don't remember being heartbroken at twenty-two. I remember being disappointed.

When I see her climbing up the ladder and getting out of the pool, I'm struck by how beautiful and lean her body is. Her breasts point upward, of course, and are shaped like the round top on my grande nonfat no-whip iced mocha. Did I ever look that good naked?

She wraps a colorful beach towel around her and rolls and tucks it across her chest. That's when she sees me through the kitchen window. She waves and walks in through the patio door.

"Hey, Mom," she says, and bends over to kiss me on my right cheek. She's inches taller. "I'm going to miss that pool. Won't you?"

"I'm going to miss a lot of things. How're you feeling today?"

"Refreshed. Clearheaded."

She sits on a stool at the end of the island and puts both elbows on the counter. "So I spoke to Dad."

"How'd you manage that?"

"He's out."

"I thought he was supposed to be in there for five years?"

"It's *been* five years," she says.

Really? "So where is he?"

"He lives fifteen minutes from here, right around the corner from Aunt Wanda and Uncle Nelson."

"You've got to be kidding me."

"Off Skyline."

"So should I be jumping for joy or what?"

"He's offered to let me live with him and his wife."

"What wife?"

"Where've you been for the last eight years, Mom? He got married way after you guys got divorced."

"What do you call 'way after'?"

"A year."

"Anyhow, I haven't exactly kept him on my radar all these years, but I don't like the idea of your even considering living with your ex-convict father and his wife."

"It was a white-collar crime, Mom."

"Oh, my bad," I say with intentional hip-hop sarcasm.

"Just because you don't like him, that doesn't mean I shouldn't."

"I've never suggested that you not like him, Frankie. He's your father. I just thought you hadn't been in touch with him that much."

"Stelle and I figured out a long time ago that it was best not to mention our dads, because when we did, your mood always took a nosedive."

"Well, thank you both for sparing me, but you didn't have to lie."

"I didn't lie. I just withheld the truth. Anyway, he's picking me up sometime this afternoon so I can meet Allegra and see their home. They have a tiny guesthouse, too, which is where he said I could stay for a while."

"Exactly how long has he been out?"

"Almost a year now."

"Are you fucking kidding me? And why didn't you ask if I minded if he came over here?"

"What's the big deal? He used to live here, and it used to be his house, too. It's not like he's going to start stalking you, Mom."

Right now I'm glad I only have two ex-husbands, because they both seem to have been reincarnated and are coming back to haunt me.

"I don't want to see him. At least not today."

"Oh, so you want him to honk? I thought you were an adult. But my bad!" And she storms past me and runs up the stairs.

I follow her.

She slams the door.

I use the L-shaped key to unlock it and barge in. She has the nerve to put her hands on her hips before she flops down on the foot of her platform bed.

"Let's be clear about something, Frankie. You need to understand that in two days you've sprung quite a lot on me, and now you're telling me your dad's out of prison and you might go live with him and his wife? And what—I'm supposed to feel warm and fuzzy? It's not always about you, Frankie."

"I know that, Mom. I'm sorry for inconveniencing you and getting you so worked up."

"It's what kids do even when they're twenty-two, I suppose. Anyway, as an FYI, your Aunt Wanda and Uncle Nelson said you're welcome to stay in their guesthouse if you want to."

"Thanks, but no thanks. I'm not crazy about Aunt Wanda. Wait. That's not true. I just find her and Uncle Nelson boring as can be, and she's also nosy. Now, if it were Aunt Violet, I'd sleep in her garage."

"Carport. What makes you think you can live under the wing of your estranged father after not having seen him in six years?"

"What makes you think I haven't seen him?"

"So this is one more thing you've kept from me."

"You divorced him, Mom. I didn't."

"You mean you visited him in prison?"

"Yes."

"When? How? And why didn't you tell me? I wouldn't have tried to stop you from seeing him, Frankie. Come on."

"What difference does it make now, Mom? He didn't kill anybody. And he didn't rob a bank. As far as I'm concerned, he went to prison for his stupidity and arrogance, which doesn't make him like a dangerous criminal. He's paid for his mistakes. I wish you would let it go and stop indicting him."

"It's a preexisting condition."

"Mom."

"What?"

"Do you have a life? I mean, are you seeing anyone?"

"No."

"I didn't think so. I wish you'd find someone. You seem so testy, or maybe you're just lonely. And I can understand why you don't want to live in this big house by yourself, I really do."

"I'm not selling this house because I'm lonely."

She just looks at me. "I really hope it's not too late for you to find love, Mom."

"What would make you think that?"

"Well, because you're old. No offense intended."

"And what do you call 'old'?"

"Over fifty." She looks at me again as if she might have gone too far.

"Well, let me say this, Miss Forever Twenty-Two. Love doesn't have an age limit, and it can find you at any time in your life. It can also just as soon leave you in a ditch. Look what it's already done to you."

"But how do you meet old men, Mom? You don't go on those dating sites, I hope."

"I really don't feel like having this conversation with you right now, Frankie. But let me also say this. You can be a woman and be happy without a man and without love. Of course your life has more octane when you have someone to share it with. But I am not lonely. Well, that's a lie. I *am* lonely, but I'm not miserable. This is just one more reason I'm getting the hell out of this house and why I'm leaving my dull-ass career and taking a train ride and might even go back to school."

This time her eyes are bulging, but it's accompanied by a smile, and then she holds up her right hand so her palm comes near me, and I slap mine against hers.

"This gives me hope, Mom."

"What does?"

"That changing the direction of my life isn't crazy if you're still willing to do it at your age."

"I'm not even almost old, Frankie. Now, what time is the ex-meteorologist coming to pick you up, so I can make sure I'm not here?"

"C'mon, Mom."

I put my hands on my hips, look out the window, then back at her.

"Look. I'm deliriously happy for him, Frankie, and I won't run and hide. Maybe we could even catch up. Find out what happened during those lost years. Find out how much fun prison was. What time should we expect Father of the Year?"

"In about an hour," she says. "I didn't know you still had so much anger toward him, Mom. That's sad."

"I'm not angry."

"Maybe he can just say hello at the front door."

"Lord, no! Now I want to see him. And not to worry. I'll be the nicest ex-wife he's ever seen," I say, and head back downstairs.

# White Light, Red Light

I T STARTED IN MY CHAIR. NILES CAME IN FOR A COMPLETE examination because his vision had suddenly become blurry. I've always been professional with patients, even good-looking men who aren't wearing wedding bands. I had to admit he was handsome in an offbeat kind of way. I assumed he was probably mixed-race, because his nose was broad, his lips full, and his eyes were light brown even though his skin was dark. The color and texture of his hair were contradictory. I wasn't studying him; I was just noticing who was standing in front of me.

"Hello, Mr. Boro," I said, motioning him to "Have a seat."

"I would prefer to stand, if you don't mind," he said, and then chuckled.

"Please be seated, Mr. Boro," I said in my best good-natured-but-professional voice.

He sat. "Please, call me Niles."

I just looked at him as if to ask, *Who do you think you are, coming into my office and getting personal? This isn't a blind date.* He smiled and crossed his legs. He was dressed like he'd just stepped off a page from *GQ*. Even his cuff links had his initials on them: NB. His shoes looked satiny, as if he never walked anywhere they might get dusty. And he smelled like chocolate. He was already a problem.

"So, Mr. Boro, you're complaining about eyestrain and blurriness."

"That's an understatement. But it's my fault, because I haven't had my eyes checked in two years."

"Why not?"

"Pure laziness. And I don't trust doctors."

I just looked down at him.

"Only kidding."

"So you're a meteorologist?"

"I am. But you haven't seen me on the six-o'clock news."

He didn't stop talking as I performed each of the various tests, and right before I was about to dilate his pupils, he felt compelled to tell me his life story. He was from Boston. His father was Nigerian, his mother Norwegian. He got his master's from the University of Massachusetts, was divorced after three years of marriage, had a five-year-old son who lived with his mother in the Berkeley Hills. For some reason he felt it important that I knew they parted ways amicably, but I would later find out this was a lie. His son's name was Homer. Like Homer Simpson.

I gave him a prescription, told him to pick out a pair of frames and that a tech would fit him.

"Can you help me choose a frame?"

"That's not what I do," I said.

And then he looked right through me. "Have you ever dated a patient?"

This threw me for a loop. "No. Never."

"Could I be the first?"

"I said never."

"I'll make a liar out of you, Dr. Young," he said with too much confidence. This is when I should've known. He'd already put some kind of spell on me, because right after he walked out with his prescription, I heard a sound coming from my chest. It was me: purring.

He sent me a dozen peonies the next day.

The note with them said, "I was blind, but thanks to you, now I see."


I DON'T KNOW HOW this whole love thing happens, but I wish that—in addition to white light—a red one would come on to warn you that the white light is only temporary. That it's meant to blind you, but of course it's too late because you're already sinking and not think-ing, which is when you find yourself wanting to scream, "Oh, Lord, not again!" Just when you think you're dead, some stranger comes out of nowhere and resuscitates you. When you find yourself giggling, not laughing but giggling. You're lighter, even though you weigh the same. Yes. You have fallen off that cliff into the sea of lust, the first cousin of love, and the two strongest drugs on earth.

In a matter of weeks, I found myself singing in elevators.

I couldn't walk. I had to skip.

I was Snow Black.

Estelle, who was twelve, said, "Mom, whatever it is you're drinking, keep drinking it!"

We both laughed.

"What's his name, and when can I meet him?" Wanda asked.

"Niles. And I don't know."

"Ask him if he has a brother," Violet said.

At first he did everything right.

He called me baby.

"Good morning, baby."

"How you doing today, baby?"

"Good night, baby."

"I love you, baby."

"Will you always be my baby?"

"Aww, baby."

"Oooh, baby."

"Give it all to me, baby."

"You make me feel so good, baby."

"I miss you, baby."

"Do you miss me, baby?"

"I've been thinking about you all day, baby."

"I need a hug, baby."

"I need me some you, baby."

"Come to Daddy, baby."

"I'm sorry, baby."

"I DON'T LIKE HIM," Ma said right after she met him. And then, after a few more meals, "If you marry this one, you'll be making a big mistake."

"How can you say that, Ma? He's been nice to you. And good to me and Estelle."

"He's phony as hell. He's too perfect. Wait until you find out he expects the same from you."

"Why didn't you warn me about Michael?"

"This is different. Something is missing in Niles. Something I don't think you see."

Always listen to the parent who doesn't like who you love. They can smell a mistake. Of course, you don't find this out until you realize that the person you fell in love with is different from the person you married. Some men are good at fooling you.

After Michael I had no intention of getting married again. I told Niles that if he cheated on me, I would definitely kill him. He thought that was funny. I also told him I didn't want to have another baby. He said that was fine, because he already had a son. But he changed his mind. When your husband says he wants you to have his child, you're supposed to be flattered. We had, of course, just finished making love, if that's what you'd call it. At first Niles was an active participant for a solid half hour, but then he started dropping down to twenty minutes and then fifteen, and even then I found myself doing most of the work. I pretended not to hear him.

"Say something, Georgia."

"I heard you."

"I love Estelle, believe me, I do. But I really want us to have a child of our own."

"I thought we agreed we were both happy the way things were."

"I don't remember saying that. So don't go putting words in my mouth."

"What made you change your mind?"

"You. Me. I want it to be us."

He was as full of shit as a Christmas turkey.

"Estelle is part of us."

"Figuratively, yes. But she doesn't have my blood in her veins."

I wanted to bitch-slap him for saying that, but instead I took the high road.

"It would've made more sense five years ago, Niles."

"I didn't know you five years ago."

"I know."

"A lot of women are having children in their forties. I'm begging you, Georgia."

Shit. Damn. Fuck. Niles was adamant, and because I was 90 percent certain we were going to spend the rest of our lives together, I surrendered.

But I also learned. Don't assume anything.

He decided to name our daughter Francine, after his dead grandmother, and he decided how we should parent her, and before she could walk is when I realized that Niles had morphed into a man I didn't know and didn't like.

He was a control freak.

He was a clean freak. (Later I would drop something on the floor just to see if he would pick it up. Of course he did.)

The garage had to be carpeted.

Everything had to have order and symmetry.

He had no friends.

He was a workaholic.

He didn't like my two best friends, Wanda and Violet. They pretended to like him.

He rarely had anything nice to say about most people.

Everybody had a hidden agenda. Including his family.

He hated the IRS and did everything he could to pay as little in taxes as he could get away with. He hoarded his money, liked to pay cash for as many things as possible. He even insisted we file our taxes separately, and we did, which would ultimately be what saved me.

AFTER EIGHT YEARS of marriage to Mr. My Way or No Way, I realized I didn't like Niles because he was unlikable. He lost his luster and that Mr. Nice Guy façade disappeared, which is when I started seeing neon signs that read MAYBE I SHOULDN'T HAVE. I hated knowing that this marriage wasn't going to last unless I did everything he wanted the way he wanted. But I couldn't. His love started to hurt. Because he had become my enemy.

"Wake up, Georgia."

"Did you get my suit out of the cleaners?"

"I can't."

"This house is never clean."

"Are you deaf?"

"I'm tired."

"I'm not interested in going."

"Your friends bore me."

"Turn over, would you?"

"Have you thought about how unattractive those extra pounds are?"

"Why don't you get a weave?"

"I think you should trade in your Lexus and get an SUV."

"I'm not interested in politics."

"You're not making any sense."

"Your focus is much narrower than you think."

"I don't like your mother, and I can't apologize for it."

"I don't like that dress."

I threw a whole roll of Bounty at him once. No: twice.

"I didn't know you were this rude, Niles."

"I didn't know you were not a nice person."

"I didn't know you were so selfish."

"I also didn't know you were going to be so boring."

"I work for a living, too, and I'm educated, too, you know," I finally said.

"You don't have to remind me. It's hard for me to look into your eyes anymore. There's nothing in them."

"Well, I'm tired of being married to someone who only talks about the fucking weather. From here on out, whenever the clouds turn gray I will probably always think of you."

That was cruel. But it took me a long time to be as cruel to him as he had been to me.

One night he was drying dishes to make sure there were no hard-water stains.

"We need to talk," I said.

"That's pretty much all you do, isn't it, Georgia?"

"You missed a spot," I said, knowing he hadn't. The glass he was holding up to the light was immaculate.

"So we're done, then?"

"I believe we are."

He moved out the next day. It felt like he'd been packed a long time. Of course he insisted I buy him out, which I did. The one good thing that our marriage produced was Frankie.


I GET OUT of the shower and hear a series of knocks on my bedroom door. "Mom, open up!"

I grab a towel and wrap it around me, which unfortunately leaves no room for error, so I hold it together with my thumb and index finger and run to the door and open it. "Either he's early or not coming—which one is it?"

"He's not coming."

"And why not?"

"His wife doesn't want me to stay in the guesthouse."

"I know he's not listening to his wife, a woman, after all these years."

Frankie rocks her weight to one flip-flopped foot and crosses her arms. "Apparently he's a kept man and has no power."

"You don't know that, Frankie."

"Well, she didn't bother discussing with him that she'd already promised her grandson he could stay in it."

"Then why are you upset with him?"

"Because he said she doesn't have a grandson."

"So when are you going to see him?"

"I don't know. I hung up on him."

"You need to slow your roll, Frankie. It wasn't his fault, and he was trying to help you."

"Well, he didn't. He's disappointed me too many times, and now I have a general idea why you divorced him."

# Cardboard

AS SOON AS I GET HOME FROM WORK, I HEAR FRANKIE yelling upstairs on her phone.

"You're sorry?"

A moment of silence.

"You expect me to believe that?"

Niles?

"So what? You're still a cheater, and I don't want to love someone I can't trust!"

Not Niles.

"You better not come out here!"

I have to stop myself from yelling, *Please come!*

Pause.

"Hunter?"

Pause.

"Fuck."

When I hear her door swing open, I beeline it to the kitchen and pretend I'm looking for something in the pantry.

"Mom, I've got good news and bad news."

I walk out and look at her eyes. They're glassy, but I can't tell if anything has fallen from them. I cross my arms and lean against the refrigerator. "I'm listening."

"Hunter's probably on his way out here to fetch me."

"Fetch?"

"He said the girl tricked him."

I can't tell if this is supposed to be the good or the bad news.

"Really?"

"He got drunk at his buddy's dorm and slept with this chick and had a blackout, and she told him she was pregnant, but turns out she made it up. So he still loves me and wants me back."

"Wants you back or wants you to come back?"

"I'm not sure."

"Where's he plan on staying?"

"I don't know. But would it be possible for him to stay here for a few days? Because by then we will have figured out what we're going to do."

"You must think everybody's in college, Frankie."

"Hunter's not."

"What?"

"He got his bachelor's in digital engineering. He's a geek freak."

"Well, that's good to hear. It means he's employable."

"True, but he just got into the master's program, and it's all about app development and software design and blah, blah, who cares?"

"And now you want me to turn your room into a honeymoon suite so you can rekindle what you swore to me was lost?"

"I said I was mad at him. I didn't say I didn't love him anymore."

"What on earth do you think you know about love, Frankie?"

"The same thing you did when you were my age, Mom."

"Which was nothing."

I shake my head and walk past her. I would like to hug her and slap her at the same time. I understand the spell she's under, but now I'm anxious because so much is happening and I don't know if I'm handling it the right way or not. I don't know how you're supposed to know. Nevertheless, I walk out to the garage and look at the stool I haven't touched. I'm not thinking about Percy or staging when I get a clean rag out of the drawer and dust it. Of course here she comes again.

"What now, Frankie?"

"Can I ask you a personal question, Mom?"

"How personal?"

"How many times have you been in love?"

"Five. And two to grow on."

We both laugh. I'm glad we can.

"Is that considered a lot?"

"I have no idea. I haven't done any surveys."

We laugh again.

"Just so you know, Hunter's pretty handy and can help you do anything you need help with."

"That's nice to know. So is this what you came out here to tell me?"

"No. A lot of things are going through my head, which is why I was wondering if it would be possible to borrow your car?"

"To go where, if you don't mind my asking?"

"The reservoir. I could use a run."

"Of course. But can I have your father's phone number?"

"What?"

"You heard me."

"Why do you want his number?"

"Because I would like to talk to him."

"I told you, I can't go live there now with—"

"It's not about you. It's about me, sweetie."

"I don't get it."

"Can you just write the number down and leave it on the kitchen counter for me, please?"

"Promise you won't tell him about the whole Hunter situation."

"Go run," I say, and start looking for some tarp.

I unfold the garment box I bought from one of those storage places, use the Shop-Vac to blow accumulated dust off the stool, and put it inside the small opening that allows me to slip inside. I put on a mask and goggles and stand there like a prisoner looking at the stool. I can't paint. It feels so unimportant right now. Ludicrous. It also feels like a waste of time, because what am I going to do with this stupid stool if and when I ever finish painting it? I cover it with a beige drop cloth and back out of the cardboard entrance.

As I head back inside, the garage wall phone rings, so I reach over to answer it.

"Hello, Georgia," a gravelly voice that sounds like Percy's says, immediately followed by an avalanche of coughs.

When he manages to stop, I say, "Percy, you sound horrible. Why're you calling me if you're sick?"

"I apologize for coughing your ear off and for not being in touch sooner, but I've had bronchitis the last couple of weeks. It's just this stupid cough that takes forever to clear up, but I'm talking to a doctor. So anyway, how are you, Georgia?"

"I'm fine, Percy. And I'm sorry you're sick. Bronchitis is nothing to fool with, so you can take me off your worry list if that's what this call's about."

"It is and it isn't. We've run into a little problem. Not major. But minor. Would it be possible to meet next week so I can both explain and show you why we may have to delay our start date?"

"How much of a delay?"

"Up to a month."

"A whole month?"

"I'm so sorry, Georgia, but it's been one thing after another, and I assure you this is not my style."

"Are you okay?"

"I will be."


I LEAVE FRANKIE the car. Take BART to the office. Work is the same. New patients, old patients, but I'm nervous all day about what to expect when I get home. Lily's fallen in love with another stranger online. Marina just shakes her head. It's a good thing she still lives with her parents, or we'd worry about her safety. I feel sorry for her because she's a dingbat when it comes to men, but she's smart as hell when it comes to business. At forty-four she's never been married and doesn't understand why.

I haven't mentioned anything to Lily about wanting to sell my part of the practice, because not only is there no rush, but I don't have any idea how I'm going to make a living. Lily, who's Filipino, comes from a family of doctors, and thanks to her parents, she's a 60 percent partner to my 40. After my father passed away and left me a sizable inheritance, more than I ever expected, she and I quit the hospital where we were on staff and joined forces.

During lunch I walk to Union Square and meet with a travel agent for real. I tell her why I want to take a train trip and that I'm not sure about the length of time—two, maybe three weeks tops—and that I would love to stop at a few points along the way, sightsee, and possibly stay overnight in a luxe hotel. I tell her I'm not exactly sure about the when either, and she tells me the rail schedules are fixed and not to worry. I tell her I'm interested in seeing as much beauty as possible, starting with the California coastline. I tell her Vancouver is on the top of my list, and even though I don't exactly dream about Canada, it's a breathtaking country and I would certainly dig ending up in Toronto and then hopping onto a plane to fly home. When she asks if I'll be traveling alone and I tell her yes, instead of asking why, she gives me a high five.

I float back to the office and am breezing through my afternoon appointments when Marina taps on my door and pokes her head in.

"Some guy's here to see you. Says he's an old patient of yours and wanted to stop by and say hello."

"Did he tell you his name?"

She shakes her head.

"Put on some lipstick, Doc. He's not too hard on the eyes for an older guy," and she winks. "I'll tell him you'll be out in a few minutes."

Before I get a chance to tell her to ask who it is, I put on a fresh coat of Raging Red, take my lab coat off, and hang it behind the door.

I'm disappointed as hell when I see an older but still-handsome version of Niles looking at eyewear. He has on the black suit I remember buying him one Christmas. At least one of us can still fit into our old clothes. Marina, who always closes up the office, looks like she's not going anywhere anytime soon.

"It's okay if you leave on time," I say, showing off a fake smile that basically tells her I'm really hoping she stays. But she misses it and grabs her black purse and her black umbrella, since it's now raining, and nods to Niles, says she'll see me tomorrow, and leaves with an it's-about-time smirk on her face.

I turn and look down at him. "So what in the world are you doing here, Niles?"

"Well, what a wonderful hello, and good to see you, too, after all these years, Georgia."

"You didn't answer my question. And didn't you know that while you were in prison, God invented cell phones?"

He sits in the yellow chair. Holds up a black iPhone.

"I figured if I called, you wouldn't see me, and I wanted to know how you were holding up since our daughter's come home so distraught."

"She's not distraught. She's in love."

"Same difference."

And then we just look at each other, unsure of what to say. I want him to leave and come back after I've had time to figure out just what to say to him.

"She'll be okay."

"That's easy for you to say, Georgia. Don't you remember how hard it felt being brokenhearted?"

I do, even though he didn't really break my heart—he just disappointed me. But I say, "Of course I do." And then I sit down in a gray chair, three seats away.

"And this is where we met," he says. "Updated quite a bit. Nice touches."

"So how was prison?" I ask, wishing it hadn't slipped out like that. I couldn't think of anything else to say, and I know it was cruel. "I'm sorry, Niles. I didn't mean to say that."

"To be honest, it was probably the best thing that's ever happened to me, besides you and Frankie. It was an enlightening and humbling experience. I learned a lot."

"Like what?"

"That I was an unbearable asshole."

I nod. Loving this already.

"That I don't always have to be in control."

I try to wipe the smirk off my face.

"That I'm not always right."

Silence.

And more silence.

"That's it?"

"Well, I think everything else falls under the same general umbrella. Don't you?"

"I'm not one to judge."

"Oh, but that's one thing you were always pretty good at, Georgia."

I turn my head like Linda Blair in *The Exorcist*. "If you came here to indict me like you were indicted, you can leave now, Niles. I've got enough problems dealing with our daughter without being ridiculed by the ex-husband I haven't seen in years. This is quite a hello."

"I'm sorry," he says, with the utmost sincerity. "But I came because I want to know what I can do to get off your most-hated list."

"I never hated you, Niles."

"You sure had me convinced."

"I stopped liking you."

"What's the difference?"

"You went to college. You know there's a difference."

"They both mean that a person holds a great deal of disdain, which can become toxic. And it's what I sensed you felt about me."

"True. But not in the beginning. I just felt like you conned me."

"Conned?"

"You misrepresented yourself to make me believe you were this kind and gentle and caring person, when in fact you wanted a woman you could control, but by the time I figured this out, I was already the mother of your child, which I also didn't want to do—have another baby—at least not as soon as when you talked me into it—but as the clock ticked, I started realizing how much I was doing to please you, how you set the rules for how I was supposed to show you I loved you, but you never quite got around to caring how I might want to be loved."

"Wow. Did you just press Play somewhere?"

"I think I might have."

"Because, like I said, I was an asshole. However, I will say that I learned a lot of this from my father, who as a Nigerian ran his household and his wife like a drill sergeant. It was all I knew. And I'm sorry."

"Well, those are two words I've never heard you say."

"I've said them a lot over the years. It's just taken me this long to say them to you, which is why I decided to show up unannounced."

"Well, I'm sorry, too. That things turned out the way they did."

"I'm a more easygoing guy now. And how about you?"

"I was always easygoing."

He's shaking his head. "We had more in common than you realized. We were like Darth Vader and Princess Leia."

"Oh, really?"

"I hope you've softened up, but it docsn't sound like you have."

"You know, you've got a lot of nerve dropping by my office after a century without any advance notice with the sole purpose of criticizing my character. You haven't changed as much as you think you have."

"I've never criticized your character, Georgia. I just thought mine was more important. But you were struggling to be you without knowing how to stand up for yourself, so it was easy to get you to bend, but I see you've hardened up."

"I haven't hardened, Niles. Let's not revisit our civil war, how's that?"

"First I want you to let me have it once and for all."

"Okay," I say, with a long sigh. "Once I realized it was impossible to please you and how much of myself I'd lost trying to do just that, I had to make a choice, and I chose me. There."

"I'm far less self-centered," he says. "And I don't expect to be your BFF just because our daughter's going through a bout of anguish, but I'm willing to do whatever I can to help her, and it would be nice if we could bury the hatchet."

"Consider it buried," I say, and pop him upside the head.

He starts laughing.

And I crack up, too.

"So are you happy?" he asks.

I hate when anyone asks me that. It's such a loaded fucking question. Are they talking aggregate years? Doesn't it depend on the day, the moment? Or are they referring to last year or last month?

"I'm hopeful. And you?"

"Well, I'm trying to recognize it."

"You've remarried."

"I have. And she's a wonderful person. However, she reminds me of me back when."

"I hear she's loaded."

"You don't know anything about her."

"Well, wait a minute. Can I just ask you something totally off topic, Niles?"

He nods.

"What made you cheat on your taxes?"

"Excuse me?"

"You heard me."

"It's a long story, Georgia."

"I've got a few minutes before I kick you out."

"It wasn't my intention to cheat. I did two things that were stupid. I withheld pertinent information and then just didn't file for two years."

"But why, Niles? Between the two of us, we made a good living."

"Honestly?"

"No, please bullshit me after all these years."

"Because you earned at least four times more than me, and I didn't like the idea of it, so I simply availed myself of more of my income with the intention of paying my taxes at a later date. It was stupid."

"Did you really think you wouldn't get caught?"

"I didn't think that far ahead."

"What did your parents say?"

"My father hasn't spoken to me since the conviction. My mother wrote to me, but she kept it under the radar so my father wouldn't know. In fact, it was my mother who helped me pay off the IRS."

"So you don't owe them?"

"Not a dime."

"Good for you, Niles. What are you doing now?"

"That's a great question. I'm not a meteorologist, that's for sure. Felons aren't sought after by headhunters, you know."

"Then back to my original comment: your wife must be loaded."

"She does okay."

"What does she do for a living?"

"She's an interior designer."

"Really?" is all I say with feigned enthusiasm. I suppose I was hoping she was a doctor or something stiff or uninteresting. How'd he manage to find someone artistic?

"I've got a number of business plans in the works. And please don't ask me what they are."

"To be honest, I don't really care, Niles. Well, that was mean. I should say I'm not that curious, but I hope you're happy and doing well, and from the looks of it, you are."

"Thank you. You do, too. You've added a few pounds, I see, but they become you."

"Whatever, Niles."

"Anyway, are you dating? I know *you* haven't remarried."

"Yes, I'm dating."

"Anything serious?"

"Time will tell."

I stand up. And then he stands up.

"Would you like to grab a bite?" he asks.

"Maybe some other time."

"Seriously?"

"No. But it sounded nice, didn't it?"

"I hope you never forget that you did love me once, Georgia."

"I suppose I did, Niles, but unfortunately, it's not what I remember most."

I don't want him to hug me, but he does anyway. And he feels like cardboard.

# Sightseers

'M STROLLING ALONG FOURTH STREET IN BERKELEY. IT'S block after block of amazing restaurants, artsy shops, and hip boutiques—everything you need for the mind, the body, and the home. The scent of candles and handmade soap escapes from doorways, but I walk into my wet dream: the Builders Booksource, and head straight to my favorite section: shelf after shelf of the best up-to-the-minute books and magazines on interior and furniture design. I have been known to spend hours in here, and it usually feels like minutes.

I'm not looking for anything in particular, just waiting for something to grab my attention, which always happens, and I've got shelves of proof at home. I pull out a big book on how to restore old furniture and feel a pang of excitement as soon as I open it. I sit on the floor in a corner and turn the pages like it's a juicy romance novel. I buy it and head down the street to my favorite diner, where I stand in line along the sidewalk for another thirty minutes.

I feel my cell phone shivering in my pocket. I'm hoping it might be Frankie, who I would like to strangle for leaving me in the dark with the exception of a single text that said, GREAT NEWS COMING YOUR WAY!

No. That would be too much like right. It's my mother.

"Hi, Ma," I say, trying for enthusiasm.

"We'll see you in about five hours, Georgia, depending on how many times we have to stop. You know Dolly has a weak bladder, and I refuse to go more than five miles over the speed limit."

"Hold on a minute, Ma! What are you talking about? We never discussed or confirmed a date for you to come up!"

"I've left you two or three messages on your landline, as Estelle was kind enough to tell me they're called now. It sounds like you didn't get it. Don't you listen to your messages?"

"Of course I do. But sometimes I get busy, Ma, and I don't check the landline that often. Have you left already?"

"We're about to gas up. It's just Dolly and me. The boys finally landed jobs, if you can believe that. Hauling. Don't ask me what, and Dolly just hopes they make enough to move out."

"Ma, I need to put you on the schedule, because I can't just have you and Dolly drop in for a checkup."

"I don't see why not. You're the boss."

"I'm only one of the *bosses*."

"Well, I won't go blind this weekend, and there's always LensCrafters. To be honest, we just wanted to get out of Bakersfield for a few days, and we thought we could stay for a long weekend and spend a little quality time with you, since you never seem to have any time to come see any of your family here."

"Ma, I'm coming down for your birthday."

"I know that. And what's to stop you?"

"Absolutely nothing," I say, trying not to laugh. I love her.

"So are you still catching that train?"

"I am. Just not sure of the exact date yet."

"And you're still going by yourself?"

"I am."

"That's sad. By the way, I opened my big mouth and told Dolly, and I don't even want to tell you what she said."

"Then don't. Anyway, I have a dinner date this evening, so you might beat me home." Of course I'm lying through my teeth. I can't remember the last time I had a date, but it sounds good, and I want my mother to think I have a social life and one that involves the opposite sex.

"Well, how long could that last? I know you're not having sex anymore."

"You do not know that, Ma."

"Whatever. If there was somebody special in your life, I'd've heard it in your voice. But not so much as a lilt."

"You didn't hear a word I just said."

"What's the big to-do?"

"I've got a lot going on up here, Ma."

"Like what?"

"Frankie might be there with her boyfriend."

"And what's that got to do with us coming? I haven't seen my granddaughter since last Christmas. It'd be nice to see her. Estelle already gave me the lowdown. No biggie. She's just young and in love."

"Okay, but do me a huge favor, please. Have a little chat with Dolly and tell her to keep her thoughts to herself when she gets here, or before she knows it, she'll be staying at a Motel 6."

"Oh, baby. She's just jealous of your success, and she can't help it. Anyway, I want the guest room. Dolly can sleep in Estelle's room, which I always thought felt like a disco, or she can sleep with you in that big, empty bed! Bye! Here she comes now, and that better not be a beer in that bag!"

"Ma!"

"What now?"

"Just keep in mind you have to go home by Tuesday at the latest, because I might have movers coming to pack up some of my things to put in storage. And if you beat me home, please tell Dolly no scrounging through my closet and asking me for stuff, or no free glasses for her."

"No problemo."

"Bye, Ma. Drive carefully. Look forward to seeing you."

Right after I hang up, it dawns on me this is the weekend I was planning to do a few more of my searches and that I'd left the list of the first and last names of all five men in red Magic Marker on my desk. I know how nosy Ma is, and I certainly don't trust Dolly.

I call right back.

"Ma, I forgot! Please don't go in my office, because I have some very personal things in there that I don't want you or Dolly to see."

"Is it my present?"

"Yes," I sigh.

"Then I'm going to need you to make me another one, and you already know what it is, so don't ask."

"I know. Lobster mac and cheese."

"And don't worry. I'll make sure the door stays closed and I'll watch Dolly like a hawk. I want to be surprised. Now, good-bye for the last time!"

MA'S WHITE CADILLAC is parked in the driveway, right next to my Prius. She must've been on the road already and testing me to see if I'd try to stop her from coming. I get out of the taxi I took from the BART station, walk up the driveway, and ring the doorbell just to freak them out. I'm about to ring it again when Dolly slings it open. She's wearing my white bathrobe and my red slippers!

"Hey, cuz!" she says, and wraps about two hundred pounds around me, enough to make me lose my balance. She grabs my hand and pulls me into the house. "Before you ask why I'm wearing your stuff, you won't believe this, but I was so busy trying to make sure the boys had everything they needed that I forgot my suitcase. I hope you don't mind. I'll wash everything before we leave. Unless you wanna take your broke-ass cousin to the mall."

And she laughs.

"She's always broke," Ma says. I realize she's sitting on the sofa, reading a book, even though I can hear the television blasting from the downstairs guest room.

"So you two must've flown."

"Well, we just got here a little less than an hour ago, because Dolly Parton wanted to stop at Eagle Mountain to play the slots."

"Did you win?" I ask, trying to sound like I care.

"Of course not. She never wins," Ma says.

"That's not true, and I don't know why you're saying 'never,' Aunt Earlene, like I go all the time, which I do not, because I don't have no gambling money."

"Is Frankie here?"

"I don't think so. At first we thought you beat us here when we saw your car in the driveway."

I just smile and walk across to her. "Hey, good-looking," I say, and step down into the living room, bend over, and rope my arms around her. My mother is still beautiful. Her hair is bright white, her skin the color of ripe pecans and somehow still smooth; even her cheekbones are tight, which makes her look like she's always about to smile.

"I hope she didn't drop out of college because of this boy."

"No, she's just taking a little hiatus."

"It's always a dude," Dolly says. "Even the smart ones will fuck over you, pardon my French.

"Why didn't you drive your car to work?" Dolly asks.

I give her a *look*.

"Go check her room," Ma says. "And your various voice mails. I doubt she's up there."

Of course she's not. I run up to her room anyway to see if her designer luggage is still there. Unfortunately, it is. I dig inside my purse for my phone, and to my disbelief she's left me a genuine voice message: *"Hi, Mom. Hunter and I have come to terms and realize we're still on the same team. We're driving to Tahoe to spend a week or so at a small resort until we can figure out what to do next. Love you."*

A whole week? Does it take that long to figure anything out? And what's she going to wear?

I call Estelle to see if she's heard anything.

"She only shares good news with me to throw it in my face, so to answer your question, no, I haven't heard from her."

"Your grandma's here. With your favorite third cousin."

"I know. Hope I get to see them before they leave."

"I'm concerned about Frankie, Estelle."

"Don't worry about her, Mom. Everyone always does. Just let her play this out."

"To be totally honest, right now I wish I were on the upper deck of a train riding across Canada. And I've just received a text from Amen telling me we got an offer on this house and that I have forty-five days to move out."

"Is that where you want to take the train ride?"

"Maybe."

"Sounds cool to me. I'd take a train ride to anywhere about now."

"So are things still not good?"

"No. Everything's looking better. I've just been doing a lot of paperwork getting the girls in school and setting up my hours, and I'm exhausted."

"What about Justin?"

"He's up to his neck in everything. Getting some good freelance gigs until he lands something permanent. Working late. The girls like going to school but can't understand why they're the only black kids in their class."

"What'd you tell them?"

"That it makes them special."

"And they bought that BS?"

"Not even close. They want to go to the school Beyoncé went to when she was their age."

I can't help but laugh.

"It's not funny, Ma."

"I'm not laughing because it's funny. I think it's sad that they had to bring it to your attention because *they* noticed it. I just don't think it's healthy for black kids to go to all- or predominantly white schools."

"It wasn't by choice, Ma. It's one of the reasons I homeschooled them. But situations change."

"Let's hope."

"How'd we get on this topic?"

"All I'm saying is that it's important they don't grow up confused about their identity."

"Me and Frankie turned out okay the last time I checked, and we were in the minority. But anyway, look, Mom, I've got a deadline in four hours, and this is taking me way out of the zone."

"Then hugs to everybody, and talk soon."

I run back downstairs.

"What's the verdict?" Ma asks. "And I want to hear how your dinner date went."

"She's not up there. And my dinner date went well."

"Yeah, I'll bet it did," Ma says.

"I bet Frankie eloped," Dolly asserts. "That's what rich black kids do now, you know. Just like the white ones."

Sometimes I would like to take a handful of intelligence pills and drop them in her drink.

"Watch your mouth, Dolly," Ma says. "Didn't we have this conversation on the way up here?"

"My bad. No harm meant. So what we doing tomorrow? I was hoping we could go to Fisherman's Wharf and eat some cotton candy and some shrimp and maybe ride on one of those boats to anywhere but Alcatraz 'cause I don't need to see no prison even if ain't nobody in it. Whatcha say?"

"Did anybody ask me what *I'd* like to do?"

"What would you like to do, Ma?"

"Find a pretty dress to wear to my party. Ride across the Golden Gate Bridge and stop at Vista Point so I can take some pictures with my new iPhone. It has a very good camera, you know. I want to text them to Grover."

"Who is Grover?" I ask, sitting down next to her.

"My boyfriend."

I'm about to laugh when I see she's totally serious.

"She's telling the truth. They're cute together, and they both can still walk. Which they do a lot of."

"That's why I'm in better shape than you, Dolly."

"Where'd you meet him?"

"He lives in my facility."

"That's nice. When did he become your boyfriend, Ma?"

"I'll tell you another time. Dolly knows too much of my business as it is, and you run your mouth too much."

"Curious minds wanna know, Auntie. It ain't like you gon' get on *Inside Edition* with all the hot stuff you and Grover be doing."

"Anyway, I'm glad to hear you've got a friend, Ma."

"He's my boyfriend. I'm not saying it again."

I jump up. "Okay. So let's do this. I'm tired, and if you guys want to hang out tomorrow, let's get a good night's sleep. Does anybody need anything?"

"You got a nightgown I can sleep in?"

"I don't wear nightgowns, Dolly. And Lord knows you can't fit any of my pajamas."

"You got some nerve, cuz. What about some sweats and a T-shirt?"

I nod.

"It's nice to see you both," I say.

"Stop lying," Dolly says.

WE SPEND ALL DAY on or near water. Ma takes a ton of pictures, and I show her how to text them. Dolly wears the brown corduroy pants she wore up here and my Philadelphia Flyers hockey shirt. "No, you can't have it," I told her when she professed her admiration for it.

"I've had enough fun," Ma says after hours of circling the Bay Area looking for treasures. She found a long black dress at Macy's, and I bought Dolly a pair of decent jeans and a big white blouse because I wanted to.

Dolly turns to look at Ma, who's out cold in the backseat. "I need to ask if you could do me a big favor, cuz."

"What kind of favor?"

"Don't lend her any money," Ma says. "You'll never get it back. Take it from someone who knows."

And she closes her eyes and pretends to be asleep again until I hear her snoring.

"Don't listen to Auntie. I am in somewhat of a jam though, cuz, and you know I don't like asking for help unless I really need it."

"Well, that's understandable," I say, being sarcastic, but of course Miss Crossword Puzzle misses it. "How much do you need, Dolly?"

"Need?" She reaches inside her pleather purse and whips out a stick of gum, puts it in her mouth but doesn't chew. "If I told you that, we'd have to rob a bank. But five hundred would damn sure help, even though seven-fifty would fix a lot of the problems I'm having right now 'cause I've been waiting on a—"

"Don't tell me. A check."

"I am! Didn't Auntie tell you when this drunk dude rear-ended me last year?"

"She did. But she also said he didn't have insurance."

"He didn't. But I'm not talking about that accident. *This* huzzy had liability and collision, which almost made me glad she hit me."

"Did you get injured?"

"Of course I did. I go to physical therapy and everything."

"I'll write you a check for five hundred, and it's not a loan, but don't ask me for another dime for the rest of the weekend, Dolly, and don't go in my closet asking me for anything else, got it?"

"Got it. I'm also very grateful for this nice outfit you bought me. Thank you, again, cuz."

On Sunday afternoon we drive to Napa but don't go to any wineries because Ma's not interested and Dolly said she doesn't drink anything less than 45 percent because it's a waste of energy. We eat baked artichokes with drawn butter and spareribs and coleslaw and honey cornbread. Ma buys another dress to be on the safe side, one more like Wanda would wear, along with a pair of cheap rhinestone earrings and a pair of Merrell walking shoes.

On Sunday night Ma turns in early, leaving Dolly and me to have yet another deep conversation.

"Why don't you have no man?" she asks. We're in the kitchen eating popcorn, and I'm having a glass of wine while she's drinking a gin and tonic in a water glass with two ice cubes.

"Because I don't have one."

"Have you turned into a lesbian? I mean, if you have, it's cool with me."

"No, I haven't 'turned into a lesbian,' Dolly."

"I didn't really think so, 'cause I found your long brown friend and some of his friends in your bathroom cabinet."

"What were you doing— Oh, never mind. But do me a favor, Dolly. Stop rambling through my shit when you come to my house, would you?"

"My bad. I was just looking for some sponge rollers, but I guess you don't need 'em for all them wigs. Sorry, cuz."

"Forgiven."

"So back to my original train of thought. Why don't you have no man?"

"Because I haven't met anybody I like lately."

"According to Auntie you been going through a drought for quite a few years now. You too picky. That's what it sound like to me."

"Did anybody ask you?"

"No, which is why I'm just gonna come on out and say it. You need to stop being so scared 'cause you married the wrong motherfucker twice and get the fuck over it and stop being so stiff and uppity and loosen up or you gonna end up being one of those spinster women and die lonely as hell, and hell, even Auntie got herself a boyfriend, and she old as dirt."

"Anything else?"

"No. I didn't mean no harm, cuz."

"No? Well, thanks for the good advice. Now, get to sleep."

On Monday morning I go to work. By midafternoon I decide to call to see how they're doing, and notice I've got a voice message on my cell: *"Georgia, this is your mother, and we decided to head on back home because we've had enough activity to last us. I'll send you a text when we pull into town! No word from Frankie, and Dolly said to tell you thanks for everything. See you for my birthday! Come prepared to party!"*

PERCY IS DRESSED like he's going to a polo match. All he's missing is a fedora and a mint julep. He gives me two phony pecks, one on each cheek, and heads straight to the kitchen like he lives here.

I offer him coffee.

He refuses.

I offer him a glass of wine.

He refuses.

I offer him a bottle of water.

And he refuses.

"Okay, then, Percy, so now that I know you're not thirsty, can you tell me what's going on?"

"Where to start?" He sighs, and instead of sitting down he walks over to the alcove and starts circling the pounded stainless-steel table.

"My partner of fifteen years passed away two weeks ago, and I've been unable to function, if you want the God's honest truth."

I sit down in one of the chairs, as does Percy. When I look into his eyes, there's just a sea of sadness.

"I'm really sorry to hear this, Percy. Really."

"Thank you. So I've fallen behind on ordering some of the items we definitely need, and there's also a backlog on too many things for me to mention right now, but I wanted to see you face-to-face because I couldn't explain this over the phone and I didn't want you to think I was BS'ing. The bronchitis hasn't helped any, and I don't want to inconvenience you any more than I have already, but I also don't want Amen to hire another stager, because I'm enjoying working with you."

And he starts crying.

I walk over and rub his back, which I know isn't going to do much good, but fifteen years is a long time. "The staging can wait, Percy."

"Are you sure? I gave you a start date, and I believe that Amen said you were already making travel plans, and my fear is that I've screwed them up."

"I'm still in the planning stages, but another month won't ruin anything. Are you sure this is enough time?"

"Honestly?"

"Honestly, Percy."

"After the holidays would be so much better."

"Well, it's not like I'm getting evicted," I say, trying to lighten it up a little, but Percy looks too weighed down.

"Thank you for understanding, Georgia."

"It's all good, Percy."

"You're very nice, and you seem to be an understanding and forgiving person, so I read you right. Thank you."

"I'm not as understanding and forgiving and nice as you think I am, but I'm trying."

# Not Always in Black and White

G UESS WHO'S PREGNANT?" VIOLET ASKS, SIPPING ON A
gin and tonic. It's barely noon.

I don't need to guess. I'm surprised it took this long. We're
sitting outside on the top deck of this houseboat, which she—like the
four hundred other idiots who live on these things—refers to as a
"floating home." What I'm more shocked by than Velvet's pregnancy is
Violet's hair. She has gone and cut off that weave, which is a sure sign
of something tragic. But I don't think it's just the pregnancy.

"I could kill her."

"But hold on a minute. Why'd you cut your weave off?"

"I was tired of it. And I don't feel like talking about hair."

"Anyway, I like it. You can see your whole face again, which I forgot is pretty."

"Go to hell, Georgia, but thank you."

"You're welcome. Anyway, having a baby isn't a tragedy," I say as I
take a long swallow of sparkling water.

"It is when you're not sure who the father is."

"Come on, Violet."

"Supposedly it's between two, but I wouldn't be surprised if it's not
three guys, since she lies about almost everything."

I'm not even going to bother asking why Velvet doesn't use protec-
tion, because the question's already been answered.

"How many months?"

"Too many to change her damn mind. I knew there was a reason
Ms. Thang suddenly stopped jogging and going to the gym."

"Pregnant women still exercise, in case you hadn't noticed."

She just sucks her teeth and rolls her eyes at me.

"Where are they going to live?"

She rolls her eyes at me again. "You think I'd trust her with a baby?"

"What's that supposed to mean, Violet?"

"I'm selling this damn houseboat and will probably lease a real house on your side of the bay. They can live with me until something else happens, but Velvet will take her stupid ass back to college or my name isn't Violet."

"Doesn't she have some kind of relationship with any of these guys? And don't roll your eyes at me."

"How in the hell would I know? She parties. I don't think any of these dudes take her seriously. It just breaks my heart."

"Well, at least she's got some college credits."

She downs the rest of her drink and then goes to pour another one. I look out at the slow blue-green waves sloshing against wooden pilings. I can almost understand why she's lived on this boat for five years. After her sons went off on their own, she thought she was free, and of course when Velvet dropped out of college number two or three, she turned her home office back into a bedroom, because what was she supposed to do? I've got some nerve, but there comes a point where you just can't change your plans and your life to accommodate your grown kids.

"I think I *will* have a drink," I say, and get up to go grab a beer out of the fridge, something I rarely drink. This place is really cute, and were it not for the water out front, you might not even know you were on a boat. Thank God Violet's taste in home decor isn't half as raunchy as her taste in clothes.

I walk back out to the deck but stand in the doorway.

"I'm curious about something, Violet. Are you seeing anybody, since you haven't mentioned anybody in a while?"

"I'm taking a mancation."

"Why?"

"Because. I don't need any more drama right now. What about you?"

"Nope. Maybe he'll fall from the sky."

"All the companionship I need for the moment is in my top drawer, and the batteries are getting low."

"It's why I buy rechargeable."

We ha-ha. Then watch and listen to the seagulls. For real.

"What about your search for the blasts from the past? How's that going?"

"I'm not in any hurry. You ever just jump off this fucking deck and go swimming?"

"Are you insane? Don't you read, Georgia? There are sharks out in that water. Look, there's one now!"

And I jump to a standing position as if Shamu is about to fly up onto this deck! I slap her thigh. We both laugh. And I sit back in my chair and put my feet up on the wooden railing. We say nothing again. Just sit there. And relax. I let the breeze seduce me. I inhale it.

"Have you heard from Frankie and what's-his-name?"

"Nope. And his name is Hunter."

"I've always liked that name. I was going to name Landon that, but his daddy wasn't having it."

"I don't care what his name is. I just hope he's good to and for my daughter if they're going to try to play this out."

"How're Estelle and Justin?"

"If I believe her? Fine."

"They all lie. Why I do not know, because the truth always comes out, and then we have to deal with it."

"I'm trying not to worry, but I'm worrying."

"Well, I'm not wasting my energy worrying. I've made a decision, and I'm going to take the next step and see what happens. That's all we can do."

"Easier said than done."

"Can I ask you something? And promise not to get pissed?"

"I'm listening," I say, downing the rest of my beer. I do not feel even a tiny buzz.

"Why do you have to go on a train ride? I don't get it."

"I don't *have* to. I want to."

"What's the point?"

"The same reason people take vacations, Violet."

"But what's the point of going by yourself?"

"I'm tired of saying this, I really am. So for the last time: because I want to. Maybe I'll pick up a stranger."

"Funny."

"Then stop asking me a question you already know the answer to."

"But your situation has changed, Georgia."

"What are you talking about?"

"Frankie. She's back home. Why can't she go with you?"

"Did she tell you she asked me?"

"Of course she did."

"Her situation is the one that's changed, and now her little boy-friend might be in the picture—so what do you suggest? I get the family plan and take them both along for the ride?"

"I was just asking. Maybe he'll drag her back to New York."

"That would be my dream."

"I wish I'd had three boys, because girls are a pain in the ass."

"You have never lied, girl."


BEFORE I LEFT for work, Frankie sent me a text and said they'd be here by six. I had only two patients, so I took the afternoon off. I went to Neiman's and Nordstrom's and then Saks and back to Nordstrom's to find something flattering and pretty to wear to Ma's birthday bash. That killed a couple of hours.

I'm now in my home office ordering a few books I hope to read in this century. I look out the window at a doe and her fawn. Wonder if they'll have dating issues one day. They dart up the hill. I turn my attention to my love list, which is in the same exact place I left it, but I'm not in the mood to search for any men right now. Maybe it would be better if I weren't here when Frankie and Hunter arrive. Give them a chance to loosen up, get comfortable, and decide how or what they're going to tell me. I hope it's that they're moving back to New York and that Frankie's changing her major to, say, hell, whatever inspires her. Something where her personality might find a way to surface. Or maybe Hunter will decide to spend the summer here, get a job, and then by Labor Day they'll drive to New York for the thrill of it. Hunter will get there just in time for his classes, and Frankie will call from the road and say, "Guess what, Mom? I know how I want to spend the rest of my life." I'll listen with open ears, and no matter what she says, I'll applaud her like I did when she was a little girl, when she got accepted at NYU, when she decided to major in media studies in her sophomore year even though I never quite understood the allure or the point.

I change my mind about having dinner out and decide to run to Whole Foods, because a home-cooked meal could help ease the tension regardless of what kind of news they're going to share. You'd think they'd've come to some kind of amicable terms after being holed up an entire week together. But they're young. You never know. I wonder if Hunter's a vegetarian. I'll get seafood. I'd love to stir-fry my Latin-spiced prawns, but what if he's allergic? Or Jewish? I'll decide when I get there. Which is my favorite way to cook anyway—see what appeals and then improvise. I leave a note on the floor just inside the front door: *Hope you guys are hungry. Gone to Whole Foods. Making dinner. No meat. No shellfish. Back shortly!!*

I DECIDE ON Chilean sea bass because I love the meaty texture and the fatty content that absorbs whatever spices or sauces I use. Asparagus: stir-fried with minced garlic, crystallized ginger, and Korean soy sauce. Fingerling red, purple, and Yukon Gold potatoes rolled in olive oil and rosemary: baked. Spring greens with my sneaky homemade basil vinaigrette dressing. I buy some sourdough, but I'm not touching it. I buy crème brûlée and an assortment of those little French cookies—I forget what they're called. I'm not even going to sniff them.

It's almost seven, and I'm in the kitchen with everything spread out on the island watching Rachel Maddow sign off on MSNBC when I hear the door open. "Mom, we're here! Where are you?"

"In the kitchen!" I yell, pressing the lettuce spinner, scrambling to turn off the water that's running over the potatoes and the asparagus, and sliding the wok to the back eye.

"You beat us here! Great note!" Frankie says as I hear them kick off their shoes and head down the hall. Just as I'm about to wipe my seasoned fingers on my yellow apron, standing in the doorway is my daughter and a chocolate brown Hunter! I'm trying not to act surprised he's black, but of course I wasn't expecting him to be, so I just say, "Hello there, Hunter! I've heard so much about you! Welcome!"

I stand on my toes to give him a hug, and then I give Frankie one, too. With his wild, unkempt Afro, he reminds me of someone, but I can't think of who it is. He's handsome in an offbeat kind of way.

After we break apart, I realize they're holding hands like those wedding-cake figurines, which is when I glance down and see what looks like a pull tab from a beer can on her left ring finger.

"It's very nice to finally meet you, Dr. Young."

"Hunter, I think it's safe to call her Mom now!" And Frankie holds out her left hand to display what is definitely a faux wedding band.

I almost want to collapse, but it's not worth it, so instead I just say, "Well, congratulations to you young newlyweds. The parents are always the last to know, I suppose."

"We were definitely in the moment, Dr. Young—I mean, Mom. We drove to Reno, and the only way I could get Frankie to understand how much I really love her and how sorry I was for my error of bad judgment was to make a lasting commitment. So this is my fault, not hers."

"Fault?" Frankie says, turning to him. "Are you kidding me?"

"I know what you mean, Hunter. And it's fine. Children are good at surprising parents, but you two are adults, so I'm sure you've got everything figured out, especially about your next move. Correct me if I'm wrong."

"Mom, are you making dinner for us? That's so sweet of you! My mom's an amazing cook," she says to Hunter.

Hunter turns his attention to me. "I can already tell. Thank you, Dr. Young. Mom."

"So, to answer your question, Mom, we have and we haven't narrowed down our next move," Frankie says, looking gorgeous, happy, and sixteen.

"Well, Hunter, I'm sure Frankie has told you what's going on with the house, so you two won't be able to honeymoon here," I hear myself say, and immediately regret saying it.

"Oh, no, Dr. Young—Mom—we wouldn't dream of imposing."

"Can you give me an example of just a portion of one of your carefully thought-out plans?" I look at the daughter I would like to put in time-out for about a year.

"Well, the master plan is we're seriously contemplating the benefits of staying here in California to finish getting our degrees, and of course I'll get a job," Hunter says.

"Really?"

"My parents have agreed to help pay for out-of-state tuition should I decide to get my master's, which I intend to do, but I just don't see the urgency right now."

"Really?"

"His parents are the best," Frankie says.

Make that two years in time-out.

"And what about you, missy?"

"Not sure. I might go to San Francisco State. Maybe enroll in their creative-writing program."

"Their what?"

"Haven't you read any of her stories, Mom?"

"What stories? I've never heard you say you write anything except term papers. Stories?"

"And poetry. Why haven't you shown them to her, Frank?"

"I don't know."

"They're good. She'll get published one day, and I'm not just saying this because I love her. I know good writing."

"Really?" I say. This is getting better and better by the minute.

"They're not polished, Mom."

"So what? I'd love to read some, Frankie. And you lied," I say.

"About what?"

"That you were confused about what you like."

"Well, I didn't lie. I just failed to admit it, because I thought it would sound lame."

I pop her upside the head. "Like I said, the parents are the last to know."

And then they stand there, looking homeless and hopelessly in love.

"So what about tomorrow and next week?" I ask.

They just look at each other for an answer that neither of them has.

"Where's your stuff, Hunter?"

"In the car."

"Why don't you go get it?"

"Really, Mom?" Frankie says.

"Really."

We have a great meal. I learn that Hunter hails from Seattle. His father does something I can't repeat at Microsoft, and his mother is a painter. He's an only. I decide to let them stay in the honeymoon suite for the next three weeks because, hell, what are parents for?

I MAKE SURE my door is locked, and I call Wanda.

"Married? Please don't tell me she's pregnant."

"Who in the hell knows? They never tell the whole story, you know."

"No, I don't know."

"Well, Velvet sure is," I say.

"That's old news. I can keep a secret when I want to. I can't believe that Hunter is black! Isn't this just too fucking ironic?"

"That's one way to describe it."

"Anyway, as an FYI, Nelson and I won't be able to make it to Mama Early's birthday bash, because it's the same day as the fund-raiser we're having for homeless shelters in West Oakland. But I'll send her love and a gift card."

"You know she loves gift cards. And you know I'll make a donation."

"Of course, and we thank you. But one last thing. If and when you kick your daughter and her new black husband to the curb, they can stay in our guesthouse. And I'm not saying it again."

"I'M GETTING MARRIED, Georgia," Michael calls to tell me. I'm in Bakersfield, helping to decorate the Rec Center for Ma's party. She's having a Chippendale's affair for all her hot senior friends.

"Is this contagious?" I ask.

"Are you getting married, too?"

"No! But Frankie just eloped."

"Well, what's wrong with that?"

"Nothing. Anyway, so why are you calling to tell me this?"

"I just wanted you to know."

"Are you in need of a flower girl or something, Michael?"

He laughs.

Since I saw him, there hasn't been a month that's gone by he hasn't left me a voice message or a text to say "Hello, how are you? Was just thinking about you." It's been only on rare occasions I've bothered to acknowledge them, like when I knew it was his birthday and I was hoping just to leave a shout-out, but he picked up before I had a chance to say the *M* in Michael.

I sling a strip of black-and-white crepe paper over a rafter. Why folks have color schemes at parties I do not know. What exactly is the point? It's going to look like a room full of senior penguins, myself included.

"I would really like if you would come," he says.

Before I laugh and say something sarcastic, I realize that Michael is serious as cancer. That's not a good analogy, but it's the best I can do standing on the fifth step of this ladder.

"What on earth for, Michael?"

"Because I want you to see for yourself that it's possible to find love later in life."

"You mean it's still possible to be recycled?" I shouldn't have said that. But I've already said it.

"I thought you'd be happy for me, Georgia."

"I *am* happy for you, Michael."

"I thought you said we were friends."

"I said we can be friendly, but that didn't mean you were going to be my BFF, Michael."

"I know that. But I thought we'd put some salve on those old wounds, didn't we?"

"We did."

"Doesn't sound like it. Do I still detect scar tissue?"

"Not even close. What's her name?"

"Sandra."

"Well, look, I'm very happy for you, Michael, but I'm in Bakersfield helping to decorate for Ma's party, and—"

"I know. Eighty-two years young. I bought her a new pair of glasses."

"You did what?"

"Hold on, little lady. I called her to ask what she'd like, and she'd just come from LensCrafters, so she chose some snazzy sunglasses she'd seen there and texted me a picture of them. They're nice."

"Well, that was very thoughtful of you."

"One last question. No, two. Are you seeing anyone?"

"Yes," I said.

"Glad to hear it, Georgia. Is it serious?"

"Too soon to tell. Look, I've really gotta scoot."

"Okay. But just so you know. Estelle is coming. And it would be nice if you would, too. Bring your new boyfriend."


THE SOLES OF my feet are numb from standing on this ladder so long. I climb down and walk around until I feel the tile. I look around this big square room. All this floating crepe paper and plastic everything else is endearing because it's for my mother.

As I head over to my hotel to get dressed, I realize I can't believe not only that Michael is getting married again but that he actually invited me. Of course I have no intention of going to his wedding. Once was enough.

# Generations

I CAN'T WAIT FOR YOU TO MEET MY FIANCÉ," MA SAYS TO me. We're in her condo. I'm helping her decide which black dress to wear, the one with short sleeves that she bought at the Lane Bryant outlet store or the one with the balloon sleeves that she got at Macy's. They both go to the floor. She also insisted on wearing a tiara over her frosted gray wig.

"You did just say 'fiancé,' didn't you, Ma?"

I swear to God, she's blushing like a teenager. Her cheeks look like scoops of chocolate ice cream.

"You are talking about Grover, I assume?"

"Now, who else would I be talking about? I'm a one-man woman."

"I thought you said he was your boyfriend?"

"He was. But we've evolved into something much deeper."

"Since when?"

"Since we did, that's when."

"I'm confused. Since you *what*?"

"Fell in love! Do I have to spell it out for you?"

"How can you get married at eighty-two, Ma?"

"You know, for you to be so smart, you ask a lot of stupid questions."

"I didn't mean to offend you, Ma. I'm sorry."

"Let me say this to get it out of the way. You can fall in love at any age, but you have to be willing to give your heart permission to let the love in. I hope you get to feel it again one day. Now, zip this dress up." As she sucks her belly in and holds her breath while I pull, I'm also thinking that I hope I feel love again, too. I step back. I don't like the puffy sleeves. She looks like a fairy godmother, but she's *my* mother, so I'm going to keep my mouth shut and let her decide how she wants to look.

"So where is Grover?"

"He'll be here in a half hour to drive me over to the center."

"But you can see it out your window."

"He's a gentleman."

"How long have you known Grover, Ma?"

"Fifty-two years."

"What? Well, where's Grover been hiding all this time?"

"Alaska. He worked on the pipeline, and he stayed over there until he got arthritis, and at seventy-six he's retired."

"Does he have kids?"

"Three. Two are older than you. They're from Bakersfield. And before you ask, his wife died of lung cancer ten years ago, even though she never smoked."

"That's been happening a lot, it seems. And he's only seventy-six?" I say jokingly.

"Yes, so that makes me some kind of cougar, right?" She cracks up.

"Did Daddy know him?"

"Of course he did. They were good friends."

"Really? You didn't fool around on Daddy, did you, Ma?"

"Of course not. Anyway, we're getting married in Reno right after Grover recovers from hip-replacement surgery."

"You are serious, then, aren't you?"

"Why wouldn't I be?"

"I don't know how comfortable I am about this."

"I'm almost a century old, Georgia, so I don't need your approval. We have a long history and probably a short future, and we're going to make the most of our forever."

I admit I'm quite touched by what she's just said that I almost want to crumple over.

Instead I say, "Where does Grover live again?"

"In the building next door."

"And he's driving over here to pick you up?"

"I've already told you. Some men still understand how important etiquette is to a woman."

"But why do you have to marry him?"

"I like the other dress better. Would you please unzip this one for me and stop asking all these stupid questions?"

"Can you just answer my question?"

"Because I want to."


TURNS OUT ESTELLE'S already met Grover and approves. Why she never bothered to tell me, I don't know. She's also seen her grandmother more than I have in the past eight months. I'm ashamed of myself for postponing visit after visit, and now it may look as if the only reason I'm here is because it's her birthday. Which is true. And shame on me. I'm acting like she's always going to be here. I promise to be a better daughter.

"Knock, knock."

I hear a deep but raspy voice coming through the kitchen window.

Princess Tiana is hiding in her bedroom, waiting to make her grand entrance. "Let him in!" she whispers loudly. "This dress is hot!"

I walk over to the front door, and there stands my mother's future husband. Even with his head partly obscured under his derby, through the peephole I can see that Grover is a good-looking, silver-haired giant of a man and he's wearing a tuxedo! He's waving and smiling at me in what looks like a set of beautiful dentures. I open the door, and before I can reach out to shake his hand, he takes off his derby and bends down and gives me a hug.

"Hello, Miss Georgia, very nice to finally make your acquaintance. So is my queen almost ready?"

"I'll be out in a minute, Grover!" she yells from around the corner. She must think she's in a movie or something. I must say I'm enjoying this whole scenario, because in all honesty my mother has more action in her life than I do.

"I would like to tell you, Miss Georgia, that your mother is in good hands, and I promise to love and protect her until we float to a higher place, which won't be anytime soon. Until then let's get this party started!"

And before I can respond, here comes my mother, living out a much-deserved fantasy in her black taffeta evening gown with the sheer sleeves and her tiara resting gently on top of her wig.

"Hi, Grover," she says. Blushing again!

I look at Grover, whose eyes are lit up like he's hit the love jackpot. He walks over and takes her by the hand, kisses it, then gives her a soft kiss on her cheek and says, "You look so pretty, Earlene. Happy birthday. Your present is in my pocket, in case you're wondering. Now, shall we go? My chariot awaits."

"Isn't he funny?"

I nod.

"You need to hurry up and get yourself on over to the center, Georgia. It'll only take you five minutes to walk. Grover and I are taking the long way."

UNLIKE YOUNG FOLKS, the elderly show up on time to a party. The place is already full, with well over a hundred sparkling senior citizens and some middle-agers who must be the children of my mother's friends. Folks who grew up and probably still live in Bakersfield. I couldn't breathe here, which is one reason I fled for the crisp, cool air in the Bay Area.

I wave when I spot my daughters and new son-in-law seated at the table that has the number 1 perched on top of a metal rod sticking out through a cluster of black and white balloons, and I make my way over. Frankie and Hunter drove down with Estelle, who has given Hunter four out of five stars and told me they're also staying at a three-star hotel. Thank God she left the twins at home with a stranger, a.k.a. their father, because according to Estelle, Justin's been MIA a lot lately and doesn't seem to like being interrogated. Estelle has even fessed up by telling me she thinks he might be cheating on her, but when she confronted him, Justin vehemently denied it.

The deejay, who must be in his late sixties, is testing his speakers. His hair is slicked back and stops at his neck. He's wearing a tuxedo. I can't wait to hear what he's going to play and see who's going to dance, because there's a fair share of people in wheelchairs, but even most of *them* look like they're ready to party.

I bend down and kiss my daughters. Estelle is wearing black and Frankie white. "You both look gorgeous," I say.

"Thank you, Mamacita," Estelle says without standing, and she reaches up to kiss me back. God, does she look like a female version of her dad when he was young. She's wearing a dress I gave her for Christmas a few years ago. A silk scarf is wrapped around her neck like clouds.

"Hi, Mom," Hunter says, pretty dapper in a black suit and a white shirt. "You look very nice," he says to me.

"Thank you. And you clean up well!"

He grins wide.

"So, Mom," Frankie says, "you're looking pretty sexy—and I'll take that dress off your hands when you get tired of it. You ready to get down?"

"Yes I am. I'll just pretend this is Studio 54."

"What's that?"

"Never mind," I say.

"This is sweet," Estelle says, glancing around at all the elderly folks who look like they're thrilled to be all dressed up, ready to drink punch and eat some cake. Grover took care of the catering. There's ham and fried chicken, collard greens, potato salad and corn bread, and not a drop of anything to drink with a percentage symbol on the bottle. (Of course I brought the mac and cheese I promised, and it's sitting in a deep dish in my mother's fridge with a bow on top of the aluminum foil.)

"Has anybody heard a peep out of Dolly? She should be here by now, you'd think," I say to the girls.

"She's not coming," Estelle says, trying not to laugh.

"And why not?"

"She's sick."

"What kind of illness is it this time?" I ask.

"Grandma said she's got shingles and hates having to miss the party."

Two tall men who are Grover clones walk over to our table and stop. This is obviously a generational party.

"Hello," the one who has to be closer in age to me says. He bends down to shake my hand, and all I can think of is that he sure smells good and is not too bad on the eyes, but I stop myself.

"Hello," we all say to both of them.

"I'm Grover Jr., and this is my son, Grover III," he says, and smiles.

"I'm Georgia, and these are my toddlers, Estelle," I say—and she nods, and then I turn—"and this is Frankie, who was going to be named after her dad had his name been Frank. And this is my brilliant new son-in-law, Hunter."

We're all laughing when in walk the birthday girl and the future groom arm in arm. "Isn't She Lovely" starts playing, and I swear that if Miss Early weren't my mother, I'd be cracking up, but she is my mother and she does look lovely and happy.

Everybody stands up and applauds, but then Mr. Grover releases her and lets my mother waltz out into the middle of the room, under the black-and-white crepe bouquet hanging from the chandelier, and she waves to everybody and then blows us a kiss like she's on a float in a parade. Grover follows her out to the dance floor, gives her a twirl, and then walks over to their very own table.

"Those two are something, aren't they?" Grover Jr. asks, but he's not really asking.

I smile and nod yes, as do the girls. His son isn't feeling any of this and is obviously here out of respect, and a few minutes later, after he excuses himself to go to the restroom and comes back with a sudden mood change, he looks like he could stay all night.

My mother is surrounded by well-wishers as she comes off the dance floor, and then we sit as our dinner starts being served. Lou Rawls's "See You When I Get There" comes on, and I apparently am pantomiming the lyrics, which is when Grover Jr. blurts out, "You don't remember me, do you?"

"Should I?"

He chuckles as my daughters settle into these uncomfortable folding chairs, hoping to hear something juicy. This would make three of us. Hunter's just digging the old-school music.

"Middle school: Mrs. Hill's science class and Mr. O'Connor, music. You liked dissecting, but you couldn't carry a note."

That's funny to everybody. Including me.

"I need more details."

"I was the only eighth-grader on the junior varsity basketball team."

I don't want to, but I decide to give him a long, hard look, and all I see is the handsome man he's turned into and the shoulders he must have inherited from his father, not to mention his Barry White baritone. He's not wearing a wedding band, but not to worry, since he's soon going to be my stepbrother.

"I didn't like basketball back then," I say. "What other reasons would make you memorable?"

"I kissed you once."

Everybody's eyes light up, and his son gives him a high five. My daughters both look at each other and then at me and then at Grover and back at each other. Everybody's wearing a smirk. Hunter goes to get us all more punch.

"I have never kissed you in my life because I didn't kiss any guys until high school."

"Did you kiss girls before then?" his son blurts out, his eyes now dreamy.

His dad places his hand on top of Grover III's. "Watch yourself, son."

"I didn't mean it the way it came out, ma'am. I'm sorry."

"No harm done."

And this is when the party starts.

We eat dinner. OD on punch. The kids watch these seniors dance to songs by Barry White and Sam Cooke and Al Green and Nancy Wilson and Aretha, and when Gladys Knight's "Midnight Train to Georgia" comes on, before I can think about shaking my head, Grover Jr. gets up and walks around to my chair and holds out his hand and says, "We have to dance on that song, or how will we ever forgive our-selves? May I?"

And I get up from my chair to dance with my new brother.


WE SING THE traditional birthday song and clap as Ma blows out the 8 and the 2 and a tiny white candle to grow on. She cries when she opens the scrapbooks that I finally had digitized and presses her hands softly on top of them and then pats them. Of course there are boxes and boxes of See's candy that I pray she doesn't eat. At least five Lee Child thrillers, because she says she loves Jack Reacher. And cash, because she's told everybody she couldn't be bothered with gift cards. Grover gives her a small diamond ring that she holds up before putting her hand on her chest.

The party is supposed to be over at ten, but my daughters and Hunter leave about nine thirty, because Estelle says she needs to be on the road by six the next morning. Ma and the elder Grover are over by the door saying their good-byes, and I've been sitting here trying not to fall in love with Grover Jr. every time he smiles, which has been a lot, and I'm surprised when my breasts start throbbing after he tells me he lives in New York and was a stockbroker for almost thirty years but took early retirement because he was simply burned out.

"How'd you know you were burned out?"

"Well, maybe burned out isn't entirely accurate. I was tired of think-ing about money. I was tired of being driven by it. Tired of worrying about it. But especially tired of losing it."

"So does that mean you don't have any?" I ask in a tone meant to produce another smile, and it does.

I hope this doesn't constitute flirting, but if it does, I'm certainly not doing it on purpose. At least I don't think I am.

"I'm not as dumb as I might look," he says. "I still invest, but now I'm trying to find a new road to travel on. How about you? My dad told me you're an optometrist."

"I am."

"Well, that's a respectable profession and probably low on the stress Richter scale."

"True almost to a fault. I'm not burned out, just bored and hoping to try my hand at something else next year."

"Try your hand at what?"

"That is the question I'm hoping to find the answer to."

"Well, if you had your druthers, what would you rather be doing?"

"I don't know what makes sense."

"Why does it have to make sense?"

"Well, I'm not rich. I can't just decide to start doing watercolor. What about you, Grover?"

"I'll admit it. I'm confused as hell about what to do next with my life, but I know I've still got time to find it."

"That's a healthy attitude."

"I don't have much of a choice, because I'm not ready for a rocking chair. Like father, like son!"

I laugh at that one.

"Seriously, do you have any hobbies?"

"Nothing I do on a regular basis."

"I didn't ask you that, did I?"

"Isn't that what a hobby is?"

"Not in my dictionary. I'm talking about something you do that you get a lot of pleasure from when you're doing it. And not sex."

We both laugh at that one.

"What about you?" I ask.

He slides that rickety white chair a little farther away from the table. We're both noticing how few people are left and the small crowd gathered around our parents by the exit door. "Okay, while you think about it, I'll go first."

"I'm all ears," I say.

He taps his fingertips a few times on the table. Smiles. And suddenly stops. "Back in the day, I used to love coaching youngsters in basketball every Saturday morning without fail. But then I was in a bad car accident and broke my femur and tibia and didn't know if I'd lose my leg. As you can see, I didn't, but I just haven't gotten back to those kids."

"Why not?"

"I don't know. Too preoccupied with my own problems, and I suppose I've just become entirely too damn lackadaisical."

"Doesn't sound like it."

He waves his hand as if to blow me off.

"So think for a minute about something you used to do or wish you could do more of if you had the time or took the time that you'd get a major charge out of if you didn't have to worry about money."

"Who doesn't have to worry about money?"

"Okay. Pretend for a moment that you don't."

"Then it would definitely be painting furniture and making pillows and some kind of decorating."

"So when was the last time you did any of them?"

"Don't ask."

"I just asked."

"Suffice it to say it's been a while. I've got a lot going on in my life."

"And this makes you unique?"

"If I had all the time in the world and could do any or all of these things or even discover new things to create, I would, but I can't make a living doing any of them."

"You don't know that, now, do you?"

"No, I don't. But I'm also in my prime and speeding right on through it."

He just shakes his head at that.

"It sounds like we should both go to one of those places in Santa Fe with Deepak or on one of those Eat, Pray, Love excursions until we find ourselves."

I snicker.

"Are you two going to sit here all night?" Ma says when she and the elder Grover come to the table hand in hand. "The party's over, if you haven't noticed."

"Maybe not for everybody, Early. Did you have a good time, son?"

He nods a yes.

"Did you remember him, Miss Georgia?" his dad asks.

"No, she did not," Grover Jr. blurts out.

"Well, if she's anything like her mother, you have to give her a good reason not to forget you. Good night, you two."

"Good night, and happy birthday again, Ma," I say. "And I'll see you later." As I stand up to kiss her, she gives me a *Really?* look.

"I'll see you tomorrow, Dad."

And our parents waltz outside.

"Are you staying with your father?"

"There's not enough room in his place for two big men."

I can't even comment.

"I'm staying at the Four Points. Are you staying with your mom?"

"Nope. I'm at the Four Points, too."

"Great! You feel like having a drink?"

"Where?"

"There."

"Isn't there something illegal and unethical and immoral about this? I mean, aren't you about to be my brother or something?"

He gets up from his chair and walks over and pulls mine out. When I stand up, my knees feel shaky. I am too damn old for this, and I know it. I haven't felt slutty in years, and yet it feels so good. I don't know if I remember how to have sex with a real man, and I certainly can't let him see me with the lights on. As I turn around and this hunk of a man hands me my black clutch, I realize I don't even think there's enough space between my thick thighs to let anything slide in there. But I'll give it the college try.

"I just asked if you'd like to have a drink. Where's your mind, young lady?"

"Young?"

"That's what I said."

I follow him to the hotel, and we have a drink, and I must sound like I have Tourette's, because I just can't seem to shut up. He must be able to tell what's been going through my mind when he says, "Relax,

Georgia. I don't want anything from you except friendship. I'm a happily married man. Your mother is marrying my dad, so we're almost family."

WTF?

I close up like a clam.

But this isn't Grover's fault. How was he supposed to know I'm a hard-up, horny woman who hasn't sat next to a man at a bar in years?

I turn down the second drink and tell him that I'm exhausted but how nice it was meeting my soon-to-be stepbrother.

"Same here," he says, and walks me to the elevator. "So I guess I'll see you at the wedding?"

I get on the elevator, smile, and wave good night.

Welcome to the goddamn family.

And I push 10.

"SO WHAT DO you think about your soon-to-be stepdad?" Ma asks as I drink a parting cup of coffee. She's having mac and cheese for breakfast. "This is so good I might have to hide it from Grover!"

"He seems very nice. And I can tell he cares a great deal for you, Ma."

"Cares? Are you crazy? He *loves* me. And the feeling is mutual. He makes me tingle. In fact—and please don't laugh—he makes me feel seventy!"

I smile and giggle for her, with her.

"Well, I just feel much better knowing you're not going to be living alone anymore."

"What are you talking about? Grover's not moving in here, and I'm certainly not going to be living in his unit. We like visiting each other."

"I didn't know."

"We're close enough."

"I see. Well, if it's not getting too personal, do you two ever have sleepovers?"

"If you're asking if we have sex, the answer is 'As close to it as we can get.' I just enjoy the warmth of his body next to mine. I like it when he gives me a kiss. That's all I need. Does that answer your question, missy?"

"Yes, it does. On another subject, his son was very nice, and I had no idea we were in middle school together."

"He's a good man. Too bad he's snagged. We could've made this a double wedding! That would've been fun."

"Okey-dokey, Ma. I'm going to have to get on the highway."

"What's your hurry?"

"I've got a lot of things to do."

"Like what?"

Right then I realized I *didn't* have anything pressing at home, I'm just used to saying it. "I might go look at houses."

"You haven't sold yours yet, so what's the hurry?"

"It's been a long time since I've looked at houses, and I figured I might as well get some idea what money can buy."

"Do you not watch *60 Minutes* or read the paper? Don't you know how long you could be sitting on your house, especially in that bracket?"

"Of course I do."

"Why would you want to buy another stupid house when it's only you?"

"I said I was starting to look. And I might not be by myself by the time I move."

"Don't tell me you're dating?"

"I've had a few here and there."

"Stop lying, Georgia. Not only don't you look like you haven't been on a date, but tell me this: When was the last time you had sex, missy?"

"That is none of your business, Ma."

"How many years?"

"What makes you think it's been years?"

"Because you've got that unsatisfied look, and you've had it about four years. I've been counting."

"It hasn't been that long."

"It's not healthy to go this long without love, Georgia."

"Well, I can't put a For Sale sign on me, now, can I?"

"You need to do something about it."

"I'm trying to."

"No you're not. But heck, maybe I'm wrong. Some women forget all about love when they haven't felt it in a long time, and I believe they're called spinsters. Is that what you're aiming for?"

I shake my head no.

"Then you need to let somebody know what you want."

"Come again, Ann Landers?"

"Times have changed. You'll be as gray as me if you sit around waiting for your prince to pick you out of a lineup and sweep you off your feet. Men are stupid, you know. And they can't see for looking. How do you think I snagged your daddy and now Grover?"

"I didn't know you had those kinds of skills."

"Seriously, Georgia. There is nothing wrong with asking a man out. All he can say is no or that he's not interested. It won't be the end of the world. Men are used to rejection, but it doesn't stop them from asking. Learn from them."

She walks over and kisses me on the forehead, then gives me a big hug.

"Are you going to Michael's wedding?"

"He told you he intended to ask me?"

"He divorced you, not me. Yes. I hope you go. I always liked him, even though I know he hurt you. But you survived, because you're strong and smart. You need some joy in your life, Georgia."

"And you think I'm going to find it at Michael's wedding?"

"If you can be happy for him, that would be a yes. Now, get out of here. Grover's taking me to Victoria's Secret! Just kidding. J.C. Penney is having a sale on everything. And now that I've got all this extra cash, I want to spend some of it. Call me when you get home."

# And So It Went

EFORE YOU SAY NO, JUST SAY YES," WANDA INSISTS. "Hold that thought. Nelson's calling to ask a silly question he already knows the answer to."

I'm in downtown Oakland driving around Lake Merritt looking for a new BBQ place that's supposed to be close to where I get my hair done when I get it done. I don't know why they call this a lake when it's really a lagoon. And a gorgeous, heart-shaped one that's almost three and a half miles in circumference, smack dab in the middle of Oakland. I used to jog around it when I was in grad school. Berkeley's only a ten-minute drive from here. And right now the sun is setting and the water's surface looks like orange glass. I pass joggers and bicyclists and am once again overcome by yet another staggering sense of how-lazy-I-am shame. There's no valid reason I shouldn't be doing some form of exercise. People much older than me are doing yoga. I'm five pounds away from being fat, and I don't want to be fat, but I also know that since menopause has come and gone, it's been harder to lose weight. My long list of excuses is plentiful, but at some point reality is just reality. I finally get why it's so hard for drug addicts to kick their habit even when they want to. So from this day forward, I'm not going to keep using the same lame-ass excuses for not taking care of myself. And that's final.

"Georgia, you still there?"

"Yes. But the answer to your question is no," I say, and start laughing. "Are we talking about another blind date?"

"You're the one who's blind, sweetheart. Anyway, I've seen pictures of him, and he's right up your clichéd alley: tall, dark, and handsome."

"You and Nelson should let me check your eyes again, because your vision is clearly distorted based on all the other sex symbols you've tried to throw at me."

"You need to stop thinking you still look like a Playboy Bunny, because the last time I saw you, your days of stopping traffic are long gone, Miss Thang. So shut up."

"Some of them still slow down because they like thick chicks, so *you* shut up," I say, being more sarcastic than anything. "Anyway, what's this one's name, and what's wrong with him?"

"His name is Richard Cardoza."

"Is he Puerto Rican or Cuban or what?"

"Why? Do you have something against either? But to answer your question, he's Puerto Rican."

"Well, if he looks anything like Ricky Martin, I'll pick him up at the airport. So tell me his story."

"You're just too cynical, and I wish you'd stop, Georgia."

"Okay. But you know how many times I've been through this, Wanda? You have no idea how much energy it takes and what it feels like to be in my shoes, going on blind dates at my age, hoping I'm going to meet someone wonderful, and it never goes anywhere. It's exhausting."

"Oh, stop whining, would you? Have you ever thought maybe it might be you who has unresolved issues? You're not Miss Perfect, you know."

"I know I'm not perfect, and I'm trying to own up to some of my shortcomings, which is one of the reasons I wanted to look into the men from my past to see if maybe they saw then what I'm just learning now or if I inherited some of my unnamed issues from them. So cut me some fucking slack, would you?"

"Okay. I'm sorry. I'm on your side, baby. But anyhoo, Richard is an interesting and decent man, and that's all I have to say. Google him when you get home. And by the way, we're having a few friends over for dinner to welcome him on his impending move to the Bay Area. He's an old colleague of Nelson's."

"Aren't they all?"

"See what I mean? I wish I could slap you through this phone. It's next Saturday. Usual time. And wear something that proves you put some thought into it. Bye."

"Wait! Don't hang up, Wanda! I need to talk to you—or a priest."

"Is it about a child, an ex-husband, an ex-lover, or a house?"

"Maybe all of the above. How close are you to Lakeshore?"

"Why?"

"I was looking for that new BBQ place, but I've changed my mind, and now I don't know where I want to eat."

"I can't believe you're turning down barbecue! Meet me at the Sushi House on Grand. See you in ten and order me some sake. Please."

I'm proud of myself for turning down tender, succulent barbecued ribs with candied yams and potato salad, collard greens and corn bread, and probably peach cobbler to go. Nope. I'm having raw fish instead.

When I stop at the light, it's starting to rain, and I look over at the Grand Lake Theatre, my favorite art deco place to watch a movie. On top of it, the gigantic GRAND LAKE neon sign is lit up, because it's Friday. The lights stay on until the last show on Sunday. I'm glad some things that are old haven't been replaced.

I'm lucky and snag a parking spot right in front of the restaurant. I don't bother getting my umbrella, since my hair is synthetic and I'm wearing a trench coat. It was close to seventy degrees a couple of hours ago, but I'm sure the temperature has dropped at least twenty degrees. This is one of the things I appreciate about living in the Bay Area. You don't burn up. You learn to dress in layers or keep a sweater or a jacket in your backseat at all times. This is the beginning of the rainy season, which you live for if you're a skier, because three short hours north you'll be seven thousand feet up and can get out of your car and make a snow angel.

When I walk in, it's quiet and serene, and of course they're playing Japanese music that always sounds as if the singer is in pain. The waitress bows after I tell her that there will be two of us and no, I don't want to sit on the floor, because if I did, I probably couldn't get up.

I order a carafe of sake and pull my chopsticks out of the paper wrapper. As I'm looking over the menu, I hear a man's voice say, "Georgia Young?"

When I look up, I see a tall, somewhat good-looking black man in a black suit and wearing a nice pair of black-framed glasses. He looks vaguely familiar, but when I'm caught off guard like this, I'm off guard, so I just say, "Yes," with some skepticism.

"You don't remember me, do you?"

"I'm trying. But forgive me."

I hate it when people ask me that. I just played this guessing game with Grover Jr. I'm getting too old to remember everybody I used to know or once met, especially patients. I pretend like I'm trying to remember him. But what I'm really doing is praying I never fucked him back in the day when I drank too much. No. Because whoever he is, I know he's not on my list.

"I'm James Harvey. We were at UCSF together. You dated an old friend of mine for about two weeks before you slept with me."

I'm trying not to laugh out of pure embarrassment, but I can hardly speak.

Then *he* starts laughing. "I'm just kidding," he says. "We didn't go to any college together. Do you remember breaking your ankle at Vail, when we were both members of the black ski club?"

"Yes, I do. But I was pushed."

"Maybe you were, but it was me who picked you up and stayed with you until the ski patrol came. How's that leg doing?"

Now I remember. Michael didn't want to go. He thought skiing was too bourgeois, even though he golfed—and this was probably before Tiger was in kindergarten. "Well, I'm able to put a little more weight on it."

He doesn't react. I really need to stop being so self-deprecating.

"Do you still ski?" he asks.

"Nope. Gave it up years ago."

"Well, I've seen you around over the years, with one or two husbands, but I didn't have the guts to say anything. Some men are insecure about other men knowing their wives in past lives."

"Well, they're both casualties, or maybe I should say I'm a casualty. But oh, here comes my good friend who I'm meeting here. Do you have a card?"

"I do. I know you're an optometrist. I've wanted you to check my eyesight, just didn't have the nerve. But seeing you now tells me this may not have been accidental."

"You might be right," I say. But what else can I say?

I look down at his card. He's a cardiologist. In private practice. Did everybody in our age group go to law school and medical school or what? I want to meet a plumber or an electrician or a contractor. A man who does normal stuff for a living. Even still, I can't help but notice there's no ring on James's left hand.

"Hello there," Wanda says, sizing him up before she takes off her red rain poncho, the one I find embarrassing. "I'm Wanda, Georgia's best friend and confidante. I should know you, but I don't. Are you a relative or an interested party?"

I grab her by the arm.

James is laughing.

I'm not.

"I'm not a relative, that much I'm sure of. We're old acquaintances, but I'm hoping to get reacquainted if at all possible."

He looks down at me. If I were white, I'd be blushing.

"Would you like to join us?" Wanda asks.

"I'd love to, but I can't. You see that young man over there looking bored? He's my son. He's a college dropout. Biology wasn't his thing. But we're here to celebrate, because he's also a pretty good pianist and just got accepted to the Berklee College of Music."

"Hot damn," I say, and then, "I'm sorry. I meant to say that's wonderful."

"Congratulations to your son," Wanda says, trying to sound dignified for a change.

He smiles and winks. "At any rate, would you mind if I gave you a call sometime in the near future?" He pats those long cardiologist fingers on his black lapels and smiles. "I'm harmless."

"No, she doesn't mind," Wanda says, and I kick her under the table. "May I have your card, too?"

"Absolutely," he says, and gives it to her.

She is not even close to being slick.

"That would be nice," I finally say to him. "Do you live here in Oakland?"

"I do. Piedmont."

"With your family?" Wanda blurts out.

I kick her again.

"He's my family," he says, and smiles. "Enjoy your sake and sushi."

"Wait, one last very personal question," I ask. "Who makes your glasses?"

He chuckles.

"I have no idea. They're twenty-nine-dollar readers I buy online and then have my prescription put in. Good?"

"Smart," I say as he heads over to sit with his son.

"Damn, so is he a blast from the past you never told me about, or is picking up strangers your new middle-aged move? Regardless, he's not so bad on the eyes, I must say."

"Shut up, Wanda. He's not my type. Anyway, I met him years ago but didn't remember."

"We've been through this before. But I don't think you know what your type is, and you need to forget it whatever it is, since there's no line of any type trying to get all up inside your castle, sweetheart."

"And throw that ugly poncho away, would you?"

And after a couple more sake shots and no sushi, she says, "Maybe you'll have two men fighting over you. Okay. So anyway. I'll just tell you. Richard's a nonpracticing accountant and a practicing divorce attorney who lives in L.A. but is relocating up here."

"Oh, Lord, not another fucking overachiever. Is he *from* L.A.? Because if he is, I'm not interested."

"What a bitch you can be. But to answer your question: no. He grew up in New York, but his family lives in San Francisco."

"Then be honest. What's wrong with him?"

"He's lonely, just like you."

"Fuck you, Wanda."

"No, I'm doing okay in that department. Nelson's on that little blue pill. You're the one who could use a magic wand."

"You know what? I'm thinking maybe I should just settle for a loser, or someone who doesn't have any credentials at all. Or, even better, maybe I should find myself a revolutionary. Someone who believes in something besides himself. Like a cause. Someone who stands for something, sees the need for change, and keeps me up at night because he's trying to help me figure out the role I can play in changing the world, too."

"That would make you Michelle Obama."

"In all honesty, I'm probably better off by myself, because when I get on my own fucking nerves, I can just change the channel."

"What are you talking about?" Wanda asks.

"I don't know, but this sake has more kick than vino."

"Alcoholic beverages sure make you lose your inhibitions and say stupid shit like you just did. Let's order two cappuccinos with an extra shot before we think about getting behind a fucking wheel," she says.

"You're right," I say. "Do you think we swear too fucking much?"

"Who the fuck cares? The only time we get to talk this fucking way is when we're together, right?"

"That's so true. Let's never stop fucking swearing, okay?"

"Okay!" she yells.

And we give each other high fives.

"So when is your stupid dinner party again?"

"Next Saturday. And please don't wear that stupid fucking wig. I know you've got a head full of thick, nappy hair under there, so why not let the world see it?"

"Shut up, Wanda. You don't have to comb it."

"Then cut it off! That's why God made beauty salons."

"Any other suggestions?"

"Yeah. Bake a fucking cake. I don't care what kind. Wait. Yes I do.

Wait. I can't remember. Damn. Oh, yeah. That black-walnut pound cake. Make that one."

I realize I forgot to eat my sushi and only ate the rice with the teriyaki sauce on it and not the salmon. I wave my hand for the waitress, and she glides over to us and clasps her hands like she's praying. I wonder if she's this timid in bed.

"We'll have two cappuccinos, please, with extra shots."

"No more sake?"

"Do we look like we need more sake?" Wanda asks. Then she turns back to face me. "Hold on a minute, huzzy. I want to hear about the Niles tragedy and any other juicy stuff you feel like sharing in your slow-motion life. So spill it."

"Well, I'll start with the house."

"Oh, hell, I'm getting tired of hearing about your goddamn house. Sell it already! What about those daughters?"

"They're both fucking pregnant. Wait. I don't want to use the F-word on them. They're both pregnant."

"What? Frankie's only been married ten minutes and her black husband is unemployed, and what's Estelle trying to prove over there: that eight is enough?"

"My feelings exactly. And please stop saying Hunter's black, okay?"

"Okay. How pregnant are they?"

"I don't know. They keep so many secrets and lie about so much stuff that I'll just wait for them to tell me when the little crumbsnatchers are going to pop out of their ovens."

"This is why I'm glad I never had children."

"Shut up, Wanda. I wouldn't trade them for the world, even though they get on my last fucking nerve sometimes."

"So what about Niles?"

"He came to the office."

"You're bullshitting me! And?"

"I slapped the shit out of him."

"You're not fucking serious, Georgia."

"Of course I'm not."

I try to skip over the details, but she's not having it, so we down our coffee and order another one.

"Well, all I have to say is it's a good thing you only had two fucking husbands," and then she hands me the fucking check.

I PULL INTO Wanda and Nelson's circular driveway, and it's even colder up here because their house is on the highest peak. They have a five-bridge view, and I find myself staring out at the heavenly fog rolling in.

I don't bother knocking. Nelson spots me before Wanda does. He reminds me of an older Sidney Poitier. His hair is white, even though he's not even sixty. He's about an inch or two taller than me, and Wanda is about two or three inches taller than him, without heels, which is why she hardly ever wears them. Nelson, however, could care less if she towers over him.

"Hi, sugar," he says after hugging me and kissing me on my forehead. "I thought you might bail on us because you think we're trying to play matchmaker—and you'd be right. We want you happily hooked up and married, and if the two end up being the same, all the better. Richard should be here in five or ten minutes. Get yourself a drink. Wanda's going to strip later."

I pop him upside the head. He's like a brother, and he's a good man. It's refreshing to see that some folks fall in love when they're young and just know it's the right fit.

I don't see Violet and wonder why. She's usually the first one here. Wanda saunters over, looking pretty and precious in a lacy frock that screams Neiman Marcus Last Call.

Hugs.

"Where's the cake?"

I cover my mouth.

"You forgot it?"

"Well, no and yes. I set it on top of the car, and I'm sure some wild animals are probably getting drunk in the driveway right now. I'm sorry, girl."

"I know you're just excited, and I see that you can do wonders with gel and a rubber band, and I forgot you have cheekbones, and that outfit at least suggests you might be available. You look nice."

"So do you, huzzy."

"Anyway, you know almost everybody here, and the few you don't, act friendly."

"Where are your adorable dogs?" I ask. She knows I'm being sarcastic.

"I sent them to the Doggie Hotel for the weekend."

"You must be on something."

"Nope. Nelson and I are flying to Palm Springs tomorrow to look at more condos and see Gladys Knight. You wanna come? We've got an extra ticket."

"I love Gladys, but no thank you. Where's Violet?"

"I didn't invite her. Sometimes she's not good with a small audience, and she never shuts up. So please don't slip and tell her."

"My lips are sealed, even though that's very tacky, Wanda. It's not her fault she looks good and some of your old lady friends get jealous when their husbands feast their eyes on all her feline assets. Okay, so where's Mr. Dream Lover?"

"Coming in the door right now. And be nice, Georgia. Introduce yourself, because Nelson has already told him everything about you that he needs to know. You can lie about the rest."

I don't even want to look, because I don't feel like being disappointed. I decide to walk through this house of earth and jewel tones, stopping to say hello to folks, mostly couples I've known for years but never have much else to say to except "Long time no see," "You look good," and "You just got back from Dubai or Maui or Cape Town," and "Maybe one day we should," and "Yes, I had to get my firewood early this year," and "No doubt I'm excited about the World Cup," and "Of course I'm going to work on President Obama's campaign if he runs again, which I'm sure he will—oh, my bad, you're a Republican. Wow, I would never have guessed, but we all have our belief systems, and it was nice chatting with you, too."

I walk out to one of the balconies because I'm nervous about meeting this Richard character, and moments later I hear the door open and a deep voice say, "Why are you out here in the cold by yourself?"

Before turning around, I pretend I'm in a movie and say, "Because I'm so warm inside I don't even feel it, and a woman needs a cool breeze every now and then." And because it's clear I'm just pulling his leg and having fun, by the time I turn around and see this tall, handsome what looks to me to be a black man who's laughing and showing the most beautiful set of teeth under the shiniest mustache I've ever seen, I follow it up with, "Nice to meet you, Richard. I'm Georgia, soon to be your new wife."

"It's so nice to meet you. I knew this was going to be love at first sight."

Then I come to my senses and hold my hand out to shake his, but he simply rubs his on top of mine and says, "That was probably the best introduction I've ever had. It really is nice to meet you, Georgia."

"I was just having fun and trying to break the ice, and it's nice to meet you, too, Richard."

"This is a setup, you know."

"Of course it is. Which is why they never work."

"Not so fast," he says. "We're not even married yet. And as a divorce attorney, I know all the right things we should do so we never have to see one."

"Well, how's that worked out for you?"

"I'm a fast learner. So once."

I hold up two fingers. "Apparently I was in the remedial class."

"Would you like a drink?"

"I'm not so sure. I'm feeling slightly intoxicated."

"That would make two of us."

ON THE DRIVE HOME, I can't wipe the grin off my face, because I can't believe that in less than a week I've met two men who've piqued my interest. Of course I don't want to start thinking about whether we should elope or have a fairly simple but intimate affair, and because all orgasms are not created equal, as I've learned over the years, perhaps I should at least wait until we have sex before deciding which one will become my betrothed.

# Fortunes

SANTA'S COMING TO TOWN TONIGHT, AND I'VE BEEN IN-vited to spend Christmas Day with my daughters, their husbands and children, born and unborn, over in Palo Alto. I don't have a Christmas tree. I have stars. White, red, and silver perforated paper stars perched on thin white metal poles that light up the windows. I bought a container that emits the scent of pine just for effect and maybe for nostalgia. I know Christmas is about the birth of Baby Jesus, but in my house it was also about baking cookies and making eggnog and watching Frosty and Rudolph and the Grinch and listening to Nat King Cole sing about chestnuts roasting and those velvet notes floating all the way up the stairwell into the girls' rooms. I loved watching them put the poorly wrapped gifts under the tree and on Christmas morn-ing hearing them gallop downstairs in their red-and-white candy-cane pj's with the feet in them. They slid across the floor on their bellies and would sit up not knowing what box to open first. Their delight was contagious.

Years passed, and no cookies were left out for Santa, and it got to the point where they were bored with toys and preferred clothes that they wanted to pick out themselves and then gift cards, which caused the white felt tree blanket to look lonely under the shrinking Doug-las fir. They lost interest in Santa and wanted to spend Christmas Eve with their boyfriends and sometimes didn't show up until the after-noon. Kids grow up.

I've already sent the twins two of those gigantic Fathead posters for their wall: Tiana, the first black princess from *The Princess and the*

*Frog,* and Cars, since they love to drive and have miniature versions of real ones in the garage. What a complete waste of money. I also got them one purple and one mint green princess dress even though I have no idea who they're supposed to be.

Estelle and Frankie have insisted on doing all the major cooking, and I'm just going to walk in with a peach cobbler, a bouquet of flowers, gift cards from Nordstrom's and Macy's for my daughters, one from Sports Authority for Hunter—who I've learned is Mr. Outdoors—and a Robert Graham shirt for Justin, who seems to be addicted to them. Between basketball games I will be Mrs. Santa, Grandma, and Mother and take my time setting the table and listening and chatting and catching up while trying not to get in the way as I observe how beautiful my family is and how blessed I am to have them.

"SO WHAT ARE you doing on this unusually cold Christmas Eve afternoon?" Wanda asks me.

It's hard to describe boredom, but here goes:

"Watching *Celtic Woman: Believe.*"

"You're not serious."

"I am, but I'm not."

I can't help but laugh as three of the women prance out onto an empty stage in 1980s evening gowns and sway a little bit before singing in soprano voices that make me wonder why so many people like this music.

"Seriously, what are you doing?"

"I'm about to open fifteen bags of frozen peaches and boil them in six to eight inches of water before I add some sugar and butter and vanilla and almond extract and cinnamon and nutmeg and let them soak overnight."

"If I wanted to learn how to make it, I'd have asked a long time ago, so just be sure you bake a baby cobbler for me and Nelson, please?"

"For a large fee, of course."

"Leave it in the mailbox, and this time put a Post-it on the door so you don't forget. Anyway, Nelson and I are having a hard time choosing a condo because they're all so gorgeous."

"This is what you called to tell me on Christmas Eve?"

"You're the one who's watching *Celtic Woman,* so shut up."

"You guys aren't really planning on living in the desert full-time, I hope."

"What do you think retirement means, Georgia? You seem to forget I'm almost two years older than you, because *I* didn't skip any grades and Nelson's got two years on me and—"

"Hold on a minute, Wanda. I'm getting another call. Oh, Lord, it's Richard!"

"Don't say anything stupid. You could have a date for New Year's! Call me after you finish talking to him, and I hope it's not in a few minutes. Bye!"

My heart is pounding like a teenager's as I click over.

"Hello?" I say, as if I don't have caller ID.

"Merry Christmas, Georgia! It's Richard. Am I catching you at a good or a bad time?"

"Merry Christmas to you, too, Richard. I just finished taking a peach cobbler out of the oven and was just about to start wrapping a few gifts. How are you?"

"Exhausted, but otherwise I'm fine. I'm officially a Bay Area resident."

"That's great. So where are you living?"

"Well, I'm staying with my parents in San Francisco until I can find something to buy."

With his parents?

"It's a buyer's market, that's for sure," I say.

"I know. But I'm not in any major hurry. My parents own a fabulous Victorian, and they rarely come upstairs because of their health."

Is he serious?

"So how long have you been here?"

"A couple of months now. I needed to clear up a lot of loose ends before I left L.A., and of course everything takes longer than you think."

"Of course. Things take as long as they take. My house is going on the market in a few weeks."

"Why would you want to do something as stupid as that?"

"Excuse me?"

"That came out wrong. My bad. I *meant* in a market this bad, it would be a lot smarter to hold on to your property until things improve."

"I'm not in any hurry to sell. So. On a lighter note: welcome to the Bay Area! Maybe Wanda, Nelson, and I can take you out for a welcome dinner real soon."

"To be honest, I would prefer that you not let them know I'm here."

"What? I thought you and Nelson went way back."

"We do, but that's part of the problem. Too far back, and though he's truly a nice guy, we really don't have that much in common anymore, so I'd prefer to keep my distance."

Is this bastard for real?

"I thought you guys were friends."

"We were. But some friends you outgrow."

I'm about ready to hang up this phone. Who in the hell does he think he is? Johnnie Cochran and Jimmy Smits combined? He sure doesn't sound like the Mr. Fun Guy and Mr. Sexy that I met. What a phony son of a bitch.

"This is true," I say. "So why'd you come to their dinner party, which he and Wanda had on your behalf, portraying yourself as a longtime friend?"

"Because he insisted after I decided I was moving up here. Might as well reach out."

Reach out?

"Okay."

"So, Georgia, I called because I was wondering if you'd like to have dinner sometime?"

"This year? Next year? Could you be more specific?"

"Is that sarcasm I'm detecting?"

"I think it is, Richard. You came across as a different kind of guy when I met you."

"And what kind of guy was that?"

"Funny. Quick. Warm. Intelligent. And lighthearted."

"Well, sorry to disappoint. Good talking with you. Maybe we'll run into each other this year. Or next."

And the bastard hung up.

I don't call Wanda back. I'm too pissed off, not to mention disappointed. This is why it's so hard to find a decent man. When you finally meet one you feel a twinge of excitement about and it feels mutual, before you get a chance to even start what you think might maybe could possibly end up blossoming into a potential relationship, he does or says something so stupid or arrogant or dumb or ignorant or insulting or reprehensible or disrespectful or all of the above that reflects his legitimate personality traits, which are so unappealing or a complete turnoff that it becomes crystal clear there's not much he can do to make you want to turn that knob back to the On position. Richard is a perfect example. And after years of going through this, it wears you out.

Of course Wanda calls back. I'm now in my pj's drinking a glass of wine.

"So do you have a date for New Year's or what?"

"No."

"What the hell did you say to blow it, Georgia? I thought you guys hit it off quite well at our dinner party."

"He's phony as hell. Arrogant as hell. And he completely misrepresented himself. I don't know why Nelson counts him as a friend."

"To be honest, Nelson doesn't really like him. He was kind of a jerk when they were in business school together, and he was getting his J.D. at the same time, but he was always too slick for Nelson's taste."

"Then why in the hell did you guys want me to meet him?"

"Because we thought maybe he'd matured."

"He's aged."

"Did he mention anything about getting in touch with Nelson and me?"

"No he didn't."

"Good. Here's hoping we don't run into him anywhere. Be just our luck."

"So what are you guys doing for New Year's?"

"Probably watching the ball drop. To be honest, we usually TiVo it, because sometimes we just can't hang."

"Remember when we used to go to one party after another and get home the following day astonished it was a new year?"

"Yes, I do."

"And we danced all night, and our feet hurt so bad we walked down the street barefoot carrying our pumps?"

"Some of my favorite memories, honey."

"And we stumbled into some all-night diner, had another drink to wash down breakfast, and then threw up."

Wanda sighs. "Those were the good old days."

"Well, I might put on my jammies, make some popcorn, and drink champagne and smoke a joint and dance right along with the young folks partying on television."

"Did you just say smoke a joint?"

"I was just kidding. It sounded cool, though, didn't it?"

"Not really."

"Well, I would like to make a promise to you, Wanda."

"I'm listening."

"This is the last New Year's Eve I'm sleeping alone."

"Forgive me for bringing this up, Georgia, but didn't you say the same thing last year?"

Ho, ho, ho.


ON CHRISTMAS MORNING I bake two peach cobblers, put one in the mailbox for Wanda and Nelson, and leave early for Palo Alto. Estelle and Justin's street is so perfect it feels straight out of *Pleasantville,* and I'm just waiting for the No Coloreds sign to pop up out of nowhere. The trees look like they're staring at the cars passing by, their leaves so motionless it feels like earthquake weather. Their house is one of the smallest on the block, but still not small. The garage door is up. I park behind their two SUVs and next to Frankie and Hunter's used red RAV4.

The twins must be able to hear through wood, because that door flings open and the purple and mint green princesses run out into the garage and wrap their polyester arms around me and say, "Merry Christmas, Granny!" and then "Thank you for our Fatheads and these beautiful princess dresses! We love them!"

And they both take me by the same arm in an attempt to drag me inside, but my car door is still open because the flowers are sitting on the front seat. When we get inside, my pregnant daughters, who are both finally starting to *look* pregnant, are wearing Santa hats and tight jeans and T-shirts, and we hug and hug. Hunter, who was engrossed in a basketball game, runs to give me a squeeze, and then Justin runs down the stairs to do the same. We are one big happy frigging family.

"Merry Christmas, everybody!"

My daughters are pretending to cook in the kitchen. There must be at least four cookbooks spread out on any empty counter space.

"What happened to the peach cobbler?" Justin asks.

"It's in the car. Feel free to go get it. It's on the backseat, but it weighs a ton and it's still warm, so be careful."

"I'm hoping some of the juice spills, Mom," he says.

"Can I help?" I ask the cooks.

"We've got this covered, Mom," Estelle says.

"We've been up all night," Frankie says.

"You mean you and Hunter spent the night?"

"Why are you so surprised, Mom?"

"I'm not. Just asked."

"So sit. Relax. Have a glass of wine. Watch some basketball with Hunter."

I don't like basketball, but I like Hunter, so I sit next to him and the twins curl up next to me, and I try not to laugh at their beige Uggs sticking out from under the hems of those princess dresses.

It smells like Christmas. It even looks like a gingerbread house in here. Estelle is old-fashioned and loves white and jewel tones and stained glass and fat, stuffy sofas and things made out of brass and copper. I recognize a golden turkey and an already baked honey-baked ham and what I know are au gratin potatoes and those creamy green beans I've never quite understood the appeal of and rolls just waiting to go into the oven.

We have a wonderful meal.

"Dinner was delicious," I say.

"We can burn," Frankie says.

"We sure can, and thanks, Mom," Estelle says, looking somewhat preoccupied. I assume it's hormonal.

"So how're you both feeling these days?"

"I feel pregnant," Estelle says.

"I feel fat," Frankie says with a smile.

"It's because you're getting fat," Estelle says.

"No she's not," Hunter says from the family room. "She's getting rounder, and she's beautiful."

Frankie has a *So there!* look on her face, and Estelle passes a phony smile back to her brother-in-law, who's now jumping up and down because of a three-pointer.

I pass on the cobbler but opt for coffee. I'm ordered to sit and sip and not to help clean up. My cell phone rings, and I can't imagine who it could be, and I answer it without looking.

"Hello?"

"Merry Christmas, Georgia. It's James. Harvey."

I stand up, and my daughters are apparently wondering who's causing what feels like a smile.

"Merry Christmas to you, too, James. How are you?"

"Good, good, good. Skiing in Tahoe until after the New Year and wondered if you'd like to have dinner sooner rather than later. My treat."

"That sounds like a plan. Do a black diamond for me."

He laughs.

"Will do, and have a happy New Year."

After I press End, I look over at my daughters, both of whom have their hands on their hips with a smirk and a question on their faces.

"Well?" Estelle asks.

"He's a friend."

They give each other high fives.

As I back out of the driveway, Estelle and Frankie wave good-bye like I'm leaving them on Gilligan's Island. I know that look of uncertainty, and I sure wish I could give them a handful of joy. They don't seem to understand that babies aren't a remedy for unsolved problems. I know I have no right to be upset. But I am upset. About both of them deciding to have a baby under the circumstances. But I've also resolved to mind my own business and not offer any advice unless they ask for it. I'm just curious how they're going to pay for all these children and, in Frankie's case, where in the hell they're going to live. They can't raise a child in my friends' guesthouse. I'm also starting to think Frankie was probably pregnant when she came home. But so what? I did it my way. And they're doing it theirs.

I forgot the flowers. They're still on the front seat, but they've fallen over. As I head down the street, the leaves on the trees seem to be waving in slow motion as if I should've stayed longer.

I get home in less time than it took me to get there, and I'm so glad I forgot to unplug my stars. They are still bright. They welcome me home.

ON NEW YEAR'S EVE, I order Chinese. Combination chow fun, because I love the soft, wide noodles and that light gravy. Egg rolls because I like and hate the way the hot mustard burns my tongue and opens my nostrils. Salt-and-pepper shrimp just because I like the way they smell and you get the best of both worlds. And garlic spinach because I need a vegetable. I'm not a pig. I believe in leftovers.

I light two of my favorite red-currant candles, take a shower with my new lemongrass-and-bamboo scrub, and put on a pair of white velvet pajamas. I pop the cork on a bottle of French champagne and pour myself a glass. I walk over to my laptop and open Facebook. I also turn on the television and decide I'll wait up for *Dick Clark's New Year's Rockin' Eve* and watch the ball drop, which is when I hear someone say for his New Year's resolution he is going to smile more. When I turn around, the man who said it is gone and an ASPCA commercial comes on, with Sarah McLachlan singing that beautiful but depressing song

I don't want to hear on New Year's Eve. I donate enough money to rescue about twenty dogs a month and have enough ASPCA T-shirts to last, so I change the channel.

I don't believe in making New Year's resolutions because I read in *Forbes* magazine that only 8 percent of people even keep them. I wonder how they know that? I suppose resolutions are more like reminders of things you've been meaning to do that you haven't gotten around to. Or they're like secret weaknesses you want to turn into strengths. I don't really see any harm in making them, except most people don't just pick one big thing they want to improve or change, because most of us know just how imperfect we are. Which is probably why the list of our perceived shortcomings is so long, because what they really seem to want is to be somebody else, and besides, it's like promising you're never going to get drunk again until you remember you were drunk when you said it.

My Chinese food gets here before I have a chance to finish my second glass of champagne that was worth every dollar I paid for it, and I eat standing up and put the rest in the fridge. I take all four of the fortune cookies I never eat over to the desk and crack them open one by one. Number one says, "Good news will come to you from far away." Number two says, "A cheerful message is on its way to you." Number three says, "You have an important new business development shaping up." Number four says, "We must always have old memories and young hopes."

It would sure be cool if just one of these fortunes were to shock the hell out of me by coming true. I eat number four. Decide that music would add even more flavor and energy to this evening, so I open iTunes and press "Green Light" by John Legend with that sexy Andre 3000. I turn up the volume so all my neighbors can hear it if they're at home, and I jump up and start dancing like I'm thirty—no, twenty-five—and by the time the song is over, here comes Tina Turner asking "What's Love Got to Do with It" and I do what used to be called the cha-cha and pop my fingers and rock my hips from side to side and then yell out to Tina, "Everything and nothing!"

I attempt to pour another glass of champagne and am surprised to discover that the bottle is empty. Although I'm not drunk, I suppose this means I've had enough.

I finally open Facebook and decide tonight might be a good night to see if any of the remaining Talented Five can be found.

I try Carter first. He saved my life. And never knew how his bravery turned my heart into a warm, wet sponge. Will you look at those emerald mountains? What a backdrop. Apparently Carter has become the old man in the shoe, because he's got eight kids, twenty-two grandkids, and five great-grandkids, which might explain why his hair is white and his skin looks like old leather. He's a retired chief of police in Charlotte! Still married to the same woman he was married to when I met him.

Oh. Oliver. A minister? See what giving up drugs can do! Not! As the young kids say, LOL. Seriously. Oliver was quite the philosopher. I learned a lot about life from him. A lot of which I think I forgot. Or failed to apply. I mean, here I am half drunk, and what am I celebrating? A new year. He would tell me I could come up with a better reason than that. And Lord, did he wear me out with the orating. It was definitely his mind I loved, because he wasn't all that heavenly in bed. I had to work too hard for an orgasm. Look! He's married! No children. And lives in Chicago? I forgot. He was from Chicago.

Lance isn't on Facebook. Which means he's probably behind bars. He was a smooth operator, who conned me—and Lord only knows how many other young women—to fall in love with him. How'd he do it? With that smile. He was smart as hell and could outtalk you on almost any subject. I can't leave out the unbelievable sex. Or I should say that what he did with his tongue would make any woman or man fall under his spell. But I pretended not to care about him and made him think I didn't take him seriously and was just doing to him what he was doing to me: using him for sex. I failed at faking. Last I heard, he'd gotten busted for selling cocaine. He told me he was doing field studies for his postgraduate work in sociology.

And there's the too-good-to-be-true David, who after months of on-again, off-again dating called out of the blue and told me he was moving to New York to work in theater and would not be in touch because he found me too insipid and uninteresting but wished me a good life and then hung up. He wasn't exactly a thrill a minute either, and a one-trick pony in bed. But he was socially wild and fascinating, which is what kept me wanting to spend time with him. A few months later, he called from New York to apologize for his crassness and said he was just having an *episode* and was now taking his medication. Well, it looks like he got clear and found his true calling. He's a television producer in Toronto. Been married since 2005. To a Canadian woman.

And here's Eric. The man responsible for resuscitating me after my post-Michael divorce hiatus. His status is blank. Hold on! He's standing in front of one of my favorite restaurants: Toulouse Petit! I don't believe this! It's right here in San Francisco and within walking distance from my office. I've eaten there at least ten times since it opened a few years ago and never saw him. I think I'll move Eric to the top of this list.

But this is what I really want to know: Where in the hell is Waldo—a.k.a. Abraham?

Oy vey.

I realize I may in fact be drunk, so I slam the lid of my laptop shut, and it makes a sound like it's letting all the air out of its computerized soul. I laugh at this. I look out the window, and it's raining again. I cup my chin inside my palm, and I bet each one of these guys is probably ringing in the New Year with the one they love.

# Time and Money

I'VE GOT MOLD ON THE HOUSEBOAT AND HAVE TO MOVE the hell out of there as soon as possible because it can harm the baby and our lungs, and on top of this I'm having problems with work, and I'm around the corner at the Waterbar. Can you meet me for a drink after your last patient? Please?"

I'm almost at a loss for words.

But I call her back and say, "Give me an hour, Violet. Are you okay?"

"I've been better. Get here when you get here. And thanks, girl."

Mold?

Right after I finish with my last patient, Marina taps on my door. I tell her to come on in. She stands there and crosses her arms. Her hair is up in a big black knot. "Guess who just quit without giving any notice?"

"Jamie. I'm surprised she lasted this long. Did she say why?"

"You don't even want to know, Doc."

"I do since you put it that way."

"She's moving to Hollywood to become an actress."

I try not to laugh but I can't help it. "At least she won't be needing a reference from us. Well, you know what to do. See if you can find us somebody with a personality this time."

"Will do. Nobody liked her anyway. And she's going to starve down there. Have a good evening, Doc."

And out she goes, but before she has a chance to close the door, Lily pokes her head in.

"Got a minute?"

"I do. Meeting a friend for dinner in about an hour, but if it's important, sit."

"It can wait until tomorrow," she says. But the somber look on her face tells me this may not be true.

"Talk to me, Lily. What's going on?"

She sits down and crosses her legs. Through the opening of her lab coat, I can see her cobalt lace top and the floral slacks with rhinestones surrounding each petal. Her orange heels match one of the flowers. She leans forward and places her left hand on the desk.

"My parents haven't been doing so well."

"I'm sorry to hear that, Lily."

"I know. My mom's seventy-seven, and her dementia is at the point where I can't care for her at home anymore. My dad's been fighting me, but he has to have a hip replacement. So all this is to say I'm going to need to take about a month off to manage all the changes that need to happen since I'm the only one who can do it."

"Do whatever you need to for your parents, Lily."

"I just want to find a good place for my mom. I don't know what my dad's going to do without her there. I really don't. He's been postponing this hip replacement for so long that now he's having a hard time getting around."

"How soon, honey?"

"Well, that's the thing I'm not sure about right now. Suffice it to say in the next two weeks for sure, because I can get Dad scheduled, but I'm going to visit a number of facilities before deciding which one'll be best for my mom. I also think I should get a temp to help Marina let all my patients know I'll be away and reschedule. How's all this sounding to you?"

"The office should be the least of your concerns. Marina and I will handle it. You do what you need to do, Lily. If it were my mother, I wouldn't give this a second thought. Take as much time as you need."

"Did you have any plans in the next month or so? Because I can try to postpone it for maybe a week."

"No, nothing that can't wait," I say.

She stands up. "Let me ask you something, and be honest with me."

"I'm always honest, Lily."

"You ever thought about not practicing one day?"

I'm thrown for a loop by this, and without thinking I just say, "Yes. I've thought about it."

"So have I. What would you do instead?"

"Not real sure. Why'd you ask me this?"

"Just curious, because depending on what happens with my parents' health in the next year or so, I might want to sell my interest in the partnership."

"Really? You've thought that far ahead?"

"Haven't you?"

"As a matter of fact, I have. But let's talk more about this when you get back."

I give her a hug and return to my office. When my cell moves across my desk I answer it. "I'm walking out the door right now!"

"Georgia, it's me, Percy. Happy New Year!"

"Happy New Year to you, too, Percy."

"Sounds like I've caught you at a bad time."

"No. Talk to me."

"Well, I'd like to first thank you for agreeing to the cost. It's usually such a challenge convincing sellers just how important it is to make their home look as amazing as possible to potential buyers."

"I'm a believer, Percy."

He laughs. "Okay, so did you not see my e-mail?"

I scroll down my in-box, and there it is.

"Sorry, it's been busy around here. Just tell me what it says, Percy. I need to be out the door in ten minutes."

"Well, I've got great news! All of the materials are in, and I've even hired a new assistant who's a godsend, so we can get started as soon as three or four days from now."

"What?"

"I knew you'd be excited to hear this! You don't have to do a thing except pack, because we'll schedule the movers, and we know what needs to go in storage. But the other even better news is that because all our ducks are now in a row, we can have you back in your fully staged home in seven to ten days."

"You mean completely finished?"

"Yes! Aren't you thrilled?"

"I'm overjoyed," I say, trying to sound enthusiastic. "But, Percy, I think I'm going to need about a week to make some arrangements."

"I totally understand. Still, read over the e-mail. Get back to me tomorrow, and you have a great evening, and thank you so very much for your patience, Georgia. I can't wait to get started!"

Well.

I sit here and don't move. I'm trying to process what has just happened in the space of ten minutes. If Lily's going to be out of the office for at least a month and she's probably not even leaving for another two weeks, then this also means Percy could conceivably be finished before she even leaves, which also means I have to find somewhere to live, and this also means I won't be able to go on any train ride anytime soon.

Shit.

It's now raining nine-millimeter bullets, and I don't know if it makes much sense for me to meet Violet, but she'll have a stroke if I use rain as an excuse for not coming. I valet-park. When I spot Violet inside, I stroll over. She looks like she's in a trance, staring at the tropical fish in one of the floor-to-ceiling aquariums.

"Earth to Violet," I say, and when she turns, it's hard to believe those cool little porcupine quills are really her hair. One day I'm going to burn all my wigs.

"I'm surprised you came out in all this," she says, and lets her arm sway and float like she's Vanna White showing a vowel or a consonant. "I was waiting for you to cancel."

"It's just rain," I say. "Besides, I love this place, and I might just stay in the city tonight. I don't feel like driving in this. So talk to me, Violet."

"Talk," she sighs.

"I ordered you my drink of choice, and they're bringing over some oysters even if you don't feel like eating them. Sit."

And I sit. "So tell me what's going on? This obviously isn't just about mold on the houseboat."

"Nothing and everything."

"Look, V. I didn't drive over here in fucking torrential rain to play guessing games with you. Talk to me."

"Mold is inside the walls and beneath the floors of my entire houseboat. As you know, it can be deadly, so I have to get Velvet and my unborn grandchild out of there immediately."

"Then let's find you a new place!"

She stares at me so hard that her eyeballs look like they're going to pop out.

"What?"

"I'm having financial difficulties."

"What kind of financial difficulties?"

"What difference does it make? How many types are there?"

"Look, Violet, either you're way ahead of me or you've lost me."

"I need a loan."

"How much of a loan?"

"Ten thousand."

I almost cut myself on the oyster shell. It's right up there with asking me to cosign for that Range Rover because she was already overextended.

"I just spent way too much having my house staged, Violet."

"Which was a complete waste of money."

"Oh, so I should've asked if my sports-attorney girlfriend might need it?"

"I said it's a loan."

"What is it you do with your money, Violet? Tell me that, would you?"

"Ever heard of college tuition?"

"Ever heard of fathers?"

"Ever heard of defaulting on student loans and getting behind in mortgage payments and being too embarrassed to tell your friends because they'll get on your case and interrogate you about what you've done to ruin your credit and then have nowhere else to turn but them?"

"Ever considered making your daughter get her own apartment and maybe that thing called a job and not buying her luxury cars and the latest of everything?"

"She's my daughter."

"She's also twenty-five."

I down my mojito. "I don't get it, Violet. You're a fucking sports attorney!"

"Not anymore."

"What!"

"I'm under investigation by the bar for purportedly violating two codes of professional conduct."

"Are you serious?"

She nods but doesn't look at me. She's staring at the empty shells. "Yes."

"For doing what?"

"It's total bullshit."

"Answer the question, Violet."

"For purportedly accepting gifts from a client or two and for sexual misconduct, and I'm not getting into any details. I'm going to fight it."

"Really? So you're sitting here saying you didn't do any of this shit?"

"Everybody does it but I'm just being singled out."

"Oh, so the bar doesn't like you, is that it?"

"I don't need a lecture, Georgia. I'm just trying to figure out my next steps and how to do what you're doing."

"Which is what?"

"Reinventing yourself."

"Who said I was trying to reinvent myself?"

"You're a middle-aged woman attempting to sell your beautiful home for no legitimate reason except that you're bored and trying to start a new career when the one you have is perfectly fine, and then to top it off you're looking up all your old boyfriends hoping you can hook back up with one of them since you can't seem to find one right here in the Bay Area."

"How many drinks have you had?"

"Not enough."

"So I'm not even going to address what you just said. But back to your request. I can't afford to lend you ten thousand dollars right now, Violet, especially since my own financial future might be tenuous."

She rolls her eyes at me.

"When do you think you might be able to pay me back?"

"How in the hell do I know?"

"I could do five."

"That won't cut it."

"You're really scaring me, Violet. You've just laid some heavy-duty shit on me, and a few minutes ago my partner did the exact same thing, which means I'm going to have to postpone my so-called reinvention, as if you care. What did you do with the ten grand you borrowed from Wanda?"

"I told her not to tell you!"

"Well, she told me. So what are you going to do about it? We love your stupid ass, and you can take my offer or leave it."

"Wanda and her big fucking mouth. You know what? I'm done with both of you bitches."

I stand up after this. "I'm not hungry. And I don't think you should drive home in this rain," I say.

"I drive a fucking Range Rover," she says, standing up, and I plop back down.

"Look. I said I'd lend you five thousand."

"I'm not going to beg for your help. And as of this moment, this friendship is officially over."

And she storms out.

I've barely had a chance to process what Lily and Percy have told me, and now in the very same hour one of my oldest friends has just laid some hard-core shit on me by throwing a temper tantrum worthy of the twins. Violet's got a lot of nerve. But she's been pulling similar stunts like this for years. She thinks the world revolves around her and her needs. She never asks what anyone else might need. And she's not drunk. She's dramatic. But I'm about to put a few away until I simmer down. This is all too much to process at once.

I have one more mojito, call the Hyatt and a taxi, and send Frankie a text telling her what's going on with the staging and why she should call Aunt Wanda. I also tell her I'm feeling a little under the weather and not sure if it's contagious, so I'm going to spend the night at the Hyatt.

In the morning I don't feel like going to work, so I call in sick. I also don't want to go home. So I don't. I call this a vacation, but I think it's probably better known as a breakdown.

I tell Marina the truth. She says, "I've been there, too, Doc. Sometimes you just need to pause. And it's not like your patients are sick. Just stock up on the Splenda for me."

I put on the terry-cloth bathrobe and fall across the bed and look up at the ceiling. For some stupid reason, there are tears falling from my eyes, so I wipe them with the sash. But then here comes more of them, and I decide to just let them roll. I need to feel what I feel and stop pretending I don't feel it.

A few months ago, I was hopeful. Excited. I was going on a train ride. I was selling my home. I was trying to decide when it would make sense to tell Lily I want to sell my partnership. I was thinking about when and how to consider starting a whole new career. I was even thinking about taking classes that might not add up to anything. I was going to start exercising. I was thinking of looking up old loves just to see how they were doing, to make amends, to let them know I hadn't forgotten them. Maybe acknowledge what I might have learned.

And here I am holed up in a hotel room acting like my world is caving in on me or about to end when neither is true.

On day three I perk up. My pity party was fun, but it's over.

I clean out the tub and soak for an hour in lavender bath crystals. I put on a clean robe. I throw my wig in the trash and wash my hair. I don't wash out the conditioner. I put the Do Not Disturb tag on the door and realize I'm hungry. I stare at the bag of Lay's potato chips staring back at me and reach for a big green apple instead. To my surprise, it's tasty. I get a hundred-dollar bottle of sparkling water from the minibar and sit down at the desk and open my laptop and am astounded when I see I actually have four comments.

The first is from Saundra Lee Jones, a girl I went to middle and high school with in Bakersfield. She looks worse than I do. I didn't like her because she was shady. She would smile in my face and then talk about me like a dog behind my back to someone else who also didn't like her, but she didn't know it, and they'd run back and tell me what she said. It was always about me acting like I was so smart. But I *was* smart. Or how nice my parents dressed me, but I couldn't help it if we weren't poor. And how many boys liked me, even some Mexican and white boys, which apparently made her feel like scratching her fingernails on that green chalkboard, something she actually did on quite a few occasions. My hair was thick and long, and hers was stringy and thin, which made her complain about why ponytails were overrated. I was also a good dancer, and Saundra had issues with rhythm, which is why she always stepped on her partners' toes and preferred not to slow-dance unless it was unavoidable. Saundra also didn't like being black.

> Hi there, Georgia! I finally found you! Just wanted to say hello and wondered if you were planning on attending our 40th high school reunion coming up late August, since you've missed all the other ones except the tenth, if memory serves me correctly. From your picture, let's hope we'll both have lost a few pounds by then. It would be nice to catch up. I live in New Orleans. I never had children, but my most recent husband of five years passed on Christmas Day of 2008. We were late bloomers, but he was my sole mate. I see you're an optometrist. I skipped college, but I do enjoy selling cars. I'd never figure you'd go the medical route, although it's an honorable profession. You seemed suited for something more flamboyant. Hope to see you in Bakersfield! Be in touch, but I doubt if I'll hear from you, because I know you didn't like me forty years ago. Maybe you will now that we're both old.

Once a bitch. Always a bitch.
Since I'm not dead, I feel obligated to respond.

>Good to hear from you, Saundra! Thanks for reaching out!
>Looking forward to seeing you at the reunion.

I scroll down to the next person I do recognize. It's my daughter Frankie.

>Mom, what up? Say something to the world! Let them know
>you exist! What are you thinking about? What bothers you?
>What do you find fascinating? What's that itch you have yet
>to scratch? Who do you love?

Is she serious? Why in the world would I put any of this on Facebook for people I don't know and who don't know me to read? I hit the Reply button.

>Because if I wanted to share my personal feelings about
>anything I certainly wouldn't put it on social media to be
>scrutinized. And who cares what I care about and what I
>think? Anyway, I am in the process of giving that itch some
>thought. I love you. And whomever else I may or may not
>love is nobody's damn business. Please don't do this again.
>Next time just call or text me. Love, Mom.

Next is Mona Kwon. What on earth is *she* doing on Facebook?

>Hello, Dr. Young! I can't believe you finally got on Facebook!
>You will find it exciting and a wonderful way to interact with
>friends and strangers who can become friends. Or perhaps
>find your third husband!! ☺ I appreciate the good care and
>attention you give my eyes! And I totally dig all the cool
>frames you sell, especially my new Tom Fords! ☺ See you
>soon!

When did Mona buy a pair of Tom Fords? And when did she get hip? And how in the hell does she know how many husbands I've had?

I know that Marina didn't tell her. This is one more reason I don't trust social media. And sometimes even Google. It's like people can peek right through your windows even when the curtains are drawn.

I decide it's best not to respond to Mona. Her comments and Frankie's were posted months ago, and Mona hasn't mentioned it. If she does, I'll just play dumb.

Right below Mona is a picture of a well-preserved man whose name is Warren Flowers. I have no idea who this guy is. Maybe he thinks I'm a different Georgia Young.

> It's been centuries, Georgia, and from your photo I see you're faring well. Not sure if you remember me, but to remind you, I was one of the pharmacists at the hospital where you interned back in the day. I always said hello when you got your car out of the parking structure. At any rate, I see you still live in the Bay Area, as do I. I'm now at Walgreens in Walnut Creek.

I do not recall ever meeting Warren, not even after staring at his picture and trying to remove the creases in his face and the gray hair. I delete his comment, because if I don't remember him, why should I try to?

WE HIRE A new tech. We've never had a black one before. Don't know why. He's over six feet tall and weighs about the same as me. He wears suspenders on top of shirts that will be a different color on the color wheel almost daily; Urkel plaid or pin-striped pants with white socks and expensive loafers; add to all of this some shiny manicured dread-locks that look like a container of extra-large black french fries from McDonald's and white-framed Prada glasses, making him look very British. The first thing he says to me is weird: "I like girls." I just say, "Suit yourself." His name is Mercury Jones. Yes, he tells me, it's his real name. Marina loves him. He's also a part-time student at the Academy of Art. Major: digital illustration.

During our five-minute interview, I asked him why he wanted to work here. "Because I need a job," he said, and smiled. He then went on to tell me he took a year to get certified as an optometric technician mostly because he wanted to get a respectable and somewhat interesting job that allowed him to deal with the public and in an environment that was aesthetically pleasing and, in this case, one that was within walking distance from the academy, where he'll get his degree in two years, which is how long he hoped he'd be able to work here.

I already like Mercury. Mostly for his honesty, but I also dig the way he dresses. And being a tech is really 50 percent public relations, 25 percent salesmanship, and 25 percent anything else that needs to be done. There are not a lot of technical skills needed to be a technician, but I'm relieved we're now all one big happy optometric family.

# Loss of Use

FRANKIE AND HUNTER MOVE INTO WANDA AND NELSON'S guesthouse two days before Percy starts doing his thing. I decide to just stay at the Hyatt, because they've given me a corporate rate. I go home and pack enough things to hold me for a week or so, including my chocolate penis. I take one last glance around just to remember what my home looked like before it gets de-Georgia-ed. Violet cashed my check without so much as a thank-you. Wanda hasn't heard a peep out of her either. I'm pissed at her, but I hope she's okay.

After a week I'm already tired of living in a hotel. I call Wanda.

"You wanna meet me in the city for dinner?"

"Why and where?"

"Toulouse Petit. Because I haven't seen you since your dinner party."

"That's not the real reason. Should I invite Nelson?"

"No."

"Something's going on, then. What is it?"

"I'm not saying."

"Come on, Georgia, just tell me, what's the occasion?"

"Didn't you say you remembered Eric?"

"Of course I do. He's one of the Talented Five. And of the bunch, he's the one who got away. Why?"

"He owns Toulouse Petit."

"Get the hell outta here! How'd you find that out?"

"Take a wild guess."

"Facebook. He sure has good taste. Get it?"

"No, I don't."

"So are you going to corner him or what, girl?"

"Get serious. I have no idea what I'm going to say, but I don't re-member ever seeing him when we've eaten there."

"Maybe he was back in the kitchen. Anyway, I'll make the reserva-tion so we keep it on the down low. Seven work for you?"

"Yes, it does. But there's also the possibility of potentially good news. And don't ask. I'll see you there."

I do not know what has possessed me to do this, but I'm not going to back out or get cold feet. I hadn't really thought about the likelihood or even the possibility of seeing any of these men face-to-face. I decide to write Eric a note, because there's no way I'd put anything this per-sonal on Facebook. I use a soft font. Ironically, it's called Georgia.

> Hello, Eric! I just learned that you're the owner of the amazing restaurant I've been patronizing since its opening! I've never seen you there, and I'm heading over for dinner this evening. In case you're not there, I just wanted to let you know how proud I am of you, and I'm thrilled that you've done so well for yourself. I also want you to know that I've never forgotten you, our short but amazing time together, but mostly the joy we shared when we were younger even though you kicked me to the curb so you could attend that chef school in Paris and of course I had this thing called a job, but it appears you made the right decision! I looked you up on Facebook, but you don't offer much personal information. You still look good. Healthy. And I hope this means you're happy. Would love to see you! I've aged! Estelle is almost thirty, and my younger daughter is twenty-two. I'm twice divorced. So that's my story, and I'm sticking to it! I'm enclosing my card. My office is minutes away, so maybe we could have coffee or I could get a free meal out of you! If I don't hear back from you, I'll understand that you probably have a good reason. At any rate, just wanted to tell you how happy I am for you,

knowing that your dreams did come true. Here's a bear hug
for old times' sake. Warmly, Georgia Young.


P.S. BTW: No one has ever called me baby the way you did!


Okay. So it's not a note, it's a letter, but if he's there and available, I'll
give him the abbreviated version to his face. If he's not there, I'll simply
leave it with the maître d'. I put it in a sealed white envelope and write
his name: Eric Francois.

I do my best to look as good as I possibly can. I wear light blue.
Black pumps. My hair is now kinky-curly and short. Of course Wanda
beats me here. She waves to me like she hasn't seen me in years.

The restaurant is dramatic. Wood and rattan and floor lamps and
floor-to ceiling tinted windows. Red velvet drapes hang in front of
some tables, giving them privacy. We sit out in the open.

"He's not here," she says.

"Who'd you ask?"

"That gorgeous hostess over there with the short blond Afro."

I turn to look. She is striking.

"Maybe *I* should go blond!" I say.

Wanda sucks her teeth.

"Will he be here sometime this evening?"

"Nope. Apparently he's a marathoner and is in some country being
Forrest Gump."

I let out a sigh of relief. "BTW, I'm not drinking tonight."

"Me either," she says.

We order.

Wanda: A yellow beet salad. Cauliflower, asparagus, and white
truffle soup with Dungeness crab.

Me: Heirloom tomato salad. Barbecued shrimp with hominy grits.
We share a roasted duck.

"So aren't you excited that your house is finally going on the market?"

"Yes and no."

"I know it screws up your train ride, but this is the reason God invented vacations, Georgia! You can still catch that midnight train to whenever and wherever the hell you're planning to go. Choo-choo!"

"Vancouver. And all across Canada to Toronto."

"Why in the world do you want to go to Canada?"

"Because I want to. We've already had this conversation, so please stop asking me."

"Well, you could probably get the same results after five days on the beach in Cabo. Just sayin'."

I roll my eyes at her. Our non-drinks come.

"I'm skipping the subject. So now that your house is going on the market what would you do if somebody offered to buy it, like, immediately?"

"I'd have to move out."

"And go where?"

"Again, we've had this conversation."

"But I don't remember where you ended up. Was it Dubai?"

"Ha, ha."

"Answer the question."

"I'll cross that bridge when I get to it."

"I think you should just keep your ass right here in Oakland, because it's not only a beautiful place to live, as you well know, but it's also ethnically diverse and culturally alive and it's full of smart, educated people and just enough crazies to keep it real."

"Then why are you and Nelson leaving?"

"I've already told you. We want to slow our roll, golf every day, and breathe in nothing but hot air."

When our food arrives, we finally stop talking and clean our plates. We would eat them, too, for the flavor alone. I wish Eric had been here so we could tell him this to his face.

"Have you thought about when you're going to sell your partnership? I mean, have you discussed it with Lily yet?"

"Vaguely. She's got a lot going on with her mom and dad. When she gets back."

"Something is missing in that chile. Why hasn't she ever been married?"

"I don't know."

"And she dresses like a ho, and I bet she doesn't even have sex."

"Well, she spends a lot of time online."

"Cybersex is not real sex."

"Anyway, enough about Lily. I signed up for an upholstery class."

"For a what class?"

"Upholstery?"

"Why?"

"Why not?"

"When was the last time you upholstered something?"

"Never. Which is why I'm takin' the class, Wanda. Duh."

"This sounds even more boring than being an optometrist."

"Check, please!"

"Hold your thongs! Did you paint that stool yet?"

"I can't mess up the garage now!"

"Finally, a valid reason and not one of your bogus excuses. Okay. So. This may sound stupid, but I'm going to suggest it anyway. Why don't you whip out that nineteenth-century sewing machine and make some damn pillows. That's what you should be doing. Sewing. I know you could sell those suckers."

"Sewing is messy, too."

She shakes her head like she gives.

"This food was almost too good. Tell him that if and when he gets in touch."

As we're on our way out, who's walking in the front door with at least five scarves wrapped around his neck, wearing purple glasses, with his arm draped around the shoulders of a girl who looks just like him? Of course it's Mercury, who has the biggest smile on his face when he sees me, and he opens his long arms for me to walk into. "Hello, Dr. Young! So nice to see you in real clothes! This is my sister, Neptune, and yes, our parents were on something. How are you?" he asks after he lets me go.

"I'm glad to meet you, Neptune, glad to see you, Mercury, and this is my BFF, Wanda."

"Nice to meet you, Ms. Wanda. Anyway, see you under those

fluorescent lights tomorrow, Dr. Young," he says, and they go to sit at the bar. Wanda walks outside to get her car, and I hand the envelope to the maître d' and ask if she would be kind enough to give it to Eric for me.

"Will he know who you are?" she asks.

"Yes. I think he will."

ERIC BACKED INTO my bumper by accident.

He had just moved into the building I'd lived in for years with Michael and Estelle, who was four at the time.

We both got out to see how much damage had been done.

"I hope you have insurance," he said. "I'm Eric. Nice to meet you."

"I hope *you* have insurance. I'm Georgia. I don't think this is a good way for us to meet, *Eric.*"

"Well, I'll let you slide, because I don't see a scratch."

"I don't either, to be honest."

"I think it's because we were meant to meet. Aren't you on the fourth floor? You live with your gorgeous little girl?"

"How do you know so much about me?"

"Because I'm a stalker who lives on the fifth floor, and I see you taking her to school, and I know you've been divorced a year and counting, and I'd like to welcome you to the divorce club."

"So you weren't lying about the stalker thing."

"No, a few neighbors gave me the 411 on everybody in the building. Anyway, maybe we could grab a bite sometime."

"Who are you?"

"I'm a man who wants to cook you dinner."

And that was how it started.

He was a southern gentleman.

Born and raised in New Orleans.

Married four years, no children.

He said she "drop-kicked" him to the curb for another man.

He was hurt.

He recovered.

He forgave her.

He said anger is a termite to your heart.

He became my insecticide.

He showed me how to forget to remember what hurts.

He was honest.

He offered me tenderness.

He brushed my hair.

He helped me live in the present.

He made me laugh out loud.

He admired me for being smart.

He was thoughtful toward my daughter.

He did not sleep in my bed unless Estelle was not home.

He talked to me about my hopes.

He talked to me about his. That one day he wanted to open his own restaurant.

Michael didn't like him. And he didn't like Michael.

Ma liked him right off the bat. "This one is worth keeping," she said.

Nine months went by fast.

He said he loved me.

I told him I loved him, too.

But when he was accepted into a famous cooking school in Paris, I knew he had to go.

And he knew I couldn't.

We had a marvelous farewell.

I felt lighter.

We both declared how glad we were that he backed into me. That we were able to part ways without leaving a scratch or a dent.


"DOC, THERE'S a woman here to see you, and she says it'll only take a minute."

"What's she look like?"

"Like a movie star. She has a short platinum Afro and earrings to die for. What do you want me to do?"

Now I'm worried, because I know it's the maître d' from Eric's restaurant. How does she know who I am and where I work?

Oh, Lord, this means she opened my letter and read it! Goddamnit. Now I'm both angry and worried that maybe something happened to him, or maybe she's got a gun and is here to blow my brains out. But she didn't strike me as being crazy.

"You can send her on back."

A few seconds later, in walks the homecoming queen from the eighties. I stand up to greet her.

"Hello," I say. "Have a seat. I remember you from Toulouse, of course. Is something wrong?"

"I'll just stand, if you don't mind," and she reaches inside her big black purse and pulls out the unopened envelope I'd given her to give to Eric.

"Is something wrong?" I ask again.

"I'm not sure. Eric is my husband. We've been happily married for twenty-two years, and I'm just curious about what's in this envelope and if it's something I need to know about."

I'm shaking my head.

"Not at all. Please. Sit."

And she does. And I tell her how I know her husband and what I'm in the process of doing and that her presence at the restaurant and now here has answered my biggest question.

"And what's that?" she asks.

"That he's happily married and to a beautiful woman."

"Thank you, Dr. Young. And my name is Sofia. I think what you're doing is admirable, and to be honest there're a few skeletons in *my* closet it might pay me to revisit."

"Well, I only have a few left. I didn't mean to cause any problems, and I apologize if my gesture has offended you in any way or made you uncomfortable."

"Not at all. I was just curious why a beautiful sister was giving me a confidential envelope to give my husband, but I respect his privacy, and had it not been for that young kid, I wouldn't have known who you were or where to find you."

"Mercury."

"Believe me, I know all about Mercury. Anyway, now that you've explained what you're doing, I'm fine with it. And as soon as Eric gets back from Switzerland—yes, I said Switzerland—he races all over the world, Dr. Young—I'll give him your letter, and I hope the two of you will be able to have dinner or something, but just not at Toulouse Petit."

She stands up.

"Thank you, Sofia. And please call me Georgia."

"Good-bye, Georgia. You have a blessed day."

And she leaves. And I feel much better.

A few minutes later, I hear a tap-tap at my door. "Dr. Young, I have something for you," Marina says.

"Come on in."

And when she does, she hands me that envelope.

# Previously Accepted Limitations
# No Longer Apply

I CAN'T BELIEVE YOU FINALLY SAID YES," JAMES SAYS.

"I've had good reasons for saying no," I say.

"Well, I hope I don't give you any more. Cheers," he says, and presses his wineglass against mine.

He looks better than I remember. Even in broad daylight. We're at a seafood restaurant in Jack London Square. There are all kinds of boats rocking in their berths and pelicans marching up and down the dock.

"So," James says, crossing his arms. He's wearing a pink polo shirt that I think is sexy and brave. Nice broad shoulders and solid muscles stare at me. "Do you date much?"

"No. How about you?"

"Depends on the month or year," he says, and chuckles. "I thought I was in a serious relationship but learned over the holidays that her perception of serious differed from mine."

"Sorry to hear it."

"Don't be. I'm a free agent hoping to find a new team, if you don't mind that terrible analogy."

"Finding the right 'team' isn't easy as we get a little older."

His thick eyebrows go up as if to say, *Ya think?*

We smile. Nibble on sourdough and take our time eating our big bowls of clam chowder.

"How's your son?"

"Wow. Thanks for asking. He's fine. He likes Berklee. Says it fits."

I don't really know what to talk about without getting too personal, and even though he's pleasant, he's not exactly arousing my curiosity or lifting the hem of my dress so far.

"How do you feel about camping?" he asks.

"You mean in a cabin or a tent?"

"Do you have a preference?"

"I prefer hotels, but it's because I'm afraid of what lurks in the great outdoors."

"What about water?" he asks, pointing to the boats. "How do you feel about floating—or I should say cruising—up the coast?"

"I'm open. Why, do you have a boat?"

"I do. A cabin cruiser. Small, but it's good for my soul. Operating on hearts takes a lot out of you, and boating is one of my sources of comfort."

"I'd go on your boat."

"Really?"

"But not too far. I have to be able to see the shoreline."

"Does this mean we might have a second date?"

"We haven't finished this one yet," I say.


"AND?" WANDA ASKS after I tell her I went on a real date.

"He was pleasant enough."

"Pleasant? What the hell does that mean?"

"He was nice. I didn't feel any sparks, but he's a good conversation-alist."

"What'd you talk about?"

"Life."

"Well, that pretty much narrows it down. What else?"

"I told him in less than five minutes that I was selling my house, but I didn't bother to get into leaving my practice, because it just didn't feel appropriate."

"Good. He probably wouldn't understand anyway. So do you want to fuck him or not?"

"Probably. When I go on his boat."

"Well, at least you'll already be rocking, so you'll get a head start."

JAMES HELPS ME onto his boat, which is really a yacht. He's wearing white everything, including the baseball cap with a big *A* on the front, and I don't dare ask what team it's for.

"Welcome aboard," he says. "You look lovely in yellow."

"Thank you," I say. "It feels a little bright."

"You need a hat," he says, and whips out one just like his from a bin under the long blue seat cushions. He puts it on me. He smells good.

"This is a big boat," I say, because I can't think of anything intelligent.

"I'm a big man," he says, and laughs. "I sleep on it from time to time. Go on below deck and take a look. You might want to put your life vest on now, too. I set it on the table for you."

"Aye, aye, sir." I head down into an area that is sleek and modern and full of smooth wood. It's equipped with everything you'd have in a studio apartment but in miniature, except the bed. It's a real queen. I put on my orange life vest, grab a nectarine and a bottle of sparkling water, and head back up when I hear the engine.

"How much time do you have?" he asks.

"How much time do we need?"

"That's a pretty loaded question, but I like to go out the bay, then out through the Carquinez Strait and up the Sacramento River, so it could take three or four hours if that's okay with you."

"That's fine. But what about when we get hungry?"

"All taken care of."

And out we go.

It's breathtaking, of course, and other boats, especially sailboats, pass by, and everybody waves. The swells are thick and sloshy, and after an hour we eat fancy finger sandwiches, sweet pickles, cheese, dried fruit, and have a glass of wine.

"I've got some great news to share, even though you might not find it as thrilling as I do," James announces.

"I'm listening. I love good news."

"I've just gotten a research grant, so I get to spend four months in India."

"India?"

He nods as the boat rocks from side to side. "Yes. I'm thrilled."

"Well, it sounds like an amazing opportunity. How soon?"

"We have to work out the dates. But because I have my own practice, I've got colleagues I trust who'll cover for me."

"Cool," I say, and try to stand up.

"You want to steer?"

"I don't think so."

"Come on up. It's fun. It's like driving a car."

He takes my hand, and I step up. When I get close, he gently ushers me in front of the steering wheel and stands behind me and puts his long arms around me, takes my hands under his and places them on the metal rim and leaves them there. He's warm and he feels good. All of this feels good.

"See how easy it is?"

He leans down and kisses me on the cheek and then softly on my neck. This feels even better.

"I don't want to lose control," I say.

"It would be okay with me."

And for the next ten minutes, I do my best to keep my eyes on the water and the boats around us and the hills to the right until I feel my belly turning flips. As I'm about to say, *I think I'm getting sick,* I throw up all over the steering wheel and let go.

"It's the waves," he says, and grabs a towel. "Don't worry, this happens. But I know how you're feeling, and I'll get us back to shore as soon as possible."

And he does.

"GEORGIA, GREAT NEWS! *We've got some very interested buyers who've seen the house twice. They want to come by today about eleven just to take one more look at the backyard, and if they can do what they're hoping to do back there, they said they'll make an offer today.*"

I listen to the message again.

My heart is beating like a snare drum.

Amen did say "today," like in today, didn't he? I look at the little clock on my phone. It's 12:19. Shit! I play the second message.

*"Georgia, when I didn't hear back from you, I took the liberty of bringing the couple over this morning, since there was no need to go inside. I hope you don't mind, but the good news is that they've made an offer."*

I call Amen back, with some wariness because I don't quite believe this. It was too easy.

"Well, hello, Georgia! I was hoping to hear from you right away. I apologize for going into the backyard without your permission, but I knew they were serious, and they had to catch a plane back to Seattle. Aren't you excited we got an offer so soon in this market? I certainly am."

"Should I start packing?" I ask, obviously with a ton of sarcasm.

"Not yet. I have to tell you that their offer is below our asking price, which I explained I'd have to discuss with you after telling them that you're not underwater nor are you under any pressure to sell."

"How much below the asking price?"

"About sixty thousand. But of course buyers always come in low for wiggle room."

"Wiggle room? This is insulting."

"I agree, but it's a start. As soon as I get their app, we can go from there."

"They live in Seattle?"

"They do."

"Why're they relocating?"

"Divorce."

"Then who is 'they'?"

"They're now a blended family. Not married yet, but each has a child from a previous marriage."

"How old are they?"

"Who? The kids or the buyers?"

"Well, the kids will give me some idea how old the parents are. Not that I really care, but if they're little, this hillside isn't the best place for them to play."

"The kids are seven and nine. The parents are in their mid-forties.

I should know more in the next day or so, but sometimes these negotiations can take a little longer. Keep your fingers crossed that we can make this happen."

"They're crossed," I say, and shake them out as soon as I press End. I close the garage door and enter the house I'm now grateful I don't have to speed-clean.

I suppose I should be happy, but as I walk down the hallway and into the entry, I sit on these metal stairs and look around. Am I going to have to move out of my home of thirteen years for real? Where am I going to live? And how soon will I have to move? And who *are* these people that want to live in my house? Sleep in my bedroom? Swim in my pool? Park in my garage? Use my toilet? Hell, I was just starting to get used to the idea that it was even for sale.

And although it doesn't look like my home anymore, it is. And it has a history. I've lived in here with my children and a husband, and now they're all gone. There are thousands of memories like brown ghosts in every room. I'm beginning to wonder if I really want to move. The whole idea has been like dreaming out loud, but this is no dream. Is this how it feels when you get what you asked for?

I don't hear from Amen for three days.

On the fourth day, I call him.

"What's going on, Amen? I thought I'd hear from you by now."

"I thought you would, too. I was just about to call you, as I've finally heard from the buyers—who aren't buying."

"What?"

"They changed their minds."

"But why?"

"Their broker claims they found another property in the same area that better suits their needs."

"Oh, really. Just like that?"

"Just like that."

"Wow. Well, I imagine this is how a bride might feel being left at the altar."

"I'm really sorry, Georgia. But as brokers we really have no control how buyers decide what home they love enough to marry."

"Well, I'll call the movers and tell them to hold off." I follow it with a chuckle.

"You don't sound all that disappointed."

"Because I'm used to disappointment."


I'M ON INTERSTATE 5 heading down to Bakersfield. I needed to get away from my faux home but also to see Ma and Grover. Apparently they decided to postpone the nuptials until after Grover recovers from hip surgery, and they've been shacking up because he couldn't be left alone. Ma told me she does not sleep in the same bed with him, as he's too fragile. He's got one of those hospital beds right next to hers. God understands, she said.

When I hear the first few chords of "Slave Driver" by Taj Mahal, I know it's Frankie. I'm hoping the baby's not here early, but if he or she is, I'll turn this car around.

"Are you at or on your way to the hospital?"

"No, Mom! The baby's still baking! But I've still got some awesome news to tell you!"

"Then spill it! Nothing like good news, honey."

"Hunter got a job at a start-up in San Francisco, and he's going to be making megabucks, Mom! And guess what else?"

"I'm too happy and excited to guess. Spill it!"

"We just found an adorable little bungalow-type house to rent in Bernal Heights, not far from his job. Is this cool or what?"

"It certainly is. I'm so doggone happy for you two I could shout! Yeah, yeah, yeah!"

"I didn't want you to think we've just been sitting around twiddling our thumbs when we've got a baby on the way. Hunter's very responsible, and we just wanted to wait until we had something solid and concrete to report. I think this qualifies!"

"It certainly does. So will you be able to move before my grandson or granddaughter arrives?"

"How does next week sound?"

"That soon?"

"Yessiree! Where are you now? I called your landline first."

"On the 5 heading to see your grandma and her betrothed!"

"Well, tell them hello and that I love them both! Hugs!"

This is the kind of news that makes me not need music.

After another hour of bumper-to-bumper traffic, I look at my phone and see there's a text from Wanda: *Nelson's not breathing right and feeling pressure in his chest, so the paramedics are taking us to emergency. I'll call you as soon as I know something definitive.*

I stare at the text a few minutes until I hear the trucks behind me start honking. I pull over and call Wanda back.

"Is Nelson okay?"

"I told you I'd call you, Georgia! Yes and no. Apparently he might have had a mild heart attack. But he's going to be okay."

"How do you know that?"

"Because the medic said it was a mild one."

"A medic? They're not doctors!"

"But they have EKG equipment, and they know how to read it. Anyway I don't feel like debating right now, Georgia."

"I'm sorry. But what can I do to help?"

"Just be careful driving, and I'll call you later or tomorrow. Sorry for scaring you. He's going to be fine."

But then I hear her crying.

"I'll see you in a few hours."

# What to Do When You Don't Have a Calling

WISH I HAD A CALLING," I TELL WANDA AS WE SIT ON A bench outside Nordstrom Rack. We're in Petaluma. At one of her favorite outlets, which she dragged me to in an attempt to cheer me up after Amen persuaded me to drop the price on the house by forty thousand dollars, since we haven't had a decent offer in four months. The good news is we're also celebrating Nelson's having made a full recovery. It turns out his blood pressure was off the charts, and he's going to have to get more physical besides just swinging a golf club, and he might even have to start cutting that little blue pill in half and stop trying to be such a sexual tyrant.

"Did you hear what I just said, Wanda?"

"No. Repeat it. My mind is on the dress I saw in this very store last week and didn't buy. I'm pissed because they don't have it in my size, and I should know that beautiful things disappear in seconds when the price is too good to be true. So what were you saying?"

"I said I wish I had a calling."

"Oh, would you please stop whining, Georgia? You're getting on my nerves with this shit," she says cheerfully.

"What shit?"

"Tell me why you quit your little upholstery class?"

"Because it wasn't fun. It was actually boring. The only thing I did like was the staple gun."

"What'd you expect, Martha? You put some new fabric on an old couch or chair. Duh. I told you it sounded about as exciting as watching Korean TV, but you never listen to your smart BFF, so I'm not saying another word about any of your brilliant ideas."

"I don't blame you. I'm getting on my own nerves. Change is hard, and sometimes I think I should just turn to drugs and stay high and not worry about a damn thing."

"Sure, let's pick up some crack on the way home, why don't we?"

"Shut up, Wanda. You don't understand what it feels like to be dissatisfied with yourself. To not know if you're really good at something."

"You know what, Georgia, there are millions of us who don't have a damn calling. And some people just do what they do and keep doing it until they retire and don't worry about it. Some folks don't even know what a fucking calling is."

"I know that, Wanda."

"I mean, either you're born some kind of prodigy or you're not. But some people do get lucky and find what they love doing by accident. I also know for a fact that a lot of people turn their hobbies into careers."

"Not at my age, they don't."

"Look at Martha! She started out on Wall Street and then started decorating her old barn house, or maybe it was just the damn barn, but anyway, then she started baking cookies and shit, and by the time she was in her forties, Martha was cooking her ass off and published that book on hors d'oeuvres and spending Christmas with her, and she got rich, and of course she had that little prison stint for doing what men who do the same fucking thing get away with scot-free, but then Martha came out and went back to doing what she loves, and the rest is history. So don't tell me what can't happen." Wanda then throws her hand up.

"Okay! I get your point. But who would hire someone my age?"

"You know, sometimes, you don't sound like you even went to college, Georgia. That is about the stupidest shit you've said this week. I didn't think you were going to be *looking* for a job."

"I didn't mean it that way."

"Look, huzzy, when you cash in from selling your house and your partnership, you should be okay for a while, don't you think?"

"At this rate there might not be any money from the house, and as long as I get most of my investment back from the practice, you're right, it should buy me some time."

"You don't know how lucky you are. A lot of people would kill to be in your position. And for lack of a better cliché: Rome wasn't built in a day. I don't get the urgency. You need to make something and just have fun making it. Then see what happens."

"I'm taking another class."

"Please don't tell me it's making corny jewelry or lopsided pottery or that boring tie-dye that only babies wear or herbal soap with weeds inside it that makes no bubbles or those musty-smelling aromatherapy candles that stink up the house, because if you do, I'm going to take a macramé and a glass-blowing class, too."

"What do you call your needlepoint?"

"It's called a hobby. But I'm not interested in making more of it than that. Besides, I know that most of them are ugly as hell and serve absolutely no purpose, which is why I let the dogs sleep on them and give most of them to friends like you, who put them in low-traffic areas so as not to hurt my feelings. You have no idea how many of them I donate."

"Then why don't you find another hobby?"

"Because I like this one. It doesn't require much imagination, but it's relaxing, which is invaluable if you ask me."

"That's not a good enough reason if you ask *me*."

"I *didn't* ask you. Look, Georgia, everything you do doesn't have to lead to something bigger. So what class?"

"I'm thinking about furniture restoration."

"Really? That sounds dirty and rough and loud and cancerous and disgusting, and you have to use heavy tools. What about your acrylics?"

I look at her. Then down at my nails.

"Whatever happened to that stool you were going to paint?"

"It's locked in a cabinet in the garage. I can't do any painting out there until I know where I'm going to be living in the near or far-off future."

"Then why don't you get yourself a little studio?"

This time I roll my eyes. "Get real, Wanda. How many stools can a woman paint?"

"Then paint something else! Damn. You are so small-minded, Georgia. I used to think you had vision, but I'm on the verge of losing faith in your ability to think outside the box."

"I need a latte," I say.

"I think I'd much rather have a double shot of gin."

Wanda buys another Golden Girls jogging outfit and a pair of last year's Reeboks but cannot find a dress she likes for some award dinner she has coming up. I don't buy anything.

On the drive home, we stop by a fruit stand.

"Have you spoken to Violet lately?" Wanda asks as we go from fruits to nuts to olives and cheese.

"Nope. She doesn't return my calls."

"You know Velvet had that baby a month ago."

"I figured. What'd she have?"

"A little boy. And he *was* little. Only weighed five pounds."

"And she couldn't tell anybody?" I ask.

"You're still on her shit list."

"Anyway, what's the baby's name?"

"I can't remember it. I think it's a natural disaster or a planet or some kind of vegetation or something. You know how these young kids name their kids after anything."

"Is she working anywhere?"

"I'm not sure, and I'm not sure what she can do if she can't practice law."

"Do you have her address?"

"Yes."

"I want to send something for the baby."

"I already did. From both of us."

She pulls up to the drive-up Starbucks and orders our usual.

"Let's talk about something light," I say.

"I haven't heard you mention any of the Talented Four in months. What happened, you changed your mind?"

"I'm not feeling as enthused about it as I was."

"Why not?"

"Because it was probably a stupid idea."

"That hasn't stopped you before. I never thought it was a stupid idea. I still think it's a very large idea."

"Maybe. But I've got a lot more pressing things going on in my life these days, as you very well know."

"And this makes you special?"

"It's nothing but the past, and it's over."

"Well, what a surprise that is."

"I'm trying to focus more on my future."

"Well, I thought it was you, Ms. Psychology Today, who said your motive was not to try to hook back up with these men but to see how they've fared after all these years and to let them know you hadn't forgotten about them and that you were glad they were a part of your life or some shit like that."

"But I *had* forgotten them. And apparently they've forgotten about me, too."

"How do you know that?"

"Because I'm easy to find."

"Oh, stop, would you? You are really getting on my last nerve today, and here I was trying to cheer your ass up."

"Well, you asked."

"You should think about what Jesus went through, and then maybe you'll understand what real suffering is about and how the past does play a role in our present. Look the rest of the men up, Georgia. Finish what you started."

"You may have a point."

"To be very honest, I really don't care one way or the other, but this was your bright fucking idea, and if you don't look them up—since Nelson isn't acting like he's sick and shut in anymore and I've got a lot of free time on my hands—I might track the bastards down myself and send them a questionnaire, and this is what I'd ask them: *Do you remember a Georgia Young? Was she a good lay? Was she crazy? Did she have a lot of unresolved issues? Did you love her? What made you stop? Was she a bitch? And what the hell happened to you? How are you these days? Did you become successful, or are you a failure? Did you learn anything from her? Have you ever thought about the huzzy after all these years? I mean, has she ever crossed your mind? And if so, would it have killed you to look her up just to tell her, "Hey, how you doing? I hope you're happy and have found your place in the world and a man or a woman to love and treat you the way you deserve to be treated, and I hope you're healthy, and it was nice having you in my life for that little bit of time we spent, and God bless you, Georgia"?*

"Okay! Damn."

THE OFFICE IS QUIET. Everybody's left for the day except Marina and me. We often turn my office into happy hour. White wine.

Marina, who now has midnight blue streaks in her hair that I absolutely love, is twirling a clump of it around and around two fingers. Her lips are red. She takes a sip of her wine and sighs.

"Can you keep a secret, Doc?"

"Sure I can."

"Mercury has to quit, but he's afraid you'll be pissed."

"No I wouldn't. How soon?"

"Like so soon it may have already happened."

"Spit it out, Marina."

"He was offered a position in the men's department at Neiman's that he applied for centuries ago, and he said yes."

"Good for him. So we'll just have to find a replacement. You know I'll miss him. Won't you?"

"We've become quite close."

"How close?"

She rolls her eyes.

"You mean you slept with him?"

She nods, pivots, downs the rest of her wine, winks, and says good night.

But I'm not ready to go just yet.

I'm hungry. So I order Chinese.

I flip through a catalog I picked up outside my local grocery store:

> Lifelong Learning: Personal Enrichment. As thoughts turn to
> warmer days, why not consider doing something just for you?
> Studies, time and again, show that at any age staying active
> both physically and mentally benefits both body and mind.
> Why not sign up for a class just for fun? Thousands of com-
> munity members, your friends and neighbors, have taken and
> continue to take classes through our extension. Sign up! Get
> enlightened!

The yellow booklet is a little more than fifty pages. Knowledge is
cheap. The least expensive class is thirty-nine dollars and the highest is
two hundred. I have to admit I'm impressed by the categories: *Professional Development.* The first course listed is certified in IT networking
to help you decide if you might want to pursue a real career, and it's
offered by Cisco no less. Under *Enrichment,* you can learn how to sew,
make soap and candles, tie-dye, bake and cook and even paint. You
can become the next Ansel Adams: nature photography; learn how
to understand your dreams, clean a house, and even how to stop pro-
crastinating. They have a fiction-writing class that Frankie might like,
and there's beginning belly and tap and line dancing! Decisions! Decisions! If for nothing else, it would give me something interesting to do
on a Saturday morning.

I hear two sounds at once. The buzzer at the front door. And a
*ding* on my computer letting me know I've got an e-mail. I open it, and
there's a notice from Facebook telling me I have a new comment. Not
seen this before. I click to see who it's from and cannot believe my eyes.
Abraham.

> Where have you been for most of my life? Here's my number:
> (415) 555-1155. Please call me sooner than is convenient.

I hear the buzzer again.
Whoever it is, can't they see we're closed?
I'm now hyperventilating.
I start fanning myself like I used to do when I had hot flashes, but

now, like then, it's not helping, so I walk out into the reception area and turn the air up, and standing at the front door is the older Chinese gentleman in his white apron waving my bag in the air. I sprint over and open it. "My apologies. I was on the phone and didn't hear the buzzer."

"No problem, Dr. Young. You must be busy this evening. No more patients, I hope!" And he chortles as he hands me the bag and his little pad with my credit-card receipt. I add the tip, and he says thank you twice and "Have a good night, and don't forget to lock," as he points to the door. I do. And although I usually eat in our tiny lunchroom, I'm so wired right now that the smell of my salt-and-pepper prawns and beef chow fun and garlic spinach is making me nauseous.

I dash back to my office and sit down but jump back up and run to the kitchen and grab a big cup from the cabinet and then a container of vanilla-bean gelato and blood-orange sorbet from the tiny freezer, dig out two medium-size scoops of each, but this time I tiptoe back to my office, sit down with grace, and click on his photograph as I slowly push my chair backward. Which takes me directly to his Facebook page, and there he is, bigger than life on my screen: an older but still-handsome-and-sexy-as-hell version of the young Abraham. I truly don't know what to do, so of course I call Ms. Ghostbusters.

"He's on Facebook!"

"You can only be talking about Abraham," Wanda says.

"He looks healthy and hot, and he sent me a goddamn message!"

"Well, what else?"

"I don't know. He gave me his phone number and asked me to call him!"

"Then why in the hell are you calling *me*?"

"Because I haven't looked at his page or whatever they call it, to see who he is now."

"Well, you're talking to the wrong person. Try it and see. And don't call me back. Nelson's half pill is about to kick in."

As I eat my frozen sex, I look at Abraham's eyes and melt. The whites are still creamy and show no signs of hard drinking and drugging or worrying or lack of sleep. His skin still looks like dark brown satin. He has not gotten rid of his Afro, though it's now about two inches high and mixed with gray. And those lips—Lord have mercy— still thick and smooth and looking as if they haven't been bored. For a split second, I think I smell the Aramis he always wore.

I look to the left of the screen and click on his profile to see what he's chosen to reveal to the world. He studied at UC Davis: Horticulture. Master's: Cornell, agronomy. Work: Horticultural biologist. (What in the world does that mean?) Lives: Lafayette, Louisiana. Relationship Status: Ask. (I don't know if I want to. Or, if I should.) There are no photos. Nothing about his family or life events. Nothing under Contact and other basic information. Just the facts.

"So, Abraham," I say to him, "looks like you finished what you started. Good for you. Good for you."

And then I sit there and wait for him to jump through the screen or something just to say, "It's okay. Relax. I'm still the same guy." But he's not moving. I know this is silly and ridiculous, but after all these months of my hoping to find him, he's found me, and I have no idea what to say to him. And what an idiot he is for putting his phone number on the Internet. I hope he's not still smoking reefer. I take a deep breath and exhale it slowly, then dial his number.

He answers on the first ring. "Hello."

That voice. He still owns it.

"Hello, Abraham," I say, trying not to moan.

"Well, well, well. Long time not hearing your voice, Dr. Georgia Young, unless you lied on Facebook about what you do. How are you, sweetheart?"

Sweetheart? Don't. Please. Don't.

"I'm fine," I think I say, but nothing comes out.

"Georgia?"

I clear my throat. "Sorry, Abraham, I think I might be coming down with something. How are *you*?"

"I'm good. I'm in San Francisco."

I try to swallow the lump that just moved into my throat.

"You're kidding?"

"I try to get back here two or three times a year, since my mom's up here. She's in the hospital. Her kidneys aren't holding up, even with dialysis. But she claims she's feeling good. She lies."

"I'm glad to hear she's still with us. And that you're still a good son. How long are you in town for?"

"Five or six more days. Why do you want to know?"

"I was just curious."

"So tell me, are you a married woman or a divorced one?"

"Didn't you look me up on Facebook?"

"I'm new to Facebook, but to answer your question: yes. And to be honest, you were the first person I searched for. But all it said was you're an optometrist and absolutely nothing about your personal life."

"And that's on purpose, just for stalkers like you. Anyway, I'm divorced. Twice."

"That would make two of us, then. Kids?"

"Grown."

"How many?"

"Two. Daughters. One grown. One almost. College dropout."

"So how are you after all these years? In one word."

"I need to think about that."

"Okay. Make it two words."

"Reinventing myself."

"What was wrong with your old self?"

"Anyway, how about you, Abraham?"

"I'm good. So where are you right now?"

"In my office."

"Which is where?"

"The Embarcadero."

"Have you eaten?"

"As a matter of fact, I'm on my way to have dinner with friends."

I do not know why I just lied. Yes I do, because I'm nervous as hell and can't believe I'm even hearing Abraham's voice after all these years.

"Cancel it."

"What?"

"Cancel it. Tell them one of your old boyfriends is in town and that we've got a lot of catching up to do, because you broke his heart when he was hoping you would be his wife one day, and you need to see him to make up for it. How's that?"

"Okay," is all I can utter.

# Whew

F I'D BEEN SMARTER WHEN I WAS YOUNGER, IT WOULD'VE been—or should've been—obvious that breakups are inevitable. Soft ones, which are rare, mean you don't hate each other when you call it quits. You both know you've given it your best or worst and wish the other person well but be gone. Yet what if you broke his heart? What if you sent him off and he disappears on a cable car and you don't see him again for thirty-four years? I don't know if I was really in love with Abraham, although I have to admit I have never quite managed to reach that plateau since. Close. But how do you compare degrees of love? Even though it does seem to happen in different temperatures. Abraham created a furnace in me, and his power scared me, because at first I just thought he was a tall, black, fine, multiple-orgasmic-inducing, marijuana-smoking man who probably didn't have a future, and before I fell all the way into every inch of his heart—or I should say let him fall inside mine—I opted out. He wanted to marry me?

Right now he's about fifteen minutes away. I've agreed to meet him here at the office because it's the furthest we can get from even thinking about touching, not that I'm thinking anything like that. Liar. No matter what, he will never see the inside of my house nor a hotel room with me in it. I would probably break his back were he to find his way inside me, because I would probably never want to stop moving. I don't look anywhere close to what I used to look like, and all that most men want is a centerfold anyway. This is one more thing that bothers me about most men, and especially black men: they don't get fat. They also don't seem to age the same way we do. They don't have babies. They don't have C-sections, and I've never seen a man with stretch marks. Well, that's not completely true, because my daddy got fat, and Ma said he had more stretch marks than she did later on. Oh, who cares? I'm not taking my clothes off or having sex with a man I haven't seen in thirty-four years.

But then I think about that. Why the hell not?

You can smell the Chinese food, so I spray Febreze, which doesn't quite cut it, so I shove it back into the bag it came in and grab a plastic one from under the sink and tie the ties so tight it makes my fingers red. I dash down the hall to our private restroom and get a can of neutralizing spray and blast it from the front door, around the reception area on back past the exam rooms, and into my office. I inhale, but I don't know what nothing smells like.

I go back to the restroom and brush my teeth and floss and put on a thin layer of pancake makeup along with a little blush, but not enough to make him think I just put it on, and I wipe off and then replenish my red matte lipstick, which I add a thin coat of gloss on top of, and rake my fingers through my hair, look in my purse and get out my favorite hand cream and rub it on my neck and arms. Thank God I wore a black knit, and just when I run back to my office to put the long jacket on, the phone rings. It's him. He's probably changed his mind. I deflate.

"Hello, Abraham."

"Georgia, I'm so sorry to have to do this, but can we get a rain check? My mom is having a hard time this evening. One of the reasons I came home this time was to make sure she gets in-home care, since my trifling siblings aren't helping."

"No problem, Abraham. I'm really sorry to hear this. But you do what you need to do."

"I might end up staying longer," he says. "Will you be in town all this week?"

"Yes I will. How old is your mother?"

"Eighty-six."

"Mine's eighty-two."

"And how's she doing?"

"She's engaged."

He chuckles.

"That just made my day. Let me ask you what might be an inappropriate question at an inappropriate time, but would you ever consider remarrying?"

"Only if I were sure it would be the last time."

"Nice to hear. I'll be in touch in a day or so, if that's okay."

"That's fine. Take care of your mother."

Whew.

I wipe the perspiration from my brow and put my head down on my desk. Then get up and go dig my Chinese food out of the trash. I don't bother to read my fortunes.


"TO HELL WITH all the other ones, girl, just marry Abraham and be done with it."

"I'm going to look for my dress first thing in the morning, Wanda."

"Please fuck him, Georgia. For old times' sake if for nothing else. You've been on that petrified list too long, and you know you could use a good lube job—although I wonder if your engine will even start."

"I think I'd like to kick things off with an old-fashioned blow job."

"You sure you remember how?"

"Some things you don't forget, Wanda. Anyway. Seriously. I'm not thinking about sex."

"Then something is wrong with you. I thought you take hormones."

"I do. Low doses."

"Then run and buy something to make it easier for him to slide inside that tunnel."

"He could be happily married."

"So what? Is she here with him?"

"I don't know, but I could get myself in a lot of trouble if I have sex with him and like it half as much as I used to."

"Oh, girl, please. Just be a middle-aged woman who hasn't had any in years! Take it any way you can get it."

"You're sounding more and more like Violet."

"I'm just messing with you, Georgia, but don't be such an old lady. Men do this shit all the time."

"And what's that?"

"Get it whenever with whomever they can. We can learn from them, and especially you about now."

"I'm just excited about seeing him after all these years. I think I'd be happy just to hug him."

"Hug him? He's a goddamn man, not your long-lost son."


I'M TOO WIRED to fall asleep, so I take a Tylenol PM. Detective Goren's voice wakes me up. I don't find him sexy anymore. He's too predictable. I know he's going to solve the murder after he humiliates the hell out of the perpetrator. I grab the remote and press the button that allows you to see the programs you record as a series. I delete the five episodes waiting to be watched and then press that button twice to stop recording the series. I'm tired of crime. And I'm tired of being entertained. I turn the television off.

In the morning I decide I'm going to walk the reservoir. It may be for the wrong reasons, because it feels like I'm really just killing time hoping to hear from either Abraham or Amen, but I'm praying it's Abraham today. Right now I don't care if the house never sells. When I'm almost halfway around, my phone rings. It's Abraham. I let it ring twice.

"Are you free for lunch?"

"I can be. How's your mother?"

"Better. All things considered. My sisters are with her. So. I can't believe I'm actually talking to you, Georgia. You sound the same."

"You do, too."

"Is there someplace you like to have lunch?"

"Would you mind driving to the East Bay?"

"Not at all. You live on that side?"

"I do. Right behind the Claremont."

"It's nice over there. Green. Quiet. Lots of wildlife. So how about lunch, then?"

"That sounds great. We can meet at the Claremont."

"What's a good time for you?"

I look at my phone. It's already eleven.

"How about one, if that works for you?"

"I'll see you then and there."

As soon as I hit End, I realize I'd meant to warn him that I don't look the way I used to look. But as I walk the last mile and a half, I realize I don't have to apologize for anything.

When I get home, I pick out something flattering to wear, and when my wig box falls on the floor, as if I'm on autopilot I gather all nine of them in my arms like dirty laundry, walk down to the kitchen, shake out a white trash bag, and toss them all inside. I walk out into the cold air and drop them into the trash bin. On the way back in, I see three wild turkeys on the hillside staring at me.

"They're wigs," I say. "I'm done."


HE BEATS ME THERE.

He's sitting on a long leather sofa and wearing a burgundy sports coat, a burgundy T-shirt, and jeans, and when he sees me, he stands up like a king and holds his arms out for me to walk inside them. Which I do. In fact, I believe I could sink in deeper if my heartbeat weren't so loud. "Hello, Abraham," I say, trying not to sigh. He looks better now than he did thirty-four years ago. He kisses me on both cheeks. I didn't even know I had two.

"Georgia." He *does* sigh. "Time is on your side, baby. You're still beautiful," he says, and I try not to act as if I know he's lying.

Baby? Please don't. Yes. Do.

"Thank you."

"Once more with feeling."

"I know I look different."

"Like I don't?"

"Well, there's a lot more of me."

"And? You say it like it's a bad thing. We've been in the world a half century, so no need to apologize. Look at this," he says, and he opens his jacket and takes my hand and presses my palm against his stomach. Which is firm. And warm. I pull my hand away like I just got burned.

"Please." Now I sigh as well.

"It's so nice to see you, Georgia. I can't believe we're really standing here together, to be honest."

"You?"

"I mean, have you ever thought about me?"

"Let's sit down first."

"Answer the question first."

"Of course. Every time I read the Bible," I say, laughing. He takes me by the hand, the way he did years ago, and we follow the waiter to an outdoor table. It's chilly out here, but I'm too warm inside to put on my jacket. He pulls the chair out for me, and I swear to God a man has never looked so good in a pair of blue jeans, and those legs go on forever. He sits down and looks at me, and I look out at the Bay Bridge.

"Miss Georgia," he sighs.

"Please don't stare at me, Abraham. You're making me nervous."

"What do you expect me to look at?"

"Okay."

"You're still feisty, I see."

They bring our water, and I drink too much at once and start choking. He gets up and comes around to pat my back and then lifts me to a standing position and pulls me inside his arms like I'm a little girl and pats my back some more.

I could almost cry. "Thank you for saving me," I say with light-heartedness.

"If you ever really needed to be, you could count on me."

"So why the South?" I ask.

"Why not?"

"It wasn't a rhetorical question, Abraham."

"I like the soil down there. I'm a farmer, you know."

"You mean a real farmer, like in living on a farm?"

He nods. "Does that shock you?"

"Well, yeah. Considering you grew up in San Francisco."

"If we all stayed where we were raised, we would never branch out and spread our roots."

"Have you spread yours?"

"Well, I've got three sons. One lives in Seattle—he teaches high-school biology. Another one lives in Atlanta—he's an interior designer, and yes, I'm proud to say he's gay in case you're wondering. And the youngest still lives with me. He's physically challenged, but he's a big help and, like me, loves to cultivate and grow anything we can eat."

"Wow. That's pretty amazing. What about your wife?"

"Which one?"

"I thought you said you'd been divorced twice."

"I have. But I'm engaged to a wonderful woman who reminds me of you."

Well, so much for that fantasy.

"I'm flattered."

"So what about you? I know you have two daughters and two ex-husbands and you've got a thriving optometry practice in San Francisco. Are you involved with anybody?"

Involved? I try not to cut my eyes at him, because he means well.

"I was a while ago, but not recently."

"How long ago?"

"Why?"

"Because I want to know how long it's been since you've been in love or been loved."

Oh, Lord, help me. It doesn't pay to lie, because then you have to tell another one to make the previous one sound valid.

"What difference should it make to you, Abraham?"

"Because I just want to know if you're happy."

"Well, I'm not."

I can't believe I just said that!

Abraham doesn't look all that surprised. "I didn't think so."

"What would make you say that?"

"Because there's no light in your eyes."

"Maybe I need glasses."

He doesn't chuckle at that. "Talk to me."

"I am talking to you."

"You know what I mean. I'm harmless, and we go too far back to have to play any head games. I don't want anything from you. I'm not going to go on Facebook and blab anything you say to me, which is one reason it took me so long to go on it. My sons forced me."

"My daughter," I say, pointing to my chest.

"So are you lonely?"

"I don't feel comfortable saying if I am or not. I haven't seen you in years, Abraham, and here you come out of nowhere trying to get all inside me like time hasn't passed."

"If you are, it's not something you need to be embarrassed about."

"Shouldn't we order?"

"I'm not that hungry," he says. "Are you?"

I shake my head no. I feel like I'm sinking. Like I'm going to slide under this table onto the floor and curl up into a ball forever.

"How close is your house?" he asks.

"Why?"

"Because I want to know."

I point.

"I'd love to see where you live and how you live."

"I don't know if that's such a good idea, Abraham."

"I think it's a very good idea," he says, and stands up and takes my hand. He reaches inside his pocket and puts a twenty on the table.

The waiter comes over and doesn't even ask.

# Listening to Your Brain

AFTER I APOLOGIZE FOR THE BLANDNESS OF MY HOUSE and tell him why I'm selling it and how I'm trying to figure out what to do next, or with the rest of my life, Abraham says, "You explain far too much, Georgia."

Oh, Lord.

"Let me help take some of your worries away today," he says.

Oh, Lord.

"You can't possibly do that," I say.

"Oh, I think I can," he says. "I just heard what you said. You're trying to figure out how you want to live the rest of your life. You sound conflicted and yet sure you're doing the right thing, just like when you kicked me to the curb it was the right thing to do, even though I knew you were in love with me."

"No I wasn't."

"I beg to differ, sugar. You loved me so hard you couldn't take a chance on having my baby, because you were afraid I wouldn't live up to your expectations and I'd change the course of your entire life. And that scared the hell out of you. You can admit it now."

"I admit to that."

"Can't believe it took more than thirty years to hear you finally agree with me about something."

"To be honest, I was worried. But I also think it was probably more about lust than love."

"Anyway, call it whatever you want to call it, but I was pretty fucked up for almost a year. Didn't date. Jerked off so much that both of my wrists almost needed casts."

We both crack up at that.

"I loved me some you, young lady, but I also learned a lot from you."

I'm surprised to hear him say this.

"Like what?"

"That you have to listen to your brain and not just your heart, even if it hurts. At first I wanted to shake you until your teeth fell out, but time went by, and it took me almost two years to take my stupid ass back to school. When I graduated, I realized how much smarter than me you were. Our future would've been rough, and you saw that. So you helped me grow up, and for that I thank you, Miss Georgia."

"I wish I could say you're welcome, but I think I see it a little differently. I was afraid of the power you had over me, and it made me feel weak and defenseless, and I didn't want to feel weak and defenseless. You made me understand how you can lose your mind because someone makes you feel like butter. Plus, you were so damn good in bed."

"You were the conduit, baby."

"Please don't call me 'baby,' Abraham."

"I'm sorry. So do you have anything to snack on around here? I'm starving."

We head to the kitchen. We eat flatbread crisps with Gouda cheese and sweet pickles and drink tomato basil soup while we stare out at the pool.

"This is a beautiful home you have, Georgia. I don't know why you think you need to move just because you don't have a husband."

"Did I say that?"

"No, but it's pretty obvious. I know you probably lived here with your last husband, right?"

"And?"

"And you had to buy him out, yes?"

I nod my head slowly up and down, wondering where this is going.

"And now your daughters are on their own, and here you are all by yourself in this house, and you can't stand the thought of being in here all alone."

I nod again.

"Which is such bullshit."

"What do you mean by that? First, would you like a glass of wine?"

"No. I'm good. Iced tea would be nice, if you have any."

"It just so happens."

"So thanks for interrupting me and trying to break my train of thought, but it's not going to work, sweetheart. I'm going to get personal."

Sweetheart. Baby. Sugar. Stop it.

He looks at me and raises his bushy eyebrows like it's a question.

I raise mine like, *Just say it!*

"How many years do you have left on your mortgage?"

"Five."

"Damn, Georgia! You won't even qualify for Medicare yet! Seriously. Let me say this. This house isn't too big for you, and besides, you've got grandkids, and there's no doubt in my mind you're going to meet the man you're supposed to meet when you're supposed to meet him, and chances are the two of you'll run off into the sunset, and this house won't have a damn thing to do with it."

"I'm not moving because I'm not in a relationship."

"I didn't say that, did I? Don't go putting words in my mouth, darling. Honestly. I'd pay this sucker off and sit tight until the market changes, then give it to one of your kids. You're going to lose a lot of money if you sell it now. It's just a thought."

"I'll give it some thought, Abraham."

"I have to say this, though. I thought you had pretty good taste in college, and next time you might want to do your own staging, because your little studio had more charm and energy than this."

I look around and am glad that someone sees what I see. "So what about you?"

"Look at these hands," he says, and holds out what look like dark brown baseball mitts. "I'm a farmer. Own five hundred acres of the most beautiful land you'll ever see. I supply soybeans, rice, and sweet potatoes to the likes of Whole Foods and other natural markets. I have about forty employees I pay fairly, and I fight for the rights of black farmers. Which means I go to D.C. quite often. I love my life. And I love my fiancée, even though it's not the kind of wild and crazy love you feel when you're in your twenties."

"I'm happy for you, Abraham," and I say that honestly. "This is just what I was hoping for, for you. And of course I know what you're saying about the good old days, but I'd really like to hear you tell me exactly how loving someone at our age is different. And maybe even better now."

"Well," he says, and he takes a sip of his tea as he looks out at apparently nothing. "We know each other's habits. We know how far we've come in our lives. We know each other's shortcomings and weaknesses and don't hold each other hostage because of them. We don't have to apologize for not being perfect. And we give each other what we know the other needs. We don't have to ask. And we don't need to be reminded. We know we're in this for the long haul, because we see this as our arc. No more drama. It's a waltz. And sometimes a cha-cha-cha. It's about all I could ask for. All I've ever wanted. That answer your question?"

"Well, yeah. I'm touched. She must be an amazing woman."

"Most women are amazing. They just need to be with someone who makes it easy for them to express it. I think it's called respect."

"Well, the line is long."

"I just wanted to tell you the truth so you know what's in store for you. Don't give up."

"I haven't."

"But right now, if you wouldn't mind strolling down memory lane, it would sure be nice to spend the next twenty-four hours with you so we can memorialize what we once had. You up for that?"

"I think so," I say.

"We don't have to if you don't feel comfortable. But how often will we get the chance to enjoy a fantasy?"

"I want to," I hear myself say. "But I don't want you to look at me."

"Are you serious?"

"Yes I am."

"That's not going to happen. And we're not hiding under the covers. We're not turning off all the lights and drawing the shades. You're a fifty-four-year-old woman who's had two babies, so you might not look like you did in your twenties, but that doesn't stop you from being appealing now, okay?"

"Okay."

I get him another iced tea. And one for me, too.

"You want to watch a movie?" I ask.

"Sure, since I'm going to be your husband for twenty-four hours. Let's play house. What movie do you want me to watch?"

"*Before Sunrise.*"

"We'll see, won't we?"

We walk down to my bedroom and sit on the floor and lean against the bed and watch the entire movie.

With our clothes on.

I don't sit close enough to touch him. I'm scared to touch him, but I don't want to *act* like I'm scared. So I talk. What I always do when I'm nervous, and I tell Abraham about my plans to take a train ride that I've had to postpone.

"Regardless of if and when you retire from your practice or if you decide to sell this house or keep it, go on the doggone train ride, Georgia. It's not like you're trying to be Amelia Earhart. Sounds like a gift you should give yourself when you want to."

"Oh, I'm going," I say.

"Go everywhere you've always wanted to."

"You sound like my father."

"You know what?" he says, looking down at me. "I'm afraid to touch you."

"And I'm afraid what'll happen if you do," I say.

"Both of us are at a crossroads in our lives, don't you think?"

I just nod.

"I'm starting over, and this is going to be it for me," he says, and puts his arms around me and squeezes me. Rubs my arm up and down as if he's trying to comfort me from a fall I just had. "I really can't believe I found you on Facebook."

"Well, you weren't on it when I first looked, Abraham."

"Why were you looking for me?"

I tell him he wasn't the only one, and try to explain why.

"So I found you," he says.

"Yes you did."

"But what were you hoping would happen when you found me?"

"I just wanted to know you were still alive, if you were happy and healthy, and you are, and I'm glad."

"But I want to know why it was so important to you after all these years."

"Honestly?"

He just looks at me.

"Last year I found out that someone I once cared a lot about had passed away, and I never told him how I really felt about him."

"I'm sorry to hear that, but you never told me either."

"No I didn't."

"I'm all ears."

And he crosses his arms and looks down at me, and it takes all the courage I have to look him in the eyes and say, "I want to thank you for the time we spent together, because even though it was brief, you made me feel good, and you made me happy, and I did love you and wished there'd been a way we could've rode it all the way out. I'm also grateful to you for being the first man to cause me to have multiple orgasms, which I've learned aren't that easy to come by."

He starts laughing, and I rock back and forth against him.

"And I also want to say I'm sorry."

"For how you dogged me in the end?"

"That, and not telling you why I couldn't have your baby."

"You don't have to apologize for that. You don't think I knew why? We would've been screwed. We were too young, and I was glad you didn't go through with it, to be honest."

"Really?"

"Really."

We sit here for another few minutes. It's so quiet it's almost scary.

"So how many men have you done this with—unless it's too personal?"

"My two ex-husbands. And now you."

"How many do you have left? Again, don't answer that if you don't want to."

"Four. Maybe three."

"Wow. Is there a ranking?"

"No!"

"Hell, I was hoping I came in first after those husbands."

"A close second."

"So after you find them, then what?"

"Then nothing."

"Really?"

"Well, I think some relationships ended badly and some weren't finished. And in the case of someone we loved, after the relationship ends, it's like they disappear or just die. I just wanted you and them to know I didn't forget you."

"I suppose there are a few women I could look up, too, and even apologize to. Though some were skanks."

We both burst into laughter over that one.

"Well, I'm not wasting my time looking up the dogs or the major mistakes or the losers or the ones I just slept with—and don't ask how many."

"I've found quite a few relatives and old friends, too."

"I haven't done that yet. But hopefully I still have time."

"So can I be honest with you?"

"Stupid question, Abraham."

"I'm so proud of what you've done with your life and what you're still trying to do, and I'm glad you're not one of those women in their fifties who're bitter because past relationships or marriages didn't work out, and you haven't thrown in the towel and given up on men and love, and I'm thrilled you've still got the same fearlessness you had in college, because here you are thinking of giving up a lucrative profession to jump out into the abyss. Try a whole new path. You still rock, lady, as my youngest says."

"Thank you, Abraham. Here's my testimonial: I'm glad you didn't become a pothead and that you took horticulture seriously, and I respect and admire what you're doing for black farmers, because I know how they got screwed by the government. I'm even more thrilled that you stand for something, and even though it might feel as if we missed the boat, we didn't. I don't think we need to go back. And I'm happy you found a woman who makes you happy."

"Thank you, sugar."

"Please stop with the sugar, Abraham."

"Okay, Georgia, so what are you saying?"

"I would so much love to have sex with you, but I'm afraid that if I do, I would probably want to pretend like we're nineteen and on my Murphy bed and that I'm about to hit number four. I can't believe I'm saying this, but I think we should keep our clothes on."

"See what I mean? You're still using that amazing brain, and I'm still thinking with the one in my pants, although I was just about to tell you that this would probably be a mistake, because I still and always will love you, and it would be selfish of me to hurt Maya."

"This is music to my ears. A man with a conscience. And I am thrilled to finally admit to myself and to you that I have loved you for thirty-four years, so there."

He pulls me up to a standing position, and I walk him to the door.

"But," he says, looking down at me, "may I pretty please just have one of those deep, juicy kisses I used to love, for old times' sake?"

And he bends down, and I stand on my toes, and his lips are sweet and warm and soft, and as soon as I feel that waterfall, I gently push him away, and he steps back the same way he did right before he walked out of that restaurant, handsome and strong.

"It was good seeing you, Abraham."

"It was more than good seeing you, Georgia. Thank you for not forgetting."

I watch him get into his car and disappear down the hill.

I close the front door.

And lean back against it.

I should've married him.

# When Bad News Is Good News

W ELL?"
  "'Well' what, Wanda?" I ask back. I'm finally doing laundry. Something I've almost forgotten how to do.

"Don't play with me, Georgia. Did you give it up or not? Did he get rid of the cobwebs? Did you fall back in love? Is he the same or better or worse after a thousand years?"

"We hugged. And he's much better."

"Hugged? Clothes off or on?"

"On."

"Don't tell me Abraham's gay?"

"No. But he's engaged."

"And? That's not the same as married."

"I told you I wasn't trying to hook up with him, Wanda. My goodness."

"Did he want to or he didn't want to?"

"Oh, he wanted to. We both did. But it would've been dangerous for both of us."

"You know what? Don't even bother explaining. I don't know any man in his right mind who would turn down some free pussy."

"You can really be crass sometimes."

"Yeah, well, it's for your ears only. Anyway, so how'd he look? And what's he been up to?"

"He looks better now than he did back then. He's a farmer."

"A what?"

"He owns a farm. He grows soybeans and rice and sweet potatoes and fights in Congress for black farmers. And he lives outside of New Orleans."

"You sure that's all he grows?"

"Let me say this. It was cathartic for both of us."

"Well, that's just great. And pretty fucking boring. I'm very disappointed that nothing came out of this. Not even a single orgasm. What a waste."

ESTELLE HAD TO GO and have another girl, and Frankie had a boy three weeks later. I understand that the twins aren't crazy about Dove. In fact, they said they wish she'd fly away. With those two she-devils running around, Dove's going to have to be one cool baby sister.

I volunteered to take a few days off to help Estelle, but she insisted it wasn't necessary. I asked her how Justin was adjusting to his new daughter, and she just said that Justin's making all kinds of adjustments and asked me to give her a few weeks to get settled into more mothering, so what else could I say?

Levi, my grandson, looks about thirty when I lay eyes on him. Even though he's black, he looks Chinese, but he smells new. His eyes are tiny black marbles.

I've been holding him in his mint green blanket for a half hour, and he's just fallen asleep. I like the way Levi feels in my arms, so I don't put him in his crib. Frankie's decided to take advantage of my grandparenting presence and has beelined it to Target to buy a few things and get a Starbucks.

I look around their Hansel-and-Gretel house and can't imagine how they pass each other without bumping.

OMG! This little boy is snoring!

I try not to laugh as I push myself up from this crunchy rattan chair, but it takes another attempt before I'm standing. Levi isn't fazed as I walk into his parents' room and put him in his crib. There's about six inches between his bed and theirs. This room is the size of my walk-in closet, but—like mother, like daughter—it's full of color. The walls are turquoise, but the ceiling is pale orange. They painted the door goldenrod, which doesn't make much sense to me, but then again I don't have to live in this tiny box they call home.

I shouldn't judge.

While he sleeps, I go into the kitchen to get something to drink and see what looks like a pile of typewritten papers on the cute little IKEA table. It's one of Frankie's stories. It has no title. As soon as I start reading, I realize it's written in the voice of an elderly woman who has magical powers and can make pain evaporate in those who don't deserve it. This is my daughter. I'm only up to page ten when I hear her pull up, and I quickly straighten the stack as neatly as it was and go sit in the living room.

I hope she changes her major again.

Hunter was right.

I open the front door for her. "You need help?"

"Nope. I'm good."

"Are you sure? You shouldn't be lifting anything heavy yet, Frankie."

"These Pampers are weightless, and so is my latte. How's my little man doing?"

"He's fine. Frankie?"

"Yes, Mom."

"I read some of your wonderful story, and I wasn't snooping, but I just want you to know how impressed I am, and if what I read is any indication of how good you are, please don't stop."

Her eyes open wide, almost in disbelief. But then she sees the sincerity in mine and relaxes.

"That means so much to me, Mom," she says, and gives me a strong hug.

I head into their room to check on the little man, and those sparkling black eyes are wide open, and I swear he's smiling at me. I'm pretty sure sweet Levi already knows who his grandma is.

"I'M AFRAID I'M NOT the bearer of good news," Marina says at the close of business, which seems to be the only chance we get to talk about anything. I should've known that something was up, because for the first time in almost five years she's not wearing black.

"Come on in and have a seat," I say, since my door isn't closed. I lean back in my chair and want to cross my arms, but it might make me look like I'm upset, which I'm not. I knew that this day was coming. I'm just surprised it's taken so long.

"I'm moving to New York," she says as she eases into the chair in front of my desk, sliding it back to make room so those long legs don't bump into it.

"This sounds like good news to me."

"I need a change. Haven't you ever felt like that, Doc?"

"I think I have."

"I mean, seriously. When every day feels the same and the needle just doesn't move?"

"It's the reason I've been divorced twice."

"I heard that," she says.

"Would you like a glass of wine?"

"About to pop that cork now."

She goes over to my hidden refrigerator and whips out a bottle of something good.

"Yes, I believe in product replacement," she says, laughing. "Sometimes after everybody's gone, I've sat in here and blasted Pandora and only leave the lighting on in the cabinets, and I'll be honest, I've had sex with a few boyfriends in the lunchroom, on the floor behind the reception counter, and even in the exam-room chairs—which is fabulous, I might add."

"And you think this shocks me?" I ask, amused.

She runs to the lunchroom and comes back with two plastic glasses, even though I have real ones in the cabinet. She pops the cork and pours us both a full glass of sauvignon blanc.

"You've got good taste in wine, Doc."

"Glad you approve, Miss Thang," I say, and try to get the smirk off my face but then decide I want her to see it. I take a very long swallow, then cross my legs as if I'm waiting for her to tell me the real reasons she's ready to leave the Bay Area. "So I want to know what you're going to do in New York, which is even more expensive than San Francisco, but I'm not asking to be discouraging so don't take it that way."

"I'm not! Do you know where I've been living all these years?"

"With your parents?"

She nods.

"It's embarrassing, but I've had the freedom to come and go as I please, and I've managed to save up a bundle. I've got a cousin in New York who lives on Roosevelt Island, and I'm going to try to find a job in fashion. It's always been my passion. I've been taking merchandising and fashion-design classes at the Academy of Art on weekends and evenings, so I'm bringing something with me."

"Why haven't you ever said anything?"

"Because I didn't want you to think I had another agenda. Like some fine man I know."

"You thought Mercury was fine?"

"Hell to the yeah."

"I'm glad you've *had* an agenda, because I know you had so much more going for you, Marina. I'm thrilled you're finally taking a risk on yourself."

"Give me an example of a big one you took. Wait, hold that thought," she says, and jumps up to head over to the fridge. "You don't mind today, do you? Since we're celebrating, aren't we?"

"Drink whatever you want to. I can put you in a cab if you get too buzzed."

On that note she refills her glass, and I gulp the rest of mine down and hold it out. She pours, sits back down, and puts her elbows on my desk. All ears.

"This is about you, Marina."

"Okay, forget about the risk bullshit. How do you make changes when you get old— My bad, again, Doc. I meant 'older.' Forgive?"

"Forgiven. But let me just say this. When you get older, you have the understanding that it would be stupid to change what's been working for you, but sometimes you come to your senses and realize you're not happy, you're bored and lonely, you haven't been laid in years, and on top of all this you admit that your profession is dull and unfulfilling and you just decide you're going to break up the monotony and sell your big-ass home and you're going to take some classes in anything that excites you and you're also going to sell your interest in your practice and then figure out what the hell you're going to do next."

"No shit?" And she holds her hand up to give me a high five. "How many years?"

"How many years what?"

"Since you've been laid."

I count four fingers.

"You've gotta be fucking kidding me!"

I now realize I'm almost drunk and should never have admitted to that and especially to a thirty-year-old, sexually active, attractive, six-foot-tall Japanese woman! But: too late.

"I wish I were. But you don't die. It only feels like you're dying. Which is why I'm about to become a whore!"

And we both slap the desk too hard with our palms, and we're not that drunk because it stings both of us, and we can't stop laughing. But then we do. And a kind of sadness suddenly takes the laughter's place.

"So does this mean you're seriously planning to leave optometry?"

"Yes."

"Good. This is one boring fucking profession."

"It is."

"When?"

"Next year, hopefully."

"And what are you going to do?"

"Paint stuff. Make stuff. Turn tricks."

"Ha! What kind of stuff would you paint and make?"

"Don't know yet."

"Paint something cool, but please don't make any curtains or shit like that!"

"I won't."

"So since this probably is going to be like our last hurrah, can I ask you something that might sound corny, since you're old and full of wisdom?"

I'm just going to go ahead and be old this evening. "Nothing is corny, Marina."

"Okay. So. What do you wish you'd done differently when you were young?"

"Whoa. Wow. Why?"

"I just want to know, when I get old—I mean older—if I'll have like a long fucking list of regrets. I don't know why I can't stop swearing, and I hope I'm not pissing you off."

I shake my head. "Well, I think we have regrets at every age. But can you be a little more specific?"

"No, I can't. Just say whatever comes out, Doc."

"I need a minute to think about that."

"Hold that thought! I need to pee. I mean go to the bathroom."

"Wait! I hope you're giving us at least a two-week notice."

"Try three months from now. I'm Japanese. I plan my life in advance. Plus, I wouldn't stick you and Dr. L."

And she dashes off.

I don't know if I can answer her question right now. I'm feeling a little tipsy myself, but I take another sip anyway. This is fun. And she's back! Marina must pee like a bird.

She flops down in the chair and leans on her elbows and stares those glassy eyes into mine. "I'm listening."

"I don't know. I wish I'd read more so I'd know more."

"Are you fucking serious? That's the first thing that comes into your head? Come on, Doc, rattle 'em off like you've got Tourette's or something—and I mean no offense to anybody with Tourette's, God."

"I probably wouldn't have majored in biology and would not have gone to optometry school. I would've traveled more, and I still intend to, and I'd probably live in a foreign country for a while and maybe have tried dating outside my race and learned to speak French and Italian and maybe not married my second husband."

"Have you ever dated anybody besides black guys, Doc?"

"Nope."

"They're no different from the rest of them. Trust me. I've fucked just about every ethnicity known to mankind."

"I did have sex with a white guy when I was in college."

"And?"

"He was pretty good. But I was worried what would happen if I liked him."

"Duh. This is America. You're too old-school. I date anybody I find interesting. I don't believe in discriminating."

"Duh yourself. That was like the 1970s, and the world was a mess."

"Okay, I'm getting tired or maybe a little drunk, but what would you have chosen to do had you not gone the whole seeing-is-believing route?"

I want to answer, but I don't think I have it in me to explain another thing.

"Oh, to hell with it, Doc. But I'll bet you a pair of Prada sunglasses you'da made a terrible talk-show host."

And we both laugh. She chugs the remaining three ounces of her wine and almost misses the desk when she plops it down. Now I know why she got plastic.

# Why I'm Calling

"Y OU STILL HERE?" THE SAME PIZZA KID SAYS WHEN I open the door.

He not only appears to be two or three inches taller but also has what looks like a fuzzy mustache and a dirty chin.

"You still delivering pizzas?" I ask lightheartedly.

"Yep. But I'm in school full-time now. Going to Laney College. You moving? I've seen that For Sale sign in your front yard for months, and I was thinking of stopping by just to say hi and give you some free breadsticks. How you doing, Dr. Young?"

"I'm doing fine. And it sounds like you're doing well, Free."

"You remembered my name?"

"How could I not?"

"Did you stop eating pizza, or you stopped liking ours?"

"No, I just haven't been in the mood."

"Well, I'm glad to see you. I ain't—I mean, haven't got a tip like the one you gave me since then. Hey! Did you get robbed or something?"

"No, I had to put most of my stuff in storage."

"Why?"

"To make the house more appealing to buyers."

"You mean to white folks. You don't even gotta say it. It's ugly, no offense. This sure wouldn't make me wanna buy this crib. It look just like the rest of these houses I deliver pizza to. Except for the ladies next door. Their crib is ultra-cool. Anyhow, I liked yours the way it was. Did you do this?"

"No. Someone else did."

"I hope you didn't have to pay 'em."

"I did."

"Did you pay somebody to make it as hip as it was before?"

"No."

"Then you got skills, Dr. Young. Where you trying to move to, if you don't mind my asking?"

"Don't know yet, Free."

"What you mean, you don't know? You too old not to know where you going—no offense. Even *I* know where I wanna go, so I know *you* gotta have some idea."

"I'm just not sure what I'm going to do next."

"Well, at least you got options. Some folks don't. This pizza's on the house for you being so nice to me last time."

"No, you don't have to do that."

"I know I don't have to, but I want to. And hurry up and eat it, 'cause these pizzas are nasty when they get lukewarm, and forget about microwaving it unless you put a half cup of water in there, or your teeth'll get stuck in the crust. You'd be SOL if you had dentures!" And he cracks up.

"Thanks, Free," I say.

"You're welcome. And guess what? Eighteen months I'ma be able to transfer up to Sac State, which is where my daddy live. Anyway, Dr. Young, I hope your crib sell fast and you figure out where to go."

"I will. And good luck in college, Free."

"Luck is for fools. I'm working my tail off, 'cause one day I wanna have more than one option, like you. Can I give you a hug?"

"Sure," I say, and he squeezes me like he hasn't been hugged in a very long time.

Which would make two of us.

I ONLY EAT two slices, because it's greasy and doesn't taste like pizza. In fact, it makes my throat feel thick. I crush the box with the remaining pizza in it and push it inside the metal trash can. I surprise myself by scouring inside the fridge and finding some salad fixings and make one, and I'm shocked it's not only tasty but filling. I grab a bottle of sparkling water and put on my brand-new pink-and-black dalmatian pajamas and go sit in front of my computer. I Google every course and degree program offered in the Bay Area that deals with every type of designing imaginable, and as I carefully read every single description, it becomes crystal clear to me that I want to make things folks will appreciate touching or find cool or interesting and maybe even useful. I want to make things that are one of a kind. Things you might not find in a conventional furniture store. And I don't want it to function as furniture. In fact, I'm hoping it might be considered art.

I feel ten pounds lighter.

My house phone rings and makes me jump. I was enjoying this carefree zone I was in, and who interrupts the flow of it? My mother, who else? "Hi, Ma. What are you doing calling me at nine o'clock at night? Where's your fiancé?"

"You mean husband," she says, chortling.

"Okay, so you eloped?"

"I guess you could say that. Since Grover is just starting to get around good, we went downtown to the courthouse. But we're legal."

"Well. Congratulations. What's your new last name?"

"If you think for one minute I'm changing my last name after fifty-three years, think again, sister. It's Young, and I'll always be Young. Grover's last name is Green. And don't say anything smart."

I try not to laugh when I hear it in my head but I blurt it out. "Grover Green. Green Grover."

"Anyway, he certainly is a nice addition to my life."

"I'm so glad to hear it, Ma. Really."

"Now I don't have to worry about dying alone."

"Please don't say that!"

"His son thought you were nice, too."

"He was interesting enough, but I'm not interested."

"Anyway, Grover just told me yesterday that Grover Jr.'s wife left him for a man almost half her age."

"Wow. I thought he was happy."

"He was. But now he's not. So what were you doing when I called?"

"Looking for my future on the Internet."

"Good luck. They say you can find just about anything on there. Bye-bye, baby."

I make the love sound.

My phone rings again and scares the hell out of me. I'm tempted not to pick up, but when I look down and see that it's Michael, I go ahead and answer. Talk about not being able to get rid of the past. "Is the wedding off?" I ask jokingly.

"As a matter of fact, it is, Georgia."

Shit.

Sometimes I need to learn not to say what I'm thinking just because I'm thinking it. I often say the wrong thing at the wrong time to the wrong people, but apparently I have yet to learn from my mistakes.

"I'm sorry, Michael. And I apologize for being so tactless. I had no idea."

"It's okay. I got punked, as Ashton Kushner would say. It was all about money."

It's Kutcher. But this is no time to correct him.

"What happened?"

"She didn't like the ring I chose. She wanted to live behind gates, and she insisted we go to Dubai and Bora-Bora for our honeymoon."

"What's wrong with that?"

"I'm not rich, Georgia."

"Does she have money?"

"Not unless she hid it under her mattress."

"Well, at least somebody managed to get married."

"Who?"

"My mother."

This makes him chuckle.

"Is there anything I can do?"

"Seriously?"

"Seriously."

"Would you like to have sex?"

"No, Michael."

"I didn't mean to ask you that. Well, I did, but I didn't expect you to say yes."

"You know, you can always buy some comfort if you need it that bad."

"I've just lost a stranger, don't think I want to go looking for another one."

It's marathon call night, because no sooner than I hang up do I see it's an alien. Violet. I'm almost afraid to answer it, since she put a price tag on our friendship. I do miss her, and I've been worried about her well-being, but she refuses to return my phone calls and even Wanda's.

"Hello, stranger," I say.

"Hello back," she says. "How are you?"

"I'm fine. And you?"

"Well, I had a lump."

"You had a what? Repeat that. I'm not sure I heard you right."

"I said I had a *lump*."

"You mean as in a breast-cancer lump, Violet?"

"Yes. But it's gone. And they took my right breast. But I had it reconstructed."

I almost can't breathe.

"Georgia?"

"I'm here. I don't know if I should just be happy or mad as hell at you for not telling me, Violet. When did all this happen?"

"Not long after I moved."

"And you're okay now?"

"Yeah. I'm pretty much recovered."

"Does Wanda know?"

"No."

"Why didn't you fucking tell us?"

"Because I just didn't feel like it."

"What the hell do you think friends are for?"

"Well, that's why I'm calling."

"Do you need some help?"

"No."

"Are you sure?"

"I'm sure."

"What about Velvet? How's she doing?"

"Still trifling and unemployed."

"And the baby?"

"He's good, finally up to ten pounds."

"Thank God. So tell me, Violet, what I can do for you?"

"Be my friend again."


WANDA AND I are in Tahoe. The snow is long gone, but we drove up here to gamble and gaze at the snowcapped mountains and look for bears and, of course, stop at the Vacaville outlet on the way back. We invited Violet, but she said she had to babysit her grandson. We did not believe her. We have tried to learn everything about recovering from having a mastectomy and breast augmentation, and we realized Violet's probably depressed, but despite our efforts to reach out to her and tell her that we understand how she might be feeling—even though we really don't—and that we're here for her, she won't let us in. Wanda and I have decided we're going over to her house when we get back. We don't care what she says.

"Let's do that breast-cancer walk," I say to Wanda as we unpack the back of her SUV.

"Violet won't care, and you know I did it last year, but you were too lazy."

"Yeah, well, I'm not feeling lazy now, and Violet will care, and she's coming with us, even if all she can do is be our cheerleader."

"It's thirty-nine point two miles, but we can do twenty-six," she says.

"I want to go the distance."

"Then let's do it."


WE RING VIOLET'S doorbell until she answers.

"What do you two want from me?"

"We're doing the walk, and if you're not able, we just want you to come out to support us."

She starts crying. We all cry. And hug. And together Wanda and I start what will be the most grueling eight weeks of my life. Violet isn't as strong as we are yet, but she can ride a bicycle. We follow the training program. I wake up when it's still dark and meet them at the safe walking trails. We walk six miles the first day. Do a recovery walk for fifteen short minutes the next. Then three miles. Then I haul my ass to the gym and use up some of that personal-trainer credit. I'm surprised how much I like exercising, how good it makes me feel. I have more energy, my spirits are rising, and at the end of the eighth week, when I walk into my closet to try on a dress I always wear, it's too big. I hadn't thought of how this walk would also benefit me.

Of course we're among thousands on the perfect fifty-five-degree day when we walked twenty-six point one miles, then thirteen point one the next, and I can't believe I actually did it. I really don't know how. Wanda's not surprised. I've never been this high in my life, and I've also never seen so many shades of pink and purple and blue, nor have I ever participated in anything this meaningful with so many people who have so much in common and all gathered for the same reasons.

We meet women in recovery. Women who are walking with cancer still alive inside them. We had hoped Violet would've come, but she said she didn't think she was strong enough to cheer us on for all those miles. We meet men who are the sons, brothers, fathers, and husbands of women who did and didn't survive.

I vow to do this again next year.

I vow to keep exercising.

Wanda does, too. Even though at the end of the walk, when we're heading to the parking lot, she tells me she and Nelson have made an offer on the condo they liked in Palm Desert and chances are they're going to be moving down there for good next year.

I have no intention of losing my friend. But what in the world am I going to do without her?

# The Dreaded Reunion

I FORGOT MY HIGH-SCHOOL COLORS.

Ma told me to go anyway, before everybody's dead. That was comforting. I look over the itinerary, and it seems ridiculous that so little activity could fill two whole days. Ma wants me to stay with her, but I'm afraid to. I'm told that Grover Jr. is back in town, but who wants to be around a man whose wife just left him? Besides, he's my frigging new brother!

"Good thing you lost all that weight," Ma says when I stop by a few hours before the Icebreaker Cocktail Party.

"I've lost thirteen pounds," I say.

"Well, it looks like twenty-five. Keep doing whatever you're doing, because it's flattering to see less of you."

She chuckles.

"So looks like little Levi is finally getting cute," Ma says.

"Little boys always seem to have to grow into their looks."

"Some do. Some don't. So what's the 411 on Estelle and Justin?"

"What do you mean?"

"Heard it's not paradise anymore," she says. "And they might be in counseling. They picked a heck of a time to have another child. What do you think is going on, Georgia?"

"I don't know," I say, although I believe in my heart he's probably cheating. Men stop being nice to you when they're having an affair. "Where's your husband?"

"At his place, and don't ask me why, because we like our setup. He'll be over later to watch *Iron Man 3* or maybe even *4*. I don't know."

"There is no *Iron Man 3* or *4*, Ma."

"We're asleep before the credits roll anyway. Who cares which one it is? I don't like robots to begin with."

"Well, maybe I'll stop by after all the icebreakers melt and before someone falls off the stage during karaoke."

"Wait a minute. You're not going to this festivity by yourself, I hope."

"Yes. What's wrong with that?"

"You're supposed to have an escort. Hell, somebody. You do not want to walk into your forty-year reunion by yourself. That much I do know."

"Why not?"

"It just sends the wrong message."

"And what message is that?"

"That you didn't have anybody to bring."

"I don't care what these people think."

"You *should* care. Why don't you take Grover Jr.? His social calendar is blank. Believe me."

"I don't want to take anybody, Ma. And I'm not the least bit embarrassed to go by myself."

"Who're you going to dance with?"

"Dance? Who said anything about dancing?"

"You have to dance, Georgia."

"Okay! What's his number?"

"He's right across the parking lot. In Grover's unit."

"How long is he staying?"

"Not sure. He said he likes Bakersfield."

"Oh, Lord."

"And by the way, it's nice to see your hair again. Short and curly is so much more flattering. You looked like you were wearing a Russian hat all these years."

"Why didn't you ever say anything?"

"I figured when you got tired of looking like wooly bully, you'd come to your senses."

"You always know what to say."

"Can you please call Grover Jr.?" she says, and hands me her cell phone, which has pictures of all four of her great-grandchildren on the screen.

"Nice," I say.

"I had it made. I'll give you the website if you want it."

I just shake my head, and then I hear that deep voice.

"Hi, Grover, this is your new sister, Georgia. How are you?"

He says fine. He's lying, of course.

"Look. I'm here to attend my hundredth high-school reunion and was just advised that I should have a date."

Ma is staring me in the mouth.

"Yours was in June? . . . You did? . . . You will? . . . All day. . . . That's great."

Ma makes a charades gesture and points at her heart and then moves her arms like she's steering.

"How about I pick you up about six? It should be over about nine, ten at the latest. And we can talk about day two also."

Her eyes turn into sunny-side-ups.

"Do you golf? . . . Me either. But there's the long dinner and the dreaded speech during dessert and the awards for best this and that and the PowerPoint of those who aren't with us anymore and then, so as to end the evening on a high note, the faux dancing. It's going to be a long night. . . . No kidding? The last five? . . . I don't want to say. . . . I'll see you in a few hours then, Grover. And thanks."

"Wear something as close to sexy as you can find in that garment bag," Michelle Obama says.

"Ma, please."

"He is not your real brother. Just keep that in mind. And if he's anything like his daddy, you won't be disappointed."

I have nothing to say to that.


GROVER JR. LOOKS better now than he did at Ma's birthday. It could be that olive green shirt he's wearing with those long black slacks. From under his sports coat, even his belt is dark olive leather. His shoes are black. The toe almost pointed but not quite. He could pass for gay considering how put together he is, but I sometimes forget that straight men also have good taste.

I'm in tangerine and turquoise because I said to hell with trying to look conservative. I'm not conservative, and I'm not putting on a front for people I probably won't even remember. Jacket. Straight skirt. Silk tee. Size twelve. All new because those fourteens are finally too big.

"Wow, you look amazing," he says to me when I get out of the car to greet him. Hug. Hug.

"So do you," I say. Hug. Hug.

He gets in the passenger side.

"Dig this Prius," he says. "So how've you been?"

"I've been fine. Sorry to hear about what happened."

"She left me. I'm hurt, but I don't hate her for it."

"Really?"

"No. I'm heartbroken, of course, and I'm not thrilled this is how my marriage had to end, but I've heard you can recover. Right?"

"You can even do it twice."

"So," he says, and pats both palms on those beautiful, tight, brotherly thighs. "Now it's time to travel back forty years."

"I suppose it is. And I'll say this right now: if it feels like we're the only ones not in a coma, we give each other the look and bail for a fun bar."

"You got it."

THIS BAR IS already packed. With mostly white people. There are about fifty or sixty people here and more behind us. I get my badge with my name on it. It does not look good with my outfit, but I wear it anyway. There were only forty-two black students in our graduating class of three hundred. I don't see any of them.

We have a drink.

I don't recognize a soul in here. That is, until I hear a man's voice say, "Georgia Young!" and I turn around and there's Thomas, the jerk who ditched me at the senior prom and left with another girl. He looks

like Bill Cosby and is all gray and wearing bifocals. I can spot them
from across a room. I pretend I don't recognize him. He then takes his
glasses off so I can get a better look, smiles, which is when I haul off
and slap him hard on the arm.

"Hi, Thomas. Long time no see," I say.

"I deserve that," he says. "Feel better now?"

"Yes," I say. "How are you?"

"Well, I'm here. Is this brother your husband?"

"No, he's my brother."

"No he isn't. I knew your brother."

"His father married my mother."

"Then he's not even a relative. I'm Thomas, and you are?"

"Grover. How are you, Thomas? So you must've done something
unforgivable for her to have clipped you after all these years."

"She can tell you about it later. I had some undiagnosed issues back
in the day. So are we drinking tonight?"

"I suppose we are," I say.

For the next hour, I walk around bumping into people I don't
recognize and remembering bits and pieces of why we didn't know
each other or why did I sit in the back row or the front row and did
I remember when and how could I forget, but then by the time everybody's drunk, they start doing karaoke. Most of the songs are rock
and roll and country, all from the seventies, which certainly doesn't lift
my hem. I didn't want to be the Carpenters or Helen Reddy or Olivia
Newton-John or Cher or Judy Collins, but when Tina Turner's "Proud
Mary" comes on, Grover looks at me and I look at him and we go for
it. We rock the place, of course, because we've got soul, and I wish
I had my wig on, but afterward we get huge applause. When these
alcoholics start spilling their drinks and falling off their stools, I give
Grover "the look."

I drop him off without incident.

The following morning I go on the tour of our high school, without Grover (saving him for dinner), along with about seventy other
reunion-goers. Except for the die-hard golfers, everyone is hungover.
We walk out onto the football field, which feels weird, and of course

I get a little nostalgic looking at the empty bleachers. I go on the tour bus. We have the option of getting off and on where we want because the bus circles back around until each venue closes. I'm really enjoying just riding on the bus and marveling at how much there is to see and do in Bakersfield. There's the Museum of Art, the Fox Theater, the Buck Owens Crystal Palace, and more and more. A lot more than I remember.

At dinner Grover wears a serious black suit with a yellow shirt and a purple-and-yellow tie. We match by accident. I'm wearing my purple suede Manolo pumps with a kelly green dress. It's tight. And I'm glad.

We're now having dinner in the Sequoia Room, which is just four white-and-gold doorways away from the Grapevine, because a few more people RSVP'd at the last minute. The rows of tables are lined up like those in an orphanage. It feels odd. When I locate my table number and spot my three-by-five high-school photo on a short wooden stick, I'm not happy about it. I looked like I had too many things on my mind and was trying to figure out which one to address but had failed. My lips looked like they were upside down. My hair looked like a turkey plume. My long, skinny neck didn't look like it could handle the weight of my head. I do not remember being anorexic. But there was only half of me. Maybe I would've looked better if it had been in color. It's a shame we didn't have Photoshop back then.

And of course whose photo is sitting on the other side of me? None other than Miss Walkie-Talkie herself: Saundra Lee Jones. I'm praying she's called in sick or something. I don't feel like reminiscing with her, because we don't have a plateful of good memories, and I also don't feel like lying about how much fun we used to have. I couldn't stand her ass. I bet they only seated us together because we're both black.

I'm also hoping the after-dinner speech is short but I'll applaud and laugh on cue. That the awards are short. And the PowerPoint of those who are no longer with us is even shorter. My goal is to dance through this night and cha-cha right on out into the parking lot without being missed. Grover's game for anything.

"Hello there, Georgia." I hear that familiar voice from behind me. It's my girlfriend Saundra Lee. I turn around and look up and cannot believe my eyes. She's gorgeous! She should change that tired picture she has on Facebook.

"Saundra?" I ask, standing up and giving her a big squeeze.

"It's me. I had a makeover. You're looking pretty snazzy yourself, girl. Change that picture you have on Facebook. Here," she says, and hands me a gift bag with a yellow flower on it.

I open it, and it's a picture of the two of us when we were both skinny and about to get into trouble. I think it was in our sophomore year. Before she started getting on my nerves. And here she is now. Being nice. I'm going to throw the ugly where it belongs.

"Why, thank you, Saundra! We were terrors, weren't we?"

"It's so good to see you. You know, I asked to be seated next to you, since there were so few of us, and it looks like even fewer of us turned out. And who's this?" she asks, trying not to give Grover the gaga eye, but she's giving him the gaga eye, and he stands up and looks down at her like he's just made a discovery. Men are such whores.

"This gentleman is my stepbrother, but we've dropped the 'step.' "

Saundra shakes his hand like she means it and without looking away from his eyes. She was always a loosey-goosey, and age has apparently not affected her. Something tells me there's going to be a whole lotta shaking going on.

And so the reunion officially begins.

I see groups forming.

The once-pretty, skinny blondes who were cheerleaders are still skinny and blond but not even close to pretty, because they've had too much work done. They're huddled in a tight circle with their arms around one another, hugging and giggling, stuck in time.

I see the same snobs whispering as they move through the banquet hall. They thought they were hot shit then, but they just look like shit now. I'm being mean. They all pretend like they remember me. But they don't. I'm sure they've all looked at the little bios in the catalog and know I'm a doctor. I wonder when white folks will realize and accept that black people are just as smart and as educated as they are and in some cases smarter and more educated and that we don't have to apologize for it and that they should just respect us and accept it, because we now are and always have been equals. So yes, I'm a fucking doctor, and I don't even want to be one anymore. I take a pretend chill pill.

Everybody mingles.

"Really? You were a lifer in the army?"

"You still twirl a baton?"

"You own a McDonald's?"

"You're an embalmer? Wow."

"Sorry to hear you've been laid off after fifteen years. Yes, the economy is in shambles and scary. And you think it's all President Obama's fault."

"Of course I'm an empty-nester."

"Yes, I did end up graduating from college. Twice."

"You've got prostate cancer?"

"You've got high blood pressure and high cholesterol?"

"You're a breast-cancer survivor?"

"Yes, my mother's still alive."

"Sorry both of your parents have passed on."

"You're retired?"

"You lost a son in Afghanistan?"

"You lost a daughter in Iraq?"

"So that's how you met your third husband?"

"And prison wasn't as bad as you thought?"

"You never left Bakersfield?"

"Why would you?"

"You have sixteen grandchildren?"

"This is only your second face-lift?"

"No, I haven't been to Greece, but it's on my bucket list."

Dinner is tasteful and tasty. Our reunion money was well spent.

I excuse myself and head to the ladies' room. All I do is powder my nose, because what I really needed was to breathe. It's hard being on. As I head back into the ballroom, I hear a man's voice say, "Hello there, Georgia."

I turn and see an older Bruce Gardner who was in my English class three years in a row. He was somewhat cute then, but he's definitely handsome now.

"Bruce Gardner?"

"I can't believe you remember me."

"Of course I remember you. You didn't talk in class. I did. We sat next to each other. I think you cheated on a test once."

"I've never cheated at anything."

I smile. He smiles.

"You look fabulous," he says, and without pausing, "So I read up on you, Georgia. You've done well for yourself, not that I'm surprised, and don't freak out, but there's something I've been wanting to tell you after all these years."

"I'm all ears."

"I had a mad crush on you in high school."

I get a very thick lump in my throat.

"You don't have to say anything. I've looked for you at the last four reunions and was very disappointed not to see you. But here you are, and I just thought I'd tell you this, and you don't have to react or respond, because it was worth getting it off my chest and finally out of my heart."

"Wow."

"That's good enough," he says, and bends down and takes my hand and kisses it.

"Hold on a minute, soldier, we can do better than that," I say, and walk up close to him and drape my arms around him, and he does the same to me.

"Wow, so were it not for racial politics back in the day, you mean to tell me I could've felt you in my arms like this all these years?" he asks as I step away from him.

"Who knows?" I say. "It's really nice seeing you after such a long time, Bruce. And thank you for telling me how you felt. I'm flattered. Hope to see you again in ten."

And off he goes to sit three tables away from mine, next to a handsome woman I know must be his wife. They both wave, and I wave back. I'm now sitting in Grover's seat, because he and Saundra are engrossed in a conversation.

And then the awards and applause: for longest marriage, oldest child, youngest child, the most grandchildren and best dancer, which I was shocked to win, as I was no Janet Jackson back in the day. We see remnants of the sports teams and the cheerleading squads. They pose for pictures. And then there's the slide show of the twenty-six classmates who've passed away. I recognize almost all of them.

When I hear the announcement that the speaker's going to give his talk soon and I hear them say Bruce's name, I'm quite surprised. I never gave him a minute's attention, and now he's a senator who forty years later tells me he had a crush on me in high school. I'm all ears.

"Well, hello, class of '72! I know you've all been sitting out there thinking you feel younger than everyone else looks. But guess what? Forty years from now, the class of 2011 will be full of old ladies with tattoos. It's good so many of you were able to make it this year. Instead of reminiscing I thought I'd say something about where we are now and how we managed to get here. Wherever we are. Because the fact that we are here means we should be celebrating our lives. I know many of us have had a series of ups and downs. And after fifty we get not only the face we deserve but the life we deserve. It may not be the life we wanted, but we all got the life we have as a result of choices we made. Some of us who haven't been so lucky probably look back at our lives and wish we could put them on videotape so we could get an instant replay, but then others might just want to erase theirs. Don't even think about it, because everything we've done, every bad and good decision we've made is what's shaped our lives and brought us here tonight. Know that we're the only people who knew you when you weren't a father or a mother. We're the only people who knew you when you didn't have a profession or a career. We knew you when you were young and vibrant. Some of us didn't like each other back then. Some of us got bullied. Some of us fell in love but were too afraid to admit it. Some of us got our hearts broken because we did. But I'm here to tell you folks something you probably already know. It's not that complicated. All we can do is aim to leave this world a little bit better than we found it. So let's not listen to that domestic devil. Let's continue to be the change we want to see in ourselves and in the world. And regardless of how many times you've been divorced or if you're still looking for that special someone or you wish you'd chosen a different career, don't give up just yet. If you're still looking for your purpose, don't stop until you find it. Because guess what? For lack of a better cliché, it ain't over till it's over. We've still got some good years left to dance to the song known as our lives at whatever rpm we choose. Some of us like to tango. Some want to waltz. Personally, I still like to rock. I'm just so glad we're all still here, and as my granddaughter likes to say, it's all good! Now, let's party like it's 1972!"

And off the stage he goes. I'm in tears. I'm standing like everyone in this banquet room is. We're applauding Bruce, but we're also applauding ourselves. Our lives.

And then we dance.

To all those songs from the seventies on up to right now.

I dance with Bruce and his wife.

Saundra dances with Grover.

The floor is packed with middle-agers who came here to celebrate and applaud one another. As we head out, everybody says good-bye to everybody, and some of us—people I assumed didn't remember me and whom I didn't remember—acknowledge one another. Some of us hug and squeeze hands, and by the time I get into the car, as much as I didn't think I would, I have to admit I had fun.

# Already Home

'M ON MY KNEES WEEDING THE FLOWER BED WHEN NAOMI comes over.

"Hi, Ms. Georgia. How's everything?"

"Everything is everything. And you?"

"Well, looks like I'm single after nine years."

I wipe my gloved hands together, then brush the mud off my apron and stand up. "You mean you and Macy are splitting up?"

"Split. She moved out."

"When? I never saw any moving trucks."

"She left everything with me. Except Rascal. He was hers."

"I don't want to pry, but why?"

I can tell she's been drinking, but who can blame her?

"According to the headlines, she ran into a blast from her past, and apparently they've rekindled those old flames. I'm sick. Deep inside sick."

And she starts crying, and the Indian feathers on the front of her red sweatshirt begin jerking around like waves. I untie my wet apron and let it drop to the sidewalk and walk over and give her a motherly hug. I take her by the hand, and we go sit on the steps.

"I'm really sorry to hear this, Naomi. Truly sorry. What are you going to do?"

She shakes her head back and forth, rakes her fingers through her short blond hair, and then starts twirling her small gold hoop earrings with two fingers. "I suppose I have to divorce her."

I'd forgotten they were one of the first hundred same-sex couples standing outside the courthouse in San Francisco on that June day in 2008 and were lucky to get legal marriage licenses. They were married on the courthouse steps. I saw them on the news and was happy for them. And of course it was all halted months later, and we'll just have to wait to see if the Supreme Court ever comes to their fucking senses and gives these couples the same rights as the rest of us.

"Don't think about that yet. People go through things. Sometimes they come to their senses when they realize what they've lost."

She shakes her head even more vigorously. "Not Macy."

"You want to come in for coffee?"

"Sure, if you can put a kick in it?"

"You bet."

"Wow," she says after following me in. "This is proof that all gay men don't have good taste."

"He did his job. But I couldn't agree more. Come."

And she follows me to the kitchen and sits on a barstool. I step down to the bar and hold up a bottle of Maker's. She nods.

"She was a complete bitch anyway," she says.

Here we go with alcohol honesty.

"But enough about her," she says, leaning on the island with both elbows. "Have you gotten any offers yet? If not, mine will be on the market in a few weeks. So they'll have twins to choose from!"

"No offers that've stuck."

"But say if your house were to sell later today, where would you want to move, Miss Georgia Peach?"

"New York," I say for the hell of it.

"Don't be ridiculous. Californians don't have the heart or the chutzpah to live in or even appreciate the high octane that New York has to offer, just like New Yorkers don't like living in sunny, picture-fucking-perfect, beautiful, superficial, yes-the-clichés-are-all-true California. Except none of them apply to the Bay Area. We're the East Coast of the West, and we rock!"

She holds her hand up, and I pat it with my palm.

"Face it, you like trees and grass and digging up worms and weeds in your fucking flower bed. You should keep your straight black ass right here and put some money into this fucking 1985-flashback kitchen. Wait until you're like a real senior citizen and then sell this son of a bitch. Hey, you want to come to my divorce?"

"No," I say, and put her arm over my shoulder and walk her sluggishly down my sidewalk up her driveway and inside her and Macy's very hip and art-filled house, which is floor-to-ceiling glass with a view of San Francisco to die for.

I walk her over to their gunmetal leather sofa and help her sit, and she falls to one side. I pick her up by both feet and slip one of many silk pillows under her head and then take the yellow mohair throw and place it over her.

"You're such a cool neighbor, Georgia Brown. Don't fucking move to New York. You're already home."

And she's gone.

And she's right.

I finish weeding and clean up, then go to every single art store I want to. I buy paint. Broken glass. Sand. Seashells. Pebbles. Black roses. Black rocks. Feathers. Ribbon. Burlap. Leather. And more. By the time I get home, it's dark. I leave everything in the car until I decide where I'm going to put it. I am happy.

Although it's probably not even fifty degrees outside, I open the door, turn on the pool lights, walk back inside, and grab two folded bath towels from the laundry room, come back and sit on a chaise lounge and throw the towels over me like a blanket. I watch the small navy blue waves flow like they have a destination. Through the fog I can still see the Bay Bridge lit up as if it's celebrating itself. I turn around and look inside my home, my house, then close my eyes and recline.

A chill wakes me up. I walk back inside and out the front door and pull that For Sale sign out of the ground. I can feel the roots applauding. I drop it inside the trash bin that's sitting on the curb, and when I go back inside, the door closes slowly and the whoosh of the air sounds like it's whispering thank you. I go into the kitchen and just stand there. Look around. All the stainless steel suddenly looks cold and old and outdated. Naomi was right. I toss the towels over a barstool and

make myself a strong cup of coffee. I turn off the lights that lead down
to my office and look over at the fireplace and decide to light it.

I'm tired of waiting. Feeling anxious all the time. Tired of strangers
traipsing through my house, tired of hearing what they like and don't
like, what they would change. How they would rip out the floors. And
why would anybody put concrete and leather on the floor? We'd have
to carpet all this. We'd definitely put a real chandelier over the stairwell, and is that a boat? And that metal stairway would have to go; it's
too cold and industrial. At least the walls are all white, so we wouldn't
have to paint. Not sure if we like that black-bottomed pool, it's too dramatic. Water should be turquoise.

Sorry, Georgia, that family from Seattle couldn't qualify. Sorry,
Georgia, the couple hoping to relocate didn't qualify. Sorry, Georgia,
sorry, Georgia, sorry, Georgia. Well, I know who does qualify. Georgia. And right now, were I to pay off what's left on my mortgage after
I sell my partnership, I'll be free. I can't even believe this. Stupid is as
stupid does. I don't know what I was thinking. I didn't even know
where else I wanted to go. As I look around, I realize I like living in
this house. It's my home. And it wasn't the house I needed to change.
It was me.

# How to Fall In and Out of Love
# in Three Easy Steps

'M HOLED UP IN A THREE-STAR HOTEL WHILE PERCY GETS all that ugly furniture out of my house and I have most of the walls repainted with energy. In five days I'll be able to move back into my old new home.

I've also come to the conclusion that trying to reconnect with the remaining three men I purportedly once loved feels like a waste of time. I think I was just melancholy and nostalgic after finding out that Ray had passed away. I will, however, send these men a shout-out and call it a day. After reuniting face-to-face with my ex-husbands, I admit it was touching, but I'm not so sure that if I'd never laid eyes on either one of them, I would have really missed out on anything. Although I couldn't stand Michael for years and can now tolerate him, what would I have lost had I never forgiven him? It's not like I sat around year after year thinking about how I wished I'd pushed him off the Golden Gate Bridge or like I lost sleep wondering how things were going with his new wife. And Niles. Mr. Narcissisto. After seeing him I could not remember what it was that made me fall in love with him.

I'm no anthropologist, but it has become clear that as a middle-aged woman, I've spent more time and energy on mistakes than I have with men who lived up to their image and kept their promises. It doesn't seem to matter how educated or smart they were—since the two aren't synonymous—although the geniuses I've met seem to think they've been blessed with holy water, which is one of the major reasons for, causes of, and contributors to their shortcomings.

As I swivel in this chair, I open Facebook and stare at my home page. I'm getting bored with Facebook, but if I say I'm going to do something, I usually do it. It may take a while, but I like to finish what I start. Right now, however, this is what I'm thinking: if I'd just gone on and had Abraham's baby and married him and ended up on a farm in Louisiana growing stuff, I probably would've been happier and wouldn't need to go scrounging around on Facebook looking up these blasts from my past, and Abraham would still be my boo.

Which is why I wish I'd just gone ahead and seduced him and not run my mouth so much talking about old times and his life on the farm and how much we once meant to each other. I'm too old to fall in love because I have a few orgasms. Those days are so 1980. And so what if I had? It would've been worth the suffering and longing I felt after he went back home to plant soybeans and sweet potatoes with his earthy new wife.

I click on Carter.

In bold blue letters across those velvety green mountains is a caption: IN MEMORY OF CARTER GLENN RUSSELL. There are comments from at least thirty people expressing how much they're going to miss him and what a great uncle/brother/cousin/father/friend/colleague he was. I click on About, and all it says is, "Our father passed away on January 1, 2011, surrounded by his friends and family. Please share a photo and any memories you have about him on his timeline. He would like that."

This is what I remember about him.

I lived in an iffy neighborhood on a busy street my first year in optometry school. One night while I was trying to get my key in the door, some guy comes out of nowhere and snatches my purse and runs. Carter, who was patrolling the area, saw this and took off after the thief. He was able to corner him, and the man tossed my purse into some bushes. I saw Carter draw his gun and then say, "Go in those bushes and get the lady's handbag, right now, son, and don't make me say it again." The man, who was in his early twenties, did as he was told. "Now, walk back down the street to where you see her standing and give it back to her, and then I want you to apologize for scaring her half to death." And he did. "I'm sorry for stealing your purse, ma'am," he said as Carter shook his head, indicating that I not respond. He then pushed the guy into the back of his squad car and locked the door. "Are you okay?" he asked, and I told him I was. Carter was a big guy, at least six-five, and he gave me his card and told me if I ever needed him for anything, to feel free to call him.

For the next nine months that I lived there, almost every night Carter made sure either he or one of his partners kept an eye on me when I walked down that street. And right before I was going to move in with Michael, he showed me a picture of his wife. "Lucky woman," I said. He kissed me on the cheek and told me to take good care of myself and not to marry any man who didn't.

This is my comment:

> Carter was a brave, honest, caring, and loyal human being. He made me feel safe as a college student, and I'm honored to have known him.

And Lance. Not worth remembering, and I probably should've put him on that long list.

Oliver had a voice so deep he made you feel like you were being seduced fully clothed. Even when he laughed, it came from down deep. I used to ask him questions that required long answers just to hear him speak. He knew he was sexy, but he couldn't help it. His smile was sideways and forced a dimple to form in the crease below those cheekbones. No man should have so much to lure you in with, but he did. And on top of all this, he was smart. Much smarter than me. Or I should say he was more knowledgeable about a lot more things than I was. Oliver was a philosophy major, and when he told me that, I almost squeezed the moisture out of the plastic cup of juice I'd snuck into the library. I thought this was very cool, especially him being a young black man. Out of all the majors in the universe, I asked him, why philosophy? And he said because he had always been curious about how to live a morally awake life and about how and what we could do to elevate our character. Well, okay, I remember thinking. But wasn't that what the Bible helped us figure out? And going to church? I didn't say it—I was just thinking it. But I remember him asking me if I'd ever heard of Epictetus, and of course I hadn't, and he went on to tell me that he was one of his favorite philosophers and suggested I look him up. Which I never did, because in the nine months Oliver and I would date, I would learn more about him and a lot of other philosophers, some of whom I thought were nuts, until I started OD'ing on how to live based on a moral compass. I spent so much time trying to impress Oliver that I got lost in his way of looking at the world and the role he thought we were meant to play in it, and to ourselves.

I loved him because he lifted my heart and my mind, but I got tired of analyzing everything. Loving Oliver wore me out. He lost patience with me because, I believe, he came to the conclusion that I was just shallow. He wanted to break up because I didn't share his beliefs. I wanted to break up because he didn't respect mine.

I'm not surprised he became a minister. He's married. The father of three. One grandson. Although I'm trying not to put so much emphasis on the sex, there was a reason I didn't mind being preached to. He was extremely talented in bed, and over the years I've come to realize that there are only two schools of men: those who are good in bed and those who aren't.

> Hello, Oliver! Just wanted to let you know I recently saw a book on Epictetus and thought of you. I purchased it in your honor and believe he may very well have been onto something! I'm trying to do some of what he subscribed to. But enough about me! I'm so glad you found your calling, and it looks like you are happy, which I'm thrilled to learn. I turned to a different type of curative practice and am now ready to find a more creative one. Just wanted to let you know that after all these years I hadn't forgotten that you once held a warm place in my heart and that I'm grateful to have met you. Continued blessings to you and your family. Very best, Georgia.

Last but not least is David. He was not the most tactful. I knew it when standing behind me at the grocery store, he leaned close and said in a low voice, "You look good enough to eat, and I wish I could put you in my basket." When I turned around, he gazed at me with those dreamy black eyes. That shiny mustache couldn't hide those smooth lips that he had the nerve to lick, and I tried my best to say, "Don't be so fresh. You don't even know me." I paid for my food, and when I unlocked my blue '75 Honda, he came out of the store empty-handed and just stood there with his arms crossed and watched me open the door before he said, "Can I help you put your groceries in your Rolls-Royce?" And that pretty much did it. I let him enter my life, because he was intoxicating, and after Eric and a few hits and misses pre- and post-Niles I was due for some excitement, regardless of how racy it might turn out to be. I had the time of my life with David and fell in love like a teenager. They say you always want what you can't have, and I knew that David wasn't in love with me, but I didn't care.

He was almost always unemployed, but he was quite the socialite for someone with no money. He didn't miss a party or an excuse to go out, which was one of the reasons I started sewing again! He pretended to be creative and claimed he was going to get into theater one day, even though he never took a class. He was dramatic. And I didn't know how to read him. He would fly. And then crash. I didn't know there was a name for his behavior back then, and after six months on this emotional roller coaster, he broke up with me. I took him back. And then I broke up with him. The last time I heard from him is when he called me from New York to apologize for exiting stage left without closing the curtain.

> Hello, David! It's me, Georgia Young from the Stone Age. Was in Berkeley a week ago and passed by your old apartment and thought I'd look you up on Facebook to see if you'd dropped off the planet: glad to see you haven't. So you went from theater to television, and looks like producing was a good fit. I hear Toronto is a great place to live. Anyway, I just wanted

you to know I'm happy to see you're thriving and glad I had a chance to know you back in the day! Warmly, Georgia.

There.

I put on a pair of fresh pajamas, brush my teeth, put my hair in six braids, don't turn on the low-definition television, and pull the Clorox-smelling sheets across my breasts and stare up at the popcorn ceiling.

I might just give up on love, because I've come to realize it's the one thing that doesn't last. Too many men have disappointed me. They confess their love, and then I discover they don't really know how. There are three things I've decided might have helped if I had known then what I know now:

1. When you think you've found the Right One and you free-fall so hard you levitate and picture yourself spending the rest of your life with this person, give the relationship everything you've got, milk it, and enjoy it while it lasts, because you don't know when you might feel this way again.

2. No one is perfect. Not even you. But know how much you can tolerate and don't toil like a slave to make your relationship or marriage work. When you find yourself miserable more than you are happy, know this is not where you need to be. Figure out a way to get out.

3. When it's over, it's over. Don't look back. You never know who's behind Door Number One or who might walk into your life when you're not looking.

But then again, I ain't no Oprah.

# What Are Friends For?

"G UESS WHO'S BACK?" MARINA SAYS.

"I can't begin to," I say.

She opens the door wide, and Mercury pops his head inside. "Hi, Doc."

"Don't tell me," I say, laughing.

"I was too loud and too friendly. I tried to calm it down, but it
wasn't enough for Neiman's, and so here I am! Marina's ready to train
me to replace her if you'll take me back."

"I like loud. And I like friendly. Welcome back, young man," I say,
and walk around my desk to hug him.


I'M ABOUT TO exhaust myself for ten whole minutes stir-frying
Latin-spiced shrimp and snow peas to pour over linguine in this outdated kitchen when my doorbell rings. No one just drops by my house.

"Open the door before I break it down, huzzy."

"I'm coming!" I'm at a loss for words when I open the door, and
then, just like old times, standing there in a short leather jacket with
her hands on her hips like a middle-aged runway model, is my Violet.
She's in her animal print, but this getup is turquoise-and-black leopard
or cheetah—who knows? She's got her auburn weave back, and it's
cascading way past her shoulder blades. She's too thin, because I can
feel how pointed they are when she bends over and hugs me hard.

"I don't believe this. Come on in. Is something wrong?"

"Why does something have to be wrong?" she asks, and sashays right on past me like she's been doing for years.

"I'm just surprised to see you. Why didn't you call first?"

"Because I didn't want to. How's that?"

"What if I hadn't been home?"

"Then I would've turned around and gone somewhere else—anything to get out of that little house."

"So what brings you all the way over here, Violet?"

"It's only twenty minutes away. But for starters I've been trying to figure out how to thank you and Wanda for walking those thirty-nine miles. It meant a lot to me. I'm going to do it next year for sure. What's that you're cooking? It sure smells good, but I don't care what it is as long as you're cooking it. I'm starving," she says, and heads to the kitchen and grabs a plate from the cabinet.

"Your coming here says it all, Violet. So how's everything going?" I ask, and it must be obvious I'm looking at her chest, although I don't mean to.

"It's fine. You want to see it?"

"No!" I yell, just as she's taking off her leather jacket and is about to pull up her tight black top.

"It looks just like the old one."

"Well, I didn't see your *old* one, Violet. I'll take your word for it. But you're doing okay, then?"

"I'm moving along."

"I'm glad to hear that. I've been leaving you alone thinking you might just need some time to grieve."

"I'm done grieving. I'm moving to Toronto."

"What did you just say?"

"You heard me. Can I get a glass of wine or something to go with my dinner?"

"You've been getting what you want from the bar for years, so don't try to pretend you're a guest all of a sudden."

And she does.

"The bar has me on probation for another year. I'm done living in America."

"Oh, really, now?"

"Really," she says, and kicks off those four-inchers.

"So tell me, Violet, since when did you get tired of the whole damn country?"

I go pour myself a glass of wine. I know this is going to be like her own reality TV show, so I'm going to give her my undivided attention.

"Okay, so I'm exaggerating," she says, and uses her fork to pierce a shrimp. Chews it.

While I watch and wait.

"This is tasty. Anyway, I'm sick of my daughter. I'm sick of that baby. I'm sick of being a lawyer. I'm sick of the Bay Area. I need a clean break. So I'm taking it."

This is really hard for me to swallow. I know that Violet's oldest son, Maxwell, plays basketball in Toronto.

"So are you going to just abandon your daughter and grandson to go live with your son and his wife? Is that it?"

"Maybe. That baby hasn't changed her one bit. If I could, I'd take him with me, but he would need a passport."

"What's his name?" I ask, holding my breath as I fix both of us a plate.

"Sauvignon."

"Wanda said he was named after a fruit."

"And you know damn well that's a grape. Anyway, we just had it out, and she's freaking because I've given her until the first of the year to get her shit together. I'm tired of making excuses for her. I'm done. She had a paternity test, and the good news is the baby daddy does have a few ounces of sense, and if she doesn't watch herself, he could file for, and probably get, custody."

"Really? You would let that happen?"

She rolls her eyes at me.

We both take a few bites.

"This is so good, whatever it is," she says.

"Glad it meets with your approval. Anyway, I'm both sorry and happy to hear all this, Violet. But what are you going to do for money?"

"I'm not piss-poor anymore, Georgia. I can also work up there. You can get permits. I do have some marketable skills, although I can't tell you what they are right now, so don't ask. How in the hell are you? You look good. You must be exercising like crazy."

"Not as much as I was when I was preparing to do the walk."

"Well, don't stop now."

Between bites I tell her about the new babies, that Frankie and Hunter are doing great and that she's enrolling at San Francisco State, that Estelle and Justin are going through something.

She downs her drink and stands up.

"I never trusted him if you want to know the truth. But anyway, thanks for the meal. I just wanted to say hi and give you a hug."

"But you just got here, huzzy!"

"I've got tickets to see Oleta Adams tonight."

"I love her."

She walks over to the sink and washes her plate and glass and flatware and puts them in the dish rack. "You want to go with me?"

"I can't."

"Why not? Doesn't look like the dishwasher's out of service. And let me say this. The crib looks great. Hey, wait a minute now! This is all your stuff! And you painted! You know my mind is gone for not noticing. Does this mean you took it off the market and you're keeping your stupid ass here?"

"Yes."

"This is a good thing, especially since you've now got four grand-kids and they're going to need somewhere to sleep besides your bed. Put a fence around that pool so they don't drown. Those twins were a handful—are they finally on some kind of medication?"

Under different circumstances I'd be pissed at Violet for saying this, but I know she's just being facetious. I'm happy to have my friend back, so I laugh right along with her.

"I told you. This market wasn't changing anytime soon, even with all Obama's trying to do. This is just one more reason I'm getting the hell out of here. I don't own anything anymore, and I don't care. I'm not leaving anything to my kids, because they don't appreciate me anyway. Let them fight over the insurance. Bye. I love you, girl, and good seeing you, but I can't afford to miss Oleta."

MERCURY KNOCKS ON my office door. I tell him to come on in. I can tell something bad has happened.

"What's wrong?"

"Lily's father just passed."

"Oh, no," I sigh. "Where is she?"

"At John Muir in Walnut Creek. She had the office on speed dial. That's the reason she didn't call you directly. She's a little messed up. I thought he was doing okay after his hip surgery."

"He had liver cancer," I say.

"Oh, shit. Sorry."

"I'm sorry, too. I'm pretty sure Lily knew what stage he was in, but it doesn't matter. It's her father."

"She said she'd call you the first chance she gets, but she did ask me to relay this and said it might freak you out a little."

"Relay what, Mercury?"

"She asked me to tell you she probably won't be back in the office for the next two to three weeks, and she asked if I'd notify all her patients as soon as possible and tell them about her loss."

"I totally understand."

The following day Lily expresses to me that because of her family's tradition she's taking her father to the Philippines for his final resting place and then tells me she's probably going to need to take the whole month off to handle all of his and her mother's affairs. I ask if there's anything I can do to help. She says no. But maybe we should consider closing the practice for a month to give us both a break before deciding what we're going to do with it permanently.

I agree.

It turns out Marina's not moving to New York for another month and a half, and since she and Mercury have become rather close, they've agreed to call every single patient to reschedule. They also put a big sign on the door to explain why the office is going to be closed and for how long, along with a number to call in case of an emergency. Of course I'm saddened by Lily's loss and can remember like it was yesterday how it felt when my father passed. It takes a long time to accept losing a parent no matter how old that parent is.

I SPEND THE first week at home organizing my new "studio." I may also have done something stupid. Instead of spending money on a real studio, I paid a contractor to install a utility sink and a partition to separate both sides of the garage and also to lay down waterproof rubber flooring. I bought Formica and metal rolling cabinets and enough cans, cork, bottles, jars, brushes, glue, and glue guns to last for years. I must think I'm some kind of artist or something.

I haven't even finished painting that stool, and I had the nerve to buy two baby chairs for Levi and Dove. I only hope they won't be in college by the time I finish them.

The house phone rings.

It's Michelle Obama.

"Hi, Ma. How you doing?"

"I'm just ducky, and you?"

"Quack-quack."

"What are you doing for your birthday?"

"When is it again?"

"Funny. In twenty-seven days."

"Why? You want to take me to Bora-Bora?"

"No. You want to go to Bora-Bora? Is that on your bucket list, too?"

"Maybe."

"Anyway, Grover and I want to come up to the Bay Area and take you to dinner if you're not doing anything special, which—I hate to say it—I doubt you are."

"What if I said I was going to Bora-Bora?"

"Answer the question, Georgia. We might take the train up there. It takes almost seven hours, but we've never done it. Did you ever take your train ride?"

"Not yet. Soon. It's at the top of my bucket list."

"So are we on, then?"

"We're on. You want to stay here?"

"No. Too many stairs. Don't worry, we've already got a hotel reservation. Anyway, did I interrupt you?"

"No you didn't."

"What were you doing?"

"Nothing much. Just organizing."

"I'm not even going to ask what. Talk soon, and see you next month."

Ma has never been all that curious about how I spend my birthday, and because my daughters and Wanda haven't said anything, something is definitely going on.

I know how to find out. Play dumb.

I start with Wanda. I get her voice mail. Which is odd.

I call Frankie, who's at the pediatrician with Levi. Can she call me back? Of course.

Estelle's putting the twins down for a nap and about to breast-feed Dove. Can she call me back tomorrow?

Violet answers.

"So," she says, "what's going on?"

"How was Oleta?"

"Phenomenal."

Silence. Which is a dead giveaway.

"Why'd you call me?" she asks.

"Can't I call just to say hi?"

"Hi. So. Wanda just told me you finally saw Abraham."

"I did."

"Why didn't you say anything when I saw you?"

"What was there to say?"

"Well, how was he or how was it?"

"He was fine. Still is fine. Almost married. He's a farmer and living deep in the South."

"Did you fuck him?"

"No."

"Well, I guess after all this time it's safe to tell you that I did."

"Say that again. I couldn't possibly have heard you right."

"You heard right. I fucked him. I don't know how you left all that."

"You know, you always were a skank, Violet."

"Yeah, maybe, but so what, and just so you know, we're having a surprise birthday party for your ass, so act surprised."

"I DON'T WANT a surprise party," I said in a voice message I left for Wanda, who's just pulled up in front of my house and is sitting in her car because I told her not to come over here trying to persuade me that I'm being childish, unreasonable, and ungrateful.

"Why not?"

"Because I don't."

"Well, it's too late now. The stripper's already booked."

"Why didn't somebody ask me if I wanted a party?"

"Because we knew you would say no. Last year we sent you flowers because you pretended like you were sick so you wouldn't have to go out."

"Well, I don't want a party."

"And why in the hell not?"

"Because I'm too old to have a surprise birthday party."

"Did you take some kind of pill to depress you?"

"No."

"Then what is it?"

"Violet told me she slept with Abraham."

"That's old news."

"What did you say?"

"You heard me. I think he only did it to get back at you after you dropped him."

"So that made it okay?"

"No, but it's ancient history, Georgia."

"How would you feel if I told you I slept with Nelson before you did?"

"I wouldn't believe you."

"And why not?"

"Because you would've told me before he even looked my way. Besides, you've got too much class to stoop that low. Look, girl, we've always known Violet doesn't take morals into account when she makes a lot of decisions, so why hold it against her now?"

"Some secrets you should keep to yourself."

"I agree. Anyway, your mom and Grover and his son and his son and Dolly and her sons are all coming."

"What?"

"So is Michael."

"You've got to be kidding me."

"Niles and his wife might come. Your daughters, of course. All the folks from your office—too bad Lily might not be back in time. But that outrageous young fella Mercury and Marina, who's supposed to be leaving on a red-eye right afterward, and some of your good patients, but not Mona Kwon, who said she can't stay up that late, and even the techs said they wanted to come."

"What about President Obama and the First Lady?"

"They're busy."

"Anybody else I don't know?"

"You'll see," she says. "I know you couldn't possibly be this upset about what Violet said."

"No. I just find her timing a little questionable. I mean, why'd she have to wait all these years to admit it, especially when in the same breath she tells me about my fucking surprise birthday party? She's not my friend. Period. And I don't want to see her ass if I decide to come."

"You're going to come. And she's going to be there. And you will pretend to forgive her, and that's that."

"When is this frigging party?"

"It's a surprise."

"It's already not a surprise, Wanda."

"We'll see, won't we?"

# Surprising Surprises

H E'S GONE," ESTELLE SAYS TO ME AFTER I RETURN HER
call. I'm at the grocery store. I leave my full cart in the produce
section and head out toward the front door.

"Who?" I ask, knowing, of course, she's talking about her husband.

"Justin."

"Where did he go?"

"I don't know. And don't care. I kicked him out."

"Do you think you might be suffering from postpartum depression
or something?"

"He's got a boyfriend."

"A what?"

"You heard right. A fucking boyfriend."

"That's impossible."

"No, it's not impossible, Mom."

"Did he tell you he's gay?"

"Mom, he's got a fucking boyfriend! Not a girlfriend, so I think
that makes him gay. But I don't care what he is. The one thing I know
for sure is he's a father and he's going to take care of his children."

Justin never struck me this way, although people are damn good at
hiding all kinds of things. But why wait until she has another baby to
come out of the damn closet?

"Are you sure you're okay, Stelle? I think I need to come over there."

"No, don't come over here, please!"

"Where is Justin right now?"

"At the emergency room."

"The emergency room! What happened?"

"I just hit him in the head with a rolling pin. He'll live."

"I'm driving over there."

"Mom, please don't. I'm fine. I'm asking you to just respect my privacy right now. I had to tell you so you'll know why he's not going to be coming to your surprise birthday party. Oh, shit, now it's not a surprise! I'm sorry."

"I'm already aware of it. You know black folks can't keep a secret. How did you find this out, is what I want to know."

"He's been acting different for almost a year. He blamed it on working long hours. Which is why I was surprised when I got pregnant, and he definitely wasn't happy about it. Everything I did started getting on his nerves. He was testy. He would do and say things he knew would piss me off, but now I know why. So I would turn my back to him. And it worked. Anyway, I saw the same number on his cell over and over, so I called it. The guy's voice threw me for a loop, but when I confronted Justin, he just came out and told me. It was a dumb mistake for him to follow me into the goddamn kitchen. He should be glad we don't own a gun. And I'm sorry for swearing, Mom."

"I still think I should come over there."

"No. Please. Justin's just acting like a little bitch. He drove himself to the emergency room, which is all of ten minutes away. It's just a tiny cut."

"Where were the kids when all this was going on?"

"Sound asleep. He better be glad he's finally making some real money again, because I'm going to take all of it."

"Estelle, you're terribly upset right now, which is understandable. Look for me in about an hour."


I DRIVE FAST without any music for a half hour. I have no idea what I'm going to say to my daughter. Maybe I'll bring all of them back home with me. He's not dangerous. He's just gay.

I hope Estelle doesn't think she's to blame for this. I'm more worried about her heart. Her girls. Their future. Is she going to keep her job? Will she have to move? If so, how, and where? And what if they reconcile? But this isn't the type of thing you can negotiate. By the time I approach the entrance to the Dumbarton Bridge, she calls.

"Mom, where are you?"

"Almost on the Dumbarton Bridge."

"Please turn back around and go home."

"Why? I'm worried about you, Estelle. You need some kind of support right now."

"You're right, Mom, but just not tonight. Please. I'm not falling apart. The kids are fine, sleeping. And to be very honest, I've had my suspicions that Justin might have another side to him, and this just confirmed it."

"Are you saying you thought he might possibly be this way?"

"I don't know. I thought he might be cheating on me. What I do know is Justin loved me. I just never thought it was possible for a man to love a woman and also be attracted to men. Anyway, I need some time to think about all this without any input."

"Well, I'm here if you need me," I say. "Don't be too proud to reach out. This is what parents are for."

"Love you, Mom. Oh, and please don't tell Frankie. I want to be the one to tell her."

"I won't," I say. "And I'll help you get through this."

When I pull into my driveway, there's a car parked in front of my house. It's Justin. *Oh, Lord,* is all I'm thinking as I wait for the garage door to open. I walk out to his car, where he's just sitting like he's in a trance. I've always seen him as warm and respectful of my daughter and me, but right now he looks like he's been convicted of a crime he didn't commit and he has nowhere to go.

"I'm so very sorry, Dr. Young."

"I suppose you are," I say. "Since when did you start calling me Dr. Young?"

He wipes his eyes with both hands. I see a small railroad track on the side of his head. Dry red. "I wish I could still call you Mom. But I know that's over. I didn't do this to hurt Estelle. I swear I didn't. I just want you to understand that."

"I don't think you *did* anything, Justin. It's just really unfortunate that your timing is extremely bad. Why'd you come all the way over here?"

"Because I know Estelle hates me right now, and I needed to tell someone who knows her that I didn't do this on purpose."

"Do you want to come in?"

"No. I don't think that would be healthy, and I didn't drive over here to try to get you to feel sorry for me."

"I don't. I'm more concerned about my daughter and your children's well-being, but I can say I don't know what it's like to live a lie."

"First you have to admit to yourself that you are lying."

"Well, my first husband did a good job of it. And he's not gay."

And I start laughing. He wants to, but he just can't go that far right now.

"I hope you didn't jeopardize my daughter's health, just tell me that."

I feel myself cutting my eyes at him, and am prepared to split that railroad track in half if he gives me the wrong answer.

"I would not and did not."

"So now what?"

"I don't know. I just hope she lets me see my daughters."

"She will. Don't worry about that. But I'm sure she's going to have to get used to all this, Justin, so bear with her."

"I know, and the worst part of it is I so want to comfort her even though I'm the cause of her pain. How sick is that?"

"I get it. But let me ask you this. Are you going to be living with this boyfriend?"

He turns his head away and looks down. Shakes it no.

"Why not?"

"Because I can't."

"Don't tell me he's married, too?"

He shakes his head no.

"So this means he must be in a relationship, then, right?"

He nods.

"A live-in situation?"

He nods again.

I would really like to kick his ass right now. How dumb can you be? But this just goes to show: gay or straight, they're all the same—stupid!

"Well, that's just too bad, isn't it, Justin? So where are you going to go?"

"Probably a Holiday Inn or something until I can figure out how Estelle wants to deal with all of this. I'm so sorry."

And I believe him. I bend down and give him a hug, the hug I wanted to give my daughter, but I know he needs one, too.


I DON'T TELL Estelle that Justin came over here. I want to tell Frankie, but I have to respect Estelle's wishes. I do tell Wanda, who says she'd like to shoot him. But then she takes it back. I check in with both daughters on an almost daily basis until they tell me to relax, that they have their lives under control, and I should carry on with my own.

Estelle tells me Justin found an apartment and she's already filed for divorce, that she and the kids will continue to live in the house and Justin will, of course, continue to pay the mortgage, child care, and provide her with whatever monthly support the court tells him to. Plus whatever will make her and the girls' lives comfortable. He'll have visitation rights and promises not to subject them to anything he feels a need to explain, until they're old enough to understand.


DURING THE REMAINING three weeks left of not going to work (which I could definitely get used to), I feel like I'm possessed. I spend most of my waking hours in my garage. I paint. I glue. I sand. I make decisions. I love that I have choices. Options. Cracked glass or sand? Gravel or tiny seashells? Mosaic tiles or green grapes? Marbles or safety pins? Glass paint or metallic? Satin finish or flat? No one is more surprised than I am when I look out the only window and see daylight. This is what I hoped for.

I painted the original stool first. Flat black and then glued pennies all over it and sprayed it with a clear satin finish. No one will ever be able to sit on it, of course, but it will certainly provide some sort of interest for a dull corner. I went back to the wood-furniture store and bought two more stools in addition to two side tables, a magazine rack, and a shelving unit for knickknacks. I painted one stool metallic blue and glued broken glass on the legs but not the seat. I like it.

It's ten o'clock at night, and Naomi, who's on the long road to recovery, scares the hell out of me when she crawls under the garage door and just stands there with her hands on her denim hips and yells, "What the hell are you on? I mean, have you moved out here, or do you just not sleep anymore? And I want to buy that frigging stool with the pennies on it even if it's not for sale."

I take my mask and goggles off, then toss my gloves on top of the metal cabinet. "You know what, Naomi? You can have that stool."

"Are you fucking kidding me?" she says. "When did you become an artist, Doc? And why've you been hiding all this?" She walks over to the side table I've glued and splattered with three different shades of yellow sand. "How much is this?"

"Come on, Naomi. It's my new hobby. It's a great way to get rid of stress and confusion. I wouldn't call it art. Anyway, how are you?"

"I'm fine. I've met someone. But it's not serious. Of course, Macy's trying to crawl back in, but I've locked the door on her. What are you stressed about, unless I'm being too personal? And this *is* art, bitch."

"Just the usual. Nothing heavy-duty," I say.

"Are you sure?"

"Positive."

"Don't lie," she says. "I know what it's like to be pissed off, so if you ever feel like spilling your guts, your secret's safe with me."

"I appreciate that, Naomi, but I'm good."

"So when did you start doing this?"

"Probably before you were born. I used to sew, but I've always wanted to try making things out of wood and metal and glass because I like the idea of using materials for purposes they weren't intended. That's my story, and I'm sticking to it. I should mention I'm also having a helluva lot of fun."

"This is all just so freaking awesome. I never saw you as an eye doctor, to be honest. You should sell your work."

"My work?"

"Your art. What the hell else would you call it? It's beautiful, it's funky, it's original, and it's got the wow factor going for it. That's what art is."

"Slow down, Naomi. I'm flattered, but—"

She holds up her hand to push the air. "Just let me say this. When you get a body of work large enough to show, then we'll talk. But for now, honey, even with this cute partition you've got going, you're going to ruin this garage."

"I know. I might eventually need to find a little studio."

"You do that, and soon, but don't make it little. Isn't this addicting?"

"Yes, it is."

"And it's obvious you're strung out. You're not going to stop now that you've started. You'll soon realize it. Anyway, let me know when I can take that stool off your hands, and BTW, I'm having a birthday party next month, and lots of my—and yes, Ms. Macy's—friends are art people, and I'd love it if they could sneak over and take a peek at some of your work. Some of them have galleries. Shops. Anyway, you don't have to answer right now. You have totally fucking surprised me. I kid you not," she says, and heads back over to the garage door.

"Thanks. But hold on a minute. I'm having a surprise birthday party next week, and you're officially invited, but you just have to act surprised."

"Your friend Wanda already invited me. She's a pistol. She put the invitation in my mailbox. I might come alone. There's gotta be a single lesbian somewhere at your party who likes white women. I do not discriminate."

We both laugh as she crouches and slides under the garage door and disappears down the driveway. A moment later she pokes her head back under the garage door.

"Hey, girlfriend, who's going to be *your* date?"

"I don't have one."

"There has to be somebody you can tolerate for a few hours."

"What difference does it make?"

"It would just be fun to have an automatic dance partner. Someone you don't have to fuck unless you want to. Bye."

Maybe she has a point.

# Party Over Here

YOU HAVE A WHAT?" WANDA SCREAMS THROUGH THE phone.

"A date for the party."

"Cancel it."

"You don't tell me what to do."

"Who on earth could it be?"

"James Harvey."

"I invited him to the damn party. He didn't tell you?"

"No, he didn't."

"Well, everything's already been set up. We're picking you up in a limo. And he's not getting in it."

"I don't understand what the problem is."

"You wouldn't. Hold on a minute."

Silence.

"Wanda!"

Silence.

"There. I just texted him. He sent me a smiley face and said he understands. He'll see you at the party. So there."

I BUY A purple pencil skirt and an orange top that goes with it. I've decided to show it all and be daring, since it's my party. I can honestly say I don't want to lose another inch. I like being a size twelve. I also get my makeup professionally done. I look like a better version of myself. I like it. My brand-new beautician insists on adding a fun bun piled on the crown of my head. I love it. It's like a free face-lift. At first I choose pearls, but I forgot that Michael gave them to me, and if he shows up, which I'm sure he will, I don't want him to recognize them. I scour through one of my old jewelry boxes and notice a pair of purple, orange, and green rhinestone earrings that are so long they almost hit my collarbone. I bought them at a street fair in New York eons ago. Oh, why not? It's my birthday! To be safe, I opt for orange pumps that I know I can at least walk in. I can always kick them off if I dance.

*Beep-beep.*

Wanda's right on time, of course.

I run out to the limousine, grabbing the purple velvet stole I haven't had an occasion to wear in forever, and pray there are no moth holes in it.

"Well, you certainly look lovely tonight," the driver says. He's about seventyish and is striking in an odd way. His name tag says SHELDON.

"Thank you very much, Mr. Sheldon," and I get in after he opens the door.

"Happy birthday, huzzy," she says, nuzzling me with a cheek-to-cheek kiss.

"Thank you, Wanda. For everything."

"Think nothing of it! You sure clean up good," Wanda says, giving me the up-and-down and round-and-around.

"You don't look so poorly yourself," I say. She's in black, which is what Wanda thinks is appropriate for every occasion after dark. "Where's Nelson?"

"He's playing host. Greeting everybody to make sure they're all there. We've got time."

"What's that supposed to mean?"

"Well, we have one stop to make first."

"Really?"

"Yes, and don't ask. Why is your car in the driveway?"

"Because I'm painting in the garage?"

"Did you finally finish painting that stool?"

"I did."

"Hallelujah. I can't wait to see it."

"You probably won't like it."

"You don't know that. My taste is changing. In fact, when Nelson and I move to Palm Springs, we're leaving everything in the house."

"Seriously?"

"You heard what I just said, didn't you?"

"But why?"

"Because it's old and outdated, and our condo is new and bright, and open and we don't want it to look like a morgue. And they've got some great furniture stores in Palm Desert and Palm Springs, which you may not know are sisters."

"I think I do, and I think this is so cool, Wanda. But what are you guys going to do with your house?"

"Nothing. We're not putting it on the market, that's for sure. We'll let it sit there until we decide."

"Okay."

"Well, everybody's going to be there tonight," she says, and claps her white-gloved hands. "And I do mean *everybody*."

"Don't make me freak out, Wanda, and please don't embarrass me."

"I don't do that, and you know it."

"So where is this party?"

"None of your business, now. Just relax."

"Why are we going this way?" I ask when I look out the window and realize we're on a residential street, and I know who lives on it. I cut my eyes at Wanda. But then I realize it is my birthday celebration and today isn't the appropriate time to be a bitch. And out come Violet and Velvet! I didn't know she was coming with Ms. Thang. They're both sparkling. Their breasts would be visible to a blind person. Violet's in silver sequins, and Velvet's dress is hot pink lamé. I feel like I'm dressed more for an expensive dinner compared to these two sexy huzzies.

Sheldon opens the door, and Violet enters first, almost wailing, "Happy birthday, baby!" and then Velvet gives me a smooch on the cheek after flipping fifty of the two hundred blond braids over her shoulder and says, "Happy birthday, Auntie," and I'm suddenly touched.

"Thank you, ladies. You both look very pretty. Almost like sisters instead of mother and daughter."

They bump fists.

Wanda calls Nelson on her cell phone. "We'll be pulling up in less than five minutes," she says.

"Georgia, almost everybody knows you already know about the party, but when they yell 'Surprise!' just act surprised, okay?"

"Okay."

"But we do have some real surprises in store."

"I can only imagine," I say, and thump her head, then bend over and press my forehead against her cheek. "Thank you."

Minutes later Violet yells, "We're here!"

Velvet claps like she's at a basketball game.

I know this country club. Niles brought me here right before we parted the sea of marriage. I knew that Wanda and Nelson were going to go all out, which is precisely why she kept it a secret. She knew I would've tried to talk her out of it, and I probably would have. I'm almost afraid to walk in.

And then she exhales. Looks over at me. "We're going to rock your birthday, girl, so get ready to have some fun. I love your ass. And even though you'll hear more from me later, I want to take this opportunity to tell you privately, up close and personal, that at age fifty-five, your party is just getting started, baby. I think you know that already, but I want you to know that I—we—celebrate you because you're on a brand-new journey, and I am enjoying watching how you're continuing to improve your life and make changes some of us wouldn't dream of doing at our age. I'm proud as hell of you and proud to be your friend, your sister. Now, let's go party and tear the roof off this sucker!"

I smack her for making me lose it.

Mr. Sheldon opens my door first and says, "Happy birthday, Ms. Georgia. You must be celebrating your fortieth!" And he squeezes my shoulder like my father would. Wanda, of course, is already out of the car, almost bouncing, waiting for me to come around, and when I do, she grabs my hand and almost drags me to the double doors. After she taps on one, both open, and standing there are at least a hundred people who scream, "SURPRISE!"

And I lose it again.

I knew I shouldn't have gotten these frigging individual lashes, because when I go to wipe my eyes, I feel that hardened glue scratch. I am gang-hugged by almost everybody in here, including people I know and don't even think I know. My mother and her husband, and my daughters without husbands, squeeze me so hard I have to sit down at what is apparently "my" table in front of the entire room, on a platform, which makes me feel like I'm on a float at the Rose Parade, and behind me is a huge screen, which terrifies me. I'm pretty sure it's going to be testimonials of people lying about why they like me, but I hope and pray there are no baby pictures or photos of me from high school or college or when I was in my twenties or thirties. If Wanda did this, I'm going to kick her ass after this party. I don't want to be reminded of what I used to look like, because I look the way I'm supposed to look right now.

The place is beautiful, of course, and what a view. The tables could've come out of a magazine. The band is playing Chaka Khan's "Once You Get Started," and it appears that this is a Rainbow Coalition in here. I love it.

When the music stops, Wanda walks over to a podium and dings her wineglass to get everyone's attention. Oh, Lord, please not a speech. If so, I'm going to slide under this table. I'm already feeling lonely up here, and I wish she hadn't put me on a pedestal. I wish I had a husband sitting next to me, squeezing my hand, nodding at my guests while wrapping his legs around mine under the table behind this tablecloth. But it's just me.

"Welcome, everyone, to Georgia's fifty-fifth birthday celebration. We don't need to lie about our age, and my BFF for the past thirty-five years certainly doesn't, and I say she looks good!"

Applause.

I'm so embarrassed I hold my head down but then remember I have an audience, so I smile and hold my head up high. I almost feel like waving, like I'm indeed in a parade on a float and I'm the homecoming queen, but then I look out, and in the middle of this sea of people I see a man, a white man, a handsome white man with mixed gray hair and mustache smiling at me. He reminds me of one of those guys on a Cialis commercial, and I swear he looks just like . . . OMG! It *is*! Stanley! I feel like I'm sliding off this chair under the table, but I'm not. I cannot move. What is *he* doing here? And how did he find me? I turn to look over at Wanda, and she's winking at me and slowly nodding her head. So apparently Stanley is my surprise. I turn back to peer out at him, and he waves, then gives me a thumbs-up. What in the world am I supposed to do? I wave back like an intermittent windshield wiper, and I'm embarrassed but don't know why, and then my daughters and my mom and the entire front row of tables turn to see who I'm waving at, and Stanley smiles and nods and winks at them, and they all wink at me, and then I check out Wanda, and she's smiling like the Cheshire Cat. What a sneaky little bitch!

"So to help Ms. Thang celebrate, we're first going to watch a video of your family, close and not-so-close friends, and a few long-lost friends expressing why they love and care about you and what they wish for you on your fifty-fifth year of life. This will only take about fifteen minutes tops, because I gave everybody sixty seconds, and of course a few had to go over—you know who you are—but dinner will be served immediately afterward. So start working on your buzz, everybody, because dancing is coming up next." She turns to the screen and says, "Roll 'em."

I look back out into the audience, and Stanley is staring at me. Michael is staring at me. Niles is staring at me. Grover Sr. and my mother are smiling at me, and right next to them is Dolly, who I almost didn't recognize—she cleans up well—waving like she hasn't seen me in years, and two grown men in white shirts and ties who must be her sons, all giving me a thumbs-up. Grover Jr. is holding Saundra Lee's hand and grinning. Grover III is already whispering something in Velvet's ear, and she's blushing. Violet is sitting next to and flirting with Richard the jerk, which tells me that Wanda never told Nelson what he said, but it's all good. And there's Naomi pointing at Macy and hunching her shoulders and holding her palms up. I spot James Harvey, who just winks at me and smiles, because he's figured it all out by now. Wanda seems to have missed her calling, because she would make a great private investigator. And is that Lily? Yes it is, sitting at a table farther back with Marina and Mercury and the rest of my staff, and that looks like Mona Kwon! I thought she couldn't hang, but she's hanging tonight. Everybody's smiling. Everybody's happy. I'm happy. Although I'm wondering if there are any more blasts from my past seated at the back tables!

I listen to all the reasons that people like me and, in some cases, love and respect me. Marina is the most hilarious, because she tells how much fun we had getting drunk together, as if we did this on a regular basis. My mom is as sentimental as ever. Same with the daughters. And then Violet tells how much she admires and respects me and that she's done a few things to violate my trust and how she hopes I will forgive her. Of course I do. She's my fucking BFF. And then up come the exes. Oh, no! Michael just says how glad he was to have spent six years of his life with me, even though it was only five, and his daughter is lucky to have such a great mother. Niles pretty much says the same thing. And then to my surprise there's Stanley, on the screen, who says that he and I were good friends in college and are in the process of rekindling our friendship and how proud he is of all that I've accomplished, and that he hopes I remember him, because he sure hasn't forgotten me.

Even though I'm up on this stage, it's impossible to hide the fact that I'm blushing.

And then he winks! And he gets some serious applause! What exactly is going on here? What I remember most about Stanley happened under the covers, and that was a one-shot deal! Well, it was really quite a few shots, since I didn't go home for seventy-two hours. And I lied to Wanda. Stanley made my heart swell. But it was my little secret. I look out at him now, and he's looking back at me with that same smirk Ryan Gosling had in *Drive,* and I suddenly feel like someone needs to open a window. Fast. When I finally hear Wanda's testimonial, she pretty much says this:

"Georgia, I know you're probably wishing this party was over, because you're good at doing for others but you have yet to figure out how to accept, or I should say receive, except tonight you don't have a choice. I have loved being your friend, your sister, your confidante all these years and want you to know how much I respect your bravery, your sense of delight and fearlessness about life. You're not getting older, you're just about to reach the next plateau. You inspire me. Continue taking risks. Take that frigging train ride you've been postponing for too long, and Nelson and I hope that when you finally disembark, you get off at the right stop. Happy birthday, sis. P.S. Yes, I went over the time limit!"

The room is all laughter and applause and good spirits and even tissues zigzagging across cheeks. Plates start being set on tables, and there's not a dry chicken breast in sight. I walk down the three steps and out into the room to accept hug after hug and see Stanley standing there, on the sidelines, waiting patiently for his turn.

# Space Sailor

S O YOU'RE SUPPOSED TO BE GOING ON A TRAIN RIDE?" he asks as he sits down next to me, crosses those long legs, and then puts his arm around the back of my chair. I'm wondering if anybody's watching us, but everybody's on the dance floor, and of course Wanda and Nelson are shaking their booties, but she's got her eyes on me and Stanley with a smile, and when I glance over at my mother's table, everybody pretends to be looking at the lights on the Bay Bridge.

"I was. Am. What on earth are you doing here, Stanley?"

"Well, it's nice to see you, too, Georgia. Happy birthday."

And he smiles. Please don't smile at me like that. I shake it off and regain what I suppose would be called composure, even though I don't remember losing it.

"Thank you. One more time: What in the world are you doing here, Stanley?"

"I was invited."

"I know it was Wanda. But how?"

"She tracked me down on Facebook and gave me the update on you and what you were doing."

"But how'd she find you?"

"It wasn't that hard. Which tells me *you've* never tried to find me in all these years."

"I forgot your last name."

"What a liar you are. How could you forget DiStasio? I'm offended."

"Okay, so I didn't forget. I've been a little preoccupied."

"I know. I'm just trying to get you to relax."

"I'm not relaxed. I'm shocked. What exactly did Wanda tell you that made you want to come out here?"

"That you were looking up old friends—is how she put it, but I'm not stupid—and she didn't know if I'd made the cut, so she thought it would be nice for me to reach out to you, since you obviously never took me as seriously as I took you."

"And you're serious now?"

"Yes. Would you like to dance?"

"No!"

"Why not?"

"Because."

"Because why?"

"Because."

"If it's because I'm still white, that's just too bad," he says, and stands up and holds his hand out for me to take it, which I do with some hesitation, and we walk out to the dance floor and slowly begin to move to a beat I can't hear. I'm nervous because I've never danced with a white man before and especially in front of a roomful of mostly black people and especially with my two black ex-husbands staring at us like we're on *Dancing with the Stars*!

Stanley moves a little closer to me, and I back up a few inches, and he moves closer, and I stop, and then his feet and hips begin to swivel like he knows how to dance.

I almost can't handle this.

"Can't you dance, Georgia?"

"Yes, I can dance. But I'm having a hard time getting my rhythm right now."

"Relax. I didn't come here to upset you or bring up bad memories. But we don't have any bad memories that I know of, do we?"

I roll my eyes at him.

"Seriously, what made you come to my party, and where on earth did you come from? And who in the world are you, Stanley?"

"Well, I came because about thirty-some-odd years ago I fell in love with this beautiful college student, and her name was Georgia Young, but she was more worried about what other people would think, so I married another woman, who happened to be French, and she died ten years ago. I live in Manhattan, but my family's in Albany, and if you want to know what I do for a living, I'm not going to tell you unless you promise to have dinner with me."

I almost lose my footing.

The music stops, and Stanley just stands there. Looking down at me. Goddamn, is he handsome and sexy, and he's Italian, and did I just hear him right?

"We just *had* dinner."

"That doesn't count."

"How long are you going to be here?"

"Answer my question."

"Why should I have dinner with you?"

"Because you should."

"But you don't even know me anymore."

"Yes I do."

"No you don't, Stanley."

"All these people in this room tell me who you are. I know what you've been doing for a living, and I know you have two daughters and what's going on in their lives, and I know you've been alone too long and that you've got two husbands, whom I've met this evening, and I also know that our hearts don't forget who didn't break them. I'm here because I think enough time has passed and we're both mature enough and old enough to get to know each other—because what do we have to lose?"

"I think I need a drink," I say, and walk off the dance floor over to the bar. I can feel Stanley behind me. When I get to the bar, I turn around, and he's standing so close that I swear to God if this were a movie, I'd be putting my arms around him and giving him a long, deep kiss.

And then Stanley bends down and whispers in my ear. "I'm the same man. Only older and wiser, and this time I'm not letting you get away. I don't care what it is we don't like about each other. We'll get to like it. I came here to sweep you off your feet and love you for the rest of your life the way you've always dreamed of being loved. And I'll have whatever you're having."

I know he must be kidding.

And can he read minds?

"Are you on some kind of medication?" I ask him.

He laughs.

"What exactly did Wanda tell you, Stanley?"

"You can call me Stan."

"What exactly did Wanda tell you, *Stan*?"

"Enough. But it sounds like we've pretty much been swimming in the same sea."

I feel myself nodding but don't mean to, so I stop my head from moving.

"You know this kind of stuff only happens in the movies, *Stan,* and I don't know who you are or what makes you think you can just come to my fifty-fifth-birthday party unbeknownst to me and talk all this historical shit and assume I'm going to act like—"

"Georgia Young. Now, relax. I'm not here to kidnap you or hypnotize you. I just want to make sure you don't forget me again."

"Who said I forgot about you?"

"You never bothered to find me."

"But you also didn't try to find *me*."

"Oh, yes I have. But not until Facebook has it been possible, and I admit you took your sweet time getting on it."

"So shall we run to the justice of the peace after I blow out the candles and ride off into the sunset or what?"

"You think I'm not serious?"

"That's what's scaring me. We're too old for fairy tales."

"That's why I'm here. Because we're long overdue for one, and please stop with the 'We're too old for this' business, because we're not. Now, go blow out those candles and give it everything you've got."

I set my wine down, because my head is already spinning. As I walk over to the table where my big white cake is waiting for me, Wanda whispers in my ear. "Don't resist, bitch, or I'll kick your ass on your birthday. I got in touch with him for a reason. You forget I was there back in the day. I saw how much you liked him, and it scared you. But he's here now, so blow the candles out as if you mean it."

And I do.


I CAN'T REMEMBER the speech I gave. Of course I thanked everybody for everything, especially all the contributions for free glasses and eye exams I plan to donate to those who can't afford them. This is what I told Wanda I would most appreciate in lieu of personal gifts.

"Who is that man?" Estelle finally asked.

"You mean the white one?"

"I didn't say it, you said it. And I wasn't thinking it. Who is he?"

"An old friend from college."

"He's handsome," Frankie said.

"He sure likes you," Ma said. "And it looks like he made your knees buckle, which we all know is hard to do. Who is he?"

"I just said it. An old friend from college."

"Does he have a brother?" Lily asked after poking her head between my family members. "Happy birthday, Georgia, and . . ." She blew air onto her open palm to let me know that everything was fine, and she was thanking me for whatever I didn't do. I crossed my arms across my heart and gave her a wink and a soft smile.

"Well, where's he been hiding all these years?" Ma asked.

"Don't even bother explaining," older Grover said.


RIGHT NOW I'm sitting in the passenger side of that old friend's rental car, which happens to be a Prius, because he insisted on driving me home.

"This is a little weird," I say after we get onto the freeway.

"I'd say it's more like having an out-of-body experience."

"You look good, *Stan*. But seriously, what really made you come all the way out here?"

"I've already answered a few of those questions if you were listening and I can't answer the rest of them while I'm driving, so I'll just pull over at the next exit," he says. And he does.

As usual, San Francisco is staring at us, and for a split second I feel like a teenager about to make out, but Stanley is not a teenager, he's a grown man, and a white man, and a man who I don't know how he's making my heart turn over when I thought it was dead.

He turns off the engine.

"Look, Ms. Georgia. I took the chance of making a complete fool out of myself by getting on a plane and coming to see you. But I had to find out for myself if seeing you would conjure up any old or new feelings, and I'm happy to say that both of those were indeed the case. I didn't mean to freak you out, but I do know that you ran from me in college. But now we're older, and . . . I don't know, maybe you're in love with someone else."

"I'm sure Wanda told you I wasn't."

"No, she just said you weren't in a serious relationship."

"So what is it you do for a living? I mean, what did you grow up and become?"

"I'm a space sailor." And he smiles.

"I know you're not sitting here telling me you're an astronaut, are you?"

"Retired astronaut."

"Are you bullshitting me, Stan? My bad. I apologize for swearing."

"Don't. I use profanity on a regular basis." And he winks at me. Again.

"Seriously. You mean you've really been out there—I mean, up there—in space?" I say, looking up like an idiot.

"I have."

"You're much smarter than I thought you were," I say.

"Well, thanks for the show of faith."

"Wait a minute. You're not old enough to retire."

"You can if you saved your money the right way."

"What do you do with all your time?"

"I buy homes in run-down neighborhoods to help rebuild them."

"Where?"

"Different cities. The last one was outside New Orleans. Baltimore and D.C. are on the long list, although some parts of East Oakland I'd love to get to."

"I must say I'm impressed you even care."

"You've read some William Kennedy, right?"

"Long, long time ago. *Ironweed* is my favorite."

"Well, it was William Kennedy's accurate portrayal of heaven and hell. I've been blessed. Everybody hasn't."

"You must work with a lot of people, a company?"

"We have crews that change. I'll tell you all about it another time."

"Another time?"

"You heard right. But how about you? You're going to be giving away glasses and performing free eye exams, which tells me your heart's still in the right place."

"You didn't know me long enough to know where my heart was."

"How soon we forget. I used to love listening to your long but brilliant diatribes in our Afro-American history class. So I do have a clue. And science is a form of altruism, in case you didn't know it."

"But I want to leave optometry."

"Nothing wrong with that. We all take a path we thought we wanted to take, and then we find out there are other paths we can still explore. That's why I started rebuilding homes, and I love it."

"I hear you," is all I can say, because I agree with what he's just said and it's also so very refreshing. But I don't want to gush.

"So what road are you ready to travel down?"

"I'm not sure."

"You have to have some idea."

"It's too soon to know," I say. I'm not about to tell Stan here that as soon as I learn how much of my investment I'm able to recover, it's what's going to determine how long I can afford to play designer in my garage or my not-yet studio.

"Well, give me a hint about what you like doing."

"Painting and redesigning and decorating cheap furniture. At least that's what I've been doing in my spare time. I like to sew, but not clothing. I'm just playing it all by ear until I see what happens with my practice."

"I like using my hands, too. I just got burned out working for NASA and had enough stints being in space. I like it down here. So how close are we to where you live?"

"Ten minutes."

"Look, Georgia. To be honest, I can't believe I got on a plane to come see you, but it feels like I didn't have a choice. Do you know what that feels like?"

"I do, but I just didn't know you felt this way about me back when."

"What it felt like was unfinished business. We never had an ending because we barely had a beginning. Which was your fault."

"You've got to be kidding."

"I'm not kidding. You liked me, and it scared the hell out of you."

"That's so not true."

"Then what was it?"

"I just wanted to see if you were good in bed."

"And?"

"You were okay."

"I'm still good in bed," he says, and starts laughing. "But I had other qualities I thought you found appealing."

"I can't remember. I didn't know you that long."

"You know what, Georgia? We're too old to play these kinds of games. If you didn't feel anything at all or were appalled at seeing me tonight, why am I driving you home?"

"Because I didn't want to be rude."

"Well, you're being rude now by lying about it."

I almost choke, because he's just busted me, and how is that possible?

"Okay. I will admit I was both shocked and surprised to see you at my party, okay? But this is also kind of freaking me out, because like I said to you before, this kind of thing doesn't happen in real life, where a blast from your past just shows up and you're supposed to fall madly in love with him on the spot again."

"Hold on, now, little lady. Let's back up. Did I just hear you say 'fall madly in love with him on the spot *again*'?"

"It was a figure of speech."

"And is that what I am? A blast from the past?"

"Well, it's also a figure of speech."

"They can't both be figures of speech. Which one is true and which one isn't?"

"Both," I say, and start laughing. "But you're coming on a little strong, like we just broke up a month ago and now you're back trying to woo me. I have to admit I'm flattered by it all."

"Woo?"

"Yes, woo."

"Look. I'm not trying to be pushy, so don't think it for a minute. I'm still a gentleman."

"You weren't a gentleman back in the day. You were a flirt and a very convincing one."

"I know how to imitate my old ways, but hopefully, if you discover you still like me a little bit, we'll have plenty of time for everything."

"This is all kind of otherworldly. Maybe you were in space too long, Stanley."

"It's Stan. Now, point me in the right direction."

And up the hill we go.

What I do know is I am not taking off my clothes.

At least not in front of him.

He drives slowly. As if he's doing it deliberately. I'm feeling nervous and suddenly scared, because men don't just appear from your past, sweep you off your feet—especially a white one you slept with twice and pretended to forget.

But I didn't forget.

# More Than a Slice

"MAY I BE IN YOUR STUDY GROUP?"

"It's not my study group," I said to the fine white guy who'd been sitting next to me two weeks in a row in my Afro-American history class.

"Well, you seem to be the one organizing it."

"So why do you want to be in *my* study group?" I asked.

"Because I like the way you think."

"Everybody in this class thinks," I said.

"Some quieter than others," he said.

This was a three-unit course entitled The Afro-American Experience: From Slavery to Selma 1965. That was a lot to cover in ten weeks, and on the first day of class we were advised that midterms were in five weeks. The seminar met twice a week. We were to write an essay on one of the lecture topics up to that point. Of the ninety students, six were white. It looked as if one of them had chosen me to be his go-to person for ten weeks. Lucky me.

"What's your name?"

"Stanley. Stanley DiStasio. Which makes me Italian. But you knew that."

"No. I didn't."

"And you're Georgia Young."

"And how would you know that?"

"Because it's right there on your notebook."

"Why are you taking a class in Afro-American history, if you don't mind my asking?"

"What if I did mind?"

"Then I would just assume it's out of guilt."

"And you would assume wrong, because I have no reason to feel guilty, because I haven't done anything to feel guilty about. Except forgetting my sister's birthday."

"Are you avoiding my question?"

"Because I want to understand how Afro-Americans suffered during slavery and managed to survive it."

"You could read that in a book."

"We've *got* books for the class, if you haven't noticed. I really want to hear how— Would you mind if I said 'black'?"

"I prefer it."

"Okay. I want to hear how younger black people feel about it now, including the passage of the Voting Rights Act, which I think is just one more slap in the face."

"How so?"

"It's going to sound naïve. But after all the hell black people went through, why should they have had to risk their lives just to have the right to vote? And why did they have to have legislation passed to grant them that right when they were already United States citizens?"

"Well, we'll be up to the Voting Rights Act before week nine, and you can write your essay about it."

"It pisses me off, to be honest."

"Well, that would make two of us. My mother couldn't vote until she was thirty-six, and my father was forty."

"This is why I like the Black Panthers, if you want to know the truth. They get it."

"They're not the only ones."

"Want to know what I don't get?"

"Not really, but I'm listening."

"Why do black people call each other niggers?"

"Why do you care?"

"Because it just seems like a contradiction. I thought black people were trying to show their pride."

"Not everybody. Some people are ignorant, but that word is meant to be demeaning, which it is."

"So why doesn't it make them angry? But when a white person calls them one, they're fighting words."

"Because it's racist when they say it. Any more questions?"

"Yes, can I be in your study group?"

"I suppose we could use someone with a different perspective."

"You mean white."

"You said it. Not me."

"Wow. And I was hoping we could be friends."

And then he smiled at me sideways. I had never been this close to a white guy, and when his elbow actually touched mine, he didn't move it.

By the beginning of week three, our study group, which was made up of four other black students besides me, met once a week in an empty room on campus. Afterward we always went for pizza. Two members couldn't understand what a white boy was doing in the class, but they weren't up to asking Stanley. The other student just said she thought it was cool that he even cared.

By week four I finally said, "You are making me uncomfortable."

"How?"

"Why do you always have to sit next to me?"

"Because I like the way you smell."

I just looked at him. "You're weird."

"I'm not weird. I like you."

I turned my head like Linda Blair in *The Exorcist* and said, "What do you mean, you like me?"

"I like your vibe. You're a beautiful, intelligent black or Afro-American young woman, and I hope we can get to know each other better."

"You are serious, aren't you?"

"Did I say something to offend you?"

I grabbed his hand and put it next to mine.

"What do you see?"

"Two hands."

"What's different about them?"

"Mine is bigger."

"And what else, Stanley?"

"Yours is the color of cinnamon, and mine is light beige. So what is your point?"

"Nothing," I said.

Although he didn't act like it was an issue, I couldn't help but notice. In all honesty, it was what I had already started to like about him, which is what was making me nervous.

"I WOULD REALLY appreciate it if you would read my paper," he said.

"I've got a lot of things to do. Like studying. And finishing my own essay."

"Could you and I just confer with each other?"

"Confer?"

"Yeah. Skip study group, and would you come over?"

"You mean to your apartment?"

"Yeah."

"Are you kidding me?"

"What's wrong with that? Or I can come over to yours if that would make you feel more comfortable."

"First of all, I don't know if either one of them is such a good idea."

"What are you afraid of, Georgia? Not me, I hope."

"No, I'm not afraid of you."

"I thought we were friends."

"We're classmates."

"You said you thought I was a nice guy."

"You are, but you're pushy."

"I'm assertive."

"Same thing."

"So can I count on you or not? I'll treat you to pizza and a Coke afterward."

"Okay. But only for an hour."

"It'll take fifteen minutes to read it."

When he opened the door, I immediately knew this was not a good idea. He was burning incense! Would we need that to read? I did tell Wanda and Violet I was coming over here and that if they didn't hear from me before they fell asleep, to come find me.

"I'm glad you made it," he said. "And thank you for coming." He then politely put those long Italian arms around me and gave me a quick hug! What was I really doing here is all I was thinking, but the truth of the matter was I was curious about what he really wanted. I read his last essay, and it was good.

"I can't stay long," I said.

His apartment was one big room, but it was too small for him. It was orderly. And clean. I sat on the chair in front of his narrow desk.

"Where's your essay?" I asked.

He pointed to the desk. I started reading, even though I suddenly felt illiterate.

"May I have a glass of water, please?"

"Absolutely. Anything else? I've got chips."

I shook my head no.

He filled a glass of water from the faucet. Set it down next to my hand, stood behind me, and bent down so his face was over my shoulder. "Are you okay?" he asked.

"I'm fine. Don't get so close! And I'm in a hurry."

"You're not in a hurry," he said.

"Will you let me read, please?"

"Sure," he said, and sat down on the floor, crossing his legs. And what beautiful legs they were.

I read his paper, and to this day I do not remember what it said, but I gave him enough criticism and compliments to make him feel grateful.

"So how about that pizza?" I asked.

"Really? Right now?"

"What else did I come here for?"

"This," he said, and he leaned down and kissed me on the lips. My hands were thinking about pushing him away, but my brain refused to cooperate.

But then I stood up.

And he turned off the bright lights and turned on a black light, and the ceiling became a galaxy of stars and planets. He undressed me without touching me.

"I don't know what we're doing, Stanley."

But something made me unzip his jeans and slide them down to the floor while he pulled his T-shirt up over his head and walked up against me. His chest brushed my breasts, and he wrapped those long arms around me, and oh, what a man, what a man.

"You're sure." He sighed. "And I'm sure."

And like a magician, he made my fears evaporate.

But then he just stopped.

"Don't," I said.

"Don't what?"

And then he kissed my eyelashes and my eyebrows and my ears and my cheekbones.

"Don't what?" he asked again.

"Stop."

And he didn't. And I couldn't.

Afterward he held me like I was a newborn, and then he said, "Don't leave. I don't want you to leave."

"I couldn't if I wanted to."

And for three days I didn't.


I DREAMED STANLEY was black.

Then I woke up.

And I went back to sleep.

I dreamed about him again. But this time he was white. And I knew this was the one I had fallen in love with. I didn't dare tell him this, but I did tell Wanda what I'd done.

"So how was it?"

"It?"

"Don't play dumb with me, Georgia."

"He was amazing, and it was astounding, and he's brilliant, and we talked about everything, but I have to leave him alone."

"Why?"

I just rolled my eyes at her.

"You mean just because he's white?"

"Just? Are you serious? Never mind."

The last two weeks of class, I deliberately walked to the front and sat between two other black students. I didn't turn around until the last class was almost over, and when I did, Stanley was looking at me. He looked hurt, and I couldn't believe it. He left class early, and after it was over, he was waiting out in the hallway with a pizza box.

"I promised you a slice, but you can have the whole pie."

"I'm sorry, Stanley."

He walked right up to me. "I didn't know you were a racist."

"What are you talking about?"

"If I were black, would you be acting like this?"

"No, Stanley. I probably wouldn't."

"You didn't strike me as being a coward."

"I'm not."

"Oh, I think you are. Otherwise why are you avoiding me?"

"Is that what you think I'm doing?"

"Hell yeah. You won't answer the phone when I call. You changed where you sit. What did I do?"

"Nothing."

"Like I said. I didn't know you were such a coward."

"I'm sorry, Stanley."

"So am I. Have a good life, Georgia. And be careful who you tell you love."

He handed me the pizza, which I took so as not to cause a scene. He flung his backpack over his shoulder, and off he went. And that was the last time I saw him, until my birthday party.

ᕫᕬ

I POINT TO my house, and when he pulls into the driveway, he says, "You mean to tell me you drive a Prius?"

"I do."

He holds his hand out for me to give him a fist bump.

"Cool home. Been here long?"

"Thirteen years."

"You plan to stay?"

"Well, I tried selling, but with the economy being what it is, I just took it off the market."

"Where were you thinking of moving?"

He opens his door, and I open mine, even though he was coming around to open it for me.

"I had no idea."

"We can't plan everything, can we?"

"Sometimes we can. Although I like having some control over what happens next."

"Look at my right hand," he says, holding it out just as I unlock my front door and it swings open. There's a turquoise ring on his middle finger. It's mine.

"You forgot to put it back on," he says. "And I'm here to return it."

I'm about ready to crumble. I take a deep breath, and when we get inside, he looks around slowly and says, "Very cool pad."

"Thank you."

"I'll bet a million bucks that you're responsible for all this. Tell me I'm wrong?"

"You're not wrong. But I'd like that million as an advance against something."

"I want to see what's in the garage."

"Why?"

"Because I know that's where you do your art."

"Who told you that?"

"Your neighbor. Naomi. And so did Wanda. But they both said you're hiding it or hoarding it out here."

"Wanda and Naomi have big mouths. They don't even frigging know you."

"I'm just grateful Wanda knew enough."

"Well, I'm not sure I feel real comfortable showing it to you, Stan."

"Well, I'm not leaving until you do."

"Okay. But if you don't like what you see, just lie. You don't have to love it. Everything isn't for everybody."

He raises his eyebrows and follows me past the kitchen and out toward the garage.

I turn on the garage lights and try not to feel as if I need to explain or apologize for what I've made.

He walks all the way over to where my works in progress are and takes his time looking, touching, smiling, shaking his head, and then he turns to me and says, "Well, now. How fucking remarkable is this? So you found it, huh?"

"Found what?"

"Your second calling. I've never seen anything like this before. You're a talented woman."

"Thank you. I'm having fun, and like I said, you don't have to say anything to make me feel good."

"If I weren't impressed, I'd just say, 'Interesting.' At any rate, you don't need me to validate what you're doing, now, do you?"

"No, but it's nice to hear people say they like it."

"Why are you doing this in the garage? You don't have a studio?"

"Not ready yet."

"Why not?"

"Because I just started doing this."

"Well, look. If there's a slight chance we can rekindle what feels like a potentially amazing friendship, even though I'm pretty sure I'm going to marry you and we're going to live happily ever after, without taking into account that I'm still white and all and I'm older, then I'd be more than happy to help you find one, or build or rebuild one for you. What do you think?"

"I don't know what I think right now, Stanley."

"For the last time, it's *Stan.*"

He walks right up to me just as I'm beginning to turn off the garage light. He smells good. Like clean air. I want to back away, but I can't move.

"Well, as much as I know you'd love for me to stay over and make slow, tender, and ultimately passionate love to you, considering this meet-and-greet doesn't really constitute a second first date after thirty-some-odd years, I think I'm going to be a gentleman and not press my luck. On that note I will bid you good night and, again, sweet Georgia, a very happy birthday."

He puts his arms around me and holds me like I've wanted to be held for years. I feel his heart ticking, and my breasts are keeping it warm, and I swear I could stand here like this for the rest of my life. But then he kisses me softly on both cheeks and then on my forehead, and then I feel him press his lips gently on top of my head, and then I watch him slowly back away and stop. He smiles at me like he's known me all his life.

"So where are you staying, Stan?"

"At the Clift in the city."

"And how long are you going to be in town, Stan?"

"Until I win you over."

And then he's gone.

And so am I.

# What Is Sustainable

HAD A HARD TIME FALLING ASLEEP. IN FACT, I DON'T KNOW if I slept or not. I look up at the ceiling and wonder if maybe I dreamed that a young man I secretly slept with while in college really did reappear and sweep me off my feet in a matter of hours.

I need to go for a walk. I don't brush my teeth or make coffee. I just put on a pair of sweats and a sweatshirt and walk outside, and who's in her driveway waving at me? Naomi, of course.

"Great party! Black folks sure know how to bring it!" she says, zipping up her sweat jacket and joining me as if I'd asked her to. She has on sneakers. As always.

"That it was. Not everybody was black, you know," I say, laughing. She of course looks down at her hands.

"Oh, I know! What up this morning, girl?"

"I have no idea."

"That much I can see, because you're walking up this steep hill instead of down it."

I stop dead in my tracks. Most people have to shift gears to make it up our street. I turn around.

"Looks like somebody finally got laid."

She holds her palms up into this cold morning air. We both need gloves.

"No," I say, putting my hands inside my jacket pockets. "Something almost better than getting laid."

"Like what? Because I would sure like to order some of it."

And I tell her the whole story.

"I say go for it. You only live once, and let's face it: we're not getting any younger. He sounds like a dream, and if I liked men, I'd marry him even though we're both white!"

She cracks up and takes off her ski hat. She's dyed her hair black. It looks too severe. But I don't say that.

"I fucked up my hair, so don't say anything. I have to let it grow out. I was trying to be adventurous."

"So how're things working out for you?" I ask.

"Much better."

"And Macy's back."

She nods.

"I get it, Naomi."

"I'm going to AA."

"Why?"

"Because I needed to stop drinking."

"Well, at least you're doing something about it."

"It's what sent her running. I'm the one who turned her into a bitch. I never would've married her if she'd started out as one."

"Is it hard to stop?"

"Hardest thing I've ever done. I've lost two partners over it, but I'm not about to lose my wife. So game over."

I give her a maternal hug, even though I don't think I'm old enough to be her mother. "As always, let me know if there's anything I can do."

"I told you. Let me buy that stool."

"And I told you, you can have it. I meant it, so let's go get it when we get back down the hill. In fact, let's turn around."

"And I'm telling you I would prefer to buy it, but why don't we do this? Wait until you build up your inventory and see who wants to buy some of your work?"

"I might actually be getting a studio."

"Smart move. Let me know if you need some help finding a place."

"I think I might already have all the help I need."

She waves at me as she turns into her driveway. I trudge up mine and sit on the cold steps at the front door. When my cell phone rings, I don't look at it. I just answer.

"Is it too late for breakfast?" he asks.

"Who is this?" I feign.

"A blast from the past."

"I'm over the moon," I say. And then suddenly realize what I'm doing. Acting like some lovesick teenager when I'm more than a half century old. I need to slow my roll. This isn't some fantasy or some game I'm playing—this is real. I don't really even know Stanley. I remember him. What I do know right now is I'm all shook up, and whatever drug Stanley injected into my heart, I want to get a prescription for it. With unlimited refills.

"Would you mind meeting me in the Velvet Room at the hotel?"

Lord.

"No, I don't mind that much. It'll take me about an hour."

"I'll wait."

I really want to call Wanda, but not now, not yet. I have no idea what I'd say. I'm falling for a man I don't even know, and he's not even black, and this is scary but exciting as hell. I'm trying to open my heart and shut down my brain, which is talking me out of something that feels beautiful. I shower and put on something soft and sincere. Jeans with a creamy cashmere sweater. My lips are red.

My heart is beating so hard I place my hand over it and pat it like I would a crying baby. I take a tissue from my purse and dab my forehead, careful not to wipe off my makeup. I know where the Velvet Room is, and when I walk in, I see Stan sitting in a dark corner, on one of those long leather seats I think they call banquettes. He smiles at me in a sinister way and with his index finger motions me to come on over as he slides out and stands up and shakes my hand heartily and says, "Good morning, Miss Young. I'd first like to thank you for joining me for breakfast, but I'd also like to ask why you saw fit to make those beautiful lips of yours candy-apple red so early in the day?"

I'm glad it's dark in here, because I'm sure I'm blushing.

"Good morning, Stan," I say, and I swear I want to stand on my tiptoes and kiss him, but I wouldn't dare. "I wear red lipstick a lot. And how are you this Sunday morning?" I ask, and it almost sounds phony, because I haven't asked any man that question in years. At least not standing this close.

"I'm happy to be alive and in San Francisco with you."

He slides into his seat and turns the corner and does not let go of my hand and pulls me down close enough to him so our shoulders touch. It's already pretty dramatic in here, what with the purple lights and those floor-to-ceiling purple velvet drapes behind us, and the bar looks like one giant piece of stained glass the way the light shines through the bottles. On our table, which I know is mahogany, sits a three-foot cylindrical glass vase full of flowers I don't think I've ever seen before.

I have to admit I'm nervous as hell. I don't really know what I'm doing here and what I expect to come from this little fantasy that Wanda has tossed me into. I have to remember not to thank her when this is over.

"So," he says, handing me the menu, "what do you have a taste for?"

I look down at the menu. But first I read how the chef has partnered with local farmers and growers so he's able to produce dishes from items that've been grown in a sustainable and organic manner. Well, okay. That explains everything, but of course my eyes become transfixed when I see the Texas pecan French toast. However, I force myself to skip over it as well as the Belgian waffles with fresh berry cream and candied almonds and scroll down to the disgusting organic steel-cut oatmeal with brown cane sugar, walnuts, and golden raisins.

"What appeals to you?"

"Hard to choose."

"The French toast sounds like it should be ordered."

"I wouldn't dare."

"Please don't tell me you're on a diet."

I look over at him. Like: And so what if I am?

"Come on, Georgia. You look good. Live. Anything else you see that you might like?"

"Everything except oatmeal."

"I have never liked oatmeal. Do you like French toast?"

"Of course I do."

"Do you believe in sharing?"

"Depends."

"How about I order the smoked-salmon Benedict and the French toast for you, and let's have that ruby red juice to match your ruby lips? We can start with coffee. Yes or no?"

"Yes."

"I try to be democratic about everything."

And he orders, and the coffee comes, and we sip. I'm trying to prepare myself for something outrageous, because I know it's coming. I just do. But I decide to see if I can bring this fantasy down to reality, so I ask, "What have you been doing the last ten years of your life since your wife passed?"

"Let's cut right to it, then, shall we?" he says after he takes a sip of his juice. "Well, first of all, my wife didn't die. She was killed. Drunk driver. We had no children together, because she fixed that before we met, but she had two sons when I met her, and I'm the only father they know. One lives in Miami and the other one in London. They're thriving. Both in their mid-thirties."

He then takes a sip of his coffee and raises his hand to get a refill.

"To be honest, we'd been thinking about divorcing but just never got around to it. We'd been together for more than twenty years. Anyway, it took me a couple of years to get used to being alone, living without her, and that's when I knew it was time for me to make some dramatic changes in my life, so five years ago I retired from NASA and started working to clean up the neighborhood I grew up in, but I worked with real developers, and that's pretty much it."

"That's not all of it."

"You mean my personal life, of course. Okay. So suffice it to say I haven't had one."

"You mean you haven't dated or been in a relationship?"

"I've been on dates. It's different when you're almost fifty and even more difficult at fifty-six."

"Can you be more specific?"

"Hold on a minute. Let me interject and ask, what's your love life like? Are you dating?"

"I have no love life. I don't date because no one asks me out, and I don't know how to flirt, and I'm too afraid to go online, and old men bore me, and I'm not a cougar, so it looks like I've pretty much been waiting for you."

And I cover my mouth. Oh, no, I didn't just fucking say that! But then I burst into laughter.

He bends over and kisses me on the lips, and his are now pink. I wipe them off with the burgundy napkin.

"I can't believe I just said that. I might have to take it back if we can go to the videotape."

"As my older son would say, 'Shit happens for a reason,' and this is no accident. I've read magazine articles about how people reunite with lovers from their past, going as far back as middle school and even kindergarten if you can believe that, but I never put much weight on it. First you have to find the person to see if you feel anything."

"I feel something."

"Then this is going to work," he says, and they bring our meal, and we sit there and eat every bite.

"You feel like walking?" he asks.

"I almost walked this morning, but I'd love to walk again for real," I say.

"No. How about we take a drive across the Golden Gate and sit on a bench and then maybe do a little windsurfing with the sharks?"

"Black people don't windsurf," I say sarcastically.

"Black people do everything white people do, so let's roll."

And off we go.

The fog is almost gone, and it's cold, but Stan was smart enough to bring a heavy trench coat. We turn into Vista Point and sit on the hood of the car and look out at the sailboats in the bay and San Francisco and Alcatraz, and down to our left is the tip of Tiburon and Belvedere. The sky is an unbelievable blue, and I know for a fact that this is the coolest dream I've had in years and that I do not want to wake up.

"So when can you come to New York to spend some time with me?"

"I'm spending time with you right now, Stan."

"You want to know how I live?"

"Yes."

"Wait. Let me ask you. Do you travel much?"

"Not as much as I'd like, but I'm hoping after I leave my practice I'll have more time to, but how much I'll be able to will be contingent on how I end up making a living. Answer your question?"

"Yes it does. Okay. So I live in a hotel."

"Oh, Lord. Please don't tell me it's a shelter."

He's shaking his head and smirking at the mere thought that I would think it.

"I have plenty of shelter, and it's on the thirty-sixth floor, and I've got a hundred-and-eighty-degree view of Manhattan and the Hudson River."

"What would make you want to *live* in a hotel?"

"Because for years I lived in the big house with the yard and the pool and the three-car garage, and once I was in it alone, I realized what a waste of good space it was, and especially the energy and money it took to maintain it. Plus, I like to travel. I decided to be mobile, and this way I can do it. I love it."

"So do you have a kitchen?"

He just looks at me and then pops me upside the head.

"I think I do, but I've never cooked anything in it. Why? Do you cook?"

"Yes."

"Would you cook me something?"

"Yes. In the future. If we have one," I hear myself say.

"Don't you worry. The cards are in our favor."

"No comment. And how long do you plan on living this way?"

"Until I drop dead or run out of money. I want to spend at least two to three months a year for the rest of my life seeing every single country I've always wanted to see, and living the way I do makes this very easy to accomplish."

"I actually think it's pretty cool."

"I'm not saying I have to stay in five-star hotels everywhere I go. It's the countries I want to see, not the hotels. It's the people. And it's been an eye-opener and, I believe, has saved my life."

I just look at him.

"Don't you ever get bored?" he asks.

"Of course," I say.

"Blue?"

I nod.

"And what do you do about it?"

"It's the reason I want to leave my practice."

"Are you really going to do it?"

"I think so. Soon."

"You're scared, though, aren't you?"

"Of course I am. But it's not going to stop me."

"But don't you think that's a normal way to feel, considering you're breaking a lot of the traditional rules of what's supposed to happen when we reach middle age?"

"Well, yeah. There's a lot of uncertainty."

"Yeah, well, when you didn't eat that pizza with me that day, you were basically challenging me, and I can see that your spirit hasn't been broken."

"I don't think it has. I'm ready to just go for it."

"I think we're both due for an adventure, and I want you to go on it with me."

"Sure, let me just run home and pack."

"I won't disappoint you, Georgia. I guarantee you that. I think we've been waiting for each other."

"Maybe."

"How about this for our first one. Do you like mud?"

"What?"

"Mud? You know, as in mud baths?"

"I've only done it a few times, but it was great."

"Then how about we drive over that hill to Calistoga, take a mud bath and a mineral steam, get massages, and then you come back to my hotel. We'll order room service, you sleep next to me tonight, and then

I'll head back to New York, and you take as much time as you need to figure out if you want to hang out with me a little longer. If you're not happy being with me, then it just means the dream wasn't real. How about it?"

"Damn."

"I was hoping more for a 'Hell yeah,' but I'll let it slide," he says, and takes my hand.

I could not have made this shit up.

# The Name of This Movie

WE ARE BOTH BLACK FOR AN HOUR.
Then red for another.
We are wrapped in thin flannel blankets like mummies and do not move until we're unrolled. We find it impossible to open our mouths and utter so much as a syllable.

We go our separate ways to our respective locker rooms, both shaking our heads because of how good we feel. I feel like I've lost about five pounds. My white towel is wrapped around my head like a turban, and my arms are so limp I can't tie the sash on my white robe. I sink into a wicker chair and slowly inhale the scent of eucalyptus. I don't think I exhale. Why haven't I driven over here and done this more often? And Wanda, too, instead of spending so much time at those stupid outlets. But I don't want to think about Wanda right now, although I know she's going to freak out when I tell her what has happened to me in the past forty-eight hours. I'll bet my cell phone has a thousand missed calls and two thousand texts. When I finally open my locker and look down at it, I see I wasn't far off the mark. Her last text says: *Birthday Huzzy, are you alive? Did you get kidnapped? That Stanley looks pretty damn good. I liked him. He's not scared of you, which means he's not going to take your shit. He's the one. Nelson and I have a bet going at how long it's going to take to make it legal. He gives it a year. I give it three months. I don't like losing bets to Nelson. He never pays! Anyway, you knock the door down and call when you come up for air.*

I drop the phone back inside my purse and do my best to get dressed as fast as possible. When I look in the mirror, I notice that my hair has crinkled into a wild Afro, and I don't have the strength to pull and stretch it into a ponytail. I opt for lip gloss versus the scarlet and make my way out into the lobby, but I don't see Stan until I look outside. He's sitting in one of those eighties wicker swings. I sit close to him, and we both just start swaying.

"So, Ms. Georgia. I'm curious about this train ride you're supposed to be taking."

I look at him like this couldn't possibly be the first thing on his mind after what we just experienced.

"Why a train?"

"Because I saw it in a movie and I've had a fantasy about taking a long train ride ever since."

"So tell me, Ms. Georgia, where are you planning on going, and for how long, and when? Take your time answering."

"You are extremely nosy."

"I'm just curious."

"First of all, I'm going alone."

"You don't say? I love it. So where to?"

"Well, from here to Vancouver on Amtrak's Coast Starlight, and then I'd change to VIA Rail Canada and maybe spend the night in Vancouver and then travel all the way across to Montreal and down to Toronto and then New York City, where I'd shop and go to a few museums if I have any energy left, and then get on a giant bird and fly back to the Bay Area."

"Wow. That sounds very cool. So how long does this take?"

"It depends. It could take as little as six days, up to twelve. I haven't decided yet if I want to spend the night in Vancouver, because I can do the hop-on-hop-off thing on the train if I want to see the sites along the route, like Edmonton or Winnipeg."

"This sounds like a great adventure. Sometimes it's good to experience some things alone."

"I'm glad you get it."

"I think it speaks volumes about you. So many people wouldn't

dream of doing something like this. I don't want to say 'women,' because that would be sexist, but give me a pass this one time. Why
Canada?"

"Why not? Chances of my going there ever again in life are probably slim to zero, and also because it's breathtakingly beautiful and it's
easy to get to from here."

"So why do you want to do this? I know it's not just because you
saw it in a movie. Spill it."

"Because I want to relax and read and think and dream and imagine my future, and maybe the train ride and the scenery will help me
see what's possible during the last third of my life. I want to talk to
strangers. Look out the window for miles and see everything from the
ocean to the mountains speed by. I really think of it as kind of a long,
meditative prayer that I hope will help me not worry about the end of
my life but encourage me to keep trying to live it more like it's a verb
instead of a noun."

He holds his fist out, and I press mine against his.

I still think I may have said too much.

But he asked.

"If you think you wouldn't mind some company along the way, you
let me know. I'd love to catch up on some reading."

"We'll see. Like I said, I don't have a firm date yet."

"I'm not trying to pin you down, Miss Georgia. And to be honest, it
sounds like you'd be better off doing most of this trip alone. So you let
me know if and when you figure out when you're going to get to Toronto, and if you still like me, I'll meet you there, and maybe you can
hang out with me in Manhattan for a few days. How's that sound?"

"You are extremely presumptuous, aren't you?"

"You haven't seen anything. Are you hungry? I'm starving."

"I don't know if I am or not."

"Well, how about we order room service when we get back to the
hotel, unless you have other plans?"

"I'm for lease all day," I hear myself say.

Lord, what has gotten into me?

〜〜

THE ROOM IS PRETTY.

So are the drapes that I walk over to close.

"What are you doing?"

"There's too much light in here."

"Really?"

He sits on a candy-striped chair and crosses his legs. I just realized his eyes are almost cobalt blue. Probably because I've been avoiding them. I sit on a chair across the room. Same color.

"So are you nervous about something?"

"Well, yeah."

"What?"

"Don't ask a stupid question, Stan. Maybe I should've gone home. Maybe I'm pushing my luck. Maybe this isn't the right thing to do yet."

"What are we doing?"

"Well, you know what we're going to do."

"No I don't. We might have already done it."

"What?"

"Made a connection. It feels healthy, and we don't have to make love or have sex or . . . whatever you're thinking—but it sure would be nice to hold you without all those clothes on."

I look down at my jeans and white pullover sweater and my sheer white socks inside my favorite loafers. Okay. So I didn't dress like some sexual conquest, and it may very well have been deliberate. But I'm not prepared to undress in front of Stanley. In front of anybody.

"I really would like to, but I'm a little nervous and very self-conscious."

"I'm not nervous, and you have absolutely nothing to be nervous about. But let me take a wild guess about why you're so self-conscious. You probably think you need to lose a few pounds—which you do not—or you've got some cellulite and stretch marks and you don't think you look appealing naked like you did when you were younger. Am I right?"

"Yes. To almost all of the above. I don't really want to lose weight."

"Well, that's refreshing to hear."

"But the other stuff is right on."

"Get over it, Georgia. You're beautiful."

"You get over it, Stan."

"Look, I love your round hips," he says.

And he stands up. I cross my legs and arms and wish I were a magician and could slide into the crease between these cushions, but I can't.

"You want to see my muffin top?"

"No!" I yell, but it's too late. He's already pulling up his black sweatshirt to reveal a put-your-head-on-this beautiful chest with a few strands of gray hair on it, and I don't see any fucking muffin top or love handles. He also has muscles on his biceps, which means he works out. What a liar!

"A person could starve on that muffin."

"You need to be closer to see it," and he walks over to me and takes me by the hands and pulls me up to a standing position and wraps his arms around me, and I swear to God, I'm almost ready to burst into tears I'm so scared and nervous and embarrassed, and he says, "Georgia, Georgia, Georgia. It's so good to see you after all these years."

I can't talk, but then I make myself say in a tinny voice, "Me, too."

And he just keeps on holding me and stroking my nappy hair and running his fingers through it and then rubbing the back of my neck and sliding his hand up and down my back, and I know damn well this is not happening to me, that this is a scene from every romantic movie I've vicariously put myself into, but when he backs away and lifts my sweater over my head, I step back, too.

"You want me to stop?"

"No. I mean yes. Of course not. But, Stanley, I'm already falling over a cliff, and I haven't been near a cliff in years, and I haven't been naked in front of a man, nor have I slept with a man in quite some time, and please don't ask me how long, but you're making me remember what I've forgotten, and I'm scared as hell."

"It's Stan," he says, I suppose to make me feel better.

"Stan."

"Well, if you'd feel better going into the bathroom and putting on that thick terry-cloth robe and then crawling under the covers, I'll keep my eyes closed, but it's going to come off anyway, and I'm going to see your beautiful black skin and your thick body and rub my hands up and down, and I'm going to touch you everywhere, and you're not leaving this room until I hear you whisper or yell out my name."

And then he backs away and lets go of me.

"It's your move."

"Can we at least close those drapes?"

"No we cannot."

And then he sits on the foot of the bed and starts tapping one of his now-shoeless feet. He starts laughing. And then I start laughing. And then I just say oh, to hell with it, and I unzip my jeans that are a little on the tight side, since I've been spending more time bending over in the garage than I've been spending walking, so I have to struggle a little, which I turn into a wiggle to get them down to my feet, and then I step out of them and roll down these stupid white socks, which I am going to leave in the trash, and then Stan gets up and walks behind me and unhooks my bra and takes both of these 36Ds into his hands and massages them like they're supposed to be massaged.

He turns me around and kisses me on my forehead again and says, "You are one hot mama," and we both laugh as I walk over to the bed and try to slide under the covers as smoothly and as sexily as possible, but I get a little tangled up when he drops his jeans and my eyes grow wide, and now I remember what he gave me back in the day, and he walks over and slides under the sheets and puts his arms around me, and he takes me on a slow train ride until I hear myself yell out his name three or four times, and he softly whispers, "Oh, Georgia," in my ear, and then he wraps his arms around me, and I'm in a cocoon, and when we wake up, it's dark outside but daylight in here.

"SO. LET ME KNOW how soon your train ride is or if you'd like to come to New York before then."

"What makes you think I want to come to New York?"

I wish he would let me get out of this bed. But he is not letting me go, and if it were possible for me to move in and live under these sheets with him, I would just have room service every single day for the rest of my life and be happy.

"Because you like me. And I live in New York."

"True. Wait! What's the name of this movie?"

"*Georgia and Stan's Excellent Adventure That Will Last for a Life-time.* How's that?"

"As long as it's in high definition, I might sit in the front row."

"I just want you to know I'm not perfect," he says, after we shower and get dressed. "But you won't have to ever consider having me committed. My feet are firmly planted on the ground."

"Well, I *am* perfect, and I can't help it," I say, trying my hardest not to even snicker.

"Okay," he says. "So let's be clear about this. We're not lovestruck teenagers or twenty-somethings, we're middle-aged adults, right?"

"I suppose," I say.

"I've been lonely a long time, if you want to know the truth," he says.

"Well, that makes two of us."

"We've got a chance to remedy that, you know."

"But what if we don't like each other?"

"I already like you. And you like me, so stop pretending you don't. We've only got about twenty or thirty years left, so let's not blow it."

"It's been two days, Stan."

"Yeah? How long is it supposed to take?"

# My Brand-New Future

SOMEBODY SURE LOVES THEM SOME YOU," MERCURY SAYS.

"What are you talking about?"

"You must've put a spell on him or something."

"And who might you be referring to?"

"You know who I'm talking about. Stanley, of course. He seemed very cool and was easy on the eyes for an old guy. No offense. Marina thinks he could pass for a well-preserved movie star."

"Who told you his name?"

"He came over and sat at our table! Didn't you see him talking to me, Marina, and Dr. Lily?"

"No, I didn't. I was a little busy, Mercury."

"Anyway, we all know what 'old friend' means."

"Did Marina make it off okay?"

"Afraid not. I made her cancel it and come home with me. She's not leaving. She's enrolling in the Academy of Art full-time. We're moving in together. But she can't have her old job back. So how about them apples?"

I just smile and throw my hands up in the air. I can believe almost anything about now.

"What up with that outfit? Haven't been home yet?"

I look down. Embarrassed.

"I've got a lab jacket. Tell me who's first this morning?"

"She's at the door."

Without even turning around, I know it's Mona Kwon.

She's waving, but this morning it's in slow motion. I open the door for her.

"Good morning, Mona. What are you doing here so early?"

"I have time to kill. Dr. Young, I went out of my way to go to your party, and you ignore Mona Kwon, but very good food. Why you don't post a response to me on Facebook? Many of those comments from men. I hope you had fun at high-school reunion. Many photos posted. Very happy for you."

"I apologize, Mona, but I've been so busy with my new grandchildren, and I don't go on Facebook as often as I probably should."

"So true. But grandkids don't need you. See them anytime. But husband number three could be hiding in your friend requests. I'll bet free glasses you do not bother checking your personal messages either."

"Mercury, let Mona pick out a pair. And what makes you think I want another husband, Mona?"

"You need one, but this time it will be the final one. Mona Kwon knows things. I do need new glasses. Thank you for free ones."

"I thought you canceled your appointment?"

"True. I just came for new glasses, so mission accomplished."

Before I reach my office, Lily comes out to greet me.

"You have a minute?" she asks.

"I do. You want me to come to you?"

"Sure. Come on in."

Her office is identical to mine, except the only family photos on her walls are of her parents. The rest are of flowers and sunsets and the ocean. I sit across from her. Cross my legs.

"Everything went okay?" I ask.

"Yes. Dad is at peace. My mom couldn't stay. She wanted to come home. Doesn't know Dad's gone. Anyway, I want to thank you for all your blessings, and my family really appreciated the flowers."

"You're welcome, Lily."

She folds her hands on her desk. "The party was just wonderful. I had more fun than I've had in years. Met a very nice fellow. Grover. He said he's your new brother."

"Was he with a woman?"

"He said she was just a good friend."

What a whore.

"He's very good-looking. Intelligent. Professional. Witty."

But he's also not divorced. I can't say it. I just can't.

"He asked for my card, and I gave it to him."

"I'm sure you'll be hearing from him soon."

"I have already." She smiles.

I haven't seen this smile before.

"So you and Stanley go way back?"

"We do."

"He seems very nice. And thoughtful to have come this far for your birthday."

"And how far did he come?"

"He told us New York. Listen, Georgia. You look like you've been over the moon, and I think I have more good news."

"I'm listening."

"I want to keep the practice going, and I've already checked with a broker, and because of the fact that our equipment is only a couple of years old, it's highly probable that you can get your original investment back—and then there's also interest. How's that sound to you?"

I'm about ready to fall out of this chair. "It sounds like good news."

She nods.

"But I thought you wanted out, too?"

"No. I never really said that. Or did I? It doesn't matter. Medicine is part of my family's tradition, and before my dad got really sick, we talked about my selling the practice, and he asked me if there was any way I could keep it. It would make him feel better."

"But if you don't want to do this anymore, Lily . . ."

"I don't have any other skills, to be honest. This is what I do. This is who I am."

"Do you really believe that?"

"I'm not miserable. It may be monotonous, but the patients help me get through the day."

She leans back in her chair and breathes a long sigh, glad to finally have everything out in the open.

"Anyway, we can talk more about legal stuff and just how long this transition might take. Are you in a big hurry to do something else?"

"No. Now that I know how feasible it is."

"So what are your plans after you leave?"

"I think I'm going to try my hand at decorating furniture."

"To make a living?"

"I didn't say that, now, did I?"

"You don't have to. I get it. How long have you been doing this? And why haven't you ever shown me anything?"

"I haven't had much to show until lately."

"Cool. Maybe one day, if you ever invite me over, I'll get a chance to see some. Hint, hint."

"You just took the words out of my mouth. We're overdue, and if you like something, it'll be a parting gift."

"I'm already excited."

I stand up.

"Wait a sec. Tell me a little more about Stanley."

"All I can say is he feels like a dream come true. I'm still a little afraid to put all my trust in it."

"Well, at least he's real and not married."

"You don't know that."

"Oh, but I do."

"Really, now?"

"Just so you know, Mercury's already done a background check on him. He's good to go."

"What?"

"Apparently Marina told him to do it. She's the one who did my background checks. She's very good at it. Anyway, they both think Stanley's a keeper. I can't believe he's really been up in fucking outer space, and now he rebuilds houses in run-down neighborhoods. How fucking cool is that?"

"Very fucking cool," I say, mimicking her. I can count on one hand how many times I've heard Lily swear, so maybe therapy has finally loosened her up.

"I think you should get on over to your office. I didn't mean to talk so much, but I thought this would make your birthday even better. Now, go!"

When I open my door, the office smells and looks like a florist's shop. I can't see my desk or the chair behind it. Mercury runs in and stares at me looking like I'm in a trance, and of course he has his iPhone in one hand videotaping for Marina, and then finally he snatches the card out of my hand and rips it open and starts reading: " 'Ms. Georgia Peach. I choose you. Been a long time coming. Hope to see you soon. I say yes. And I hope you will too. Love, Stan.' "

Mercury falls backward into the door. "OMG! LHM! INNW!"

"Hold on! I know the first two, but what's this INNW?"

" 'If not now, when?' Enough said. Back to work. Hey, now!"

And out he goes.

And I'm drunk.


I NEED TO DO something to ground me, bring me back to reality, so I call my daughter. I don't even know which one until I hear Estelle's voice.

"That was some party, Mom," she says.

"That it was," I say. "But how are you doing? Seriously?"

"I'm in a daze, to be honest. If it weren't for the kids, I'd sleepwalk my way through this tunnel until I come out on the other side."

This is hard, because I'm feeling the exact opposite, like I'm in a hot-air balloon. But my daughter's feelings and what she's dealing with are real, and I don't want her to have to go through this alone.

"I know, baby," I say, picking up a pencil and batting it against my keyboard. "Would you bring the girls over this weekend? Or I'd be happy to drive over for a visit."

"I'd rather come there. This place is a mess."

"How about the three of you spend the weekend with me, then?"

"That sounds like a plan, Mom."


I LOOK AT the clock at one. Stanley should be landing soon. At two I think I'll hear from him. At three I decide to call him, but it goes straight to voice mail. By four I wonder if this was some kind of fucking game he just played on me. Was that what this reminiscing bullshit was all about? And how about these fucking flowers? Isn't this more like overkill? It wasn't a fucking funeral. Maybe he's home and came to his senses and realized I'm not the woman he thought I was going to be. I could kick myself in the ass for getting so caught up in the moment, and maybe I just dreamed this whole fucking fantasy because I've wanted to know what it felt like to be swept off my feet and touched and kissed and made love to by a man. To hell with you, Mr. Fucking Space Man.

As I leave the office at six, my cell rings. I recognize the 212 area code. It's Mr. Swoop-Down-on-Me.

"So thanks for the flowers, Stanley."

"Stanley? Did I miss something?"

"I'm not sure. You tell me."

"I forgot my cell in the seat pocket, and I had to wait until everybody got off the plane, and then, after all that, the flight attendant claimed they didn't find it, so I just walked in. Are you okay?"

Okay. So I'm a cynic.

"I'm fine. Sorry to hear about your cell. I was just having doubts about all this."

"Don't even go there."

"Are you sure about everything?"

"I'm not even going to answer that."

"The flowers are beautiful. As was your card."

"I'm glad you liked them. But look, Ms. Georgia, I'm wiped out. It's been a long wonderful weekend. Dream about me. Hope to see you in Toronto, unless you change your mind. Peace out, sweetheart."

Sweetheart?


MEET ME FOR *dinner or die,* Wanda says in a very long text. *it's been three days since anybody's heard a peep out of you, and just so you know, our friend violet, the slut, left the party with richard. they belong together. anyway, is stanley still here or something?*

I call her back.

"So?"

I tell her about Lily buying me out.

"That's great. That's one down. Get to the juicy stuff, would you?"

And then I go on and tell her almost everything.

"Well, this is undoubtedly the most gratifying five-course meal I've had in years. Get on the goddamn train as soon as humanly possible. And meet that man in Toronto."

Click.

# Spilling the Beans

'VE HEARD EVERYTHING," MA SAYS. IT'S SIX THIRTY IN THE
morning, and I was just about to go on a walk with Naomi and
Macy.

"What are you talking about?"

"Good morning to you, too, missy. Wanda told me all about
Stanley."

"Wanda talks too much."

"That's what friends are for. To tell all your business, but at least
Wanda knows who to tell it to. I'm your mother, and I'm happy for
you, baby."

"I haven't eloped!"

"That wouldn't be a bad idea, now that you mention it."

"You looked very nice at my party, Ma."

"I did, didn't I? Thank you."

"Have you had your humble breakfast already?"

"You know I'm not a racist, don't you?"

"Yes, I do."

"He was sexy."

"What do you know about sexy?"

"My Grover is sexy. You can be sexy at any age. Heck. I'm sexy. You
still have a ways to go," she says, and cracks up.

"You know, you never did tell me how the train was, Ma."

"Chile, Grover drove. Seven hours was too doggone long to be stuck
on a train and not be able to pull into a gas station or a Burger King,
you know what I mean?"

"Well, I'm still going on mine. And it's going to last a whole lot longer than seven hours."

"You always have been different," she says. "Is the space man going with you?"

"Who told you he was an astronaut?"

"He told Grover, who was giving him the third degree. He wanted to make sure he hadn't escaped from a planetarium, if you know what I'm getting at. But Grover liked him. How long was he up there?"

"I don't know."

"Find out what he saw. And if he floated without holding on to anything like you see in the movies. And ask him how'd he go to the bathroom."

"Why don't you make a list?"

"Grover's the one who wants to know. Not me."

"You tell Grover I'm glad to hear he's so curious."

"The next time you talk to him—what's his last name?"

"DiStasio."

"Anyway, the next time you speak to Stanley, you tell him he can come on down to Bakersfield if he's looking for some more neighborhoods that need to be spruced up."

"I'll tell him."

"He seems very nice, Georgia. Well rounded. Of course, being educated is a plus. And you know, nobody minds him being white."

"I don't either," I hear myself say.

"Even Dolly liked him, and you know she doesn't like any white people. And her sons didn't believe he'd really been to space until Stanley showed them pictures on his iPhone of himself up there in that space outfit. They fist-bumped him. I saw it with my own eyes."

"Well, I'm glad they came. And Dolly looked good."

"She succeeds sometimes. Anyway, let us know when you get on that train so we know how to find you."

"I will. Love you, Ma."

"You, too. Now, go walk the walk."

When my phone rings again, I answer it like a robot. "Hello, this is Dr. Young."

"Mom, you're at home!" Frankie says.

"My bad."

I hear knocking on the front door.

"Hold on a sec. My neighbors have been waiting for me to go on a walk, so don't go anywhere. I'll be right back!"

I drop the phone, and it falls to the floor.

"COMING!" And I fling the front door open.

"What in the hell is going on with you, Rihanna? Are you walking or are you talking?" Naomi, of course.

"I'm talking."

"To be honest, I'm not feeling this hill either," Macy says.

"Is it the astronaut?" Naomi asks, giving Macy a shove.

"Stop being so nosy! But no! I have to go! Sorry, I don't think I can walk with you two huzzies this morning. Maybe tomorrow."

I close the door and hear them cackling. I run back to my office. "Okay. I'm listening."

"So, Mom, Stelle filled me in about her bad news, but she's going to be fine, and we're going to try to spend more time together and let our kids get to know what cousins are, but she just told me the rocking news about Mr. Stanley, and I say get on that train and to hell with optometry. And just so you know, baby Levi is getting two teeth, and I'm done breast-feeding because he bit me. If I sound wired, it's because I'm so frigging happy you're finally getting the love and joy and excitement you deserve, and I also have to say you're the best mom that Stelle and I could have asked for, and what up?"

"I'm good," is all I can say. "But can I please call you back a little later, baby?"

"Absolutely. Love you!"

I then run out the door and catch up with my neighbors. I am so overwhelmed with joy I could use the fresh air.


DURING THIS entire week, like clockwork before bedtime, Stanley (I only like calling him Stan face-to-face) calls me or I call him. We talk about everything under the sun. I know it's a cliché, but I'm so glad I have a man with a brain to talk to. I told him about my practice. That I've set a travel date. He's excited for me. Asked if I'd mind sending him my itinerary so he'll have some idea where I am. He said he'd be waiting at the station for me in Toronto, and to let him know if I change my plans, because he's making a lot of them. Ever heard of Broadway?

THE TWINS ARE much taller. And they're not dressed alike. Thank the Lord.

"Hi, Granny!" they both yell right after they come inside.

Gabby's two front teeth are missing, and she has a thick ponytail that cascades from the top of her head. Scarlett has two braids that fall over her ears and looks like she has all her teeth. They are both in jeans and different-colored T-shirts.

Estelle looks like she did the last time she was here. Exhausted. She's carrying Dove in whatever those carrier things are called. I wish there was something I could do for her. Maybe I'll keep the little huzzies—I'm going to stop calling them this—Gabrielle and Scarlett for a weekend after I come back. Take them to the Oakland Zoo or the planetarium. Maybe teach them how to make some kind of cookies.

"It looks different in here, Granny," Scarlett says.

"Because she painted. Anybody can see that."

"Let me see Miss Dove," I say, ignoring them but trying not to act like what they're saying isn't important.

I kiss Estelle on the cheek and take the baby out of that carrier. This little girl is cute. So are the twins, but they, like Levi, started out a bit slower on the cuteness Richter scale. Levi finally looks his age.

"So . . . good to see everybody. And I have a surprise for you, Estelle."

"What?"

"I'll tell you after you get settled."

"Granny, can we watch *Judge Judy*?"

"*Judge Judy?*" Estelle asks.

"Don't even worry about it. Give me the baby, and let's go down to the family room. Anybody hungry? I have popcorn!"

"Yeah!" they say together. "We want popcorn!"

"I bought a DVD—otherwise we'd never be able to chat—and Dove's about to fall right back asleep, I can guarantee it," Stelle tells me.

And she's right. On both fronts.

When everybody's settled, my daughter and I sit at the table in the nook, and because she's still breast-feeding, she has a glass of lemonade. I decide to have one, too.

"So. Have you heard from or seen Justin?"

"Of course. I see him more now than when he was living at home. He's actually getting on my nerves."

"I think he feels terrible about what this has done to you."

"What did you just say, Mom?"

"I mean, this doesn't seem like the kind of thing you do to hurt someone deliberately."

"Well, he can't take it back now, can he? And I'll live. My girls and I will be just fine. I made him get tested."

"That was smart, but *he's* not stupid, is he?" My heart feels like it's going to jump out of my chest.

"No, he's not. He showed me six months' worth of tests."

"Six months!"

"Some of these men get a little carried away and forget they have wives."

"That just sounds so wrong."

"Anyway, Mom, I got tested, and I'm clear."

"Okay. So. I just wish none of this was happening."

"Well, when Dad cheated on you, didn't you feel violated?"

"Of course. But this is a whole lot different."

"I know that. But didn't you want to kill him?"

"Of course I did. For about ten minutes. How's Justin's head, by the way?"

"You can't even see it. I should've hit him harder."

"I'm glad you didn't. And how are the girls handling his absence?"

"They think he's on vacation."

"Well, on some level he is. You've let him see them, I hope."

"Yes. He's taken them to the movies. The park. He loves all three of them. I'm not worried about them being exposed to anything weird."

"Weird? Come on, Estelle. He's not a freak. He's just gay."

"Okay, I get it. But I have something else to tell you."

"I hope it's good news."

"I want to leave Palo Alto and move over here into a good neighborhood that has a good school district full of children of different ethnicities, and Justin's all for it."

"How? And when? What about your house?"

"I don't care about that house. In that neighborhood it'll sell before we put the sign in the grass."

"This is good news. I'll talk to Wanda about this."

"Why Aunt Wanda?"

"I'll tell you another time."

"So the astronaut landed on your planet at the right time, from what I'm hearing. I think it's so cool, Mom."

"Yep. I might maybe could actually kinda be falling in love with him."

"I know I didn't just hear you say the word *love,* Mom."

"Yes, she said LOVE!" Gabby screams. Children have ears in the back of their heads, which is why I never swore in front of my daughters.

Of course, I give Estelle another gift certificate for a massage and facial but tell her she'd better be back in this house in less than five hours, because chances are I'll be drunk if she's not.

Dove is a sweetheart. The girls act like she doesn't exist. When I hear the garage door open, because it makes a beeping sound, and I don't see the twins, I pick Dove up in her little carrier and beeline it out there.

And there they are. Looking more curious than busted.

"Who told you girls you could come out here?"

"No one. What's that over there?" Scarlett says, walking over to a chair with feathers on it.

"Where'd you buy all this cool stuff, Granny?" Gabby says.

"Your granny made it."

"You did not!" she says.

"I did so."

"It's outrageous," Scarlett says. "Can you teach us how to make something?"

"Absolutely, but not today. Come on back inside, please."

And they do, because I interrupted their flow and I could tell they were just about to touch everything, some of which is still drying. I have to admit, if little people like it, I'm hoping big ones will, too.

I make them lunch. Turkey sandwiches. Chips. Sliced apples. Juice for Dove.

We sit at the table in the nook. Dove's chilling in her carrier on the floor next to me.

"Guess what, Granny?" Gabby asks. She definitely lives up to her name.

"Can you give me a clue?"

"Our dad has a boyfriend because he's gay."

I have to stop myself from choking on my saliva. "Really?"

"Yes! He loves our mom, but he likes men better," Scarlett interjects.

Gabby: "And he can't help it."

Scarlett: "I think I want to be gay when I grow up."

Gabby: "Girls can be gay, too, you know, Granny."

"Yes, I know that."

Gabby: "They're called lesbians. I might want to be a lesbian when I grow up."

"That's nice. I know quite a few very nice lesbians."

Gabby: "You do? Where are they?"

"You'll meet them one day. So tell me, how do you two feel about your dad being gay?"

Scarlett: "I wish he could bring his boyfriend home to live with us, and then we could all be a happy family again."

"That might not work so well."

Scarlett: "I have a boyfriend."

Gabby: "No you don't! So what. I have a girlfriend. Winnie."

Scarlett: "I have two boyfriends. Fu and Hugo."

"Fu?" I ask.

Scarlett: "He's Chinese. Hugo is black. But Mom told us race doesn't matter, so I'm not supposed to be telling you that Fu is Chinese and Hugo is black, even though they are."

Gabby: "And Winnie is mixed-race."

"How do you know that?" I ask.

This is both heartbreaking and touching.

Gabby: "Because she told me. She said, 'I'm mixed-race.' And I told her I'm black-black."

"So how are you guys enjoying little Dove here these days?"

Of course I'm obviously trying to lighten things up. A little. Or a lot.

Gabby: "I'm trying to like her."

Scarlett: "She can't do anything except drink from Mom's boobs and poop and cry."

Gabby: "She's also boring. Look at her."

Scarlett: "I'll be glad when she can talk so she'll have something to say."

"Well, do you help your mom with Dove sometimes, like big girls do?"

"Absolutely!" they say simultaneously.

"What is it you do?"

Scarlett: "We let her watch cartoons on our iPads. She likes it, and it makes her stop crying."

Gabby: "And we ask her questions we already know the answers to, because we're smart, you know."

"You don't have to tell me."

Gabby: "What can we do for fun now, Granny?"

Scarlett: "Yes, because we're boring."

Me: "How would you guys like to sleep over and go to the zoo tomorrow?"

Gabby: "Can we sleep with you?"

Me: "Absolutely!"

They both applaud, and Dove wakes up.

Gabby: "What about her?"

Scarlett: "She does not like real animals."

Me: "Well, maybe she can sleep in the guest room with your mom."

Gabby: "She only likes sleeping in her bed at our house."

Scarlett: "That's true."

Me: "Well, she's sleeping now."

Gabby: "It's because she knows it's only a nap."

They win.

# Starlight

M Y TRAIN LEAVES IN TWO HOURS. AT 9:39 P.M. OF course Wanda insists on driving me to the station, which is here in downtown Oakland and butts right up to the harbor in Jack London Square. It's amazing how you can catch a train next to sailboats and yachts parked in their berths. Wanda and I have our farewell dinner at Kincaid's.

"Well, I hope it's everything you hoped it would be. You couldn't pay me to ride on a damn train by myself for ten hours, let alone twenty-three."

"It's because you don't know what to do with silence."

"Embroider. Anyway, whatever month you get to Toronto, give Stanley a hug and a fist bump, since high-fiving is passé. And please don't blow it, Georgia."

"Bye," I say, and we hug, and I leave her in front of the kiosk.

"Be in touch whenever you have service! It'll probably be a blessing to be disconnected."

"Okay," I say, and start pulling my two bags toward the station.

But of course she has more to say, and she yells it.

"And remember, don't talk to strangers!"

I just wave a hand in the air.


WHEN I GET inside the station, it hits me that I'm finally going to get on this train. But the Coast Starlight isn't your everyday train. It's famous. The scenery along the Coast Starlight's route, widely regarded as one of the most spectacular of all train routes, is unsurpassed. I can't wait to see those dramatic snow-covered peaks, the lush forests and fertile valleys and long stretches of the Pacific Ocean, which will provide a stunning backdrop for my journey. (I stole this from their website.)

I could probably sit in this station all day and just read. Or people-watch. The walls are all paned glass. Modern. The ceilings are so high that the curved steel arches make it feel and look like an airplane hangar. Metal-encased and thick-ribbed lights hang from long cables, and right in the middle of the dark-tiled floor are rows of black seating, much nicer than what you see at the airport.

I felt the same way when I left for college. I sit down and wait. Listening to the announcements. How many minutes until boarding. Thirty. The train is on time. I look around. There are hundreds of people zigzagging through this place in slow motion. I've packed a fleece blanket and an ergonomic pillow, a hooded jacket and leather gloves just in case. I also broke down and bought a Kindle, only because I couldn't decide which books to bring. Ten minutes. For once I didn't overpack. I decided that once I'm in Canada, I'll just buy new when I need something clean. I've always wanted to do this—why not now? I want to know what it feels like to be unburdened for a week. I also want to celebrate how good I'm feeling and splurge a little and not worry about it. Of course I brought my personal items, and Wanda insisted I go to Neiman Marcus and not Victoria's Secret. I brought a pair of white silk pajamas and two items I haven't worn in years: negligees. But they're not just for Stan. They're for me. And I feel amazing in them.

When I finally hear the boarding announcement, I spring up and fall in line with about a hundred or more passengers who seem to know where we're going.

I bought a coach ticket because I don't need a bedroom on a train. It won't kill me to sleep sitting up. The passengers on the Superliners get extra privileges besides miniature sleeping quarters. They also get a little shower and free drinks and a lounge and movies. But all the windows on a train give you the same view.

A nice guy who looks like a hiker helps me up the step. He hands me my two bags and points to where I can drop them off. I put one of mine with the growing pile of seventies-looking suitcases, show my ticket to the conductor—a black woman with red cornrows. She tells me to hang a left, head up the stairs, and hold on to my ticket. I look for my row. I'm sitting next to a window. I pull out my blanket and pillow and toss them onto my seat and put my bag overhead. Doesn't look like I have a seatmate.

I say hello back to folks as they pass by. People appear to be friendly on trains. This car is filling up fast. A young couple seated across from me heave their backpacks overhead. Both are blond, and both have ponytails. They smell like the earth.

"How's it going?" he asks. "I'm Travis and this is Holly."

"I'm fine. Thanks. Nice to meet you both. I'm Georgia."

I suppose they qualify as strangers. They look European, but they're American.

"Where you headed?" Travis asks.

"Vancouver."

"Which one?"

"British Columbia."

"You a hiker?" Holly asks, but then when she notices my hot pink acrylic nails, she says, "I guess not!"

And here comes a big woman who has four thin braids falling from her temples with red, orange, and white plastic beads dangling on the end of each one. When they said to dress in layers, she listened. I can't identify what she has on, but it's multitiered and confusing. She's kicking five shopping bags down the aisle, drops her backpack on the seat next to mine, and says, "Hi, I'm Calico."

"Hello, Calico," I say with as straight a face as possible. "I'm Georgia."

She chucks each of her bags up top, and I'm praying they don't touch mine. Then she pushes her backpack to the floor, pulls a tuna sandwich on white bread out of a white bag, and takes two big bites. She chews like she hasn't eaten in weeks.

WTF.

"How far you going?" she asks, and I don't look to see if she's still chewing, because I just can't.

"Seattle," I say, low enough so my hiker neighbors don't hear.

"Me, too. Going to a funeral. You look like you might be ready to vacation."

I nod.

"Where do you hail from?"

"Oakland."

She finishes her sandwich. Then digs out two cartons of Yoo-hoo chocolate drink and a narrow package of tiny powdered doughnuts and polishes those off. And then she farts! I swear to God she does. And she doesn't say excuse me. But it's exactly what I say to her when she gets up to let me out, and I take my pillow and blanket and reach for my roll-aboard, and she says, "How long are you going to be gone?"

"I'm not sure. I'm going down to the observation car to look at the stars."

"Enjoy," she says, and moves into my seat.

I hear the conductor shout "All aboard!" loud enough to be heard a block away. When I walk into the observation car, the entire ceiling is slightly tinted curved glass that drops down to a wall of windows, which are directly in front of seats that swivel. Farther down are rows of built-in rectangular tables big enough for four. The soft blue cushions are like those you'd see in a nice diner. The dining car starts where these tables end. This is where I decide I'm going to live for the next twenty-three hours.

When I feel the wheels churn and screech against the steel tracks, and the train inches its way out of the station, I feel more excited than I did when Ma and Daddy took us to Disneyland for the first time.

After the boats finally disappear, I call my daughters, Ma, Wanda, Violet, Mercury, and Marina. I save Stan for last.

"The train has just left the station," I tell them, and they applaud and offer their personal safety guidelines about what to do in case of an emergency, all of them except Stan.

"So your adventure begins," he says.

"It does."

"Enjoy every minute of it," he says. "And call or text when you can or when you feel up to it. It's already tomorrow here. But not to worry. I also love travel photos, especially the ones that look airbrushed! Just let me know when you'll be arriving in Vancouver, and this way I'll know how many miles to go before I wake."

"Will do."

I wanted to tell him I wished he were sitting next to me.

But I just couldn't.

I miss him.

And I haven't missed anybody in years.

I put my pillow on top of the table, wrap my fleece blanket around my shoulders, and lay my head down. When I feel someone shaking me, I look up, and seated across from me are Calico and a scrawny-looking older woman with short, feathery hair I can see through, smiling at me. Or maybe not.

"I thought you were coming back. Anyway, this is my new friend, Collette. Collette, this is Georgia."

"Hello, Collette."

"Were you sleeping?" Collette asks.

"Yes. It's been a long day."

"Tell me about it," she says.

"So what is it you do for a living?" Calico asks.

"I'm an optometrist."

"No shit."

Even though I don't want to know, I feel obligated to ask. "What about you two?"

"I'm currently unemployed," Calico says. "I'm disabled."

"I'm a bebop singer," Collette says.

"Really?"

"Yes. I've just discovered how much I love harmony, so I've been helping out a group in Eugene, which is where I will have to leave you ladies tomorrow afternoon."

"That sounds exciting."

I can tell these two have a lot in common. Collette's eyes are glassy.

"Are you okay?" I ask her.

"I will be as soon as my meds kick in."

"So what are you going to Seattle for?" Calico asks.

"To start a new life," I say, just to see what *they'll* say.

"Well, we all could use one," Calico says.

Collette just nods in agreement.

"Yes we do. But you know what, ladies? I'm really tired and need to close my eyes if you don't mind."

"Then sleep away," Calico says.

But they don't leave. And for the next three or four hours, they tell each other their life stories, which is like listening to every soap opera ever made rolled into one.

I FEEL THE SUN on my face, and my neck is killing me. I open one eye and see that the girls are gone.

We're in Oregon. Klamath Falls. The town's tiny brick station, though clearly pretty new, looks like something you'd see in a black-and-white movie. I go to the bathroom, brush my teeth, and wash my face with my own products. I would like to change, but I wouldn't dream of undressing in this stainless-steel bathroom.

I have a roll and bitter coffee for breakfast. There is no cell-phone service, and I'm told there won't be for hours, but it doesn't matter. For the next seven, I won't stop looking out the window, because this is what I will see:

Rain.

Mount Shasta.

A snow-covered island surrounded by a blue lake.

Rain.

Tunnels.

Forests.

Mountains.

Canyons.

Beavers.

A red sun.

Twilight.

The last of which is precisely when I'm sitting in the dining car eager to order dinner and the train suddenly stops. Other folks seem as baffled as I do, and we're all wearing that look of anticipation, which is when we hear the announcement that there's been a gas-line break outside Portland. We're going to have to stay put until it's fixed. That it might be two, maybe three hours, but they'll keep us informed.

And here come my BFFs. The hostess asks if I would mind if they joined me, and I tell her not at all. I order a burger and fries and a salad made with iceberg lettuce. My girlfriends order the same, except Collette orders hers without the bun.

"So it looks like we're stranded, huh?" she says.

"I'm in no hurry," Calico says.

"I thought you were going to a funeral."

"Did I tell you that?"

"Yes, you did."

"Then I am. Except it's probably my own."

They both think this is funny.

I almost choke on my hamburger it's so dry, and I only eat half of it. The fries are hard and yellow, and I can see a puddle of dressing on the plate after I eat a few forkfuls of the wet lettuce. Collette is still futzing with her brown burger. Calico's plate is empty.

"Are you going to finish that burger?" she asks.

I look at it.

"No."

"You mind if I finish it?"

"No," I say, shocked that she's serious.

"What about the salad?"

"Knock yourself out," I say, and push my plate closer to her.

When the waitress brings three checks, they act like they're afraid to look at theirs. I take them.

"This is my treat," I say.

"Are you shitting me?" Calico says, as if she's hit the lottery.

"Well, that's awful kind of you, Georgia. It must be nice to be a professional like yourself. Thank you so much."

"You're quite welcome, ladies. But look, I want to get a little reading in and maybe watch a movie, since we don't know how long we're going to be on this train."

I will have a chance to watch two movies before this fucking train moves, but while we wait, this is what happens on the Orient Express:

People start smoking in the bathrooms. Cigarettes and marijuana.

Children run up and down the aisles.

A young couple at the table in front of me decide to turn it into an art class and invite the children who won't sit down to sit down and paint on three-by-five index cards they whip out of their backpacks, and they even line up the watercolor trays for the kids, and for the next few hours even some adults decide they also want to be Picasso.

I decide to have a drink.

And this is who I meet while drinking champagne at the other end of the observation car:

Harriet and Raymond, both seventy-three: Celebrating their fiftieth wedding anniversary. They met on a train. They're from Sacramento.

Juice: He's trying to get off meth and figured a train ride would help aid in his recovery. He seems a little wired to me.

Marvin and Maynard: Twins, forty-two, from Saratoga Springs, New York, both recently divorced, who've decided to ride out their pain on a train around the entire United States. They don't think they're going to make it past Seattle.

June: Eighteen, a runaway from Vallejo, California. Going as far as the train goes. She has no money. I give her sixty dollars. It's all the cash I have.

People on trains will talk to anyone willing to listen. I'm fascinated by just how different our lives are. And this is what I overhear while waiting for the Starlight to move:

"I'm getting off this fucking train if you say it one more time. I swear to God."

"I love you."

"Four times? Really?"

"They're getting a divorce? He did?"

"I'm quitting my job because I hate it."

"You lived in thirteen foster homes?"

"You're not having it?"

"You just cannot trust men."

"You were born to be a slut."

"Meet me in the restroom."

I don't read a word for hours.

I don't need to.

I close my eyes after so many miles of rocking. When we stop in a station to take on new passengers, an oncoming train passes, and it feels like we're moving, too. But backward.

When the train finally does move, I close my eyes and dream about Stanley. I reenact our weekend and hit Pause at the place I want to stop it.

Each time I try to use my cell phone, it simply says NO SERVICE, so I give up.

It appears that almost everybody's asleep, but I find myself looking out the window at the deep darkness and the strong rain and at my reflection in the glass, and I'm trying to remember why I wanted to take this fucking train ride in the first place. Oh, yeah. To figure out how I was going to do the things I've either already done or am in the process of now doing.

We arrive in Seattle five hours late. I say good-bye to my friends. The hotel has given away my room. The train to Vancouver leaves in three hours, so I decide to just wait in the station until it's time to board. Four uneventful hours later, I'm finally in Vancouver. The good news is it only takes me fifteen minutes to go through customs. I look like shit, but I don't care.

I'm starting to realize how beautiful train stations are. Airports could learn something from them. Seriously. I paid for the option of spending the day sightseeing and shopping and maybe spending the night here in a five-star hotel and leaving in the morning. I could be in Toronto in four days instead of six. But I don't want to spend the day as a tourist or the night in a beautiful hotel alone. I want to see Stanley. I decide to call him. I want to hear his voice instead of just remembering it. I hope he doesn't think the train went off the track or that I had a change of heart and am blowing him off. I sit down on what looks just like a church pew and dial. It rings three times and goes to voice mail. I probably should've just stayed home and painted something, because so far the ride on this train has been disappointing, and now I have to get on another one for four or five more days before I'll even get to Toronto. I just hope I can stand being on another train that long. I feel tears welling in my eyes, and just as they're about to roll, I realize I don't have any tissue.

"Is anyone sitting here?"

I look up. And there he is.

"No," I say, trying to pull myself together.

"Are you okay?"

"I'm fine," I say, and tighten my ponytail and wipe my eyes.

"What's your name?"

"Georgia. Georgia Young."

"Well, it's nice to meet you, Georgia Young. I'm Stanley DiStasio."

"It's nice to meet you, too, Mr. DiStasio."

"Please, call me Stan."

"Stan."

"You look like you could use a hug."

"I could," I say.

And then he reaches over and pulls me inside his arms and holds me like a baby.

"I was worried because I haven't heard a peep out of you since yesterday, so I hopped on a plane and flew here. What's wrong?"

"I'm so glad to see you, and it was just horrible, and I don't care if I never get on another fucking train ever again in life!"

"You don't have to."

"You were right about the service. Mountains and wilderness don't need to worry about reception. And what a bunch of weirdos and people who don't know where they're going. And everybody's just so damn lonely!"

"Well, no one better than you to understand that we're all only trying to find a place to land."

I look at him and just blurt out, "I really like you."

"I like you, too," he says. "A lot."

"I'm glad," I say.

"I also love you," he says.

"I think I might possibly potentially but probably love you, too, Stan."

"Could you please repeat that, but without all the words that began with *p*?"

"I love you, Stanley DiStasio."

"That's much better," he says. "But it's Stan."

And we sit here on this bench a few more minutes without talking, which is when I get an overwhelming sense of where I am and what I'm doing and how implausible this really is and that it can't be happening because it feels too good.

"I can't afford to do this again," I blurt again.

"Do what again?"

"Start and stop."

"You don't have to."

"What makes you so sure?"

"Because I think we've been waiting a very long time for each other."

"Don't."

"This isn't a movie, Georgia."

I sit there and sink. "So what would you say if I told you I fell in love with you thirty-five years ago but never told a soul, not even my own?"

"I'd believe you," he says.

"What?"

"I knew when you refused to go to the pizza place with me, which is why I brought you the whole box."

"Really?"

"I knew it when you sat up front and didn't turn back to look at me."

"Shut. Up!" I lean against him and push.

"But I also knew I loved you when you let me join your study group."

He chuckles.

"It was confirmed when you let me touch you and I knew then that one day I was going to touch you again."

I hold out my hand. "Touch me again now."

And he strokes my fingers. "I'm going to love you soft and hard," he says.

"Okay."

"I'm going to make you so happy you won't know what to do except be happy."

"This sounds good to me. And I'll give everything back to you triple."

"And I'm going to listen to every word that comes out of your mouth," he says.

"I'm a talker."

"You think I've forgotten?"

"You know what I want to know?" I ask.

"I'm listening."

"How the universe works."

"You mean the planet we're on right now?"

"Including the stars. All of it."

"That's going to take some time."

"About how many days?" I ask sarcastically.

"At least a million."

When we hear them announce that my train is ready for boarding, I tear up my ticket and toss it in the trash.

He stands up and pulls my bags closer together.

I look up at him.

He looks down at me.

"So," I say. "Here we are."

"No," he says. "Here we go."

# Epilogue

WANDA WON THE BET.
   Nelson paid up.
   They moved to Palm Desert.

Estelle and the girls are keeping their old home alive in the Oakland Hills. Gabrielle and Scarlett are both single again. Dove can say, "I eat-teen months," when asked how old she is, even though she's twenty months.

Frankie and Hunter are happy and pregnant again. She says she loves being a mom, and Levi is thriving. He is much cuter than I ever imagined. She got a story published!

Mona Kwon passed. ☹

Velvet moved in with her baby daddy and is purportedly engaged and purportedly attending cosmetology school. Miracles do happen.

Violet and Richard are for sure shacking up. She's probably going to get reinstated with the bar but has decided she might do well working with battered women. She has apparently grown a conscience.

Lily and Grover Jr. are engaged and pregnant with twin boys through a surrogate. Better late than never. The practice is thriving. Two new partners. May open an office in Berkeley.

Marina and Mercury, who claimed they didn't believe in marriage, are now married. They will graduate from the Academy of Art next year, at which time they believe without an ounce of doubt they're never having children and are moving to New York.

Stan and I just had our third child.

LOL!

Seriously.

We're in Cape Town, South Africa. We've been here for six weeks. I rented optometric equipment and have been giving free eye exams and glasses to those who can't afford them. Nothing ever felt better. Will come back annually.

We went on safari. Seeing those animals up close scared the hell out of me. I prefer watching them on the National Geographic Channel. However, I loved the accommodations.

Stan and I have decided that the world is worth seeing. So two or three times a year, we plan to travel to a different country. Or place. Somewhere one of us has never been. Next up is Dubai, then Bora-Bora, then Spain and Australia. We will go back to Africa once a year regardless. Victoria Falls and Ghana and Kenya and Zimbabwe are high on the list. I should just say the entire continent. At home I have yet to see Yellowstone and the Grand Canyon. And then there's the Kennedy Space Center!

Stan and I are bicoastal. I love his apartment. I cook up a storm in that little kitchen, but I also love New York City.

I redid my own kitchen. Blue stove. Tangerine fridge. Yellow dishwasher. It rocks. Naomi and Macy totally dig it.

Stan still builds. He has quite a crew. Bakersfield is on the short list.

Stan also keeps his word. He's renovated a fifteen-hundred-square-foot studio for me in West Oakland. The garage at my house can handle two cars again.

I seem to say Stan's name a lot.

I've sold twelve stools, seven chairs, five side tables, and a ton of pillows, all of which appear to have taken up permanent residence and found lovers in a very hip home-decor shop. Naomi and Macy knew people who knew people, and those people knew even more people. I have also recently started making ottomans. Covering them with wild and beautiful fabric and getting rather carried away.

I have deactivated my Facebook account until further notice. I do not miss it. However, Mona was right. My third husband was number three of ninety-eight messages. Stan wrote this:

Hello there, Georgia! Hope you're well. I think of you often. If you're ever in NYC, let me know. Would love to take you out for a slice! Love, Stan DiStasio.

And last but not least.
I do not regret quitting my day job.

# Acknowledgments

Even though you write alone, it takes the support of, confidence in, and patience from a lot of people during the journey. I am grateful to the following: Molly Friedrich and Lucy Carson, my forever agents, for their faith in this story from the beginning and the great advice after reading the early drafts; my young, smart, insightful, and intuitive editor, Lindsay Sagnette, for her brilliance and not being afraid of me; my publisher, Molly Stern, for her faith in and general excitement for my past work and this story. I'm also grateful to Maya Mavjee, David Drake, and Rose Fox.

Solitude is precious to a writer and sometimes hard to get, which is why I appreciate Adrienne Brodeur, the creative director of Aspen Words at the Aspen Institute, for giving me a monthlong residency in a very cool house in the mountains along with Boo Boo the Bear to keep me company.

From there, I went back to Jamaica for another month, where Charlotte Wallace, manager of the Rock House in Negril, gave me a round bungalow with a sea view that helped me continue to bring this novel to life.

I lie for a living. But in the hope of telling someone's truth. I respect and admire all the women I know and don't know for their bravery in changing lanes at a later (not late) stage in their lives. This party ain't over. Yet.

# About the Author

TERRY MCMILLAN is the #1 *New York Times* bestselling author of *Waiting to Exhale, How Stella Got Her Groove Back, A Day Late and a Dollar Short,* and *The Interruption of Everything* and the editor of *Breaking Ice: An Anthology of Contemporary African-American Fiction.* Each of Ms. McMillan's seven previous novels was a *New York Times* bestseller, and four have been made into movies: *Waiting to Exhale* (Twentieth Century Fox, 1995); *How Stella Got Her Groove Back* (Twentieth Century Fox, 1998); *Disappearing Acts* (HBO Pictures, 1999); and *A Day Late and a Dollar Short* (Lifetime, 2014). She lives in California.